FRIENDLY BROOK AND OTHER STORIES

Rudyard Kipling, son of John Lockwood Kipling, the author of *Beast and Man in India*, was born in Bombay in 1865. He was educated at the United Services College, Westward Ho!, and was engaged in journalistic work in India from 1882 to 1889. His fame rests principally on his short stories, dealing with India, the sea, the jungle and its beasts, the army, the navy, and a multitude of other subjects. His verse, as varied in subject as his prose, also enjoyed great popularity. Among his more famous publications are *Plain Tales from The Hills* (1886), *Life's Handicap* (1891), *Barrack-Room Ballads* (1892), *The Jungle Book* (1894), *The Day's Work* (1898), *Kim* (1901), *Just So Stories* (1902), *Puck of Pook's Hill* (1906), and *Rewards and Fairies* (1910). Kipling, who was awarded a Nobel Prize in 1907, died in 1936.

RUDYARD KIPLING

Short Stories: 2

FRIENDLY BROOK

AND OTHER STORIES

Selected by
Andrew Rutherford

PENGUIN BOOKS

Penguin Books Ltd, Harmondsworth,
Middlesex, England
Penguin Books, 625 Madison Avenue,
New York, New York 10022, U.S.A.
Penguin Books Australia Ltd, Ringwood,
Victoria, Australia
Penguin Books Canada Limited, 2801 John Street,
Markham, Ontario, Canada L3R 1B4
Penguin Books (N.Z.) Ltd, 182–190 Wairau Road,
Auckland 10, New Zealand

First published in Great Britain by Macmillan & Co. Ltd
Published in Penguin Books in the United States of America
by arrangement with Doubleday & Company, Inc.
Published in Penguin Books 1971
Reprinted 1976, 1977, 1979, 1980

Printed in the United States of America by
Kingsport Press, Inc., Kingsport, Tennessee
Set in Linotype Georgian

Volume 2

Preface

THESE two volumes of short stories* are selected from the following five collections, which have been made available to Penguin Books by Macmillan and Co. Ltd: *Traffics and Discoveries* (1904), *Actions and Reactions* (1909), *A Diversity of Creatures* (1917), *Debits and Credits* (1926), and *Limits and Renewals* (1932). These comprise the best of Kipling's prose fiction after 1900, apart from *Kim* (1901) and the short stories collected in *Puck of Pook's Hill* (1906) and *Rewards and Fairies* (1910).

Kipling's fiction is characteristically a rich blend of invention with experience, his own or others'; and his autobiography, *Something of Myself* (1937), suggests origins for many of these tales. 'A Sahibs' War' and 'The Captive' both derive from his first-hand knowledge of British and Boer practice in South Africa; 'Little Foxes' was based on an anecdote told him by an officer who had been Master of the original 'Gihon Hunt'; 'Regulus' draws on recollections of his own schooldays at Westward Ho!; a barmaid seen in Auckland, and a petty officer's remarks overheard in a train near Cape Town, were the starting points for 'Mrs Bathurst'; his interest in Freemasonry ('In the Interests of the Brethren') dates from his induction to the multi-racial, multi-religious Lodge at Lahore in 1885; in a house at Torquay, formerly inhabited by three old maids, he and his wife had felt in 1896 'a growing depression which enveloped us both – a gathering blackness of mind and sorrow of the heart', which he attributed to the Spirit of the house itself, and recreated in the symptoms which afflict his characters in 'The House Surgeon'; while his experiences at Bateman's, their eventual home in Sussex, provided the technicalities of 'Below the Mill Dam' and the insights into rural life and character

---

A Sahibs' War and Other Stories and *Friendly Brook and Other Stories*.

7

which he drew on in stories like 'Friendly Brook', 'My Son's Wife', and 'An Habitation Enforced'.

Deeper emotional levels are suggested by Charles Carrington's official but less reticent biography, *Rudyard Kipling: His Life and Work* (1955). Behind the delicate pathos of 'They', for example, lies Kipling's grief at the death of his little daughter Josephine in 1899; and although 'Mary Postgate' was written before his only son was killed at Loos in 1915, our knowledge of his loss gives added poignancy to a story like 'The Gardener'. Such information, however, is not necessary for our understanding and enjoyment of the tales themselves; and further speculation would run counter to Kipling's own request (in 'The Appeal') that his art be judged impersonally, and his privacy respected posthumously as he made sure it was in his own lifetime:

> If I have given you delight
> By aught that I have done,
> Let me lie quiet in that night
> Which shall be yours anon:

> And for the little, little, span
> The dead are borne in mind,
> Seek not to question other than
> The books I leave behind.

This selection from five of the books he left behind presents the twentieth-century Kipling who developed from the more familiar prodigy of the eighties and nineties; and it illustrates the range, variety, and technical originality of his fiction of this period.* There are fewer tales of Empire than the popular stereotype of Kipling might lead readers to expect: as 'Little Foxes' demonstrates, he still held firmly the ideals and prejudices which had inspired much of his work in the previous two decades, but the general incompetence

---

*The poems which accompany the stories in these collections have not been included (though they are always thematically relevant), except in the case of 'MacDonough's Song', which is quoted and referred to in 'As Easy as A.B.C.', and must be regarded as an essential element of the story itself.

revealed by the Boer War diminished his confidence in Britain's ability to sustain her imperial role, while her very will to do so, or even to prepare to defend herself against hostile European powers, was being sapped, it seemed to him by decadence and political irresponsibility. Increasingly, therefore, he was preoccupied by the condition of England herself, as he rebuked her blindness, folly and complacency, and sought reassurance in groups, types, or individuals who might still redeem her backslidings. Simultaneously, he found himself involved in a fascinating process of discovery, for the countryside, its people and traditions, came as a revelation to him once he settled in Sussex: 'England,' he wrote to a friend in 1902, 'is a wonderful land. It is the most marvellous of all foreign countries that I have ever been in.' Yet even while making it peculiarly his own, he was aware (as 'Below the Mill Dam' shows) of the baneful influence of inert tradition, and the need for technological advance. For socially parasitic intellectuals, especially those of 'the Immoderate Left', he felt the savage contempt expressed in 'My Son's Wife'; but his fable of decadence in 'The Mother Hive' goes beyond this sectional antagonism to diagnose moral-political sickness in a whole community, while the suspicion of democracy which he shared with so many major authors of the century is projected into an ambiguously Utopian future in 'As Easy as A.B.C.' Such public themes bulk large in Volume 1, as his preoccupation with the Great War does in Volume 2; but these coexist with more personal, more psychological, and more spiritual interests, especially in his later years. Individual human beings, their characters, their actions, their behaviour under stress, remain his main concern; and using a remarkable variety of settings and of *dramatis personae*, he offers stories on a characteristic range of themes – stories of revenge, seen sometimes as wild justice, sometimes as an almost pathological obsession; stories of forgiveness, human and divine; stories of the supernatural, to be taken now literally, now symbolically, but never trivially as mere spine-chilling entertainment; stories of hatred and cruelty, but stories also of compassion and of love; stories of

work, of craftsmanship, of artistry; of comradeship and iso-
lation; and stories of healing, sometimes physical, but more
often moral, spiritual or psychological.

Technically, his fiction shows a comparable variety, but
for modern readers the most interesting development is
probably his evolution of that complex, closely organized,
elliptical and symbolic mode of writing which ranks him as
an unexpected contributor to 'modernism' and a major inno-
vator in the art of the short story. This mode, with its ob-
liquities and ironies, its multiple levels of meaning, and what
have been described by Miss J. M. S. Tompkins as its 'com-
plexities of substance and . . . of method', was first attempted
in 'Mrs Bathurst' and 'They', but is to be found fully developed in his later stories, especially those dated from 1924
onwards in Volume 2 of this selection. Detailed discussion
of this and other aspects of his artistry may be found in such
studies as J. M. S. Tompkins, *The Art of Rudyard Kipling*
(1959); C. A. Bodelsen, *Aspects of Kipling's Art* (1964); *Kipling's Mind and Art*, ed. Andrew Rutherford (1964); and
Bonamy Dobrée, *Rudyard Kipling: Realist and Fabulist*
(1967).

Friendly Brook

(1914)

THE valley was so choked with fog that one could scarcely see a cow's length across a field. Every blade, twig, bracken-frond, and hoof-print carried water, and the air was filled with the noise of rushing ditches and field-drains, all delivering to the brook below. A week's November rain on water-logged land had gorged her to full flood, and she proclaimed it aloud.

Two men in sackcloth aprons were considering an untrimmed hedge that ran down the hillside and disappeared into mist beside those roarings. They stood back and took stock of the neglected growth, tapped an elbow of hedge-oak here, a mossed beech-stub there, swayed a stooled ash back and forth, and looked at each other.

'I reckon she's about two rod thick,' said Jabez the younger, 'an' she hasn't felt iron since – when has she, Jesse?'

'Call it twenty-five year, Jabez, an' you won't be far out.'

'Umm!' Jabez rubbed his wet handbill on his wetter coat-sleeve. 'She ain't a hedge. She's all manner o' trees. We'll just about have to – ' He paused, as professional etiquette required.

'Just about have to side her up an' see what she'll bear. But hadn't we best – ?' Jesse paused in his turn, both men being artists and equals.

'Get some kind o' line to go by.' Jabez ranged up and down till he found a thinner place, and with clean snicks of the handbill revealed the original face of the fence. Jesse took over the dripping stuff as it fell forward, and, with a grasp and a kick, made it to lie orderly on the bank till it should be faggoted.

By noon a length of unclean jungle had turned itself into a cattle-proof barrier, tufted here and there with little plumes of the sacred holly which no woodman touches without orders.

'Now we've a witness-board to go by!' said Jesse at last.

'She won't be as easy as this all along,' Jabez answered. 'She'll need plenty stakes and binders when we come to the brook.'

'Well, ain't we plenty?' Jesse pointed to the ragged perspective ahead of them that plunged downhill into the fog. 'I lay there's a cord an' a half o' firewood, let alone faggots, 'fore we get anywheres anigh the brook.'

'The brook's got up a piece since morning,' said Jabez. 'Sounds like's if she was over Wickenden's door-stones.'

Jesse listened, too. There was a growl in the brook's roar as though she worried something hard.

'Yes. She's over Wickenden's door-stones,' he replied. 'Now she'll flood acrost Alder Bay an' that'll ease her.'

'She won't ease Jim Wickenden's hay none if she do,' Jabez grunted. 'I told Jim he'd set that liddle hay-stack o' his too low down in the medder. I *told* him so when he was drawin' the bottom for it.'

'I told him so, too,' said Jesse. 'I told him 'fore ever you did. I told him when the County Council tarred the roads up along.' He pointed up-hill, where unseen automobiles and road-engines droned past continually. 'A tarred road, she shoots every drop o' water into a valley same's a slate roof. 'Tisn't as 'twas in the old days, when the waters soaked in and soaked out in the way o' nature. It rooshes off they tarred roads all of a lump, and naturally every drop is bound to descend into the valley. And there's tar roads both two sides this valley for ten mile. That's what I told Jim Wickenden when they tarred the roads last year. But he's a valley-man. He don't hardly ever journey up-hill.'

'What did he say when you told him that?' Jabez demanded, with a little change of voice.

'Why? What did he say to you when *you* told him?' was the answer.

'What he said to you, I reckon, Jesse.'

'Then, you don't need me to say it over again, Jabez.'

'Well, let be how 'twill, what was he gettin' *after* when he said what he said to me?' Jabez insisted.

'*I* dunno; unless you tell me what manner o' words he said to *you*.'

Jabez drew back from the hedge – all hedges are nests of treachery and eavesdropping – and moved to an open cattle-lodge in the centre of the field.

'No need to go ferretin' around,' said Jesse. 'None can't see us here 'fore we see them.'

'What was Jim Wickenden gettin' at when I said he'd set his stack too near anigh the brook?' Jabez dropped his voice. 'He was in his mind.'

'He ain't never been out of it yet to my knowledge,' Jesse drawled, and uncorked his tea-bottle.

'But then Jim says: "I ain't goin' to shift my stack a yard," he says. "The Brook's been good friends to me, and if she be minded," he says, "to take a snatch at my hay, *I* ain't settin' out to withstand her." That's what Jim Wickenden says to me last – last June-end 'twas,' said Jabez.

'Nor he hasn't shifted his stack, neither,' Jesse replied. 'An' if there's more rain, the brook she'll shift it for him.'

'No need tell *me*! But I want to know what Jim was gettin' *at*?'

Jabez opened his clasp-knife very deliberately; Jesse as carefully opened his. They unfolded the newspapers that wrapped their dinners, coiled away and pocketed the string that bound the packages, and sat down on the edge of the lodge manger. The rain began to fall again through the fog, and the brook's voice rose.

'But I always allowed Mary was his lawful child, like,' said Jabez, after Jesse had spoken for a while.

' 'Tain't so. . . . Jim Wickenden's woman she never made nothing. She come out o' Lewes with her stockin's round her heels, an' she never made nor mended aught till she died. *He* had to light fire an' get breakfast every mornin' except Sundays, while she sowed it abed. Then she took an' died, sixteen, seventeen, year back; but she never had no children.'

'They was valley-folk,' said Jabez apologetically. 'I'd no call to go in among 'em, but I always allowed Mary – '

'No. Mary come out o' one o' those Lunnon Childern Societies. After his woman died, Jim got his mother back from his sister over to Peasmarsh, which she'd gone to house with when Jim married. His mother kept house for Jim after his woman died. They do say 'twas his mother led him on toward adoptin' of Mary – to furnish out the house with a child, like, and to keep him off of gettin' a noo woman. He mostly done what his mother contrived. 'Cardenly, twixt 'em, they asked for a child from one o' those Lunnon societies – same as it might ha' been these Barnardo children – an' Mary was sent down to 'em, in a candle-box, I've heard.'

'Then Mary is chance-born. I never knowed that,' said Jabez. 'Yet I must ha' heard it some time or other . . .'

'No. She ain't. 'Twould ha' been better for some folk if she had been. She come to Jim in a candle-box with all the proper papers – lawful child o' some couple in Lunnon somewheres – mother dead, father drinkin'. *And* there was that Lunnon society's five shillin's a week for her. Jim's mother she wouldn't despise week-end money, but I never heard Jim was much of a muck-grubber. Let be how 'twill, they two mothered up Mary no bounds till it looked at last like they'd forgot she wasn't their own flesh an' blood. Yes, I reckon they forgot Mary wasn't their'n by rights.'

'That's no new thing,' said Jabez. 'There's more'n one or two in this parish wouldn't surrender back their Bernarders. You ask Mark Copley an' his woman an' that Bernarder cripple-babe o' theirs.'

'Maybe they need the five shillin',' Jesse suggested.

'It's handy,' said Jabez. 'But the child's more. "Dada" he says, an' "Mumma" he says, with his great rollin' head-piece all hurdled up in that iron collar. *He* won't live long – his backbone's rotten, like. But they Copleys do just about set store by him – five bob or no five bob.'

'Same way with Jim an' his mother,' Jesse went on. 'There was talk betwixt 'em after a few years o' not takin' any more week-end money for Mary; but let alone *she* never passed a farden in the mire 'thout longin's, Jim didn't care, like, to push himself forward into the Society's remembrance. So naun came of it. The week-end money would ha' made no odds to Jim – not after his uncle willed him they four cottages at Eastbourne *an'* money in the bank.'

'That was true, too, then? I heard something in a scadderin' word-o'-mouth way,' said Jabez.

'I'll answer for the house property, because Jim he requested my signed name at the foot o' some papers concernin' it. Regardin' the money in the bank, he nature-ally wouldn't like such things talked about all round the parish, so he took strangers for witnesses.'

'Then 'twill make Mary worth seekin' after?'

'She'll need it. Her Maker ain't done much for her outside nor yet in.'

'That ain't no odds.' Jabez shook his head till the water showered off his hat-brim. 'If Mary has money, she'll be wed before any likely pore maid. She's cause to be grateful to Jim.'

'She hides it middlin' close, then,' said Jesse. 'It don't sometimes look to me as if Mary has her natural rightful feelin's. She don't put on an apron o' Mondays 'thout being druv to it – in the kitchen *or* the hen-house. She's studyin' to be a school-teacher. She'll make a beauty! I never knowed her show any sort o' kindness to nobody – not even when Jim's mother was took dumb. No! 'Twadn't no stroke. It stifled the old lady in the throat here. First she couldn't shape her words no shape; then she clucked, like, an' lastly she couldn't more than suck down spoon-meat an' hold her peace. Jim took her to Doctor Harding, an' Harding he bundled her off to Brighton Hospital on a ticket, but they couldn't make no stay to her afflictions there; and she was bundled off to Lunnon, an' they lit a great old lamp inside her, and Jim told me they couldn't make out nothing in no sort there; and, along o' one thing an' another, an' all their spyin's and pryin's, she come back a hem sight worse than when she started. Jim said he'd have no more hospitalizin', so he give her a slate, which she tied to her waist-string, and what she was minded to say she writ on it.'

'Now, I never knowed that! But they're valley-folk,' Jabez repeated.

' 'Twadn't particular noticeable, for she wasn't a talkin' woman any time o' her days. Mary had all three's tongue. . . . Well, then, two years this summer, come what I'm tellin' you. Mary's Lunnon father, which they'd put clean out o' their minds, arrived down from Lunnon with the law on his side, sayin' he'd take his daughter back to Lunnon, after all. I was working for Mus' Dockett at Pounds Farm that summer, but I was obligin' Jim that evenin' muckin' out his pig-pen. I seed a stranger come traipsin' over the bridge agin' Wickenden's door-stones. 'Twadn't the new County Council bridge with the handrail. They hadn't given it in for a public right o' way then. 'Twas just a bit o' lathy old plank which Jim had throwed acrost the brook for his own conveniences. The man wasn't drunk – only a little concerned in liquor, like – an' his back was a mask where he'd slipped in the muck comin' along. He went up the bricks past Jim's mother, which was feedin' the ducks, an' set himself down at the table inside – Jim was just changin' his socks – an' the man let Jim know all his rights and aims regardin' Mary. Then there just about *was* a hurly-bulloo? Jim's fust mind was to pitch him forth, but he'd done that once in his young days, and got six months up to Lewes jail along o' the man fallin' on his head. So he swallowed his spittle an' let him talk. The law about Mary *was* on the man's side from fust to last, for he showed us all the papers. Then Mary come downstairs – she'd been studyin' for an examination – an' the man tells her who he was, an' she says he had ought to have took proper care of his own flesh and blood while he had it by him, an' not to think he could ree-claim it when it suited. He says somethin' or other, but she looks him up an' down, front an' backwent, an' she just tongues him scadderin' out o' doors, and he went away stuffin' all the papers back into his hat, talkin' most abusefully. Then she come back an' freed her mind against

Jim an' his mother for not havin' warned her of her up-bringin's, which it come out she hadn't ever been told. They didn't say naun to her. They never did. *I*'d ha' packed her off with any man that would ha' took her – an God's pity on him!'

'Umm!' said Jabez, and sucked his pipe.

'So then, that was the beginnin'. The man come back again next week or so, an' he catched Jim alone, 'thout his mother this time, an' he fair beazled him with his papers an' his talk – for the law *was* on his side – till Jim went down into his money-purse an' give him ten shillings hush-money – he told me – to withdraw away for a bit an' leave Mary with 'em.'

'But that's no way to get rid o' man or woman,' Jabez said.

'No more 'tis. I told Jim so. "What can I do?" Jim says. "The law's *with* the man. I walk about daytimes thinkin' o' it till I sweats my underclothes wringin', an' I lie abed nights thinkin' o' it till I sweats my sheets all of a sop. 'Tisn't as if I was a young man," he says, "nor yet as if I was a pore man. Maybe he'll drink hisself to death." I e'en a'most told him outright what foolishness he was enterin' into, but he knowed it – he knowed it – because he said next time the man come 'twould be fifteen shillin's. An' next time 'twas. Just fifteen shillin's!'

'An' *was* the man her father?' asked Jabez.

'He had the proofs an' the papers. Jim showed me what that Lunnon Childern's Society had answered when Mary writ up to 'em an' taxed 'em with it. I lay she hadn't been proper polite in her letters to 'em, for they answered middlin' short. They said the matter was out o' their hands, but – let's see if I remember – oh, yes, – they ree-gretted there had been an oversight. I reckon they had sent Mary out in the candle-box as a orphan instead o' havin' a father. Terrible awkward! Then, when he'd drinked up the money, the man come again – in his usuals – an' he kept hammerin' on and hammerin' on about his duty to his pore dear wife, an' what he'd do for his dear daughter in Lunnon, till the tears runned down his two dirty cheeks an' he come away with more money. Jim used to slip it into his hand behind the door; but his mother she heard the chink. She didn't hold with hush-money. She'd write out all her feelin's on the slate, an' Jim 'ud be settin' up half the night answerin' back an showing that the man had the law with him.'

'Hadn't that man no trade nor business, then?'

'He told me he was a printer. I reckon, though, he lived on the rates like the rest of 'em up there in Lunnon.'

'An' how did Mary take it?'

'She said she'd sooner go into service than go with the man. I reckon a mistress 'ud be middlin' put to it for a maid 'fore she put Mary into cap an' gown. She was studyin' to be a schoo-ool-teacher. A beauty she'll make! ... Well, that was how things went that fall. Mary's Lunnon father kep' comin' an' comin' 'carden as he'd drinked out the money Jim gave him; an' each time he'd put up his price for not takin' Mary away. Jim's mother, she didn't like partin' with no money, an' bein' obliged to write her feelin's on the slate instead o' givin' 'em vent by mouth, she was just about mad. Just about she *was* mad!

'Come November, I lodged with Jim in the outside room over 'gainst his hen-house. I paid *her* my rent. I was workin' for Dockett at Pounds – gettin' chestnut-bats out o' Perry Shaw. Just such weather as this be – rain atop o' rain after a wet October. (An' I remember it ended in dry frostes right away up to Christmas.) Dockett he'd sent up to Perry Shaw for me – no, he comes puffin' up to me himself – because a big corner piece o' the bank had slipped into the brook where she makes that elber at the bottom o' the Seventeen Acre, an' all the rubbishy alders an' sallies which he ought to have cut out when he took the farm, they'd slipped with the slip, an' the brook was comin' rooshin' down atop of 'em, an' they'd just about back an' spill the waters over his winter wheat. The water was lyin' in the flats already. "Gor a-mighty, Jesse!" he bellers out at me, "get that rubbish away all manners you can. Don't stop for no faggotin', but give the brook play or my wheat's past salvation. I can't lend you no help," he says, "but work an' I'll pay ye." '

'You had him there,' Jabez chuckled.

'Yes. I reckon I had ought to have drove my bargain, but the brook was backin' up on good bread-corn. So 'cardenly, I laid into the mess of it, workin' off the bank where the trees was drownin' themselves head-down in the roosh – just such weather as this – an' the brook creepin' up on me all the time. 'Long toward noon, Jim comes mowchin' along with his toppin' axe over his shoulder.

' "Be you minded for an extra hand at your job?" he says.

' "Be you minded to turn to?" I ses, an' – no more talk to it – Jim laid in alongside o' me. He's no bunger with a toppin' axe.'

'Maybe, but I've seed him at a job o' throwin' in the woods, an' he didn't seem to make out no shape,' said Jabez. 'He haven't got the shoulders, nor yet the judgement – *my* opinion – when he's dealin' with full-girt timber. He don't rightly make up his mind where he's goin' to throw her.'

'We wasn't throwin' nothin'. We was cuttin' out they soft alders, an' haulin' 'em up the bank 'fore they could back the waters on the wheat. Jim didn't say much, 'less it was that he'd had a post-card from Mary's Lunnon father, night before, sayin' he was comin' down that mornin'. Jim, he'd sweated all night, an' he didn't reckon hisself equal to the talkin' an' the swearin' an' the cryin', an' his mother blamin' him afterwards on the slate. "It spiled my day to think of it," he ses, when we was eatin' our pieces. "So I've fair cried dunghill an' run. Mother'll have to tackle him by herself. I lay *she* won't give him no hush-money," he ses. "I lay he'll be surprised by the time he's done with *her*," he ses. An' that was e'en a'most all the talk we had concernin' it. But he's no bunger with the toppin' axe.

'The brook she'd crep' up an' up on us, an' she kep' creepin' upon us till we was workin' knee-deep in the shallers, cuttin' an' pookin' an' pullin' what we could get to o' the rubbish. There was a middlin' lot comin' down-stream, too – cattle-bars an' hop-poles and odds-ends bats, all poltin' down together; but they rooshed round the elber good shape **by** the time we'd backed out they drowned trees. Come four o'clock we reckoned we'd done a proper day's work, an' she'd take no harm if we left her. We couldn't puddle about there in the dark an' wet to no more advantage. Jim he was pourin' the water out of his boots – no, I was doin' that. Jim was kneelin' to unlace his'n. "Damn it all, Jesse," he ses, standin' up; "the flood must be over my doorsteps at home, for here comes my old white-top bee-skep!" '

'Yes. I allus heard he paints his bee-skeps,' Jabez put in. 'I dunno paint don't tarrify bees more'n it keeps 'em dry.'

' "I'll have a pook at it," he ses, an' he pooks at it as it comes round the elber. The roosh nigh jerked the pooker out of his hand-grips, an' he calls to me, an' I come runnin' barefoot. Then we pulled on the pooker, an' it reared up on eend in the roosh, an' we guessed what 'twas. 'Cardenly we pulled it in into a shaller, an' it rolled a piece, an' a great old stiff man's arm nigh hit me in the face. Then we was sure. " 'Tis a man," ses Jim. But the face was all a mask. "I reckon it's Mary's Lunnon father," he ses presently. "Lend me a match and I'll make sure." He never used baccy. We lit three matches one by another, well's we could in the rain, an' he cleaned off some o' the slob with a tussick o' grass. "Yes," he ses. "It's Mary's Lunnon father. He won't tarrify us no more. D'you want him, Jesse?" he ses.

' "No," I ses. "If this was Eastbourne beach like, he'd be half-a-crown apiece to us 'fore the coroner; but now we'd only lose a day havin' to 'tend the inquest. I lay he fell into the brook."

' "I lay he did," says Jim. "I wonder if he saw mother." He turns him over, an' opens his coat and puts his fingers in the waistcoat pocket an' starts laughin'. "He's seen mother, right enough," he ses. "An' he's got the best of her, too. *She* won't be able to crow no more over *me* 'bout givin' him money. *I* never give him more than a sovereign. She's give him two!" an' he trousers 'em, laughin' all the time. "An' now we'll pook him back again, for I've done with him," he ses.

'So we pooked him back into the middle of the brook, an' we saw he went round the elber 'thout balkin', an' we walked quite a piece beside of him to set him on his ways. When we couldn't see no more, we went home by the high road, because we knowed the brook 'u'd be out acrost the medders, an' we wasn't goin' to hunt for Jim's little rotten old bridge in that dark – an' rainin' Heavens' hard, too. I was middlin' pleased to see light an' vittles again when we got home. Jim he pressed me to come insides for a drink. He don't drink in a generality, but he was rid of all his troubles that evenin', d'ye see? "Mother," he ses so soon as the door ope'd, "have you seen him?" She whips out her slate an' writes down – "No." "Oh, no," ses Jim. "You don't get out of it that way, mother. I lay you *have* seen him, an' I lay he's bested you for all your talk, same as he bested me. Make a clean breast of it, mother," he ses. "He got round you too." She was goin' for the slate again, but he stops her. "It's all right, mother," he ses. "I've seen him sense you have, an' he won't trouble us no more." The old lady looks up quick as a robin, an' she writes, "Did he say so?" "No," ses Jim, laughin'. "He didn't say so. That's how I know. But he bested *you*, mother. You can't have it in at *me* for bein' soft-hearted. You're twice as tender-hearted as what I be. Look!" he ses, an' he shows her the two sovereigns. "Put 'em away where they belong," he ses. "He won't never come for no more; an' now we'll have our drink," he ses, "for we've earned it."

'Nature-ally they weren't goin' to let me see where they kep' their monies. She went upstairs with it – for the whisky.'

'I never knowed Jim was a drinkin' man – in his own house, like,' said Jabez.

'No more he isn't; but what he takes he likes good. He won't tech no publican's hogwash acrost the bar. Four shillin's he paid for that bottle o' whisky. I know, because when the old lady brought it down there wasn't more'n jest a liddle few dreenin's an' dregs in it. Nothin' to set before neighbours, I do assure you.'

' "Why, 'twas half full last week, mother," he ses. "You don't mean," he ses, "you've given him all that as well? It's two shillin's worth," he ses. (That's how I knowed he paid four.) "Well, well, mother, you be too tender-'earted to live. But I don't grudge it to him," he ses. "I don't grudge him nothin' he can keep." So, 'cardenly, we drinked up what little sup was left.'

'An' what come to Mary's Lunnon father?' said Jabez, after a full minute's silence.

'I be too tired to go readin' papers of evenin's; but Dockett he told me, that very week, I think, that they'd inquested on a man down at Robertsbridge which had polted and polted up agin' so many bridges an' banks, like, they couldn't make naun out of him.'

'An' what did Mary say to all these doin's?'

'The old lady bundled her off to the village 'fore her Lunnon father come, to buy week-end stuff (an' she forgot the half o' it). When we come in she was upstairs studyin' to be a school-teacher. None told her naun about it. 'Twadn't girls' affairs.'

' 'Reckon *she* knowed?' Jabez went on.

'She? She must have guessed it middlin' close when she saw her money come back. But she never mentioned it in writing so far's I know. She were more worritted that night on account of two-three her chickens bein' drowned, for the flood had skewed their old hen-house round on her postes. I cobbled her up next mornin' when the brook shrinked.'

'An' where did you find the bridge? Some fur down-stream, didn't ye?'

'Just where she allus was. She hadn't shifted but very little. The brook had gulled out the bank a piece under one eend o' the plank, so's she was liable to tilt ye sideways if you wasn't careful. But I pooked three-four bricks under her, an' she was all plumb again.'

'Well, I dunno how it *looks* like, but let be how 'twill,' said Jabez, 'he hadn't no business to come down from Lunnon tarrifyin' people, an' threatenin' to take away children which they'd hobbed up for their lawful own – even if 'twas Mary Wickenden.'

'He had the business right enough, an' he had the law with him – no gettin' over that,' said Jesse. 'But he had the drink with him, too, an' that was where he failed, like.'

'Well, well! Let be how 'twill, the brook was a good friend to Jim. I see it now. I allus *did* wonder what he was gettin' at when he said that, when I talked to him about shiftin' the stack. "You dunno everythin'," he ses. "The Brook's been a good friend to me," he ses, "an' if she's minded to have a snatch at my hay, *I* ain't settin' out to withstand her." '

'I reckon she's about shifted it, too, by now,' Jesse chuckled. 'Hark! That ain't any slip off the bank which she's got hold of.'

The Brook had changed her note again. It sounded as though she were mumbling something soft.

'My Son's Wife'

(1917; written 1913)

HE had suffered from the disease of the century since his early youth, and before he was thirty he was heavily marked with it. He and a few friends had rearranged Heaven very comfortably, but the reorganization of Earth, which they called Society, was even greater fun. It demanded Work in the shape of many taxi-rides daily; hours of brilliant talk with brilliant talkers; some sparkling correspondence; a few silences (but on the understanding that their own turn should come soon) while other people expounded philosophies; and a fair number of picture-galleries, tea-fights, concerts, theatres, music-halls, and cinema shows; the whole trimmed with love-making to women whose hair smelt of cigarette-smoke. Such strong days sent Frankwell Midmore back to his flat assured that he and his friends had helped the World a step nearer the Truth, the Dawn, and the New Order.

His temperament, he said, led him more towards concrete data than abstract ideas. People who investigate detail are apt to be tired at the day's end. The same temperament, or it may have been a woman, made him early attach himself to the Immoderate Left of his Cause in the capacity of an experimenter in Social Relations. And since the Immoderate Left contains plenty of women anxious to help earnest inquirers with large independent incomes to arrive at evaluations of essentials, Frankwell Midmore's lot was far from contemptible.

At that hour Fate chose to play with him. A widowed aunt, widely separated by nature, and more widely by marriage, from all that Midmore's mother had ever been or desired to be, died and left him possessions. Mrs Midmore, having that summer embraced a creed which denied the existence of death, naturally could not stoop to burial; but Midmore had to leave London for the dank country at a season when Social Regeneration works best through long, cushioned conferences, two by two, after tea. There he faced the bracing ritual of the British funeral, and was wept at across the raw grave by an elderly coffin-shaped female with a long nose, who called him 'Master Frankie'; and there he was congratulated behind an echoing top-hat by a man he mistook for a mute, who turned out to be his aunt's lawyer. He wrote his mother next day, after a bright account of the funeral:

'So far as I can understand, she has left me between four and five hundred a year. It all comes from Ther Land, as they call it down here. The unspeakable attorney, Sperrit, and a green-eyed daughter, who hums to herself as she tramps but is silent on all subjects except "huntin'," insisted on taking me to see it. Ther Land is brown and green in alternate slabs like chocolate and pistachio cakes, speckled with occasional peasants who do not utter. In case it should not be wet enough there is a wet brook in the middle of it. Ther House is by the brook. I shall look into it later. If there should be any little memento of Jenny that you care for, let me know. Didn't you tell me that mid-Victorian furniture is coming into the market again? Jenny's old maid – it is called Rhoda Dolbie – tells me that Jenny promised it thirty pounds a year. The will does not. Hence, I suppose, the tears at the funeral. But that is close on ten per cent of the income. I fancy Jenny has destroyed all her private papers and records of her *vie intime*, if, indeed, life be possible in such a place. The Sperrit man told me that if I had means of my own I might come and live on Ther Land. I didn't tell him how much I would pay not to! I cannot think it right that any human being should exercise mastery over others in the merciless fashion our tom-fool social system permits; so, as it is all mine, I intend to sell it whenever the unholy Sperrit can find a purchaser.'

And he went to Mr Sperrit with the idea next day, just before returning to town.

'Quite so,' said the lawyer. 'I see your point, of course. But the house itself is rather old-fashioned – hardly the type purchasers demand nowadays. There's no park, of course, and the bulk of the land is let to a life-tenant, a Mr Sidney. As long as he pays his rent, he can't be turned out, and even if he didn't' – Mr Sperrit's face relaxed a shade – 'you might have a difficulty.'

'The property brings four hundred a year, I understand,' said Midmore.

'Well, hardly – ha-ardly. Deducting land and income tax, tithes, fire insurance, cost of collection and repairs of course, it returned two hundred and eighty-four pounds last year. The repairs are rather a large item – owing to the brook. I call it Liris – out of Horace, you know.'

Midmore looked at his watch impatiently.

'I suppose you can find somebody to buy it?' he repeated.

'We will do our best, of course, if those are your instructions. Then, that is all except' – here Midmore half rose, but Mr Sperrit's little grey eyes held his large brown ones firmly – 'except about Rhoda Dolbie, Mrs Werf's maid. I may tell you that we did not draw up your aunt's last will. She grew secretive towards the last – elderly people often do – and had it done in London. I expect her memory failed her, or she mislaid her notes. She used to put them in her spectacle-case.... My motor only takes eight minutes to get to the station, Mr Midmore ... but, as I was saying, whenever she made her will with *us*, Mrs Werf always left Rhoda thirty pounds per annum. Charlie, the wills!' A clerk with a baldish head and a long nose dealt documents on to the table like cards, and breathed heavily behind Midmore. 'It's in no sense a legal obligation, of course,' said Mr Sperrit. 'Ah, that one is dated January the 11th, eighteen eighty-nine.'

Midmore looked at his watch again and found himself saying with no good grace: 'Well, I suppose she'd better have it – for the present at any rate.'

He escaped with an uneasy feeling that two hundred and fifty-four pounds a year was not exactly four hundred, and that Charlie's long nose annoyed him. Then he returned, first-class, to his own affairs.

Of the two, perhaps three, experiments in Social Relations which he had then in hand, one interested him acutely. It had run for some months and promised most variegated and interesting developments, on which he dwelt luxuriously all the way to town. When he reached his flat he was not well prepared for a twelve-page letter explaining, in the diction of the Immoderate Left which rubricates its I's and illuminates its T's, that the lady had realized greater attractions in another Soul. She re-stated, rather than pleaded, the gospel of the Immoderate Left as her justification, and ended in an impassioned demand for her right to express herself in and on her own life, through which, she pointed out, she could pass but once. She added that if, later, she should discover Midmore was 'essentially complementary to her needs,' she would tell him so. That Midmore had himself written much the same sort of epistle – barring the hint of return – to a woman of whom his needs for self-expression had caused him to weary three years before, did not assist him in the least. He expressed himself to the gas-fire in terms essential but not complimentary. Then he reflected on the detached criticism of his best friends and her best friends, male and female, with whom he and she and others had talked so openly while their gay adventure was in flower. He recalled, too – this must have been about midnight – her analysis from every angle, remote and most intimate, of the mate to whom she had been adjudged under the base convention which is styled marriage. Later, at that bad hour when the cattle wake for a little, he remembered her in other aspects and went down into the hell appointed; desolate, desiring, with no God to call upon. About eleven o'clock next morning Eliphaz the Temanite, Bildad the Shuhite, and Zophar the Naamathite called upon him 'for they had made appointment together' to see how he took it; but the janitor told them that Job had gone – into the country, he believed.

Midmore's relief when he found his story was not written across his aching temples for Mr Sperrit to read – the defeated lover, like the successful one, believes all earth privy to his soul – was put down by Mr Sperrit to quite different causes. He led him into a morning-room. The rest of the house seemed to be full of people, singing to a loud piano idiotic songs about cows, and the hall smelt of damp cloaks.

'It's our evening to take the winter cantata,' Mr Sperrit explained. 'It's "High Tide on the Coast of Lincolnshire." I hoped you'd come back. There are scores of little things to settle. As for the house, of course, it stands ready for you at any time. I couldn't get Rhoda out of it – nor could Charlie for that matter. She's the sister, isn't she, of the nurse who brought you down here when you were four, she says, to recover from measles?'

'Is she? Was I?' said Midmore through the bad tastes in his mouth. 'D'you suppose I could stay there the night?'

Thirty joyous young voices shouted appeal to some one to leave their 'pipes of parsley 'ollow – 'ollow – 'ollow!' Mr Sperrit had to raise his voice above the din.

'Well, if I asked you to stay *here*, I should never hear the last of it from Rhoda. She's a little cracked, of course, but the soul of devotion and capable of anything. *Ne sit ancillae*, you know.'

'Thank you. Then I'll go. I'll walk.' He stumbled out dazed and sick into the winter twilight, and sought the square house by the brook.

It was not a dignified entry, because when the door was unchained and Rhoda exclaimed, he took two valiant steps into the hall and then fainted – as men sometimes will after twenty-two hours of strong emotion and little food.

'I'm sorry,' he said when he could speak. He was lying at the foot of the stairs, his head on Rhoda's lap.

'Your 'ome is your castle, sir,' was the reply in his hair. 'I smelt it wasn't drink. You lay on the sofa till I get your supper.'

She settled him in a drawing-room hung with yellow silk, heavy with the smell of dead leaves and oil lamp. Something murmured soothingly in the background and overcame the noises in his head. He thought he heard horses' feet on wet

28

gravel and a voice singing about ships and flocks and grass. It passed close to the shuttered bay-window.

> But each will mourn his own, she saith,
> And sweeter woman ne'er drew breath
> Than my son's wife, Elizabeth . . .
> Cusha – cusha – cusha – calling.

The hoofs broke into a canter as Rhoda entered with the tray. 'And then I'll put you to bed,' she said. 'Sidney's coming in the morning.' Midmore asked no questions. He dragged his poor bruised soul to bed and would have pitied it all over again, but the food and warm sherry and water drugged him to instant sleep.

Rhoda's voice wakened him, asking whether he would have ' 'ip, foot, or sitz,' which he understood were the baths of the establishment. 'Suppose you try all three,' she suggested. 'They're all yours, you know, sir.'

He would have renewed his sorrows with the daylight, but her words struck him pleasantly. Everything his eyes opened upon was his very own to keep for ever. The carved four-post Chippendale bed, obviously worth hundreds; the wavy walnut William and Mary chairs – he had seen worse ones labelled twenty guineas apiece; the oval medallion mirror; the delicate eighteenth-century wire fireguard; the heavy brocaded curtains were his – all his. So, too, a great garden full of birds that faced him when he shaved; a mulberry tree, a sun-dial, and a dull, steel-coloured brook that murmured level with the edge of a lawn a hundred yards away. Peculiarly and privately his own was the smell of sausages and coffee that he sniffed at the head of the wide square landing, all set round with mysterious doors and Bartolozzi prints. He spent two hours after breakfast in exploring his new possessions. His heart leaped up at such things as sewing-machines, a rubber-tyred bath-chair in a tiled passage, a malachite-headed Malacca cane, boxes and boxes of unopened stationery, seal-rings, bunches of keys, and at the bottom of a steel-net reticule a little leather purse with seven pounds ten shillings in gold and eleven shillings in silver.

'You used to play with that when my sister brought you down here after your measles,' said Rhoda as he slipped the money into his pocket. 'Now, this was your pore dear auntie's business-room.' She opened a low door. 'Oh, I forgot about Mr Sidney! There he is.' An enormous old man with rheumy red eyes that blinked under downy white eyebrows sat in an Empire chair, his cap in his hands. Rhoda withdrew sniffing. The man looked Midmore over in silence, then jerked a thumb towards the door. 'I reckon she told you who I be,' he began. 'I'm the only farmer you've got. Nothin' goes off my place 'thout it walks on its own feet. What about my pig-pound?'

'Well, what about it?' said Midmore.

'That's just what I be come about. The County Councils are getting more particular. Did ye know there was swine fever at Pashell's? There *be*. It'll 'ave to be in brick.'

'Yes,' said Midmore politely.

'I've bin at your aunt that was, plenty times about it. I don't say she wasn't a just woman, but she didn't read the lease same way I did. I be used to bein' put upon, but there's no doing any longer 'thout that pig-pound.'

'When would you like it?' Midmore asked. It seemed the easiest road to take.

'Any time or other suits me, I reckon. He ain't thrivin' where he is, an' I paid eighteen shillin' for him.' He crossed his hands on his stick and gave no further sign of life.

'Is that all?' Midmore stammered.

'All now – excep' ' – he glanced fretfully at the table beside him – 'excep' my usuals. Where's that Rhoda?'

Midmore rang the bell. Rhoda came in with a bottle and a glass. The old man helped himself to four stiff fingers, rose in one piece, and stumped out. At the door he cried ferociously: 'Don't suppose it's any odds to you whether I'm drowned or not, but them floodgates want a wheel and winch, they do. I be too old for liftin' 'em with the bar – my time o' life.'

'Good riddance if 'e was drowned,' said Rhoda. 'But don't you mind him. He's only amusin' himself. Your pore dear

auntie used to give 'im 'is usual – 'tisn't the whisky *you* drink
– an' send 'im about 'is business.'

'I see. Now, is a pig-pound the same thing as a pig-sty?'

Rhoda nodded. ' 'E needs one, too, but 'e ain't entitled to it.
You look at 'is lease – third drawer on the left in that
Bombay cab'net – an' next time 'e comes you ask 'im to read
it. That'll choke 'im off, because 'e can't!'

There was nothing in Midmore's past to teach him the
message and significance of a hand-written lease of the late
'eighties, but Rhoda interpreted.

'It don't mean anything reelly,' was her cheerful con-
clusion, 'excep' you mustn't get rid of him anyhow, an' 'e can
do what 'e likes always. Lucky for us 'e *do* farm; and if it
wasn't for 'is woman –'

'Oh, there's a Mrs Sidney, is there?'

'Lor, *no*! The Sidneys don't marry. They keep. That's his
fourth since – to my knowledge. He was a takin' man from
the first.'

'Any families?'

'They'd be grown up by now if there was, wouldn't they?
But you can't spend all your days considerin' 'is interests.
That's what gave your pore aunt 'er indigestion. 'Ave you
seen the gun-room?'

Midmore held strong views on the immorality of taking
life for pleasure. But there was no denying that the late
Colonel Werf's seventy-guinea breechloaders were good at
their filthy job. He loaded one, took it out and pointed –
merely pointed – it at a cock-pheasant which rose out of a
shrubbery behind the kitchen, and the flaming bird came
down in a long slant on the lawn, stone dead. Rhoda from
the scullery said it was a lovely shot, and told him lunch was
ready.

He spent the afternoon gun in one hand, a map in the
other, beating the bounds of his lands. They lay altogether
in a shallow, uninteresting valley, flanked with woods and
bisected by a brook. Up stream was his own house; down
stream, less than half a mile, a low red farm-house squatted

in an old orchard, beside what looked like small lock-gates on the Thames. There was no doubt as to ownership. Mr Sidney saw him while yet far off, and bellowed at him about pig-pounds and flood-gates. These last were two great sliding shutters of weedy oak across the brook, which were prised up inch by inch with a crowbar along a notched strip of iron, and when Sidney opened them they at once let out half the water. Midmore watched it shrink between its aldered banks like some conjuring trick. This, too, was his very own.

'I see,' he said. 'How interesting! Now, what's that bell for?' he went on, pointing to an old ship's bell in a rude belfry at the end of an outhouse. 'Was that a chapel once?' The red-eyed giant seemed to have difficulty in expressing himself for the moment and blinked savagely.

'Yes,' he said at last. 'My chapel. When you 'ear that bell ring you'll 'ear something. Nobody but me ud put up with it – but I reckon it don't make any odds to you.' He slammed the gates down again, and the brook rose behind them with a suck and a grunt.

Midmore moved off, conscious that he might be safer with Rhoda to hold his conversational hand. As he passed the front of the farm-house a smooth fat woman, with neatly parted grey hair under a widow's cap, curtsied to him deferentially through the window. By every teaching of the Immoderate Left she had a perfect right to express herself in any way she pleased, but the curtsy revolted him. And on his way home he was hailed from behind a hedge by a manifest idiot with no roof to his mouth, who hallooed and danced round him.

'What did that beast want?' he demanded of Rhoda at tea.

'Jimmy? He only wanted to know if you 'ad any telegrams to send. 'E'll go anywhere so long as 'tisn't across running water. That gives 'im 'is seizures. Even talkin' about it for fun like makes 'im shake.'

'But why isn't he where he can be properly looked after?'

'What 'arm's 'e doing? 'E's a love-child, but 'is family can

32

pay for 'im. If 'e was locked up 'e'd die all off at once, like a
wild rabbit. Won't you, please, look at the drive, sir?'

Midmore looked in the fading light. The neat gravel was
pitted with large roundish holes, and there was a punch or
two of the same sort on the lawn.

'That's the 'unt comin' 'ome,' Rhoda explained. 'Your pore
dear auntie always let 'em use our drive for a short cut after
the Colonel died. The Colonel wouldn't so much because he
preserved; but your auntie was always an 'orsewoman till 'er
sciatica.'

'Isn't there some one who can rake it over or – or something?' said Midmore vaguely.

'Oh yes. You'll never see it in the morning, but – you was
out when they came 'ome an' Mister Fisher – he's the Master
– told me to tell you with 'is compliments that if you wasn't
preservin' and cared to 'old to the old understandin', 'is
gravel-pit is at your service same as before. 'E thought,
perhaps, you mightn't know, and it 'ad slipped my mind to
tell you. It's good gravel, Mister Fisher's, and it binds beautiful on the drive. We 'ave to draw it, o' course, from the pit,
but – '

Midmore looked at her helplessly.

'Rhoda,' said he, 'what am I supposed to do?'

'Oh, let 'em come through,' she replied. 'You never know.
You may want to 'unt yourself some day.'

That evening it rained and his misery returned on him,
the worse for having been diverted. At last he was driven to
paw over a few score books in a panelled room called the
library, and realized with horror what the late Colonel
Werf's mind must have been in its prime. The volumes smelt
of a dead world as strongly as they did of mildew. He opened
and thrust them back, one after another, till crude coloured
illustrations of men or horses held his eye. He began at
random and read a little, moved into the drawing-room with
the volume, and settled down by the fire still reading. It was
a foul world into which he peeped for the first time – a heavy-
eating, hard-drinking hell of horse-copers, swindlers, match-
making mothers, economically dependent virgins selling

33

themselves blushingly for cash and lands: Jews, tradesmen, and an ill-considered spawn of Dickens-and-horsedung characters (I give Midmore's own criticism), but he read on, fascinated, and behold, from the pages leaped, as it were, the brother to the red-eyed man of the brook, bellowing at a landlord (here Midmore realized that *he* was that very animal) for new barns; and another man who, like himself again, objected to hoof-marks on gravel. Outrageous as thought and conception were, the stuff seemed to have the rudiments of observation. He dug out other volumes by the same author, till Rhoda came in with a silver candlestick.

'Rhoda,' said he, 'did you ever hear about a character called James Pigg – and Batsey?'

'Why, o' course,' said she. 'The Colonel used to come into the kitchen in 'is dressin'-gown an' read us all those Jorrockses.'

'Oh, Lord!' said Midmore, and went to bed with a book called *Handley Cross* under his arm, and a lonelier Columbus into a stranger world the wet-ringed moon never looked upon.

Here we omit much. But Midmore never denied that for the epicure in sensation the urgent needs of an ancient house, as interpreted by Rhoda pointing to daylight through attic-tiles held in place by moss, gives an edge to the pleasure of Social Research elsewhere. Equally he found that the reaction following prolonged research loses much of its grey terror if one knows one can at will bathe the soul in the society of plumbers (all the water-pipes had chronic appendicitis), village idiots (Jimmy had taken Midmore under his weak wing and camped daily at the drive-gates), and a giant with red eyelids whose every action is an unpredictable outrage.

Towards spring Midmore filled his house with a few friends of the Immoderate Left. It happened to be the day when, all things and Rhoda working together, a cartload of bricks, another of sand, and some bags of lime had been dispatched to build Sidney his almost daily-demanded pig-pound. Midmore took his friends across the flat fields with some idea of showing them Sidney as a type of 'the peasantry'. They hit the minute when Sidney, hoarse with rage, was ordering bricklayer, mate, carts and all off his premises. The visitors disposed themselves to listen.

'You never give me no notice about changin' the pig,' Sidney shouted. The pig – at least eighteen inches long – reared on end in the old sty and smiled at the company.

'But, my good man –' Midmore opened.

'I ain't! For aught you know I be a dam' sight worse than you be. You can't come and be'ave arbit'ry with me. You *are* be'avin' arbit'ry! All you men go clean away an' don't set foot on my land till I bid ye.'

'But you asked' – Midmore felt his voice jump up – 'to have the pig-pound built.'

' 'Spose I did. That's no reason you shouldn't send me notice to change the pig. 'Comin' down on me like this 'thout warnin'! That pig's got to be got into the cowshed an' all.'

'Then open the door and let him run in,' said Midmore.

'Don't you be'ave arbit'ry with *me*! Take all your dam' men 'ome off my land. I won't be treated arbit'ry.'

The carts moved off without a word, and Sidney went into the house and slammed the door.

'Now, I hold that is enormously significant,' said a visitor. 'Here you have the logical outcome of centuries of feudal oppression – the frenzy of fear.' The company looked at Midmore with grave pain.

'But he *did* worry my life out about his pig-sty,' was all Midmore found to say.

Others took up the parable and proved to him if he only held true to the gospels of the Immoderate Left the earth would soon be covered with 'jolly little' pig-sties, built in the intervals of morris-dancing by 'the peasant' himself.

Midmore felt grateful when the door opened again and Mr Sidney invited them all to retire to the road which, he pointed out, was public. As they turned the corner of the house, a smooth-faced woman in a widow's cap curtsied to each of them through the window.

Instantly they drew pictures of that woman's lot, deprived of all vehicle for self-expression – 'the set grey life and apathetic end,' one quoted – and they discussed the tremendous significance of village theatricals. Even a month ago Midmore would have told them all that he knew and Rhoda had dropped about Sidney's forms of self-expression. Now, for some strange reason, he was content to let the talk run on from village to metropolitan and world drama.

Rhoda advised him after the visitors left that 'if he wanted to do that again' he had better go up to town.

'But we only sat on cushions on the floor,' said her master.

'They're too old for romps,' she retorted, 'an' it's only the beginning of things. I've seen what *I've* seen. Besides, they talked and laughed in the passage going to their baths – such as took 'em.'

'Don't be a fool, Rhoda,' said Midmore. No man – unless he has loved her – will casually dismiss a woman on whose lap he has laid his head.

'Very good,' she snorted, 'but that cuts both ways. An' now, you go down to Sidney's this evenin' and put him where he ought to be. He was in his right about you givin' 'im notice about changin' the pig, but he 'adn't any right to turn it up before your company. No manners, no pig-pound. He'll understand.'

Midmore did his best to make him. He found himself reviling the old man in speech and with a joy quite new in all his experience. He wound up – it was a plagiarism from a plumber – by telling Mr Sidney that he looked like a turkeycock, had the morals of a parish bull, and need never hope for a new pig-pound as long as he or Midmore lived.

'Very good,' said the giant. 'I reckon you thought you 'ad something against me, and now you've come down an' told it me like man to man. Quite right. I don't bear malice. Now, you send along those bricks an' sand, an' I'll make a do to build the pig-pound myself. If you look at my lease you'll find out you're bound to provide me materials for the repairs. Only – only I thought there'd be no 'arm in my askin' you to do it throughout like.'

Midmore fairly gasped. 'Then, why the devil did you turn my carts back when – when I sent them up here to do it throughout for you?'

Mr Sidney sat down on the floodgates, his eyebrows knitted in thought.

'I'll tell you,' he said slowly. ' 'Twas too dam' like cheatin' a suckin' baby. My woman, she said so too.'

For a few seconds the teachings of the Immoderate Left, whose humour is all their own, wrestled with those of Mother Earth, who has her own humours. Then Midmore laughed till he could scarcely stand. In due time Mr Sidney laughed too – crowing and wheezing crescendo till it broke from him in roars. They shook hands, and Midmore went home grateful that he had held his tongue among his companions.

When he reached his house he met three or four men and women on horseback, very muddy indeed, coming down the drive. Feeling hungry himself, he asked them if they were hungry. They said they were, and he bade them enter. Jimmy took their horses, who seemed to know him. Rhoda took their battered hats, led the women upstairs for hairpins, and presently fed them all with tea-cakes, poached eggs, anchovy toast, and drinks from a coromandel-wood liqueur case which Midmore had never known that he possessed.

'And I *will* say,' said Miss Connie Sperrit, her spurred foot on the fender and a smoking muffin in her whip hand, 'Rhoda does one top-hole. She always did since I was eight.'

'Seven, Miss, was when you began to 'unt,' said Rhoda, setting down more buttered toast.

'And so,' the M.F.H. was saying to Midmore, 'when he got to your brute Sidney's land, we had to whip 'em off. It's a regular Alsatia for 'em. They know it. Why' – he dropped his voice – 'I don't want to say anything against Sidney as your tenant, of course, but I do believe the old scoundrel's perfectly capable of putting down poison.'

'Sidney's capable of anything,' said Midmore with immense feeling; but once again he held his tongue. They were a queer community; yet when they had stamped and jingled out to their horses again, the house felt hugely big and disconcerting.

This may be reckoned the conscious beginning of his double life. It ran in odd channels that summer – a riding school, for instance, near Hayes Common and a shooting ground near Wormwood Scrubs. A man who has been saddle-galled or shoulder-bruised for half the day is not at his London best of evenings; and when the bills for his amusements come in he curtails his expenses in other directions. So a cloud settled on Midmore's name. His London world talked of a hardening of heart and a tightening of purse-strings which signified disloyalty to the Cause. One man, a confidant of the old expressive days, attacked him robustiously and demanded account of his soul's progress. It was not furnished, for Midmore was calculating how much it would cost to repave stables so dilapidated that even the village idiot apologized for putting visitors' horses into them. The man went away, and served up what he had heard of the pig-pound episode as a little newspaper sketch, calculated to annoy. Midmore read it with an eye as practical as a woman's, and since most of his experiences had been among women, at once sought out a woman to whom he might tell his sorrow at the disloyalty of his own familiar friend. She was so sympathetic that he went on to confide how his bruised heart – she knew all about it – had found so-lace, with a long O, in another quarter which he indicated rather carefully in case it might be betrayed to other loyal friends. As his hints pointed directly towards facile Hampstead, and as his urgent business was the purchase of a horse from a dealer, Beckenham way, he felt he had done good work. Later, when his friend, the scribe, talked to him alluringly of 'secret gardens' and those so-laces to which every man who follows the Wider Morality is entitled, Midmore lent him a five-pound note which he had got back on the price of a ninety-guinea bay gelding. So true it is, as he read in one of the late Colonel Werf's books, that 'the young man of the present day would sooner lie under an imputation against his morals than against his knowledge of horse-flesh.'

Midmore desired more than he desired anything else at that moment to ride and, above all, to jump on a ninety-guinea bay gelding with black points and a slovenly habit of hitting his fences. He did not wish many people except Mr Sidney, who very kindly lent his soft meadow behind the floodgates, to be privy to the matter, which he rightly foresaw would take him to the autumn. So he told such friends as hinted at country weekend visits that he had practically let his newly inherited house. The rent, he said, was an object to him, for he had lately lost large sums through ill-considered benevolences. He would name no names, but they could guess. And they guessed loyally all round the circle of his acquaintance as they spread the news that explained so much.

There remained only one couple of his once intimate associates to pacify. They were deeply sympathetic and utterly loyal, of course, but as curious as any of the apes whose diet they had adopted. Midmore met them in a suburban train, coming up to town, not twenty minutes after he had come off two hours' advanced tuition (one guinea an hour) over hurdles in a hall. He had, of course, changed his kit, but his too heavy bridle-hand shook a little among the newspapers. On the inspiration of the moment, which is your natural liar's best hold, he told them that he was condemned to a rest-cure. He would lie in semi-darkness drinking milk, for weeks and weeks, cut off even from letters. He was astonished and delighted at the ease with which the usual lie confounds the unusual intellect. They swallowed it as swiftly as they recommended him to live on nuts and fruit; but he saw in the woman's eyes the exact reason she would set forth for his retirement. After all, she had as much right to express herself as he purposed to take for himself; and Midmore believed strongly in the fullest equality of the sexes.

That retirement made one small ripple in the strenuous world. The lady who had written the twelve-page letter ten months before sent him another of eight pages analysing all the motives that were leading her back to him – should she come? – now that he was ill and alone. Much might yet be retrieved, she said, out of the waste of jarring lives and piteous misunderstandings. It needed only a hand.

But Midmore needed two, next morning very early, for a devil's diversion, among wet coppices, called 'cubbing.'

'You haven't a bad seat,' said Miss Sperrit through the morning-mists. 'But you're worrying him.'

'He pulls so,' Midmore grunted.

'Let him alone, then. Look out for the branches,' she shouted, as they whirled up a splashy ride. Cubs were plentiful. Most of the hounds attached themselves to a straight-necked youngster of education who scuttled out of the woods into the open fields below.

'Hold on!' some one shouted. 'Turn 'em, Midmore. That's your brute Sidney's land. It's all wire.'

'Oh, Connie, stop!' Mrs Sperrit shrieked as her daughter charged at a boundary-hedge.

'Wire be damned! I had it all out a fortnight ago. Come on!' This was Midmore, buffeting into it a little lower down.

'*I* knew that!' Connie cried over her shoulder, and she flitted across the open pasture, humming to herself.

'Oh, of course! If some people have private information, they can afford to thrust.' This was a snuff-coloured habit into which Miss Sperrit had cannoned down the ride.

'What! Midmore got Sidney to heel? *You* never did that, Sperrit.' This was Mr Fisher, M.F.H., enlarging the breach Midmore had made.

'No, confound him!' said the father testily. 'Go on, sir! *Injecto ter pulvere* – you've kicked half the ditch into my eye already.'

They killed that cub a little short of the haven his mother had told him to make for – a two-acre Alsatia of a gorse-patch to which the M.F.H. had been denied access for the last fifteen seasons. He expressed his gratitude before all the field and Mr Sidney, at Mr Sidney's farmhouse door.

'And if there should be any poultry claims –' he went on.

'There won't be,' said Midmore. 'It's too like cheating a sucking child, isn't it, Mr Sidney?'

'You've got me!' was all the reply. 'I be used to bein' put upon, but you've got me, Mus' Midmore.'

Midmore pointed to a new brick pig-pound built in strict disregard of the terms of the life-tenant's lease. The gesture told the tale to the few who did not know, and they shouted.

Such pagan delights as these were followed by pagan sloth of evenings when men and women elsewhere are at their brightest. But Midmore preferred to lie out on a yellow silk couch, reading works of a debasing vulgarity; or, by invitation, to dine with the Sperrits and savages of their kidney. These did not expect flights of fancy or phrasing. They lied, except about horses, grudgingly and of necessity, not for art's sake; and, men and women alike, they expressed themselves along their chosen lines with the serene indifference of the larger animals. Then Midmore would go home and identify them, one by one, out of the natural-history books by Mr Surtees, on the table beside the sofa. At first they looked upon him coolly, but when the tale of the removed wire and the recaptured gorse had gone the rounds, they accepted him for a person willing to play their games. True, a faction suspended judgement for a while, because they shot, and hoped that Midmore would serve the glorious mammon of pheasant-raising rather than the unkempt god of fox-hunting. But after he had shown his choice, they did not ask by what intellectual process he had arrived at it. He hunted three, sometimes four, times a week, which necessitated not only one bay gelding (£94 10s.), but a mannerly white-stockinged chestnut (£114), and a black mare, rather long in the back but with a mouth of silk (£150), who so evidently preferred to carry a lady that it would have been cruel to have baulked her. Besides, with that handling she could be sold at a profit. And besides, the hunt was a quiet, intimate, kindly little hunt, not anxious for strangers, of good report in the *Field*, the servant of one M.F.H., given to hospitality, riding well its own horses, and, with the exception of Midmore, not novices. But as Miss Sperrit observed, after the M.F.H. had said some things to him at a gate: 'It *is* a pity you don't know as much as your horse, but you will in time. It takes years and yee-ars. I've been at it for fifteen and I'm only just learning. But you've made a decent kick-off.'

So he kicked off in wind and wet and mud, wondering quite sincerely why the bubbling ditches and sucking pastures held him from day to day, or what so-lace he could find on off days in chasing grooms and bricklayers round outhouses.

To make sure he uprooted himself one weekend of heavy mid-winter rain, and re-entered his lost world in the character of Galahad fresh from a rest-cure. They all agreed, with an eye over his shoulder for the next comer, that he was a different man; but when they asked him for the symptoms of nervous strain, and led him all through their own, he realized he had lost much of his old skill in lying. His three months' absence, too, had put him hopelessly behind the London field. The movements, the allusions, the slang of the game had changed. The couples had rearranged themselves or were re-crystallizing in fresh triangles, whereby he put his foot in it badly. Only one great soul (he who had written the account of the pig-pound episode) stood untouched by the vast flux of time, and Midmore lent him another fiver for his integrity. A woman took him, in the wet forenoon, to a pronouncement on the Oneness of Impulse in Humanity, which struck him as a polysyllabic *résumé* of Mr Sidney's domestic arrangements, plus a clarion call to 'shock civilization into common-sense.'

'And you'll come to tea with me tomorrow?' she asked, after lunch, nibbling cashew nuts from a saucer. Midmore replied that there were great arrears of work to overtake when a man had been put away for so long.

'But you've come back like a giant refreshed. ... I hope that Daphne' – this was the lady of the twelve and the eight-page letter – 'will be with us too. She has misunderstood herself, like so many of us,' the woman murmured, 'but I think eventually . . .' she flung out her thin little hands. 'However, these are things that each lonely soul must adjust for itself.'

'Indeed, yes,' said Midmore with a deep sigh. The old tricks were sprouting in the old atmosphere like mushrooms in a dung-pit. He passed into an abrupt reverie, shook his head, as though stung by tumultuous memories, and departed without any ceremony of farewell to – catch a mid-afternoon express where a man meets associates who talk horse, and weather as it affects the horse, all the way down. What worried him most was that he had missed a day with the hounds.

He met Rhoda's keen old eyes without flinching; and the drawing-room looked very comfortable that wet evening at tea. After all, his visit to town had not been wholly a failure. He had burned quite a bushel of letters at his flat. A flat – here he reached mechanically towards the worn volumes near the sofa – a flat was a consuming animal. As for Daphne . . . he opened at random on the words: 'His lordship then did as desired and disclosed a *tableau* of considerable strength and variety.' Midmore reflected: 'And I used to think . . . But she wasn't . . . We were all babblers and skirters together . . . I didn't babble much – thank goodness – but I skirted.' He turned the pages backwards for more *Sortes Surteesianae*, and read: 'When at length they rose to go to bed it struck each man as he followed his neighbour upstairs, that the man before him walked very crookedly.' He laughed aloud at the fire.

'What about tomorrow?' Rhoda asked, entering with garments over her shoulder. 'It's never stopped raining since you left. You'll be plastered out of sight an' all in five minutes. You'd better wear your next best, 'adn't you? I'm afraid they've shrank. 'Adn't you best try 'em on?'

'Here?' said Midmore.

'Suit yourself. I bathed you when you wasn't larger than a leg o' lamb,' said the ex-ladies'-maid.

'Rhoda, one of these days I shall get a valet, and a married butler.'

'There's many a true word spoke in jest. But nobody's huntin' tomorrow.'

'Why? Have they cancelled the meet?'

'They say it only means slipping and over-reaching in the mud, and they all 'ad enough of that today. Charlie told me so just now.'

'Oh!' It seemed that the word of Mr Sperrit's confidential clerk had weight.

'Charlie came down to help Mr Sidney lift the gates,' Rhoda continued.

'The flood-gates? They are perfectly easy to handle now. I've put in a wheel and a winch.'

'When the brook's really up they must be took clean out on account of the rubbish blockin' 'em. That's why Charlie came down.'

Midmore grunted impatiently. 'Everybody has talked to me about that brook ever since I came here. It's never done anything yet.'

'This 'as been a dry summer. If you care to look now, sir, I'll get you a lantern.'

She paddled out with him into a large wet night. Half-way down the lawn her light was reflected on shallow brown water, pricked through with grass blades at the edges. Beyond that light, the brook was strangling and kicking among hedges and tree-trunks.

'What on earth will happen to the big rose-bed?' was Midmore's first word.

'It generally 'as to be restocked after a flood. Ah!' she raised her lantern. 'There's two garden-seats knockin' against the sun-dial. Now, that won't do the roses any good.'

'This is too absurd. There ought to be some decently thought-out system – for – for dealing with this sort of thing.' He peered into the rushing gloom. There seemed to be no end to the moisture and the racket. In town he had noticed nothing.

'It can't be 'elped,' said Rhoda. 'It's just what it does do once in just so often. We'd better go back.'

All earth under foot was sliding in a thousand liquid noises towards the hoarse brook. Somebody wailed from the house: ' 'Fraid o' the water! Come 'ere! 'Fraid o' the water!'

'That's Jimmy. Wet always takes 'im that way,' she explained. The idiot charged into them, shaking with terror.

'Brave Jimmy! How brave of Jimmy! Come into the hall. What Jimmy got now?' she crooned. It was a sodden note which ran: 'Dear Rhoda – Mr Lotten, with whom I rode home this afternoon, told me that if this wet keeps up, he's afraid the fish-pond he built last year, where Coxen's old mill-dam was, will go, as the dam did once before, he says. If it does it's bound to come down the brook. It may be all right, but perhaps you had better look out. C. S.'

'If Coxen's dam goes, that means ... I'll 'ave the drawing-room carpet up at once to be on the safe side. The claw-'ammer is in the library.'

'Wait a minute. Sidney's gates are out, you said?'

'Both. He'll need it if Coxen's pond goes. ... I've seen it once.'

'I'll just slip down and have a look at Sidney. Light the lantern again, please, Rhoda.'

'You won't get *him* to stir. He's been there since he was born. But *she* don't know anything. I'll fetch your water-proof and some top-boots.'

' 'Fraid o' the water! 'Fraid o' the water!' Jimmy sobbed, pressed against a corner of the hall, his hands to his eyes.

'All right, Jimmy. Jimmy can help play with the carpet,' Rhoda answered, as Midmore went forth into the darkness and the roarings all round. He had never seen such an utterly unregulated state of affairs. There was another lantern reflected on the streaming drive.

'Hi! Rhoda! Did you get my note? I came down to make sure. I thought, afterwards, Jimmy might funk the water!'

'It's me – Miss Sperrit,' Midmore cried. 'Yes, we got it, thanks.'

'You're back, then. Oh, good! ... Is it bad down with you?'

'I'm going to Sidney's to have a look.'

'You won't get *him* out. Lucky I met Bob Lotten. I told him he hadn't any business impounding water for his idiotic trout without rebuilding the dam.'

'How far up is it? I've only been there once.'

'Not more than four miles as the water will come. He says he's opened all the sluices.'

She had turned and fallen into step beside him, her hooded head bowed against the thinning rain. As usual she was humming to herself.

'Why on earth did you come out in this weather?' Midmore asked.

'It was worse when you were in town. The rain's taking off now. If it wasn't for that pond, I wouldn't worry so much. There's Sidney's bell. Come on!' She broke into a run. A cracked bell was jangling feebly down the valley.

'Keep on the road!' Midmore shouted. The ditches were snorting bank-full on either side, and towards the brook-side the fields were afloat and beginning to move in the darkness.

'Catch me going off it! There's his light burning all right.' She halted undistressed at a little rise. 'But the flood's in the orchard. Look!' She swung her lantern to show a front rank of old apple-trees reflected in still, out-lying waters beyond the half-drowned hedge. They could hear above the thud-thud of the gorged flood-gates, shrieks in two keys as monotonous as a steam-organ.

'The high one's the pig.' Miss Sperrit laughed.

'All right! I'll get *her* out. You stay where you are, and I'll see you home afterwards.'

'But the water's only just over the road,' she objected.

'Never mind. Don't you move. Promise?'

'All right. You take my stick, then, and feel for holes in case anything's washed out anywhere. This *is* a lark!'

Midmore took it, and stepped into the water that moved sluggishly as yet across the farm road which ran to Sidney's front door from the raised and metalled public road. It was half way up to his knees when he knocked. As he looked back Miss Sperrit's lantern seemed to float in mid-ocean.

'You can't come in or the water'll come with you. I've bunged up all the cracks,' Mr Sidney shouted from within. 'Who be ye?'

'Take me out! Take me out!' the woman shrieked, and the pig from his sty behind the house urgently seconded the motion.

'I'm Midmore! Coxen's old mill-dam is likely to go, they say. Come out!'

'I told 'em it would when they made a fish-pond of it. 'Twasn't ever puddled proper. But it's a middlin' wide valley. She's got room to spread. . . . Keep still, or I'll take and duck you in the cellar! . . . You go 'ome, Mus' Midmore, an' take the law o' Mus' Lotten soon's you've changed your socks.'

'Confound you, aren't you coming out?'

'To catch my death o' cold? I'm all right where I be. I've seen it before. But you can take *her*. She's no sort o' use or sense. . . . Climb out through the window. Didn't I tell you I'd plugged the door-cracks, you fool's daughter?' The parlour window opened, and the woman flung herself into Midmore's arms, nearly knocking him down. Mr Sidney leaned out of the window, pipe in mouth.

'Take her 'ome,' he said, and added oracularly:

'Two women in one house,
Two cats an' one mouse,
Two dogs an' one bone –
Which I will leave alone.

I've seen it before.' Then he shut and fastened the window.

'A trap! A trap! You had ought to have brought a trap for me. I'll be drowned in this wet,' the woman cried.

'Hold up! You can't be any wetter than you are. Come along!' Midmore did not at all like the feel of the water over his boot-tops.

'Hooray! Come along!' Miss Sperrit's lantern, not fifty yards away, waved cheerily.

The woman threshed towards it like a panic-stricken goose, fell on her knees, was jerked up again by Midmore, and pushed on till she collapsed at Miss Sperrit's feet.

'But you won't get bronchitis if you go straight to Mr Mid-more's house,' said the unsympathetic maiden.

'O Gawd! O Gawd! I wish our 'eavenly Father 'ud forgive me my sins an' call me 'ome,' the woman sobbed. 'But I won't go to *'is* 'ouse! I won't.'

'All right, then. Stay here. Now, if we run,' Miss Sperrit whispered to Midmore, 'she'll follow us. Not too fast!'

They set off at a considerate trot, and the woman lum-bered behind them, bellowing, till they met a third lantern – Rhoda holding Jimmy's hand. She had got the carpet up, she said, and was escorting Jimmy past the water that he dreaded.

'That's all right,' Miss Sperrit pronounced. 'Take Mrs Sidney back with you, Rhoda, and put her to bed. I'll take Jimmy with me. You aren't afraid of the water now, are you, Jimmy?'

'Not afraid of anything now.' Jimmy reached for her hand. 'But get away from the water quick.'

'I'm coming with you,' Midmore interrupted.

'You most certainly are not. You're drenched. She threw you twice. Go home and change. You may have to be out again all night. It's only half past seven now. I'm perfectly safe.' She flung herself lightly over a stile, and hurried up hill by the footpath, out of reach of all but the boasts of the flood below.

Rhoda, dead silent, herded Mrs Sidney to the house.

'You'll find your things laid out on the bed,' she said to Midmore as he came up. 'I'll attend to – to this. *She's* got nothing to cry for.'

Midmore raced into dry kit, and raced up hill to be re-warded by the sight of the lantern just turning into the Sper-rits' gate. He came back by way of Sidney's farm, where he saw the light twinkling across three acres of shining water, for the rain had ceased and the clouds were stripping over-head, though the brook was noisier than ever. Now there was only that doubtful mill-pond to look after – that and his swirling world abandoned to himself alone.

'We shall have to sit up for it,' said Rhoda after dinner.

48

And as the drawing-room commanded the best view of the rising flood, they watched it from there for a long time, while all the clocks of the house bore them company.

' 'Tisn't the water, it's the mud on the skirting-board after it goes down that I mind,' Rhoda whispered. 'The last time Coxen's mill broke, I remember it came up to the second – no, third – step o' Mr Sidney's stairs.'

'What did Sidney do about it?'

'He made a notch on the step. 'E said it was a record. Just like 'im.'

'It's up to the drive now,' said Midmore after another long wait. 'And the rain stopped before eight, you know.'

'Then Coxen's dam 'as broke, and that's the first of the flood-water.' She stared out beside him. The water was rising in sudden pulses – an inch or two at a time, with great sweeps and lagoons and a sudden increase of the brook's proper thunder.

'You can't stand all the time. Take a chair,' Midmore said presently.

Rhoda looked back into the bare room. 'The carpet bein' up *does* make a difference. Thank you, sir, I *will* 'ave a set-down.'

'Right over the drive now,' said Midmore. He opened the window and leaned out. 'Is that wind up the valley, Rhoda?'

'No, that's *it*! But I've seen it before.'

There was not so much a roar as the purposeful drive of a tide across a jagged reef, which put down every other sound for twenty minutes. A wide sheet of water hurried up to the little terrace on which the house stood, pushed round either corner, rose again and stretched, as it were, yawning beneath the moonlight, joined other sheets waiting for them in un-suspected hollows, and lay out all in one. A puff of wind followed.

'It's right up to the wall now. I can touch it with my finger.' Midmore bent over the window-sill.

'I can 'ear it in the cellars,' said Rhoda dolefully. 'Well, we've done what we can! I think I'll 'ave a look.' She left the room and was absent half an hour or more, during which time he saw a full-grown tree hauling itself across the lawn by its naked roots. Then a hurdle knocked against the wall, caught on an iron foot-scraper just outside, and made a square-headed ripple. The cascade through the cellar-windows diminished.

'It's dropping,' Rhoda cried, as she returned. 'It's only tricklin' into my cellars now.'

'Wait a minute. I believe – I believe I can see the scraper on the edge of the drive just showing!'

In another ten minutes the drive itself roughened and became gravel again, tilting all its water towards the shrubbery.

'The pond's gone past,' Rhoda announced. 'We shall only 'ave the common flood to contend with now. You'd better go to bed.'

'I ought to go down and have another look at Sidney before daylight.'

'No need. You can see 'is light burnin' from all the upstairs windows.'

'By the way. I forgot about *her*. Where've you put her?'

'In my bed.' Rhoda's tone was ice. 'I wasn't going to undo a room for *that* stuff.'

'But it – it couldn't be helped,' said Midmore. 'She was half drowned. One mustn't be narrow-minded, Rhoda, even if her position isn't quite – er – regular.'

'Pfff! I wasn't worryin' about that.' She leaned forward to the window. 'There's the edge of the lawn showin' now. It falls as fast as it rises. Dearie' – the change of tone made Midmore jump – 'didn't you know that I was 'is first? *That's* what makes it so hard to bear.' Midmore looked at the long lizard-like back and had no words.

She went on, still talking through the black windowpane:

'Your pore dear auntie was very kind about it. She said she'd make all allowances for one, but no more. Never any more. ... Then, you didn't know 'oo Charlie was all this time?'

'Your nephew, I always thought.'

'Well, well,' she spoke pityingly. 'Everybody's business being nobody's business, I suppose no one thought to tell you. But Charlie made 'is own way for 'imself from the beginnin'! . . . But *her* upstairs, she never produced anything. Just an 'ousekeeper, as you might say. 'Turned over an' went to sleep straight off. She 'ad the impudence to ask me for 'ot sherry-gruel.'

'Did you give it to her?' said Midmore.

'Me? Your sherry? No!'

The memory of Sidney's outrageous rhyme at the window, and Charlie's long nose (he thought it looked interested at the time) as he passed the copies of Mrs Werf's last four wills, overcame Midmore without warning.

'This damp is givin' you a cold,' said Rhoda, rising. 'There you go again! Sneezin's a sure sign of it. Better go to bed. You can't do anythin' excep' ' – she stood rigid, with crossed arms – 'about me.'

'Well. What about you?' Midmore stuffed the handkerchief into his pocket.

'Now you know about it, what are you goin' to do – sir?'

She had the answer on her lean cheek before the sentence was finished.

'Go and see if you can get us something te eat, Rhoda. And beer.'

'I expec' the larder'll be in a swim,' she replied, 'but old bottled stuff don't take any harm from wet.' She returned with a tray, all in order, and they ate and drank together, and took observations of the falling flood till dawn opened its bleared eyes on the wreck of what had been a fair garden. Midmore, cold and annoyed, found himself humming:

> 'That flood strewed wrecks upon the grass,
> That ebb swept out the flocks to sea.

There isn't a rose left, Rhoda!

> An awesome ebb and flow it was
> To many more than mine and me.
> But each will mourn his . . .

It'll cost me a hundred.'

'Now we know the worst,' said Rhoda, 'we can go to bed. I'll lay on the kitchen sofa. His light's burnin' still.'

'And *she*?'

'Dirty old cat! You ought to 'ear 'er snore!'

At ten o'clock in the morning, after a maddening hour in his own garden on the edge of the retreating brook, Midmore went off to confront more damage at Sidney's. The first thing that met him was the pig, snowy white, for the water had washed him out of his new sty, calling on high heaven for breakfast. The front door had been forced open, and the flood had registered its own height in a brown dado on the walls. Midmore chased the pig out and called up the stairs.

'I be abed o' course. Which step 'as she rose to?' Sidney cried from above. 'The fourth? Then it's beat all records. Come up.'

'Are you ill?' Midmore asked as he entered the room. The red eyelids blinked cheerfully. Mr Sidney, beneath a sumptuous patch-work quilt, was smoking.

'Nah! I'm only thankin' God I ain't my own landlord. Take that cheer. What's she done?'

'It hasn't gone down enough for me to make sure.'

'Them floodgates o' yourn 'll be middlin' far down the brook by now; an' your rose-garden have gone after 'em. I saved my chickens, though. You'd better get Mus' Sperrit to take the law o' Lotten an' 'is fish-pond.'

'No, thanks. I've trouble enough without that.'

'Hev ye?' Mr Sidney grinned. 'How did ye make out with those two women o' mine last night? I lay they fought.'

'You infernal old scoundrel!' Midmore laughed.

'I be – an' then again I bain't,' was the placid answer. 'But, Rhoda, *she* wouldn't ha' left me last night. Fire or flood, she wouldn't.'

'Why didn't you ever marry her?' Midmore asked.

'Waste of good money. She was willin' without.'

There was a step on the gritty mud below, and a voice humming. Midmore rose quickly saying: 'Well, I suppose you're all right now.'

'I be. I ain't a landlord, nor I ain't young – nor anxious.

Oh, Mus' Midmore! Would it make any odds about her thirty pounds comin' regular if I married her? Charlie said maybe 'twould.'

'Did he?' Midmore turned at the door. 'And what did Jimmy say about it?'

'Jimmy?' Mr Sidney chuckled as the joke took him. 'Oh, *he's* none o' mine. He's Charlie's look-out.'

Midmore slammed the door and ran downstairs.

'Well, this is a – sweet – mess,' said Miss Sperrit in shortest skirts and heaviest riding-boots. 'I had to come down and have a look at it. "The old mayor climbed the belfry tower." 'Been up all night nursing your family?'

'Nearly that! Isn't it cheerful?' He pointed through the door to the stairs with small twig-drift on the last three treads.

'It's a record, though,' said she, and hummed to herself:

> 'That flood strewed wrecks upon the grass,
> That ebb swept out the flocks to sea.'

'You're always singing that, aren't you?' Midmore said suddenly as she passed into the parlour where slimy chairs had been stranded at all angles.

'Am I? Now I come to think of it I believe I do. They say I always hum when I ride. Have you noticed it?'

'Of course I have. I notice every –'

'Oh,' she went on hurriedly. 'We had it for the village cantata last winter – "The Brides of Enderby".'

'No! "High Tide on the Coast of Lincolnshire."' For some reason Midmore spoke sharply.

'Just like that.' She pointed to the befouled walls. 'I say.... Let's get this furniture a little straight.... You know it too?'

'Every word, since you sang it, of course.'

'When?'

'The first night I ever came down. You rode past the drawing-room window in the dark singing it – "And sweeter woman –"'

'I thought the house was empty then. Your aunt always let

us use that short cut. Ha-hadn't we better get this out into the passage? It'll all have to come out anyhow. You take the other side.' They began to lift a heavyish table. Their words came jerkily between gasps and their faces were as white as – a newly washed and very hungry pig.

'Look out!' Midmore shouted. His legs were whirled from under him, as the pig, grunting madly, careened and knocked the girl out of sight.

The wild boar of Asia could not have cut down a couple more scientifically, but this little pig lacked his ancestor's nerve and fled shrieking over their bodies.

'Are you hurt, darling?' was Midmore's first word, and 'No – I'm only winded – dear,' was Miss Sperrit's, as he lifted her out of her corner, her hat over one eye and her right cheek a smear of mud.

They fed him a little later on some chicken-feed that they found in Sidney's quiet barn, a pail of buttermilk out of the dairy, and a quantity of onions from a shelf in the back-kitchen.

'Seed-onions, most likely,' said Connie. 'You'll hear about this.'

'What does it matter? They ought to have been gilded. We must buy him.'

'And keep him as long as he lives,' she agreed. 'But I think I ought to go home now. You see, when I came out I didn't expect.... Did you?'

'No! Yes.... It had to come.... But if any one had told me an hour ago! ... Sidney's unspeakable parlour – and the mud on the carpet.'

'Oh, I say! Is my cheek clean now?'

'Not quite. Lend me your hanky again a minute, darling.... What a purler you came!'

'You can't talk. Remember when your chin hit that table and you said "blast"! I was just going to laugh.'

'You didn't laugh when I picked you up. You were going "oo-oo-oo" like a little owl.'

'My dear child –'

'Say that again!'

'My dear child. (Do you really like it? I keep it for my best friends.) My *dee-ar* child, I thought I was going to be sick there and then. He knocked every ounce of wind out of me – the angel! But I must really go.'

They set off together, very careful not to join hands or take arms.

'Not across the fields,' said Midmore at the stile. 'Come round by – by your own place.'

She flushed indignantly.

'It will be yours in a little time,' he went on, shaken with his own audacity.

'Not so much of your little times, if you please!' She shied like a colt across the road; then instantly, like a colt, her eyes lit with new curiosity as she came in sight of the drive-gates.

'And not quite so much of your airs and graces, Madam,' Midmore returned, 'or I won't let you use our drive as a short cut any more.'

'Oh, I'll be good. I'll be good.' Her voice changed suddenly. 'I swear I'll try to be good, dear. I'm not much of a thing at the best. What made *you* . . .'

'I'm worse – worse! Miles and oceans worse. But what does it matter now?'

They halted beside the gate-pillars.

'I see!' she said, looking up the sodden carriage sweep to the front door porch where Rhoda was slapping a wet mat to and fro. '*I* see. . . . Now, I really must go home. No! Don't you come. I must speak to Mother first all by myself.'

He watched her up the hill till she was out of sight.

Regulus

(1917; written 1908)

Regulus, a Roman general, defeated the Carthaginians 256 B.C., but was next year defeated and taken prisoner by the Carthaginians, who sent him to Rome with an embassy to ask for peace or an exchange of prisoners. Regulus strongly advised the Roman Senate to make no terms with the enemy. He then returned to Carthage and was put to death.

THE Fifth Form had been dragged several times in its collective life, from one end of the school Horace to the other. Those were the years when Army examiners gave thousands of marks for Latin, and it was Mr King's hated business to defeat them.

Hear him, then, on a raw November morning at second lesson.

'Aha!' he began, rubbing his hands. '*Cras ingens iterabimus aequor.* Our portion today is the Fifth Ode of the Third Book, I believe – concerning one Regulus, a gentleman. And how often have we been through it?'

'Twice, sir,' said Malpas, head of the Form.

Mr King shuddered. 'Yes, twice, quite literally,' he said. 'Today, with an eye to your Army *viva-voce* examinations – ugh! – I shall exact somewhat freer and more florid renditions. With feeling and comprehension if that be possible. I except' – here his eye swept the back benches – 'our friend and companion Beetle, from whom, now as always, I demand an absolutely literal translation.' The form laughed subserviently.

'Spare his blushes! Beetle charms us first.'

Beetle stood up, confident in the possession of a guaranteed construe, left behind by M'Turk, who had that day gone into the sick-house with a cold. Yet he was too wary a hand to show confidence.

'*Credidimus,* we – believe – we have believed,' he opened in hesitating slow time, '*tonantem Jovem,* thundering Jove –

56

regnare, to reign – *caelo*, in heaven. *Augustus*, Augustus – *habebitur*, will be held or considered – *praesens divus*, a present God – *adjectis Britannis*, the Britons being added – *imperio*, to the Empire – *gravibusque Persis*, with the heavy – er, stern Persians.'

'What?'

'The grave or stern Persians.' Beetle pulled up with the 'Thank-God-I-have-done-my-duty' air of Nelson in the cockpit.

'I am quite aware,' said King, 'that the first stanza is about the extent of your knowledge, but continue, sweet one, continue. *Gravibus*, by the way, is usually translated as "troublesome".'

Beetle drew a long and tortured breath. The second stanza (which carries over to the third) of that Ode is what is technically called a 'stinker'. But M'Turk had done him handsomely.

'*Milesne Crassi*, had – has the soldiers of Crassus – *vixit*, lived – *turpis maritus*, a disgraceful husband –'

'You slurred the quantity of the word after *turpis*,' said King. 'Let's hear it.'

Beetle guessed again, and for a wonder hit the correct quantity. 'Er – a disgraceful husband – *conjuge barbara*, with a barbarous spouse.'

'Why do you select *that* disgustful equivalent out of all the dictionary?' King snapped. 'Isn't "wife" good enough for you?'

'Yes, sir. But what do I do about this bracket, sir? Shall I take it now?'

'Confine yourself at present to the soldier of Crassus.'

'Yes, sir. *Et*, and – *consenuit*, has he grown old – *in armis*, in the – er – arms – *hostium socerorum*, of his father-in-law's enemies.'

'Who? How? Which?'

'Arms of his enemies' fathers-in-law, sir.'

'Tha-anks. By the way, what meaning might you attach to *in armis*?'

'Oh, weapons – weapons of war, sir.' There was a virginal

note in Beetle's voice as though he had been falsely accused of uttering indecencies. 'Shall I take the bracket now, sir?'

'Since it seems to be troubling you.'

'*Pro Curia*, O for the Senate House – *inversique mores*, and manners upset – upside down.'

'Ve-ry like your translation. Meantime, the soldier of Crassus?'

'*Sub rege Medo*, under a Median King – *Marsus et Apulus*, he being a Marsian and an Apulian.'

'Who? The Median King?'

'No, sir. The soldier of Crassus. *Oblitus* agrees with *milesne Crassi*, sir,' volunteered too hasty Beetle.

'Does it? It doesn't with *me*.'

'*Oh-blight-us*,' Beetle corrected hastily, 'forgetful – *anciliorum*, of the shields, or trophies – *et nominis*, and the – his name – *et togae*, and the toga – *eternaeque Vestae*, and eternal Vesta – *incolumi Jove*, Jove being safe – *et urbe Roma*, and the Roman city.' With an air of hardly restrained zeal – 'Shall I go on, sir?'

Mr King winced. 'No, thank you. You have indeed given us a translation! May I ask if it conveys any meaning whatever to your so-called mind?'

'Oh, I think so, sir.' This with gentle toleration for Horace and all his works.

'We envy you. Sit down.'

Beetle sat down relieved, well knowing that a reef of uncharted genitives stretched ahead of him, on which in spite of M'Turk's sailing-directions he would infallibly have been wrecked.

Rattray, who took up the task, steered neatly through them and came unscathed to port.

'Here we require drama,' said King. 'Regulus himself is speaking now. Who shall represent the provident-minded Regulus? Winton, will you kindly oblige?'

Winton of King's House, a long, heavy, tow-headed Second Fifteen forward, overdue for his First Fifteen colours, and in aspect like an earnest, elderly horse, rose up, and announced, among other things, that he had seen 'signs affixed to Punic deluges.' Half the Form shouted for joy, and the other half for joy that there was something to shout about.

Mr King opened and shut his eyes with great swiftness. '*Signa adfixa delubris,*' he gasped. 'So *delubris* is "deluges" is it? Winton, in all our dealings, have I ever suspected you of a jest?'

'No, sir,' said the rigid and angular Winton, while the Form rocked about him.

'And yet you assert *delubris* means "deluges". Whether I am a fit subject for such a jape is, of course, a matter of opinion, but. ... Winton, you are normally conscientious. May we assume you looked out *delubris*?'

'No, sir.' Winton was privileged to speak that truth dangerous to all who stand before Kings.

'Made a shot at it then?'

Every line of Winton's body showed he had done nothing of the sort. Indeed, the very idea that 'Pater' Winton (and a boy is not called 'Pater' by companions for his frivolity) would make a shot at anything was beyond belief. But he replied, 'Yes,' and all the while worked with his right heel as though he were heeling a ball at punt-about.

Though none dared to boast of being a favourite with King, the taciturn, three-cornered Winton stood high in his House-Master's opinion. It seemed to save him neither rebuke nor punishment, but the two were in some fashion sympathetic.

'Hm!' said King drily. 'I was going to say – *Flagitio additis damnum,* but I think – I think I see the process. Beetle, the translation of *delubris*, please.'

Beetle raised his head from his shaking arm long enough to answer: 'Ruins, sir.'

There was an impressive pause while King checked off crimes on his fingers. Then to Beetle the much-enduring man addressed winged words:

'Guessing,' said he. 'Guessing, Beetle, as usual, from the look of *delubris* that it bore some relation to *diluvium* or deluge, you imparted the result of your half-baked lucubrations to Winton who seems to have been lost enough to have accepted it. Observing next, your companion's fall, from the presumed security of your undistinguished position in the rear-guard, you took another pot-shot. The turbid chaos of your mind threw up some memory of the word "dilapidations" which you have pitifully attempted to disguise under the synonym of "ruins".'

As this was precisely what Beetle had done he looked hurt but forgiving. 'We will attend to this later,' said King. 'Go on, Winton, and retrieve yourself.'

Delubris happened to be the one word which Winton had not looked out and had asked Beetle for, when they were settling into their places. He forged ahead with no further trouble. Only when he rendered *scilicet* as 'forsooth', King erupted.

'Regulus,' he said, 'was not a leader-writer for the penny press, nor, for that matter, was Horace. Regulus says: "The soldier ransomed by gold will come keener for the fight – will he by – by gum!" *That's* the meaning of *scilicet*. It indicates contempt – bitter contempt. "Forsooth", forsooth! You'll be talking about "speckled beauties" and "eventually transpire" next. Howell, what do you make of that doubled "Vidi ego – ego vidi"? It wasn't put in to fill up the metre, you know.'

'Isn't it intensive, sir?' said Howell, afflicted by a genuine interest in what he read. 'Regulus was a bit in earnest about Rome making no terms with Carthage – and he wanted to let the Romans understand it, didn't he, sir?'

'Less than your usual grace, but the fact. Regulus *was* in earnest. He was also engaged at the same time in cutting his own throat with every word he uttered. He knew Carthage which (your examiners won't ask you this so you needn't take notes) was a sort of God-forsaken nigger Manchester. Regulus was not thinking about his own life. He was telling Rome the truth. He was playing for his side. Those lines from the eighteenth to the fortieth ought to be written in blood. Yet there are things in human garments which will tell you that Horace was a *flâneur* – a man about town. Avoid such beings. Horace knew a very great deal. *He* knew!

Erit ille fortis – "will he be brave who once to faithless foes has knelt?" And again (stop pawing with your hooves, Thornton!) *hic unde vitam sumeret inscius.* That means roughly – but I perceive I am ahead of my translators. Begin at *hic unde*, Vernon, and let us see if you have the spirit of Regulus.'

Now no one expected fireworks from gentle Paddy Vernon, sub-prefect of Hartopp's House, but, as must often be the case with growing boys, his mind was in abeyance for the time being, and he said, all in a rush, on behalf of Regulus: '*O magna Carthago probrosis altior Italiae ruinis,* O Carthage, thou wilt stand forth higher than the ruins of Italy.'

Even Beetle, most lenient of critics, was interested at this point, though he did not join the half-groan of reprobation from the wiser heads of the Form.

'*Please* don't mind me,' said King, and Vernon very kindly did not. He ploughed on thus: 'He (Regulus) is related to have removed from himself the kiss of the shameful wife and of his small children as less by the head, and, being stern, to have placed his virile visage on the ground.'

Since King loved 'virile' about as much as he did 'spouse' or 'forsooth' the Form looked up hopefully. But Jove thundered not.

'Until,' Vernon continued, 'he should have confirmed the sliding fathers as being the author of counsel never given under an alias.'

He stopped, conscious of stillness round him like the dread calm of the typhoon's centre. King's opening voice was sweeter than honey.

'I am painfully aware by bitter experience that I cannot give you any idea of the passion, the power, the – the essential guts of the lines which you have so foully outraged in our presence. But –' the note changed, 'so far as in me lies, I will strive to bring home to you, Vernon, the fact that there exist in Latin a few pitiful rules of grammar, of syntax, nay, even of declension, which were not created for your incult sport – your Boeotian diversion. You will, therefore, Vernon, write out and bring to me tomorrow a word-for-word English-Latin translation of the Ode, together with a full list of all adjectives – an adjective is not a verb, Vernon, as the Lower Third will tell you – all adjectives, their number, case, and gender. Even now I haven't begun to deal with you faithfully.'

'I – I'm very sorry, sir,' Vernon stammered.

'You mistake the symptoms, Vernon. You are possibly discomfited by the imposition, but sorrow postulates some sort of mind, intellect, *nous*. Your rendering of *probrosis* alone stamps you as lower than the beasts of the field. Will someone take the taste out of our mouths? And – talking of tastes – ' He coughed. There was a distinct flavour of chlorine gas in the air. Up went an eyebrow, though King knew perfectly well what it meant.

'Mr Hartopp's sc – science class next door,' said Malpass.

'Oh yes. I had forgotten. Our newly established Modern Side, of course. Perowne, open the windows; and Winton, go on once more from *interque maerentes*.'

'And hastened away,' said Winton, 'surrounded by his mourning friends, into – into illustrious banishment. But I got that out of Conington, sir,' he added in one conscientious breath.

'I am aware. The master generally knows his ass's crib, though I acquit *you* of any intention that way. Can you suggest anything for *egregius exul*? Only "egregious exile"? I fear "egregious" is a good word ruined. No! You can't in this case improve on Conington. Now then for *atqui sciebat quae sibi barbarus tortor pararet*. The whole force of it lies in the *atqui*.'

'Although he knew,' Winton suggested.

'Stronger than that, I think.'

'He who knew well,' Malpass interpolated.

'Ye-es. "Well though he knew." I don't like Conington's "well-witting". It's Wardour Street.'

'Well though he knew what the savage torturer was – was getting ready for him,' said Winton.

'Ye-es. Had in store for him.'

'Yet he brushed aside his kinsmen and the people delaying his return.'

'Ye-es; but then how do you render *obstantes*?'

'If it's a free translation mightn't *obstantes* and *morantem* come to about the same thing, sir?'

'Nothing comes to "about the same thing" with Horace, Winton. As I have said, Horace was not a journalist. No, I take it that his kinsmen bodily withstood his departure, whereas the crowd – *populumque* – the democracy stood about futilely pitying him and getting in the way. Now for that noblest of endings – *quam si clientum*,' and King ran off into the quotation:

> 'As though some tedious business o'er
> Of clients' court, his journey lay
> Towards Venafrum's grassy floor
> Or Sparta-built Tarentum's bay.

All right, Winton. Beetle, when you've quite finished dodging the fresh air yonder, give me the meaning of *tendens* – and turn down your collar.'

'Me, sir? *Tendens*, sir? Oh! Stretching away in the direction of, sir.'

'Idiot! Regulus was not a feature of the landscape. He was a man, self-doomed to death by torture. *Atqui sciebat* – knowing it – having achieved it for his country's sake – can't you hear that *atqui* cut like a knife? – he moved off with some dignity. That is why Horace out of the whole golden Latin tongue chose the one word "tendens" – which is utterly untranslatable.'

The gross injustice of being asked to translate it, converted Beetle into a young Christian martyr, till King buried his nose in his handkerchief again.

'I think they've broken another gas-bottle next door, sir,' said Howell. 'They're always doing it.' The Form coughed as more chlorine came in.

'Well, I suppose we must be patient with the Modern Side,' said King. 'But it is almost insupportable for this Side. Vernon, what are you grinning at?'

Vernon's mind had returned to him glowing and inspired. He chuckled as he underlined his Horace.

'It appears to amuse you,' said King. 'Let us participate. What is it?'

'The last two lines of the Tenth Ode, in this book, sir,' was Vernon's amazing reply.

'What? Oh, I see. *Non hoc semper erit liminis aut aquae caelestis patiens latus.*'* King's mouth twitched to hide a grin. 'Was that done with intention?'

'I – I thought it fitted, sir.'

'It does. It's distinctly happy. What put it into your thick head, Paddy?'

'I don't know, sir, except we did the Ode last term.'

'And you remembered? The same head that minted *probrosis* as a verb! Vernon, you are an enigma. No! This Side will *not* always be patient of unheavenly gases and waters. I will make representations to our so-called Moderns. Meantime (who shall say I am not just?) I remit you your accrued pains and penalties in regard to *probrosim, probrosis, probrosit* and other enormities. I oughtn't to do it, but this Side is occasionally human. By no means bad, Paddy.'

'Thank you, sir,' said Vernon, wondering how inspiration had visited him.

Then King, with a few brisk remarks about Science, headed them back to Regulus, of whom and of Horace and Rome and evil-minded commercial Carthage and of the democracy eternally futile, he explained, in all ages and climes, he spoke for ten minutes; passing thence to the next Ode – *Delicta majorum* – where he fetched up, full-voiced, upon – '*Dis te minorem quod geris imperas*' (Thou rulest because thou bearest thyself as lower than the Gods) – making it a text for a discourse on manners, morals, and respect for authority as distinct from bottled gases, which lasted till the bell rang. Then Beetle, concertinaing his books, observed to Winton, 'When King's really on tap he's an interestin' dog. Hartopp's chlorine uncorked him.'

---

* 'This side will not always be patient of rain and waiting on the threshold.'

'Yes; but why did you tell me *delubris* was "deluges", you silly ass?' said Winton.

'Well, that uncorked him too. Look out, you hoof-handed old owl!' Winton had cleared for action as the Form poured out like puppies at play and was scragging Beetle. Stalky from behind collared Winton low. The three fell in confusion.

'*Dis te minorem quod geris imperas*,' quoth Stalky, ruffling Winton's lint-white locks. 'Mustn't jape with Number Five study. Don't be too virtuous. Don't brood over it. 'Twon't count against you in your future caree-ah. Cheer up, Pater.'

'Pull him off my – er – essential guts, will you?' said Beetle from beneath. 'He's squashin' 'em.'

They dispersed to their studies.

No one, the owner least of all, can explain what is in a growing boy's mind. It might have been the blind ferment of adolescence; Stalky's random remarks about virtue might have stirred him; like his betters he might have sought popularity by way of clowning; or, as the Head asserted years later, the only known jest of his serious life might have worked on him, as a sober-sided man's one love colours and dislocates all his after days. But, at the next lesson, mechanical drawing with Mr Lidgett who as drawing-master had very limited powers of punishment, Winton fell suddenly from grace and let loose a live mouse in the form-room. The whole form, shrieking and leaping high, threw at it all the plaster cones, pyramids, and fruit in high relief – not to mention ink-pots – that they could lay hands on. Mr Lidgett reported at once to the Head; Winton owned up to his crime, which, venial in the Upper Third, pardonable at a price in the Lower Fourth, was, of course, rank ruffianism on the part of a Fifth Form boy; and so, by graduated stages, he arrived at the Head's study just before lunch, penitent, perturbed, annoyed with himself and – as the Head said to King in the corridor after the meal – more human than he had known him in seven years.

'You see,' the Head drawled on, 'Winton's only fault is a

certain costive and unaccommodating virtue. So this comes very happily.'

'I've never noticed any sign of it,' said King. Winton was in King's House, and though King as pro-consul might, and did, infernally oppress his own Province, once a black and yellow cap was in trouble at the hands of the Imperial authority King fought for him to the very last steps of Caesar's throne.

'Well, you yourself admitted just now that a mouse was beneath the occasion,' the Head answered.

'It was.' Mr King did not love Mr Lidgett. 'It should have been a rat. But – but – I hate to plead it – it's the lad's first offence.'

'Could you have damned him more completely, King?'

'Hm. What is the penalty?' said King, in retreat, but keeping up a rear-guard action.

'Only my usual few lines of Virgil to be shown up by tea-time.'

The Head's eyes turned slightly to that end of the corridor where Mullins, Captain of the Games ('Pot', 'old Pot' or 'Potiphar' Mullins), was pinning up the usual Wednesday notice – 'Big, Middle, and Little Side Football – A to K, L to Z, 3 to 4.45 p.m.

You cannot write out the Head's usual few (which means five hundred) Latin lines and play football for one hour and three-quarters between the hours of 1.30 and 5 p.m. Winton had evidently no intention of trying to do so, for he hung about the corridor with a set face and an uneasy foot. Yet it was law in the school, compared with which that of the Medes and Persians was no more than a non-committal resolution, that any boy, outside the First Fifteen, who missed his football for any reason whatever, and had not a written excuse, duly signed by competent authority to explain his absence, would receive not less than three strokes with a ground-ash from the Captain of the Games, generally a youth between seventeen and eighteen years, rarely under eleven stone ('Pot' was nearer thirteen), and always in hard condition.

King knew without inquiry that the Head had given Winton no such excuse.

'But he is practically a member of the First Fifteen. He has played for it all this term,' said King. 'I believe his Cap should have arrived last week.'

'His Cap has not been given him. Officially, therefore, he is naught. I rely on old Pot.'

'But Mullins is Winton's study-mate,' King persisted.

Pot Mullins and Pater Winton were cousins and rather close friends.

'That will make no difference to Mullins – or Winton, if I know 'em,' said the Head.

'But – but,' King played his last card desperately, 'I was going to recommend Winton for extra sub-prefect in my House, now Carton has gone.'

'Certainly,' said the Head. 'Why not? He will be excellent by tea-time, I hope.'

At that moment they saw Mr Lidgett, tripping down the corridor, waylaid by Winton.

'It's about that mouse-business at mechanical drawing,' Winton opened, swinging across his path.

'Yes, yes, highly disgraceful,' Mr Lidgett panted.

'I know it was,' said Winton. 'It – it was a cad's trick be-cause – '

'Because you knew I couldn't give you more than fifty lines,' said Mr Lidgett.

'Well, anyhow I've come to apologize for it.'

'Certainly,' said Mr Lidgett, and added, for he was a kindly man, I think that shows quite right feeling. I'll tell the Head at once I'm satisfied.'

'No – no!' The boy's still unmended voice jumped from the growl to the squeak. 'I didn't mean *that*! I – I did it on principle. Please don't – er – do anything of that kind.'

Mr Lidgett looked him up and down and, being an artist, understood.

'Thank you, Winton,' he said. 'This shall be between our-selves.'

'You heard?' said King, indecent pride in his voice.

'Of course. You thought he was going to get Lidgett to beg him off the impot.'

King denied this with so much warmth that the Head laughed and King went away in a huff.

'By the way,' said the Head, 'I've told Winton to do his lines in your form-room – not in his study.'

'Thanks,' said King over his shoulder, for the Head's orders had saved Winton and Mullins, who was doing extra Army work in the study, from an embarrassing afternoon together.

An hour later, King wandered into his still form-room as though by accident. Winton was hard at work.

'Aha!' said King, rubbing his hands. 'This does not look like games, Winton. Don't let me arrest your facile pen. Whence this sudden love for Virgil?'

'Impot from the Head, sir, for that mouse-business this morning.'

'Rumours thereof have reached us. That was a lapse on your part into Lower Thirdery which I don't quite understand.'

The 'tump-tump' of the puntabouts before the sides settled to games came through the open window. Winton, like his House-master, loved fresh air. Then they heard Paddy Vernon, sub-prefect on duty, calling the roll in the field and marking defaulters. Winton wrote steadily. King curled himself up on a desk, hands round knees. One would have said that the man was gloating over the boy's misfortune, but the boy understood.

'*Dis te minorem quod geris imperas,*' King quoted presently. 'It is necessary to bear oneself as lower than the local gods – even than drawing-masters who are precluded from effective retaliation. I *do* wish you'd tried that mouse-game with me, Pater.'

Winton grinned; then sobered. 'It was a cad's trick, sir, to play on Mr Lidgett.' He peered forward at the page he was copying.

'Well, "the sin *I* impute to each frustrate ghost" – ' King stopped himself. 'Why do you goggle like an owl? Hand me the Mantuan and I'll dictate. No matter. Any rich Virgilian measures will serve. I may peradventure recall a few.' He began:

'Tu regere imperio populos Romane memento
Hae tibi erunt artes pacisque imponere morem,
Parcere subjectis et debellare superbos.

There you have it all, Winton. Write that out twice and yet once again.'

For the next forty minutes, with never a glance at the book, King paid out the glorious hexameters (and King could read Latin as though it were alive), Winton hauling them in and coiling them away behind him as trimmers in a telegraph-ship's hold coil away deep-sea cable. King broke from the Aeneid to the Georgics and back again, pausing now and then to translate some specially loved line or to dwell on the treble-shot texture of the ancient fabric. He did not allude to the coming interview with Mullins except at the last, when he said, 'I think at this juncture, Pater, I need not ask you for the precise significance of *atqui sciebat quae sibi barbarus tortor.*'

The ungrateful Winton flushed angrily, and King loafed out to take five o'clock call-over, after which he invited little Hartopp to tea and a talk on chlorine-gas. Hartopp accepted the challenge like a bantam, and the two went up to King's study about the same time as Winton returned to the form-room beneath it to finish his lines.

Then half a dozen of the Second Fifteen who should have been washing strolled in to condole with 'Pater' Winton, whose misfortune and its consequences were common talk. No one was more sincere than the long, red-headed, knotty-knuckled 'Paddy' Vernon, but, being a careless animal, he joggled Winton's desk.

'Curse you for a silly ass!' said Winton. 'Don't do that.'

No one is expected to be polite while under punishment, so Vernon, sinking his sub-prefectship, replied peacefully enough:

'Well, don't be wrathy, Pater.'

'I'm not,' said Winton. 'Get out! This ain't your House form-room.'

'Form-room don't belong to you. Why don't you go to your own study?' Vernon replied.

'Because Mullins is there waitin' for the victim,' said Stalky delicately, and they all laughed. 'You ought to have shaken that mouse out of your trouser-leg, Pater. That's the way *I* did in my youth. Pater's revertin' to his second childhood. Never mind, Pater, we all respect you and your future caree-ah.'

Winton, still writhing, growled. Vernon leaning on the desk somehow shook it again. Then he laughed.

'What are you grinning at?' Winton asked.

'I was only thinkin' of *you* being sent up to take a lickin' from Pot. I swear I don't think it's fair. You've never shirked a game in your life, and you're as good as in the First Fifteen already. Your Cap ought to have been delivered last week, oughtn't it?'

It was law in the school that no man could by any means enjoy the privileges and immunities of the First Fifteen till the black velvet cap with the gold tassel, made by dilatory Exeter outfitters, had been actually set on his head. Ages ago, a large-built and unruly Second Fifteen had attempted to change this law, but the prefects of that age were still larger, and the lively experiment had never been repeated.

'Will you,' said Winton very slowly, 'kindly mind your own damned business, you cursed, clumsy, fat-headed fool?'

The form-room was as silent as the empty field in the darkness outside. Vernon shifted his feet uneasily.

'Well, *I* shouldn't like to take a lickin' from Pot,' he said,

'Wouldn't you?' Winton asked, as he paged the sheets of lines with hands that shook.

'No, I shouldn't,' said Vernon, his freckles growing more distinct on the bridge of his white nose.

'Well, I'm going to take it' – Winton moved clear of the desk as he spoke. 'But *you*'re going to take a lickin' from me first.' Before any one realized it, he had flung himself neighing against Vernon. No decencies were observed on either side, and the rest looked on amazed. The two met confusedly, Vernon trying to do what he could with his longer reach; Winton, insensible to blows, only concerned to drive his enemy into a corner and batter him to pulp. This he managed over against the fireplace, where Vernon dropped half-stunned. 'Now I'm going to give you your lickin',' said Winton. 'Lie there till I get a ground-ash and I'll cut you to pieces. If you move, I'll chuck you out of the window.' He wound his hands into the boy's collar and waistband, and had actually heaved him half off the ground before the others with one accord dropped on his head, shoulders, and legs. He fought them crazily in an awful hissing silence. Stalky's sensitive nose was rubbed along the floor; Beetle received a jolt in the wind that sent him whistling and crowing against the wall; Perowne's forehead was cut, and Malpass came out with an eye that explained itself like a dying rainbow through a whole week.

'Mad! Quite mad!' said Stalky, and for the third time wriggled back to Winton's throat. The door opened and King came in, Hartopp's little figure just behind him. The mound on the floor panted and heaved but did not rise, for Winton still squirmed vengefully. 'Only a little play, sir,' said Perowne. 'Only hit my head against a form.' This was quite true.

'Oh,' said King. '*Dimovit obstantes propinquos*. You, I presume, are the *populus* delaying Winton's return to – Mullins, eh?'

'No, sir,' said Stalky behind his claret-coloured handkerchief. 'We're the *maerentes amicos*.'

'Not bad! You see, some of it sticks after all,' King chuckled to Hartopp, and the two masters left without further inquiries.

The boys sat still on the now passive Winton.

'Well,' said Stalky at last, 'of all the putrid he-asses, Pater, you are the –'

'I'm sorry. I'm awfully sorry,' Winton began, and they let

him rise. He held out his hand to the bruised and bewildered Vernon. 'Sorry, Paddy. I – I must have lost my temper. I – I don't know what's the matter with me.'

' 'Fat lot of good that'll do my face at tea,' Vernon grunted. 'Why couldn't you say there was something wrong with you instead of lamming out like a lunatic? Is my lip puffy?'

'Just a trifle. Look at my beak! Well, we got all these pretty marks at footer – owin' to the zeal with which we played the game,' said Stalky, dusting himself. 'But d'you think you're fit to be let loose again, Pater? 'Sure you don't want to kill another sub-prefect? I wish *I* was Pot. I'd cut your sprightly young soul out.'

'I s'pose I ought to go to Pot now,' said Winton.

'And let all the other asses see you lookin' like this! Not much. We'll all come up to Number Five Study and wash off in hot water. Beetle, you aren't damaged. Go along and light the gas-stove.'

'There's a tin of cocoa in my study somewhere,' Perowne shouted after him. 'Rootle round till you find it, and take it up.'

Separately, by different roads, Vernon's jersey pulled half over his head, the boys repaired to Number Five Study. Little Hartopp and King, I am sorry to say, leaned over the banisters of King's landing and watched.

'Ve-ry human,' said little Hartopp. 'Your virtuous Winton, having got himself into trouble, takes it out of my poor old Paddy. I wonder what precise lie Paddy will tell about his face.'

'But surely you aren't going to embarrass him by asking?' said King.

'*Your* boy won,' said Hartopp.

'To go back to what we were discussing,' said King quickly, 'do you pretend that your modern system of inculcating un-related facts about chlorine, for instance, all of which may be proved fallacies by the time the boys grow up, can have any real bearing on education – even the low type of it that examiners expect?'

'I maintain nothing. But is it any worse than your Chinese

reiteration of uncomprehended syllables in a dead tongue?'

'Dead, forsooth!' King fairly danced. 'The only living tongue on earth! Chinese! On my word, Hartopp!'

'And at the end of seven years – how often have I said it?' Hartopp went on, – 'seven years of two hundred and twenty days of six hours each, your victims go away with nothing, absolutely nothing, except, perhaps, if they've been very attentive, a dozen – no, I'll grant you twenty – one score of totally unrelated Latin tags which any child of twelve could have absorbed in two terms.'

'But – but can't you realize that if our system brings later – at any rate – at a pinch – a simple understanding – grammar and Latinity apart – a mere glimpse of the significance (foul word!) of, we'll say, one Ode of Horace, one twenty lines of Virgil, we've got what we poor devils of ushers are striving after?'

'And what might that be?' said Hartopp.

'Balance, proportion, perspective – life. Your scientific man is the unrelated animal – the beast without background. Haven't you ever realized *that* in your atmosphere of stinks?'

'Meantime you make them lose life for the sake of living, eh?'

'Blind again, Hartopp! I told you about Paddy's quotation this morning. (But he made *probrosis* a verb, he did!) You yourself heard young Corkran's reference to *maerentes amicos*. It sticks – a little of it sticks among the barbarians.'

'Absolutely and essentially Chinese,' said little Hartopp, who, alone of the common-room, refused to be outfaced by King. 'But I don't yet understand how Paddy came to be licked by Winton. Paddy's supposed to be something of a boxer.'

'Beware of vinegar made from honey,' King replied. 'Pater, like some other people, is patient and long-suffering, but he has his limits. The Head is oppressing him damnably, too. As I pointed out, the boy has practically been in the First Fifteen since term began.'

'But, my dear fellow, I've known you give a boy an impot and refuse him leave off games, again and again.'

'Ah, but that was when there was real need to get at some oaf who couldn't be sensitized in any other way. Now, in our esteemed Head's action I see nothing but –'

The conversation from this point does not concern us.

Meantime Winton, very penitent and especially polite towards Vernon, was being cheered with cocoa in Number Five Study. They had some difficulty in stemming the flood of his apologies. He himself pointed out to Vernon that he had attacked a sub-prefect for no reason whatever, and, therefore, deserved official punishment.

'I can't think what was the matter with me today,' he mourned. 'Ever since that blasted mouse business –'

'Well, then, don't think,' said Stalky. 'Or do you want Paddy to make a row about it before all the school?'

Here Vernon was understood to say that he would see Winton and all the school somewhere else.

'And if you imagine Perowne and Malpass and me are goin' to give evidence at a prefects' meeting just to soothe your beastly conscience, you jolly well err,' said Beetle. 'I know what you did.'

'What?' croaked Pater, out of the valley of his humiliation.

'You went Berserk. I've read all about it in *Hypatia*.'

'What's "going Berserk"?' Winton asked.

'Never you mind,' was the reply. 'Now, don't you feel awfully weak and seedy?'

'I *am* rather tired,' said Winton, sighing.

'That's what you ought to be. You've gone Berserk and pretty soon you'll go to sleep. But you'll probably be liable to fits of it all your life,' Beetle concluded. ' 'Shouldn't wonder if you murdered some one some day.'

'Shut up – you and your Berserks!' said Stalky. 'Go to Mullins now and get it over, Pater.'

'I call it filthy unjust of the Head,' said Vernon. 'Anyhow, you've given me my lickin', old man. I hope Pot'll give you yours.'

'I'm awfully sorry – awfully sorry,' was Winton's last word.

It was the custom in that consulship to deal with games' defaulters between five o'clock call-over and tea. Mullins, who was old enough to pity, did not believe in letting boys wait through the night till the chill of the next morning for their punishments. He was finishing off the last of the small fry and their excuses when Winton arrived.

'But, please, Mullins' – this was Babcock tertius, a dear little twelve-year-old mother's darling – 'I had an awful hack on the knee. I've been to the Matron about it and she gave me some iodine. I've been rubbing it in all day. I thought that would be an excuse off.'

'Let's have a look at it,' said the impassive Mullins. 'That's a shin-bruise – about a week old. Touch your toes. I'll give you the iodine.'

Babcock yelled loudly as he had many times before. The face of Jevons, aged eleven, a new boy that dark wet term, low in the House, low in the Lower School, and lowest of all in his homesick little mind, turned white at the horror of the sight. They could hear his working lips part stickily as Babcock wailed his way out of hearing.

'Hullo, Jevons! What brings you here?' said Mullins.

'Pl-ease, sir, I went for a walk with Babcock tertius.'

'Did you? Then I bet you went to the tuck-shop – and you paid, didn't you?'

A nod. Jevons was too terrified to speak.

'Of course, and I bet Babcock told you that old Pot 'ud let you off because it was the first time.'

Another nod with a ghost of a smile in it.

'All right.' Mullins picked Jevons up before he could guess what was coming, laid him on the table with one hand, with the other gave him three emphatic spanks, then held him high in air.

'Now you tell Babcock tertius that he's got you a licking from me, and see you jolly well pay it back to him. And when you're prefect of games don't you let any one shirk his footer without a written excuse. Where d'you play in your game?'

'Forward, sir.'

'You can do better than that. I've seen you run like a young buck-rabbit. Ask Dickson from me to try you as three-quarter next game, will you? Cut along.'

Jevons left, warm for the first time that day, enormously set up in his own esteem, and very hot against the deceitful Babcock.

Mullins turned to Winton. 'Your name's on the list, Pater.' Winton nodded.

'I know it. The Head landed me with an impot for that mouse-business at mechanical drawing. No excuse.'

'He meant it then?' Mullins jerked his head delicately towards the ground-ash on the table. 'I heard something about it.'

Winton nodded. 'A rotten thing to do,' he said. 'Can't think what I was doing ever to do it. It counts against a fellow so; and there's some more too –'

'All right, Pater. Just stand clear of our photo-bracket, will you?'

The little formality over, there was a pause. Winton swung round, yawned in Pot's astonished face and staggered towards the window-seat.

'What's the matter with you, Dick? Ill?'

'No. Perfectly all right thanks. Only – only a little sleepy.' Winton stretched himself out, and then and there fell deeply and placidly asleep.

'It isn't a faint,' said the experienced Mullins, 'or his pulse wouldn't act. 'Tisn't a fit or he'd snort and twitch. It can't be sunstroke, this term, and he hasn't been over-training for anything.' He opened Winton's collar, packed a cushion under his head, threw a rug over him and sat down to listen to the regular breathing. Before long Stalky arrived, on pretence of borrowing a book. He looked at the window-seat.

'Noticed anything wrong with Winton lately?' said Mullins.

'Notice anything wrong with my beak?' Stalky replied. 'Pater went Berserk after call-over, and fell on a lot of us for jesting with him about his impot. You ought to see Malpass's eye.'

'You mean that Pater fought?' said Mullins.

'Like a devil. Then he nearly went to sleep in our study just now. I expect he'll be all right when he wakes up. Rummy business! Conscientious old bargee. You ought to have heard his apologies.'

'But Pater can't fight one little bit,' Mullins repeated.

' 'Twasn't fighting. He just tried to murder every one.' Stalky described the affair, and when he left Mullins went off to take counsel with the Head, who, out of a cloud of blue smoke, told him that all would yet be well.

'Winton,' said he, 'is a little stiff in his moral joints. He'll get over that. If he asks you whether today's doing will count against him in his – '

'But you know it's important to him, sir. His people aren't – very well off,' said Mullins.

'That's why I'm taking all this trouble. You must reassure him, Pot. I have overcrowded him with new experiences. Oh, by the way, has his Cap come?'

'It came at dinner, sir.' Mullins laughed.

Sure enough, when he waked at tea-time, Winton proposed to take Mullins all through every one of his day's lapses from grace, and 'Do you think it will count against me?' said he.

'Don't you fuss so much about yourself and your silly career,' said Mullins. 'You're all right. And oh – here's your First Cap at last. Shove it up on the bracket and come on to tea.'

They met King on their way, stepping stately and rubbing his hands. 'I have applied,' said he, 'for the services of an additional sub-prefect in Carton's unlamented absence. Your name, Winton, seems to have found favour with the powers that be, and – and all things considered – I am disposed to give my support to the nomination. You are therefore a quasi-lictor.'

'Then it didn't count against me,' Winton gasped as soon as they were out of hearing.

A Captain of Games can jest with a sub-prefect publicly.

'You utter ass!' said Mullins, and caught him by the back of his stiff neck and ran him down to the hall where the sub-prefects, who sit below the salt, made him welcome with the economical bloater-paste of mid-term.

King and little Hartopp were sparring in the Reverend John Gillett's study at 10 p.m. – classical *versus* modern as usual.

'Character – proportion – background,' snarled King. 'That is the essence of the Humanities.'

'Analects of Confucius,' little Hartopp answered.

'Time,' said the Reverend John behind the soda-water. 'You men oppress me. Hartopp, what did you say to Paddy in your dormitories tonight? Even *you* couldn't have overlooked his face.'

'But I did,' said Hartopp calmly. 'I wasn't even humorous about it, as some clerics might have been. I went straight through and said naught.'

'Poor Paddy! Now, for my part,' said King, 'and you know I am not lavish in my praises, I consider Winton a first-class type; absolutely first-class.'

'Ha-ardly,' said the Reverend John. 'First-class of the second class, I admit. The very best type of second class but' – he shook his head – 'it should have been a rat. Pater'll never be anything more than a Colonel of Engineers.'

'What do you base that verdict on?' said King stiffly.

'He came to me after prayers – with all his conscience.'

'Poor old Pater. Was it the mouse?' said little Hartopp.

'That, and what he called his uncontrollable temper, and his responsibilities as sub-prefect.'

'And you?'

'If we had had what is vulgarly called a pi-jaw he'd have had hysterics. So I recommended a dose of Epsom salts. He'll take it, too – conscientiously. Don't eat me, King. Perhaps he'll be a K.C.B.'

Ten o'clock struck and the Army class boys in the further

studies coming to their houses after an hour's extra work passed along the gravel path below. Some one was chanting, to the tune of 'White sand and grey sand,' *Dis te minorem quod geris imperas.* He stopped outside Mullins' study. They heard Mullins' window slide up and then Stalky's voice:

'Ah! Good-evening, Mullins, my *barbarus tortor.* We're the waits. We have come to inquire after the local Berserk. Is he doin' as well as can be expected in his new caree-ah?'

'Better than you will, in a sec, Stalky,' Mullins grunted.

'Glad of that. We thought he'd like to know that Paddy has been carried to the sick-house in ravin' delirium. They think it's concussion of the brain.'

'Why, he was all right at prayers,' Winton began earnestly, and they heard a laugh in the background as Mullins slammed down the window.

' 'Night, Regulus,' Stalky sang out, and the light footsteps went on.

'You see. It sticks. A little of it sticks among the barbarians,' said King.

'Amen,' said the Reverend John. 'Go to bed.'

Mary Postgate

(1915)

OF Miss Mary Postgate, Lady McCausland wrote that she
was 'thoroughly conscientious, tidy, companionable, and
ladylike. I am very sorry to part with her, and shall always be
interested in her welfare.'

Miss Fowler engaged her on this recommendation, and to
her surprise, for she had had experience of companions,
found that it was true. Miss Fowler was nearer sixty than
fifty at the time, but though she needed care she did not
exhaust her attendant's vitality. On the contrary, she gave
out, stimulatingly and with reminiscences. Her father had
been a minor Court official in the days when the Great Exhi-
bition of 1851 had just set its seal on Civilization made perfect. Some of Miss Fowler's tales, none the less, were not
always for the young. Mary was not young, and though her
speech was as colourless as her eyes or her hair, she was
never shocked. She listened unflinchingly to every one; said
at the end, 'How interesting!' or 'How shocking!' as the case
might be, and never again referred to it, for she prided herself on a trained mind, which 'did not dwell on these things.'
She was, too, a treasure at domestic accounts, for which the
village tradesmen, with their weekly books, loved her not.
Otherwise she had no enemies; provoked no jealousy even
among the plainest; neither gossip nor slander had ever been
traced to her; she supplied the odd place at the Rector's or
the Doctor's table at half an hour's notice; she was a sort of
public aunt to very many small children of the village street,
whose parents, while accepting everything, would have been
swift to resent what they called 'patronage'; she served on
the Village Nursing Committee as Miss Fowler's nominee
when Miss Fowler was crippled by rheumatoid arthritis, and
came out of six months' fortnightly meetings equally respected by all the cliques.

And when Fate threw Miss Fowler's nephew, an unlovely

orphan of eleven, on Miss Fowler's hands, Mary Postgate stood to her share of the business of education as practised in private and public schools. She checked printed clothes-lists, and unitemized bills of extras; wrote to Head and House masters, matrons, nurses and doctors, and grieved or rejoiced over half-term reports. Young Wyndham Fowler repaid her in his holidays by calling her 'Gatepost', 'Postey', or 'Pack-thread', by thumping her between her narrow shoulders, or by chasing her bleating, round the garden, her large mouth open, her large nose high in air, at a stiff-necked shamble very like a camel's. Later on he filled the house with cla-mour, argument, and harangues as to his personal needs, likes and dislikes, and the limitations of 'you women', re-ducing Mary to tears of physical fatigue, or, when he chose to be humorous, of helpless laughter. At crises, which multi-plied as he grew older, she was his ambassadress and his in-terpretress to Miss Fowler, who had no large sympathy with the young; a vote in his interest at the councils on his future; his sewing-woman, strictly accountable for mislaid boots and garments; always his butt and his slave.

And when he decided to become a solicitor, and had en-tered an office in London; when his greeting had changed from 'Hullo, Postey, you old beast,' to 'Mornin', Packthread', there came a war which, unlike all wars that Mary could remember, did not stay decently outside England and in the newspapers, but intruded on the lives of people whom she knew. As she said to Miss Fowler, it was 'most vexatious'. It took the Rector's son who was going into business with his elder brother; it took the Colonel's nephew on the eve of fruit-farming in Canada; it took Mrs Grant's son who, his mother said, was devoted to the ministry; and, very early indeed, it took Wynn Fowler, who announced on a postcard that he had joined the Flying Corps and wanted a cardigan waistcoat.

'He must go, and he must have the waistcoat,' said Miss Fowler. So Mary got the proper-sized needles and wool, while Miss Fowler told the men of her establishment – two gar-deners and an odd man, aged sixty – that those who could join the Army had better do so. The gardeners left. Cheape, the odd man, stayed on, and was promoted to the gardener's cottage. The cook, scorning to be limited in luxuries, also left, after a spirited scene with Miss Fowler, and took the housemaid with her. Miss Fowler gazetted Nellie, Cheape's seventeen-year-old daughter, to the vacant post; Mrs Cheape to the rank of cook, with occasional cleaning bouts; and the reduced establishment moved forward smoothly.

Wynn demanded an increase in his allowance. Miss Fowler, who always looked facts in the face, said, 'He must have it. The chances are he won't live long to draw it, and if three hundred makes him happy – '

Wynn was grateful, and came over, in his tight-buttoned uniform, to say so. His training centre was not thirty miles away, and his talk was so technical that it had to be explained by charts of the various types of machines. He gave Mary such a chart.

'And you'd better study it, Postey,' he said. 'You'll be seeing a lot of 'em soon.' So Mary studied the chart, but when Wynn next arrived to swell and exalt himself before his womenfolk, she failed badly in cross-examination, and he rated her as in the old days.

'You *look* more or less like a human being,' he said in his new Service voice. 'You *must* have had a brain at some time in your past. What have you done with it? Where d'you keep it? A sheep would know more than you do, Postey. You're lamentable. You are less use than an empty tin can, you dowey old cassowary.'

'I suppose that's how your superior officer talks to *you*?' said Miss Fowler from her chair.

'But Postey doesn't mind,' Wynn replied. 'Do you, Packthread?'

'Why? Was Wynn saying anything? I shall get this right next time you come,' she muttered, and knitted her pale brows again over the diagrams of Taubes, Farmans, and Zeppelins.

In a few weeks the mere land and sea battles which she

read to Miss Fowler after breakfast passed her like idle breath. Her heart and her interest were high in the air with Wynn, who had finished 'rolling' (whatever that might be) and had gone on from a 'taxi' to a machine more or less his own. One morning it circled over their very chimneys, alighted on Vegg's Heath, almost outside the garden gate, and Wynn came in, blue with cold, shouting for food. He and she drew Miss Fowler's bath-chair, as they had often done, along the Heath foot-path to look at the biplane. Mary observed that 'it smelt very badly'.

'Postey, I believe you think with your nose,' said Wynn. 'I know you don't with your mind. Now, what type's that?'

'I'll go and get the chart,' said Mary.

'You're hopeless! You haven't the mental capacity of a white mouse,' he cried, and explained the dials and the sockets for bomb-dropping till it was time to mount and ride the wet clouds once more.

'Ah!' said Mary, as the stinking thing flared upward. 'Wait till our Flying Corps gets to work! Wynn says it's much safer than in the trenches.'

'I wonder,' said Miss Fowler. 'Tell Cheape to come and tow me home again.'

'It's all downhill. I can do it,' said Mary, 'if you put the brake on.' She laid her lean self against the pushing-bar and home they trundled.

'Now, be careful you aren't heated and catch a chill,' said overdressed Miss Fowler.

'Nothing makes me perspire,' said Mary. As she bumped the chair under the porch she straightened her long back. The exertion had given her a colour, and the wind had loosened a wisp of hair across her forehead. Miss Fowler glanced at her.

'What do you ever think of, Mary?' she demanded suddenly.

'Oh, Wynn says he wants another three pairs of stockings – as thick as we can make them.'

'Yes. But I mean the things that women think about. Here you are, more than forty –'

'Forty-four,' said truthful Mary.

'Well?'

'Well?' Mary offered Miss Fowler her shoulder as usual.

'And you've been with me ten years now.'

'Let's see,' said Mary. 'Wynn was eleven when he came. He's twenty now, and I came two years before that. It must be eleven.'

'Eleven! And you've never told me anything that matters in all that while. Looking back, it seems to me that I've done all the talking.'

'I'm afraid I'm not much of a conversationalist. As Wynn says, I haven't the mind. Let me take your hat.'

Miss Fowler, moving stiffly from the hip, stamped her rubber-tipped stick on the tiled hall floor. 'Mary, aren't you *anything* except a companion? Would you *ever* have been anything except a companion?'

Mary hung up the garden hat on its proper peg. 'No,' she said after consideration. 'I don't imagine I ever should. But I've no imagination, I'm afraid.'

She fetched Miss Fowler her eleven-o'clock glass of Contrexeville.

That was the wet December when it rained six inches to the month, and the women went abroad as little as might be. Wynn's flying chariot visited them several times, and for two mornings (he had warned her by postcard) Mary heard the thresh of his propellers at dawn. The second time she ran to the window, and stared at the whitening sky. A little blur passed overhead. She lifted her lean arms towards it.

That evening at six o'clock there came an announcement in an official envelope that Second Lieutenant W. Fowler had been killed during a trial flight. Death was instantaneous. She read it and carried it to Miss Fowler.

'I never expected anything else,' said Miss Fowler; 'but I'm sorry it happened before he had done anything.'

The room was whirling round Mary Postgate, but she found herself quite steady in the midst of it.

'Yes,' she said. 'It's a great pity he didn't die in action after he had killed somebody.'

'He was killed instantly. That's one comfort,' Miss Fowler went on.

'But Wynn says the shock of a fall kills a man at once – whatever happens to the tanks,' quoted Mary.

The room was coming to rest now. She heard Miss Fowler say impatiently, 'But why can't we cry, Mary?' and herself replying, 'There's nothing to cry for. He has done his duty as much as Mrs Grant's son did.'

'And when he died, *she* came and cried all the morning,' said Miss Fowler. 'This only makes me feel tired – terribly tired. Will you help me to bed, please, Mary? – And I think I'd like the hot-water bottle.'

So Mary helped her and sat beside, talking of Wynn in his riotous youth.

'I believe,' said Miss Fowler suddenly, 'that old people and young people slip from under a stroke like this. The middle-aged feel it most.'

'I expect that's true,' said Mary, rising. 'I'm going to put away the things in his room now. Shall we wear mourning?'

'Certainly not,' said Miss Fowler. 'Except, of course, at the funeral. I can't go. You will. I want you to arrange about his being buried here. What a blessing it didn't happen at Salisbury!'

Every one, from the Authorities of the Flying Corps to the Rector, was most kind and sympathetic. Mary found herself for the moment in a world where bodies were in the habit of being dispatched by all sorts of conveyances to all sorts of places. And at the funeral two young men in buttoned-up uniforms stood beside the grave and spoke to her afterwards.

'You're Miss Postgate, aren't you?' said one. 'Fowler told me about you. He was a good chap – a first-class fellow – a great loss.'

'Great loss!' growled his companion. 'We're all awfully sorry.'

'How high did he fall from?' Mary whispered.

'Pretty nearly four thousand feet, I should think, didn't he? You were up that day, Monkey?'

85

'All of that,' the other child replied. 'My bar made three thousand, and I wasn't as high as him by a lot.'

'Then *that's* all right,' said Mary. 'Thank you very much.'

They moved away as Mrs Grant flung herself weeping on Mary's flat chest, under the lych-gate, and cried, '*I* know how it feels! *I* know how it feels!'

'But both his parents are dead,' Mary returned, as she fended her off. 'Perhaps they've all met by now,' she added vaguely as she escaped towards the coach.'

'I've thought of that too,' wailed Mrs Grant; 'but then he'll be practically a stranger to them. Quite embarrassing!'

Mary faithfully reported every detail of the ceremony to Miss Fowler, who, when she described Mrs Grant's outburst, laughed aloud.

'Oh, how Wynn would have enjoyed it! He was always utterly unreliable at funerals. D'you remember – ' And they talked of him again, each piecing out the other's gaps. 'And now,' said Miss Fowler, 'we'll pull up the blinds and we'll have a general tidy. That always does us good. Have you seen to Wynn's things?'

'Everything – since he first came,' said Mary. 'He was never destructive – even with his toys.'

They faced that neat room.

'It can't be natural not to cry,' Mary said at last. 'I'm *so* afraid you'll have a reaction.'

'As I told you, we old people slip from under the stroke. It's you I'm afraid for. Have you cried yet?'

'I can't. It only makes me angry with the Germans.'

'That's sheer waste of vitality,' said Miss Fowler. 'We must live till the war's finished.' She opened a full wardrobe. 'Now, I've been thinking things over. This is my plan. All his civilian clothes can be given away – Belgian refugees, and so on.'

Mary nodded. 'Boots, collars, and gloves?'

'Yes. We don't need to keep anything except his cap and belt.'

'They came back yesterday with his Flying Corps clothes' – Mary pointed to a roll on the little iron bed.

'Ah, but keep his Service things. Some one may be glad of them later. Do you remember his sizes?'

'Five feet eight and a half; thirty-six inches round the chest. But he told me he's just put on an inch and a half. I'll mark it on a label and tie it on his sleeping-bag.'

'So that disposes of *that*,' said Miss Fowler, tapping the palm of one hand with the ringed third finger of the other. 'What waste it all is! We'll get his old school trunk tomorrow and pack his civilian clothes.'

'And the rest?' said Mary. 'His books and pictures and the games and the toys – and – and the rest?'

'My plan is to burn every single thing,' said Miss Fowler. 'Then we shall know where they are and no one can handle them afterwards. What do you think?'

'I think that would be much the best,' said Mary. 'But there's such a lot of them.'

'We'll burn them in the destructor,' said Miss Fowler.

This was an open-air furnace for the consumption of refuse; a little circular four-foot tower of pierced brick over an iron grating. Miss Fowler had noticed the design in a gardening journal years ago, and had had it built at the bottom of the garden. It suited her tidy soul, for it saved unsightly rubbish-heaps, and the ashes lightened the stiff clay soil.

Mary considered for a moment, saw her way clear, and nodded again. They spent the evening putting away well-remembered civilian suits, underclothes that Mary had marked, and the regiments of very gaudy socks and ties. A second trunk was needed, and, after that, a little packing-case, and it was late next day when Cheape and the local carrier lifted them to the cart. The Rector luckily knew of a friend's son, about five feet eight and a half inches high, to whom a complete Flying Corps outfit would be most accept-able, and sent his gardener's son down with a barrow to take delivery of it. The cap was hung up in Miss Fowler's bedroom, the belt in Miss Postgate's; for, as Miss Fowler said, they had no desire to make tea-party talk of them.

'That disposes of *that*,' said Miss Fowler. 'I'll leave the rest to you, Mary. I can't run up and down the garden. You'd better take the big clothes-basket and get Nellie to help you.'

'I shall take the wheel-barrow and do it myself,' said Mary, and for once in her life closed her mouth.

Miss Fowler, in moments of irritation, had called Mary deadly methodical. She put on her oldest waterproof and gardening-hat and her ever-slipping goloshes, for the weather was on the edge of more rain. She gathered fire-lighters from the kitchen, a half-scuttle of coals, and a faggot of brushwood. These she wheeled in the barrow down the mossed paths to the dank little laurel shrubbery where the destructor stood under the drip of three oaks. She climbed the wire fence into the Rector's glebe just behind, and from his tenant's rick pulled two large armfuls of good hay, which she spread neatly on the fire-bars. Next, journey by journey, passing Miss Fowler's white face at the morning-room window each time, she brought down in the towel-covered clothes-basket, on the wheelbarrow, thumbed and used Hentys, Marryats, Levers, Stevensons, Baroness Orczys, Garvices, schoolbooks, and atlases, unrelated piles of the *Motor Cyclist*, the *Light Car*, and catalogues of Olympia Exhibitions; the remnants of a fleet of sailing-ships from ninepenny cutters to a three-guinea yacht; a prep.-school dressing-gown; bats from three-and-sixpence to twenty-four shillings; cricket and tennis balls; disintegrated steam and clockwork locomotives with their twisted rails; a grey and red tin model of a submarine; a dumb gramophone and cracked records; golf-clubs that had to be broken across the knee, like his walking-sticks, and an assegai; photographs of private and public school cricket and football elevens, and his O.T.C. on the line of march; kodaks, and film-rolls; some pewters, and one real silver cup, for boxing competitions and Junior Hurdles; sheaves of school photographs; Miss Fowler's photograph; her own which he had borne off in fun and (good care she took not to ask!) had never returned; a play box with a secret drawer; a load of flannels, belts, and jerseys, and a pair of spiked shoes unearthed in the attic; a packet of all the letters that Miss Fowler and she had ever written to him, kept for some absurd reason through all these years; a five-day attempt at a diary; framed pictures of racing motors in full Brooklands career, and load upon load of undistinguishable wreckage of tool-boxes, rabbit-hutches, electric batteries, tin soldiers, fret-saw outfits, and jig-saw puzzles.

Miss Fowler at the window watched her come and go, and said to herself, 'Mary's an old woman. I never realized it before.'

After lunch she recommended her to rest.

'I'm not in the least tired,' said Mary. 'I've got it all arranged. I'm going to the village at two o'clock for some paraffin. Nellie hasn't enough, and the walk will do me good.'

She made one last quest round the house before she started, and found that she had overlooked nothing. It began to mist as soon as she had skirted Vegg's Heath, where Wynn used to descend – it seemed to her that she could almost hear the beat of his propellers overhead, but there was nothing to see. She hoisted her umbrella and lunged into the blind wet till she had reached the shelter of the empty village. As she came out of Mr Kidd's shop with a bottle full of paraffin in her string shopping-bag, she met Nurse Eden, the village nurse, and fell into talk with her, as usual, about the village children. They were just parting opposite the 'Royal Oak', when a gun, they fancied, was fired immediately behind the house. It was followed by a child's shriek dying into a wail.

'Accident!' said Nurse Eden promptly, and dashed through the empty bar, followed by Mary. They found Mrs Gerritt, the publican's wife, who could only gasp and point to the yard, where a little cart-lodge was sliding sideways amid a clatter of tiles. Nurse Eden snatched up a sheet drying before the fire, ran out, lifted something from the ground, and flung the sheet round it. The sheet turned scarlet and half her uniform too, as she bore the load into the kitchen. It was little Edna Gerritt, aged nine, whom Mary had known since her perambulator days.

'Am I hurted bad?' Edna asked, and died between Nurse Eden's dripping hands. The sheet fell aside and for an instant before she could shut her eyes, Mary saw the ripped and shredded body.

'It's a wonder she spoke at all,' said Nurse Eden. 'What in God's name was it?'

'A bomb,' said Mary.

'One o' the Zeppelins?'

'No. An aeroplane. I thought I heard it on the Heath, but I fancied it was one of ours. It must have shut off its engines as it came down. That's why we didn't notice it.'

'The filthy pigs!' said Nurse Eden, all white and shaken. 'See the pickle I'm in! Go and tell Dr Hennis, Miss Postgate.' Nurse looked at the mother, who had dropped face down on the floor. 'She's only in a fit. Turn her over.'

Mary heaved Mrs Gerritt right side up, and hurried off for the doctor. When she told her tale, he asked her to sit down in the surgery till he got her something.

'But I don't need it, I assure you,' said she. 'I don't think it would be wise to tell Miss Fowler about it, do you? Her heart is so irritable in this weather.'

Dr Hennis looked at her admiringly as he packed up his bag.

'No. Don't tell anybody till we're sure,' he said, and hastened to the 'Royal Oak', while Mary went on with the paraffin. The village behind her was as quiet as usual, for the news had not yet spread. She frowned a little to herself, her large nostrils expanded uglily, and from time to time she muttered a phrase which Wynn, who never restrained himself before his women-folk, had applied to the enemy. 'Bloody pagans! They *are* bloody pagans. But,' she continued, falling back on the teaching that had made her what she was, 'one mustn't let one's mind dwell on these things.'

Before she reached the house Dr Hennis, who was also a special constable, overtook her in his car.

'Oh, Miss Postgate,' he said, 'I wanted to tell you that that accident at the "Royal Oak" was due to Gerritt's stable tumbling down. It's been dangerous for a long time. It ought to have been condemned.'

'I thought I heard an explosion too,' said Mary.

'You might have been misled by the beams snapping. I've been looking at 'em. They were dry-rotted through and through. Of course, as they broke, they would make a noise just like a gun.'

'Yes?' said Mary politely.

'Poor little Edna was playing underneath it,' he went on, still holding her with his eyes, 'and that and the tiles cut her to pieces, you see?'

'I saw it,' said Mary, shaking her head. 'I heard it too.'

'Well, we cannot be sure.' Dr Hennis changed his tone completely. 'I know both you and Nurse Eden (I've been speaking to her) are perfectly trustworthy, and I can rely on you not to say anything – yet at least. It is no good to stir up people unless –'

'Oh, I never do – anyhow,' said Mary, and Dr Hennis went on to the county town.

After all, she told herself, it might, just possibly, have been the collapse of the old stable that had done all those things to poor little Edna. She was sorry she had even hinted at other things, but Nurse Eden was discretion itself. By the time she reached home the affair seemed increasingly remote by its very monstrosity. As she came in, Miss Fowler told her that a couple of aeroplanes had passed half an hour ago.

'I thought I heard them,' she replied, 'I'm going down to the garden now. I've got the paraffin.'

'Yes, but – what *have* you got on your boots? They're soaking wet. Change them at once.'

Not only did Mary obey but she wrapped the boots in a newspaper, and put them into the string bag with the bottle. So, armed with the longest kitchen poker, she left.

'It's raining again,' was Miss Fowler's last word, 'but – I know you won't be happy till that's disposed of.'

'It won't take long. I've got everything down there, and I've put the lid on the destructor to keep the wet out.'

The shrubbery was filling with twilight by the time she had completed her arrangements and sprinkled the sacrificial oil. As she lit the match that would burn her heart to ashes, she heard a groan or a grunt behind the dense Portugal laurels.

'Cheape?' she called impatiently, but Cheape, with his ancient lumbago, in his comfortable cottage would be the last man to profane the sanctuary. 'Sheep,' she concluded, and threw in the fusee. The pyre went up in a roar, and the immediate flame hastened night around her.

'How Wynn would have loved this!' she thought, stepping back from the blaze.

By its light she saw, half hidden behind a laurel not five paces away, a bareheaded man sitting very stiffly at the foot of one of the oaks. A broken branch lay across his lap – one booted leg protruding from beneath it. His head moved ceaselessly from side to side, but his body was as still as the tree's trunk. He was dressed – she moved sideways to look more closely – in a uniform something like Wynn's, with a flap buttoned across the chest. For an instant, she had some idea that it might be one of the young flying men she had met at the funeral. But their heads were dark and glossy. This man's was as pale as a baby's, and so closely cropped that she could see the disgusting pinky skin beneath. His lips moved.

'What do you say?' Mary moved towards him and stooped.

'Laty! Laty! Laty!' he muttered, while his hands picked at the dead wet leaves. There was no doubt as to his nationality. It made her so angry that she strode back to the destructor, though it was still too hot to use the poker there. Wynn's books seemed to be catching well. She looked up at the oak behind the man; several of the light upper and two or three rotten lower branches had broken and scattered their rubbish on the shrubbery path. On the lowest fork a helmet with dependent strings, showed like a bird's-nest in the light of a long-tongued flame. Evidently this person had fallen through the tree. Wynn had told her that it was quite possible for people to fall out of aeroplanes. Wynn told her too, that trees were useful things to break an aviator's fall, but in this case the aviator must have been broken or he would have moved from his queer position. He seemed helpless except for his horrible rolling head. On the other hand, she could see a pistol case at his belt – and Mary loathed pistols. Months ago, after reading certain Belgian reports together, she and Miss Fowler had had dealings with one – a huge revolver with flat-nosed bullets, which latter, Wynn said, were forbidden by the rules of war to be used against civilized enemies. 'They're good enough for us,' Miss Fowler had replied. 'Show Mary how it works.' And Wynn, laughing at the mere possibility of any such need, had led the craven winking Mary into the Rector's disused quarry, and had shown her how to fire the terrible machine. It lay now in the top-left-hand drawer of her toilet-table – a memento not included in the burning. Wynn would be pleased to see how she was not afraid.

She slipped up to the house to get it. When she came through the rain, the eyes in the head were alive with expectation. The mouth even tried to smile. But at sight of the revolver its corners went down just like Edna Gerritt's. A tear trickled from one eye, and the head rolled from shoulder to shoulder as though trying to point out something.

'Cassée. Tout cassée,' it whimpered.

'What do you say?' said Mary disgustedly, keeeping well to one side, though only the head moved.

'Cassée,' it repeated. 'Che me rends. Le médicin! Toctor!'

'Nein!' she said, bringing all her small German to bear with the big pistol. 'Ich haben der todt Kinder gesehn.'

The head was still. Mary's hand dropped. She had been careful to keep her finger off the trigger for fear of accidents. After a few moments' waiting, she returned to the destructor, where the flames were falling, and churned up Wynn's charring books with the poker. Again the head groaned for the doctor.

'Stop that!' said Mary, and stamped her foot. 'Stop that, you bloody pagan!'

The words came quite smoothly and naturally. They were Wynn's own words, and Wynn was a gentleman who for no consideration on earth would have torn little Edna into those vividly coloured strips and strings. But this thing hunched under the oak-tree had done that thing. It was no question of reading horrors out of newspapers to Miss Fowler. Mary had seen it with her own eyes on the 'Royal Oak' kitchen table. She must not allow her mind to dwell upon it. Now Wynn was dead, and everything connected with him was lumping and rustling and tinkling under her busy poker into red black dust and grey leaves of ash. The thing beneath the oak would die too. Mary had seen death more than once. She came of a family that had a knack of dying under, as she told Miss Fowler, 'most distressing circumstances'. She would stay where she was till she was entirely satisfied that It was dead – dead as dear papa in the late 'eighties; aunt Mary in 'eighty-nine; mamma in 'ninety-one; cousin Dick in 'ninety-five; Lady McCausland's housemaid in 'ninety-nine; Lady McCausland's sister in nineteen hundred and one; Wynn buried five days ago; and Edna Gerritt still waiting for decent earth to hide her. As she thought – her underlip caught up by one faded canine, brows knit and nostrils wide – she wielded the poker with lunges that jarred the grating at the bottom, and careful scrapes round the brickwork above. She looked at her wrist-watch. It was getting on to half past four, and the rain was coming down in earnest. Tea would be at five. If It did not die before that time, she would be soaked and would have to change. Meantime, and this occupied her, Wynn's things were burning well in spite of the hissing wet, though now and again a book-back with a quite distinguishable title would be heaved up out of the mass. The exercise of stoking had given her a glow which seemed to reach to the marrow of her bones. She hummed – Mary never had a voice – to herself. She had never believed in all those advanced views – though Miss Fowler herself leaned a little that way – of woman's work in the world; but now she saw there was much to be said for them. This, for instance was *her* work – work which no man, least of all Dr Hennis, would ever have done. A man, at such a crisis, would be what Wynn called a 'sportsman'; would leave everything to fetch help and would certainly bring It into the house. Now a woman's business was to make a happy home for – for a husband and children. Failing these – it was not a thing one should allow one's mind to dwell upon – but –

'Stop it!' Mary cried once more across the shadows. 'Nein, I tell you! Ich haben der todt Kinder gesehn.'

But it was a fact. A woman who had missed these things could still be useful – more useful than a man in certain respects. She thumped like a pavior through the settling ashes at the secret thrill of it. The rain was damping the fire, but she could feel – it was too dark to see – that her work was done. There was a dull red glow at the bottom of the destructor, not enough to char the wooden lid if she slipped it half over against the driving wet. This arranged, she leaned on the poker and waited, while an increasing rapture laid hold on her. She ceased to think. She gave herself up to feel. Her long pleasure was broken by a sound that she had waited for in agony several times in her life. She leaned forward and listened, smiling. There could be no mistake. She closed her eyes and drank it in. Once it ceased abruptly.

'Go on,' she murmured, half aloud. 'That isn't the end.'

Then the end came very distinctly in a lull between two rain-gusts. Mary Postgate drew her breath short between her teeth and shivered from head to foot. '*That's* all right,' said she contentedly, and went up to the house, where she scandalized the whole routine by taking a luxurious hot bath before tea, and came down looking, as Miss Fowler said when she saw her lying all relaxed on the other sofa, 'quite handsome!'

Sea Constables

A Tale of '15

(1915)

The head-waiter of the Carvoitz almost ran to meet Portson and his guests as they came up the steps from the palm-court where the string band plays.

'Not seen you since – oh, ever so long,' he began. 'So glad to get your wire. Quite well – eh?'

'Fair to middling, Henri.' Portson shook hands with him. 'You're looking all right, too. Have you got us our table?'

Henri nodded towards a pink alcove, kept for mixed doubles, which discreetly commanded the main dining-room's glitter and blaze.

'Good man!' said Portson. 'Now, this is serious, Henri. We put ourselves unreservedly in your hands. We're weather-beaten mariners – though we don't look it, and we haven't eaten a Christian meal in months. Have you thought of all that, Henri, mon ami?'

'The menu, I have compose it myself,' Henri answered with the gravity of a high priest.

It was more than a year since Portson – of Portson, Peake and Ensell, Stock and Share Brokers – had drawn Henri's attention to an apparently extinct Oil Company which, a little later, erupted profitably; and it may be that Henri prided himself on paying all debts in full.

The most recent foreign millionaire and the even more recent foreign actress at a table near the entrance clamoured for his attention while he convoyed the party to the pink alcove. With his own hands he turned out some befrilled electrics and lit four pale rose-candles.

'Bridal!' some one murmured. 'Quite bridal!'

'So glad you like. There is nothing too good.' Henri slid away, and the four men sat down. They had the coarse-grained complexions of men who habitually did themselves well, and an air, too, of recent, red-eyed dissipation. Maddingham, the eldest, was a thick-set middle-aged presence, with crisped grizzled hair, of the type that one associates with Board Meetings. He limped slightly. Tegg, who followed him, blinking, was neat, small, and sandy, of unmistakable Navy cut, but sheepish aspect. Winchmore, the youngest, was more on the lines of the conventional pre-war 'nut', but his eyes were sunk in his head and his hands black-nailed and roughened. Portson, their host, with Vandyke beard and a comfortable little stomach, beamed upon them as they settled to their oysters.

'*That's* what I mean,' said the carrying voice of the foreign actress, whom Henri had just disabused of the idea that she had been promised the pink alcove. 'They ain't *alive* to the war yet. Now, what's the matter with those four dubs yonder joining the British Army or – or *doing* something?'

'Who's your friend?' Maddingham asked.

'I've forgotten her name for the minute,' Portson replied, 'but she's the latest thing in imported patriotic piece-goods. She sings "Sons of the Empire, Go Forward!" at the Palemseum. It makes the aunties weep.'

'That's Sidney Latter. She's not half bad.' Tegg reached for the vinegar. 'We ought to see her some night.'

'Yes. We've a lot of time for that sort of thing,' Maddingham grunted. 'I'll take your oysters, Portson, if you don't want 'em.'

'Cheer up, Papa Maddingham! Soon be dead!' Winchmore suggested.

Maddingham glared at him. 'If I'd had you with me for *one* week, Master Winchmore – '

'Not the least use,' the boy retorted. 'I've just been made a full-lootenant. I have indeed. I couldn't reconcile it with my conscience to take *Etheldreda* out any more as a plain sub. She's too flat in the floor.'

'Did you get those new washboards of yours fixed?' Tegg cut in.

'Don't talk shop already,' Portson protested. 'This is Vesiga soup. I don't know what he's arranged in the way of drinks.'

'Pol Roger '04,' said the waiter.

'Sound man, Henri,' said Winchmore. 'But,' he eyed the waiter doubtfully, 'I don't quite like. . . . What's your alleged nationality?'

'Henri's nephew, monsieur,' the smiling waiter replied, and laid a gloved hand on the table. It creaked corkily at the wrist. 'Bethisy-sur-Oise,' he explained. 'My uncle he buy me *all* the hand for Christmas. It is good to hold plates only.'

'Oh! Sorry I spoke,' said Winchmore.

'Monsieur is right. But my uncle is very careful, even with neutrals.' He poured the champagne.

'Hold a minute,' Maddingham cried. 'First toast of obligation: For what we are going to receive, thank God and the British Navy.'

'Amen!' said the others with a nod towards Lieutenant Tegg, of the Royal Navy afloat, and, occasionally, of the Admiralty ashore.

'Next! "Damnation to all neutrals!"' Maddingham went on.

'Amen! Amen!' they answered between gulps that heralded the sole à la Colbert. Maddingham picked up the menu. 'Suprême of chicken,' he read loudly. 'Filet béarnaise, Woodcock and Richebourg '74, Pêches Melba, Croûtes Baron. I couldn't have improved on it myself; though one might,' he went on – 'one *might* have substituted quail *en casserole* for the woodcock.'

'Then there would have been no reason for the Burgundy,' said Tegg with equal gravity.

'You're right,' Maddingham replied.

The foreign actress shrugged her shoulders. 'What *can* you do with people like that?' she said to her companion. 'And yet *I've* been singing to 'em for a fortnight.'

'I left it all to Henri,' said Portson.

'My Gord!' the eavesdropping woman whispered. 'Get on to that! Ain't it typical? They leave everything to Henri in this country.'

'By the way,' Tegg asked Winchmore after the fish, 'where did you mount that one-pounder of yours after all?'

'Midships. *Etheldreda* won't carry more weight forward. She's wet enough as it is.'

'Why don't you apply for another craft?' Portson put in. 'There's a chap at Southampton just now, down with pneumonia and –'

'No, thank you. I know *Etheldreda*. She's nothing to write home about, but when she feels well she can shift a bit.'

Maddingham leaned across the table. 'If she does more than eleven in a flat calm,' said he, 'I'll – I'll give you *Hilarity*.'

' 'Wouldn't be found dead in *Hilarity*,' was Winchmore's grateful reply. 'You don't mean to say you've taken her into real wet water, Papa? Where did it happen?'

The others laughed. Maddingham's red face turned brick colour, and the veins on the cheek-bones showed blue through a blur of short bristles.

'He's been convoying neutrals – in a tactful manner,' Tegg chuckled.

Maddingham filled his glass and scowled at Tegg. 'Yes,' he said, 'and here's special damnation to me Lords of the Admiralty. A more muddle-headed set of brass-bound apes –'

'My! My! My!' Winchmore chirruped soothingly. 'It don't seem to have done you any good, Papa. Who were you conveyancing?'

Maddingham snapped out a ship's name and some details of her build.

'Oh, but that chap's a friend of *mine*!' cried Winchmore. 'I ran across him – the – not so long ago, hugging the Scotch coast – out of his course, he said, owing to foul weather and a new type of engine – a Diesel. That's him, ain't it – the complete neutral?' He mentioned an outstanding peculiarity of the ship's rig.

'Yes,' said Portson. 'Did you board him, Winchmore?'

'No. There'd been a bit of a blow the day before and old *Ethel*'s only dinghy had dropped off the hooks. But he signalled me all his symptoms. He was as communicative as – as a lady in the Promenade. (Hold on, Nephew of my Uncle!

I'm going to have some more of that Béarnaise fillet.) His smell attracted me. I chaperoned him for a couple of days.'

'Only two days. *You* hadn't anything to complain of,' said Maddingham wrathfully.

'I didn't complain. If he chose to hug things, 'twasn't any of my business. I'm not a Purity League. 'Didn't care what he hugged, so long as I could lie behind him and give him first chop at any mines that were going. I steered in his wake (I really *can* steer a bit now, Portson) and let him stink up the whole of the North Sea. I thought he might come in useful for bait. No Burgundy, thanks, Nephew of my Uncle. I'm sticking to the Jolly Roger.'

'Go on, then – before you're speechless. Was he any use as bait?' Tegg demanded.

'We never got a fair chance. As I told you, he hugged the coast till dark, and then he scraped round Gilarra Head and went up the bay nearly to the beach.'

'Lights out?' Maddingham asked.

Winchmore nodded. 'But I didn't worry about that. I was under his stern. As luck 'ud have it, there was a fishing-party in the bay, and we walked slam into the middle of 'em – a most ungodly collection of local talent. First thing I knew a steam-launch fell aboard us, and a boy – a nasty little Navy boy, Tegg – wanted to know what I was doing. I told him, and he cursed me for putting the fish down just as they were rising. Then the two of us (he was hanging on to my quarter with a boat-hook) drifted on to a steam trawler and our friend the Neutral and a ten-oared cutter full of the military, all mixed up. They were subs from the garrison out for a lark. Uncle Newt explained over the rail about the weather and his engine-troubles, but they were all so keen to carry on with their fishing, they didn't fuss. They told him to clear off.'

'Was there anything on the move round Gilarra at that time?' Tegg inquired.

'Oh, they spun me the usual yarns about the water being thick with 'em, and asked me to help; but I couldn't stop. The cutter's stern-sheets were piled up with mines, like lobster-pots, and from the way the soldiers handled 'em I thought I'd better get out. So did Uncle Newt. *He* didn't like it a bit. There were a couple of shots fired at something just as we cleared the Head, and one dropped rather close to him. (These duck-shoots in the dark are dam' dangerous, y'know.) He lit up at once – tail-light, head-light, and side-lights. I had no more trouble with him the rest of the night.'

'But what about the report that you sawed off the steam-launch's boat-hook?' Tegg demanded suddenly.

'What! You don't mean to say that little beast of a snotty reported it? He was scratchin' poor old *Ethel*'s paint to pieces. I never reported what he said to *me*. And he called me a damned amateur, too! Well! Well! War's war. I missed all that fishing-party that time. My orders were to follow Uncle Newt. So I followed – and poor *Ethel* without a dry rag on her.'

Winchmore refilled his glass.

'Well, don't get poetical,' said Portson. 'Let's have the rest of your trip.'

'There wasn't any rest,' Winchmore insisted pathetically. 'There was just good old *Ethel* with her engines missing like sin, and Uncle Newt thumping and stinking half a mile ahead of us, and me eating bread and Worcester sauce. I do when I feel that way. Besides, I wanted to go back and join the fishing-party. Just before dark, I made out *Cordelia* – that Southampton ketch that old Jarrott fitted with oil auxiliaries for a family cruiser last summer. She's a beamy bus, but she *can* roll, and she was doing an honest thirty degrees each way when I overhauled her. I asked Jarrott if he was busy. He said he wasn't. But he was. He's like me and Nelson when there's any sea on.'

'But Jarrott's a Quaker. Has been for generations. Why does he go to war?' said Maddingham.

'If it comes to that,' Portson said, 'why do any of us?'

'Jarrott's a mine-sweeper,' Winchmore replied with deep feeling. 'The Quaker religion (I'm not a Quaker, but I'm *much* more religious than any of you chaps give me credit for) has decided that mine-sweeping is life-saving. Consequently' – he dwelt a little on the word – 'the profession is crowded with Quakers – specially off Scarborough. 'See? Owin' to the purity of their lives, they "*all* go to Heaven when they die – Roll, Jordan, Roll!" '

'Disgustin',' said the actress audibly as she drew on her gloves. Winchmore looked at her with delight. 'That's a peach-Melba, too,' he said.

'And David Jarrott's a mine-sweeper,' Maddingham mused aloud. 'So you turned our Neutral over to him, Winchmore, did you?'

'Yes, I did. It was the end of my beat – I wish I didn't feel so sleepy – and I explained the whole situation to Jarrott, over the rail. 'Gave him all my silly instructions – those latest ones, y'know. I told him to do nothing to imperil existing political relations. I told him to exercise tact. I – I told him that in my capac'ty as Actin' Lootenant, you see. Jarrott's only a Lootenant-Commander – at fifty-four, too! Yes, I handed my Uncle Newt over to Jarrott to chaperone, and I went back to my – I can say it perfectly – pis-ca-to-rial party in the bay. Now I'm going to have a nap. In ten minutes I shall be on deck again. This is my first civilized dinner in nine weeks, so I don't apologize.'

He pushed his plate away, dropped his chin on his palm and closed his eyes.

'Lyndnoch and Jarrott's Bank, established 1793,' said Maddingham half to himself. 'I've seen old Jarrott in Cowes week bullied by his skipper and steward till he had to sneak ashore to sleep. And now he's out mine-sweeping with *Cordelia*! What's happened to his – I shall forget my own name next – Belfast-built two-hundred tonner?'

'*Goneril*,' said Portson. 'He turned her over to the Service in October. She's – she was *Culana*.'

'*She* was *Culana*, was she? My God! I never knew that. Where did it happen?'

'Off the same old Irish corner I was watching last month. My young cousin was in her; so was one of the Raikes boys. A whole nest of mines, laid between patrols.'

'I've heard there's some dirty work going on there now,' Maddingham half whispered.

'You needn't tell *me* that,' Portson returned. 'But one gets a little back now and again.'

'What are you two talking about?' said Tegg, who seemed to be dozing too.

'*Culana*,' Portson answered as he lit a cigarette.

'Yes, that was rather a pity. But ... What about this Newt of ours?'

'*I* took her over from Jarrott next day – off Margate,' said Portson. 'Jarrott wanted to get back to his mine-sweeping.'

'Every man to his taste,' said Maddingham. 'That never appealed to me. Had they detailed you specially to look after the Newt?'

'Me among others,' Portson admitted. 'I was going down Channel when I got my orders, and so I went on with him. Jarrott had been tremendously interested in his course up to date – specially off the Wash. He'd charted it very carefully and he said he was going back to find out what some of the kinks and curves meant. Has he found out, Tegg?'

Tegg thought for a moment. '*Cordelia* was all right up to six o'clock yesterday evening,' he said.

'Glad of that. Then I did what Winchmore did. I lay behind this stout fellow and saw him well into the open.'

'Did you say anything to him?' Tegg asked.

'Not a thing. He kept moving all the time.'

' 'See anything?' Tegg continued.

'No. He didn't seem to be in demand anywhere in the Channel, and, when I'd got him on the edge of soundings, I dropped him – as per your esteemed orders.'

Tegg nodded again and murmured some apology.

'Where did *you* pick him up, Maddingham?' Portson went on.

Maddingham snorted.

'Well north and west of where you left him heading up the Irish Channel and stinking like a taxi. I hadn't had my breakfast. My cook was seasick; so were four of my hands.'

'I can see that meeting. Did you give him a gun across the bows?' Tegg asked.

'No, no. Not *that* time. I signalled him to heave to. He had his papers ready before I came over the side. You see,' Maddingham said pleadingly, 'I'm new to this business. Perhaps I wasn't as polite to him as I should have been if I'd had my breakfast.'

'He deposed that Maddingham came alongside swearing like a bargee,' said Tegg.

'Not in the least. This is what happened.' Maddingham turned to Portson. 'I asked him where he was bound for and he told me – Antigua.'

'Hi! Wake up, Winchmore. You're missing something.' Portson nudged Winchmore, who was slanting sideways in his chair.

'Right! All right! I'm awake,' said Winchmore stickily. 'I heard every word.'

Maddingham went on. 'I told him that this wasn't his way to Antigua –'

'Antigua. Antigua!' Winchmore finished rubbing his eyes. ' "There was a young bride of Antigua – " '

'Hsh! Hsh!' said Portson and Tegg warningly.

'Why? It's the proper one. "Who said to her spouse, 'What a pig you are!' " '

'Ass!' Maddingham growled and continued: 'He told me that he'd been knocked out of his reckoning by foul weather and engine-trouble, owing to experimenting with a new type of Diesel engine. He was perfectly frank about it.'

'So he was with me,' said Winchmore. 'Just like a real lady. I hope you were a real gentleman, Papa.'

'I asked him what he'd got. He didn't object. He had some fifty thousand gallon of oil for his new Diesel engine, and the rest was coal. He said he needed the oil to get to Antigua with, he was taking the coal as ballast, and he was coming back, so he told me, with coconuts. When he'd quite finished, I said: "What sort of damned idiot do you take me for?" He said: "I haven't decided yet!" Then I said he'd better come into port with me, and we'd arrive at a decision. He said that his papers were in perfect order and that my instructions – mine, please! – were not to imperil political relations. I hadn't received these asinine instructions, so I took the liberty of contradicting him – perfectly politely, as I told them at the Inquiry afterwards. He was a small-boned man with a grey beard, in a glengarry, and he picked his teeth a lot. He said: "The last time I met you, Mister Maddingham, you were going to Carlsbad, and you told me all about your blood-pressures in the wagon-lit before we tossed for upper berth. Don't you think you are a little old to buccaneer about the sea this way?" I couldn't recall his face – he must have been some fellow that I'd travelled with some time or other. I told him I wasn't doing this for amusement – it was business. Then I ordered him into port. He said: "S'pose I don't go? –" I said: "Then I'll sink you." Isn't it extraordinary how natural it all seems after a few weeks? If anyone had told me when I commissioned *Hilarity* last summer what I'd be doing this spring I'd – I'd . . . God! It *is* mad, isn't it?'

'Quite,' said Portson. 'But not bad fun.'

'Not at all, but that's what makes it all the madder. Well, he didn't argue any more. He warned me I'd be hauled over the coals for what I'd done, and I warned him to keep two cables ahead of me and not to yaw.'

'Jaw?' said Winchmore sleepily.

'No. Yaw,' Maddingham snarled. 'Not to look as if he even wanted to yaw. I warned him that, if he did, I'd loose off into him, end-on. But I was absolutely polite about it. 'Give you my word, Tegg.'

'I believe you. Oh, I believe you,' Tegg replied.

'Well, so I took him into port – and that was where I first ran across our Master Tegg. He represented the Admiralty on that beach.'

The small blinking man nodded. 'The Admiralty had that honour,' he said graciously.

Maddingham turned to the others angrily, 'I'd been rather patting myself on the back for what I'd done, you know. Instead of which, they held a court-martial –'

'*We* called it an Inquiry,' Tegg interjected.

'*You* weren't in the dock. They held a court-martial on me to find out how often I'd sworn at the poor injured Neutral, and whether I'd given him hot-water bottles and tucked him up at night. It's all very fine to laugh, but they treated me like a pickpocket. There were two fat-headed civilian judges and that blackguard Tegg in the conspiracy. A cursed lawyer defended my Neutral and he made fun of *me*. He dragged in everything the Neutral had told him about my blood-pressures on the Carlsbad trip. And that's what you get for trying to serve your country in your old age!' Maddingham emptied and refilled his glass.

'We *did* give you rather a grilling,' said Tegg placidly. 'It's the national sense of fair play.'

'I could have stood it all if it hadn't been for the Neutral. We dined at the same hotel while this court-martial was going on, and he used to come over to my table and sympathize with me! He told me that I was fighting for his ideals and the uplift of democracy, but I must respect the Law of Nations!'

'And we respected 'em,' said Tegg. 'His papers were perfectly correct; the Court discharged him. We had to consider existing political relations. I *told* Maddingham so at the hotel and he –'

Again Maddingham turned to the others. 'I couldn't make up my mind about Tegg at the Inquiry,' he explained. 'He had the air of a decent sailor-man, but he talked like a poisonous politician.'

'I was,' Tegg returned. 'I had been ordered to change into that rig. So I changed.'

Maddingham ran one fat square hand through his crisped hair and looked up under his eyebrows like a shy child, while the others lay back and laughed.

'I suppose I ought to have been on to the joke,' he stammered, 'but I'd blacked myself all over for the part of Lootenant-Commander R.N.V.R. in time of war, and I'd given up thinking as a banker. If it had been put before me as a business proposition I might have done better.'

'I thought you were playing up to me and the judges all

the time,' said Tegg. 'I never dreamed you took it seriously.'

'Well, I've been trained to look on the law as serious. I've had to pay for some of it in my time, you know.'

'I'm sorry,' said Tegg. 'We were obliged to let that oily beggar go – for reasons, but, as I told Maddingham, the night the award was given, *his* duty was to see that he was properly directed to Antigua.'

'Naturally,' Portson observed. 'That being the Neutral's declared destination. And what did Maddingham do? Shut up, Maddingham!'

Said Tegg, with downcast eyes: 'Maddingham took my hand and squeezed it; he looked lovingly into my eyes (he *did!*); he turned plum-colour, and he said: "I will" – just like a bridegroom at the altar. It makes me feel shy to think of it even now. I didn't see him after that till the evening when *Hilarity* was pulling out of the Basin, and Maddingham was cursing the tug-master.'

'I was in a hurry,' said Maddingham. 'I wanted to get to the Narrows and wait for my Neutral there. I dropped down to Biller and Grove's yard that tide (they've done all my work for years) and I jammed *Hilarity* into the creek behind their slip, so the Newt didn't spot me when he came down the river. Then I pulled out and followed him over the Bar. He stood nor-west at once. I let him go till we were well out of sight of land. Then I overhauled him, gave him a gun across the bows and ran alongside. I'd just had my lunch, and I wasn't going to lose my temper *this* time. I said: "Excuse me, but I understand you are bound for Antigua?" He was, he said, and as he seemed a little nervous about my falling aboard him in that swell, I gave *Hilarity* another sheer in – she's as handy as a launch – and I said: "May I suggest that this is not the course for Antigua?" By that time he had his fenders overside, and all hands yelling at me to keep away. I snatched *Hilarity* out and began edging in again. He said: "I'm trying a sample of inferior oil that I have my doubts about. If it works all right I shall lay my course for Antigua, but it will take some time to test the stuff and adjust the engines to it." I said: "Very good, let me know if I can be of any service," and I offered him *Hilarity* again once or twice – he didn't want her – and then I dropped behind and let him go on. Wasn't that proper, Portson?'

Portson nodded. 'I know that game of yours with *Hilarity*,' he said. 'How the deuce do you do it? My nerve always goes at close quarters in any sea.'

'It's only a little trick of steering,' Maddingham replied with a simper of vanity. 'You can almost shave with her when she feels like it. I had to do it again that same evening, to establish a moral ascendancy. He wasn't showing any lights, and I nearly tripped over him. He was a scared Neutral for three minutes, but I got a little of my own back for that damned court-martial. *But* I was perfectly polite. I apologized profusely. I didn't even ask him to show his lights.'

'But did he?' said Winchmore.

'He did – every one; and a flare now and then,' Maddingham replied. 'He held north all that night, with a falling barometer and a rising wind and all the other filthy things. Gad, how I hated him! Next morning we got it, good and tight from the nor-nor-west out of the Atlantic, off Carso Head. He dodged into a squall, and then he went about. We weren't a mile behind, but it was as thick as a wall. When it cleared, and I couldn't see him ahead of me, I went about too, and followed the rain. I picked him up five miles down wind, legging it for all he was worth to the south'ard – nine knots, I should think. *Hilarity* doesn't like a following sea. We got pooped a bit, too, but by noon we'd struggled back to where we ought to have been – two cables astern of him. Then he began to signal, but his flags being end-on to us, of course, we had to creep up on his beam – well abeam – to read 'em. *That* didn't restore his morale either. He made out he'd been compelled to put back by stress of weather before completing his oil tests. I made back I was sorry to hear it, but would be greatly interested in the results. Then I turned in (I'd been up all night) and my lootenant took on. He was a widower (by the way) of the name of Sherrin, aged forty-seven. He'd run a girls' school at Weston-super-Mare after he'd left the

Service in 'ninety-five, and he believed the English were the Lost Tribes.'

'What about the Germans?' said Portson.

'Oh, they'd been misled by Austria, who was the Beast with Horns in Revelations. Otherwise he was rather a dull dog. He set the tops'ls in his watch. *Hilarity* won't steer under any canvas, so we rather sported round our friend that afternoon, I believe. When I came up after dinner, she was biting his behind, first one side, then the other. Let's see – that would be about thirty miles east-sou-east of Harry Island. We were running as near as nothing south. The wind had dropped, and there was a useful cross-rip coming up from the south-east. I took the wheel and, the way I nursed him from starboard, he had to take the sea over his port bow. I had my sciatica on me – buccaneering's no game for a middle-aged man – but I gave that fellow sprudel! By Jove; I washed him out! He stood it as long as he could, and then he made a bolt for Harry Island. I had to ride in his pocket most of the way there because I didn't know that coast. We had charts, but Sherrin never understood 'em, and I couldn't leave the wheel. So we rubbed along together, and about midnight this Newt dodged in over the tail of Harry Shoals and anchored, if you please, in the lee of the Double Ricks. It was dead calm there, except for the swell, but there wasn't much room to manoeuvre in, and *I* wasn't going to anchor. It looked too like a submarine rendezvous. But first, I came alongside and asked him what his trouble was. He told me he had overheated his something-or-other bulb. I've never been shipmates with Diesel engines, but I took his word for it, and I said I 'ud stand by till it cooled. Then he told me to go to hell.'

'If you were inside the Double Ricks in the dark, you were practically there,' said Portson.

'That's what *I* thought. I was on the bridge, rabid with sciatica, going round and round like a circus-horse in about three acres of water, and wondering when I'd hit something. Ridiculous position. Sherrin saw it. He saved me. He said it was an ideal place for submarine attacks, and we'd

better begin to repel 'em at once. As I said, I couldn't leave
the wheel, so Sherrin fought the ship – both quick-
firers and the maxims. He tipped 'em well down into the
sea or well up at the Ricks as we went round and round.
We made rather a row; and the row the gulls made when
we woke 'em was absolutely terrifying. Give you my
word!'

'And then?' said Winchmore.

'I kept on running in circles through this ghastly din. I
took one sheer over toward his stern – I thought I'd cut it too
fine, but we missed it by inches. Then I heard his capstan
busy, and in another three minutes his anchor was up. He
didn't wait to stow. He hustled out as he was – bulb or no
bulb. He passed within ten feet of us (I was waiting to fall in
behind him) and he shouted over the rail: "You think you've
got patriotism. All you've got is uric acid and rotten spite!" I
expect he was a little bored. I waited till we had cleared
Harry Shoals before I went below, and then I slept till 9 A.M.
He was heading north this time, and after I'd had breakfast
and a smoke I ran alongside and asked him where he was
bound for now. He was wrapped in a comforter, evidently
suffering from a bad cold. I couldn't quite catch what he said,
but I let him croak for a few minutes and fell back. At 9 P.M.
he turned round and headed south (I was getting to know the
Irish Channel by then) and I followed. There was no particular sea on. It was a little chilly, but as he didn't hug the
coast I hadn't to take the wheel. I stayed below most of the
night and let Sherrin suffer. Well, Mr Newt kept up this
game all the next day, dodging up and down the Irish Channel. And it was infernally dull. He threw up the sponge off
Cloone Harbour. That was on Friday morning. He signalled:
"Developed defects in engine-room. Antigua trip abandoned." Then he ran into Cloone and tied up at Brady's
Wharf. You know you can't repair a dinghy at Cloone!
I followed, of course, and berthed behind him. After lunch I
thought I'd pay him a call. I wanted to look at his engines. I
don't understand Diesels, but Hyslop, my engineer, said they
must have gone round 'em with a hammer, for they were

pretty badly smashed up. Besides that, they had offered all their oil to the Admiralty agent there, and it was being shifted to a tug when I went aboard him. So I'd done my job. I was just going back to *Hilarity* when his steward said he'd like to see me. He was lying in his cabin breathing pretty loud – wrapped up in rugs and his eyes sticking out like a rabbit's. He offered me drinks. I couldn't accept 'em, of course. Then he said: "Well, Mr Maddingham, I'm all in." I said I was glad to hear it. Then he told me he was seriously ill with a sudden attack of bronchial pneumonia, and he asked me to run him across to England to see his doctor in town. I said, of course, that was out of the question, *Hilarity* being a man-of-war in commission. He couldn't see it. He asked what had that to do with it? He thought this war was some sort of joke, and I had to repeat it all over again. He seemed rather afraid of dying (it's no game for a middle-aged man, of course) and he hoisted himself up on one elbow and began calling me a murderer. I explained to him – perfectly politely – that I wasn't in this job for fun. It was business. My orders were to see that he went to Antigua, and now that he wasn't going to Antigua, and had sold his oil to us, that finished it as far as I was concerned. (Wasn't that perfectly correct?) He said: "But that finishes me, too. I can't get any doctor in this God-forsaken hole. I made sure you'd treat me properly as soon as I surrendered." I said there wasn't any question of surrender. If he'd been a wounded belligerent, I might have taken him aboard, though I certainly shouldn't have gone a yard out of my course to land him anywhere; but as it was, he was a neutral – altogether outside the game. You see my point? I tried awfully hard to make him understand it. He went on about his affairs all being at loose ends. He was a rich man – a million and a quarter, he said – and he wanted to redraft his will before he died. I told him a good many people were in his position just now – only they weren't rich. He changed his tack then and appealed to me on the grounds of our common humanity. "Why, if you leave me now, Mr Maddingham," he said, "you condemn me to death, just as surely as if you hanged me." '

'This *is* interesting,' Portson murmured. 'I never imagined you in this light before, Maddingham.'

'I was surprised at myself – 'give you my word. But I was perfectly polite. I said to him: "Try to be reasonable, sir. If you had got rid of your oil where it was wanted, you'd have condemned lots of people to death just as surely as if you'd drowned 'em." "Ah, but I didn't," he said. "That ought to count in my favour." "That was no thanks to you." I said. "You weren't given the chance. This is war, sir. If you make up your mind to that, you'll see that the rest follows." "I didn't imagine you'd take it as seriously as all that," he said – and he said it quite seriously, too. "Show a little consideration. Your side's bound to win anyway." I said: "Look here! I'm a middle-aged man, and I don't suppose my conscience is any clearer than yours in many respects, but this is business. I can do nothing for you." '

'You got that a bit mixed, I think,' said Tegg critically.

'*He* saw what I was driving at,' Maddingham replied, 'and he was the only one that mattered for the moment. "Then I'm a dead man, Mr Maddingham," he said. "That's *your* business," I said. "Good afternoon." And I went out.'

'And?' said Winchmore, after some silence.

'He died. I saw his flag half-masted next morning.'

There was another silence. Henri looked in at the alcove and smiled. Maddingham beckoned to him.

'But why didn't you lend him a hand to settle his private affairs?' said Portson.

'Because I wasn't acting in my private capacity. I'd been on the bridge for three nights and – ' Maddingham pulled out his watch – 'this time tomorrow I shall be there again – confound it! Has my car come, Henri?'

'Yes, Sare Francis. I am sorry.' They all complimented Henri on the dinner, and when the compliments were paid he expressed himself still their debtor. So did the nephew.

'Are you coming with me, Portson?' said Maddingham as he rose heavily.

'No. I'm for Southampton, worse luck! My car ought to be here, too.'

'I'm for Euston and the frigid calculating North,' said Winchmore with a shudder. 'One common taxi, please, Henri.'

Tegg smiled. 'I'm supposed to sleep in just now, but if you don't mind, I'd like to come with you as far as Gravesend, Maddingham.'

'Delighted. There's a glass all round left still,' said Maddingham. 'Here's luck! The usual, I suppose? "Damnation to all neutrals!"'

'In the Interests of the Brethren'

(1918)

I was buying a canary in a birdshop when he first spoke to me and suggested that I should take a less highly coloured bird. 'The colour is in the feeding,' said he. 'Unless you know how to feed 'em, it goes. Canaries are one of our hobbies.'

He passed out before I could thank him. He was a middle-aged man with grey hair and a short, dark beard, rather like a Sealyham terrier in silver spectacles. For some reason his face and his voice stayed in my mind so distinctly that, months later, when I jostled against him on a platform crowded with an Angling Club going to the Thames, I recognized, turned, and nodded.

'I took your advice about the canary,' I said.

'Did you? Good!' he replied heartily over the rod-case on his shoulder, and was parted from me by the crowd.

A few years ago I turned into a tobacconist's to have a badly stopped pipe cleaned out.

'Well! Well! And how did the canary do?' said the man behind the counter. We shook hands, and 'What's your name?' we both asked together.

His name was Lewis Holroyd Burges, of 'Burges and Son', as I might have seen above the door – but Son had been killed in Egypt. His hair was whiter than it had been, and the eyes were sunk a little.

'Well! Well! To think,' said he, 'of one man in all these millions turning up in this curious way, when there's so many who don't turn up at all – eh?' (It was then that he told me of Son Lewis's death and why the boy had been christened Lewis.) 'Yes. There's not much left for middle-aged people just at present. Even one's hobbies – We used to fish together. And the same with canaries! We used to breed 'em for colour – deep orange was our speciality. That's why I spoke to you, if you remember; but I've sold all my birds.

Well! Well! And now we must locate your trouble.'

He bent over my erring pipe and dealt with it skilfully as a surgeon. A soldier came in, spoke in an undertone, received a reply, and went out.

'Many of my clients are soldiers nowadays, and a number of 'em belong to the Craft,' said Mr Burges. 'It breaks my heart to give them the tobaccos they ask for. On the other hand, not one man in five thousand has a tobacco-palate. Preference, yes. Palate, no. Here's your pipe, again. It deserves better treatment than it's had. There's a procedure, a ritual, in all things. Any time you're passing by again, I assure you, you will be welcome. I've one or two odds and ends that may interest you.'

I left the shop with the rarest of all feelings on me – the sensation which is only youth's right – that I might have made a friend. A little distance from the door I was accosted by a wounded man who asked for 'Burges's.' The place seemed to be known in the neighbourhood.

I found my way to it again, and often after that, but it was not till my third visit that I discovered Mr Burges held a half interest in Ackerman and Pernit's, the great cigar-importers, which had come to him through an uncle whose children now lived almost in the Cromwell Road, and said that the uncle had been on the Stock Exchange.

'I'm a shopkeeper by instinct,' said Mr Burges. 'I like the ritual of handling things. The shop has done me well. I like to do well by the shop.'

It had been established by his grandfather in 1827, but the fittings and appointments must have been at least half a century older. The brown and red tobacco- and snuff-jars, with Crowns, Garters, and names of forgotten mixtures in gold leaf; the polished 'Oronoque' tobacco-barrels on which favoured customers sat; the cherry-black mahogany counter, the delicately moulded shelves, the reeded cigar-cabinets, the German-silver-mounted scales, and the Dutch brass roll- and cake-cutter, were things to covet.

'They aren't so bad,' he admitted. 'That large Bristol jar hasn't any duplicate to my knowledge. Those eight snuff-jars on the third shelf – they're Dollin's ware; he used to work for Wimble in Seventeen-Forty – are absolutely unique. Is there anyone in the trade now could tell you what "Romano's Hollande" was? Or "Scholten's"? Here's a snuff-mull of George the First's time; and here's a Louis Quinze – what am I talking of? Treize, Treize, of course – grater for making bran-snuff. They were regular tools of the shop in my grand-father's day. And who on earth to leave 'em to outside the British Museum now, *I* can't think!'

His pipes – I would this were a tale for virtuosi – his am-azing collection of pipes was kept in the parlour, and this gave me the privilege of making his wife's acquaintance. One morning, as I was looking covetously at a jacaranda-wood 'cigarro' – *not* cigar – cabinet with silver lock-plates and drawer-knobs of Spanish work, a wounded Canadian came into the shop and disturbed our happy little committee.

'Say,' he began loudly, 'are you the right place?'

'Who sent you?' Mr Burges demanded.

'A man from Messines. But *that* ain't the point! I've got no certificates, nor papers – nothin', you understand. I left my Lodge owin' 'em seventeen dollars back-dues. But this man at Messines told me it wouldn't make any odds with *you*.'

'It doesn't,' said Mr Burges. 'We meet tonight at 7 P.M.'

The man's face fell a yard. 'Hell!' said he. 'But I'm in hos-pital – I can't get leaf.'

'*And* Tuesdays and Fridays at 3 P.M.,' Mr Burges added promptly. 'You'll have to be proved, of course.'

'Guess I can get by *that* all right,' was the cheery reply. 'Toosday, then.' He limped off, beaming.

'Who might that be?' I asked.

'I don't know any more than you do – except he must be a Brother. London's full of Masons now. Well! Well! We must do what we can these days. If you'll come to tea this evening, I'll take you on to Lodge afterwards. It's a Lodge of Instruc-tion.'

'Delighted. Which is your Lodge?' I said, for up till then he had not given me its name.

' "Faith and Works 5837" – the third Saturday of every

month. Our Lodge of Instruction meets nominally every Thursday, but we sit oftener than that now because there are so many Visiting Brothers in town.' Here another customer entered, and I went away much interested in the range of Brother Burges's hobbies.

At tea-time he was dressed as for Church, and wore gold pince-nez in lieu of the silver spectacles. I blessed my stars that I had thought to change into decent clothes.

'Yes, we owe that much to the Craft,' he assented. 'All Ritual is fortifying. Ritual's a natural necessity for mankind. The more things are upset, the more they fly to it. I abhor slovenly Ritual anywhere. By the way, would you mind assisting at the examinations, if there are many Visiting Brothers tonight? You'll find some of 'em very rusty, but – it's the Spirit, not the Letter, that giveth life. The question of Visiting Brethren is an important one. There are so many of them in London now, you see; and so few places where they can meet.'

'You dear thing!' said Mrs Burges, and handed him his locked and initialled apron-case.

'Our Lodge is only just round the corner,' he went on. 'You mustn't be too critical of our appurtenances. The place was a garage once.'

As far as I could make out in the humiliating darkness, we wandered up a mews and into a courtyard. Mr Burges piloted me, murmuring apologies for everything in advance.

'You mustn't expect – ' he was still saying when we stumbled upon a porch and entered a carefully decorated ante-room hung round with Masonic prints. I noticed Peter Gilkes and Barton Wilson, fathers of 'Emulation' working, in the place of honour; Kneller's Christopher Wren; Dunkerley, with his own Fitz-George book-plate below and the bend sinister on the Royal Arms; Hogarth's caricature of Wilkes, also his disreputable 'Night'; and a beautifully framed set of Grand Masters, from Anthony Sayer down.

'Are these another hobby of yours?' I asked.

'Not this time,' Mr Burges smiled. 'We have to thank Brother Lemming for them.' He introduced me to the senior

partner of Lemming and Orton, whose little shop is hard to
find, but whose words and cheques in the matter of prints are
widely circulated.

'The frames are the best part of 'em,' said Brother Lemming after my compliments. 'There are some more in the
Lodge Room. Come and look. We've got the big Desaguliers
there that nearly went to Iowa.'

I had never seen a Lodge Room better fitted. From mo-
saicked floor to appropriate ceiling, from curtain to piller, implements to seats, seats to lights, and little carved music-loft
at one end, every detail was perfect in particular kind and
general design. I said what I thought of them all, many times
over.

'I told you I was a Ritualist,' said Mr Burges. 'Look at those
carved corn-sheaves and grapes on the back of these
Wardens' chairs. That's the old tradition – before Masonic
furnishers spoilt it. I picked up that pair in Stepney ten years
ago – the same time I got the gavel.' It was of ancient, yel-
lowed ivory, cut all in one piece out of some tremendous tusk.
'That came from the Gold Coast,' he said. 'It belonged to a
Military Lodge there in 1794. You can see the inscription.'

'If it's a fair question,' I began, 'how much –'

'It stood us,' said Brother Lemming, his thumbs in his
waistcoat pockets, 'an appreciable sum of money when we
built it in 1906, even with what Brother Anstruther – he was
our contractor – cheated himself out of. By the way, that
ashlar there is pure Carrara, he tells me. I don't understand
marbles myself. Since then I expect we've put in – oh, quite
another little sum. Now we'll go to the examination-room
and take on the Brethren.'

He led me back, not to the ante-room, but a convenient
chamber flanked with what looked like confessional-boxes (I
found out later that that was what they had been, when first
picked up for a song near Oswestry). A few men in uniform
were waiting at the far end. 'That's only the head of the
procession. The rest are in the ante-room,' said an officer of
the Lodge.

Brother Burges assigned me my discreet box, saying: 'Don't be surprised. They come all shapes.'

'Shapes' was not a bad description, for my first penitent was all head-bandages – escaped from an Officers' Hospital, Pentonville way. He asked me in profane Scots how I expected a man with only six teeth and half a lower lip to speak to any purpose, so we compromised on the signs. The next – a New Zealander from Taranaki – reversed the process, for he was one-armed, and that in a sling. I mistrusted an enormous Sergeant-Major of Heavy Artillery, who struck me as much too glib, so I sent him on to Brother Lemming in the next box, who discovered he was a Past District Grand Officer. My last man nearly broke me down altogether. Everything seemed to have gone from him.

'I don't blame yer,' he gulped at last. 'I wouldn't pass my own self on my answers, but I give yer my word that so far as I've had any religion, it's been all the religion I've had. For God's sake, let me sit in Lodge again, Brother!'

When the examinations were ended, a Lodge Officer came round with our aprons – no tinsel or silver-gilt confections, but heavily-corded silk with tassels and – where a man could prove he was entitled to them – levels, of decent plate. Some one in front of me tightened a belt on a stiffly silent person in civil clothes with discharge-badge. ' 'Strewth! This is comfort again,' I heard him say. The companion nodded. The man went on suddenly: 'Here! What're you doing? Leave off! You promised not to! Chuck it!' and dabbed at his companion's streaming eyes.

'Let him leak,' said an Australian signaller. 'Can't you see how happy the beggar is?'

It appeared that the silent Brother was a 'shell-shocker' whom Brother Lemming had passed, on the guarantee of his friend and – what moved Lemming more – the threat that, were he refused, he would have fits from pure disappointment. So the 'shocker' went happily and silently among Brethren evidently accustomed to these displays.

We fell in, two by two, according to tradition, fifty of us at least, and were played into Lodge by what I thought was an harmonium, but which I discovered to be an organ of repute. It took time to settle us down, for ten or twelve were cripples and had to be helped into long or easy chairs. I sat between a one-footed R.A.M.C. Corporal and a Captain of Territorials, who, he told me, had 'had a brawl' with a bomb, which had bent him in two directions. 'But that's first-class Bach the organist is giving us now,' he said delightedly. 'I'd like to know him. *I* used to be a piano-thumper of sorts.'

'I'll introduce you after Lodge,' said one of the regular Brethren behind us – a plump, torpedo-bearded man, who turned out to be a doctor. 'After all, there's nobody to touch Bach, is there?' Those two plunged at once into musical talk, which to outsiders is as fascinating as trigonometry.

Now a Lodge of Instruction is mainly a parade-ground for Ritual. It cannot initiate or confer degrees, but is limited to rehearsals and lectures. Worshipful Brother Burges, re-splendent in Solomon's Chair (I found out later where that, too, had been picked up), briefly told the Visiting Brethren how welcome they were and always would be, and asked them to vote what ceremony should be rendered for their instruction.

When the decision was announced he wanted to know whether any Visiting Brothers would take the duties of Lodge Officers. They protested bashfully that they were too rusty. 'The very reason why,' said Brother Burges, while the organ Bached softly. My musical Captain wriggled in his chair.

'One moment, Worshipful Sir.' The plump Doctor rose. 'We have here a musician for whom place and opportunity are needed. Only,' he went on colloquially, 'those organ-loft steps are a bit steep.'

'How much,' said Brother Burges with the solemnity of an initiation, 'does our Brother weigh?'

'Very little over eight stone,' said the Brother. 'Weighed this morning, Worshipful Sir.'

The Past District Grand Officer, who was also a Battery-Sergeant-Major, waddled across, lifted the slight weight in his arms and bore it to the loft, where, the regular organist pumping, it played joyously as a soul caught up to Heaven by surprise.

When the visitors had been coaxed to supply the necessary officers, a ceremony was rehearsed. Brother Burges forbade the regular members to prompt. The visitors had to work entirely by themselves, but, on the Battery-Sergeant-Major taking a hand, he was ruled out as of too exalted rank. They floundered badly after that support was withdrawn.

The one-footed R.A.M.C. on my right chuckled.

'D'you like it?' said the Doctor to him.

'*Do* I? It's Heaven to me, sittin' in Lodge again. It's all comin' back now, watching their mistakes. I haven't much religion, but all I had I learnt in Lodge.' Recognizing me, he flushed a little as one does when one says a thing twice over in another's hearing. 'Yes, "veiled in all'gory and illustrated in symbols" – the Fatherhood of God, an' the Brotherhood of Man; an' what more in Hell *do* you want? ... Look at 'em!' He broke off giggling. 'See! See! They've tied the whole thing into knots. *I* could ha' done it better myself – my one foot in France. Yes, I should think they *ought* to do it again!'

The new organist covered the little confusion that had arisen with what sounded like the wings of angels.

When the amateurs, rather red and hot, had had finished, they demanded an exhibition-working of their bungled ceremony by Regular Brethren of the Lodge. Then I realized for the first time what word-and-gesture-perfect Ritual can be brought to mean. We all applauded, the one-footed Corporal most of all.

'We *are* rather proud of our working, and this is an audience worth playing up to,' the Doctor said.

Next the Master delivered a little lecture on the meanings of some pictured symbols and diagrams. His theme was a well-worn one, but his deep holding voice made it fresh.

'Marvellous how these old copybook-headings persist,' the Doctor said.

'*That's* all right!' the one-footed man spoke cautiously out of the side of his mouth like a boy in form. 'But they're the kind o' copybook-headin's we shall find burnin' round our bunks in Hell. Believe me-ee! I've broke enough of 'em to know. Now, hsh!' He leaned forward, drinking it all in.

Presently Brother Burges touched on a point which had given rise to some diversity of Ritual. He asked for information. 'Well, in Jamaica, Worshipful Sir,' a Visiting Brother began, and explained how they worked that detail in his parts. Another and another joined in from different quarters of the Lodge (and the world), and when they were well warmed the Doctor sidled softly round the walls and, over our shoulders, passed us cigarettes.

'A shocking innovation,' he said, as he returned to the Captain-musician's vacant seat on my left. 'But men can't really talk without tobacco, and we're only a Lodge of Instruction.'

'An' I've learned more in one evenin' here than ten years.' The one-footed man turned round for an instant from a dark, sour-looking Yeoman in spurs who was laying down the law on Dutch Ritual. The blue haze and the talk increased, while the organ from the loft blessed us all.

'But this is delightful,' said I to the Doctor. 'How did it all happen?'

'Brother Burges started it. He used to talk to the men who dropped into his shop when the war began. He told us sleepy old chaps in Lodge that what men wanted more than anything else was Lodges where they could sit – just sit and be happy like we are now. He was right, too. We're learning things in the war. A man's Lodge means more to him than people imagine. As our friend on your right said just now, very often Masonry's the only practical creed we've ever listened to since we were children. Platitudes or no platitudes, it squares with what everybody knows ought to be done.' He sighed. 'And if this war hasn't brought home the Brotherhood of Man to us all, I'm – a Hun!'

'How did you get your visitors?' I went on.

'Oh, I told a few fellows in hospital near here, at Burges's suggestion, that we had a Lodge of Instruction and they'd be

welcome. And they came. And they told their friends. And
they came! That was two years ago – and now we've Lodge of
Instruction two nights a week, and a matinée nearly every
Tuesday and Friday for the men who can't get evening leave.
Yes, it's all very curious. I'd no notion what the Craft meant
– and means – till this war.'

'Nor I, till this evening,' I replied.

'Yet it's quite natural if you think. Here's London – all
England – packed with the Craft from all over the world, and
nowhere for them to go. Why, our weekly visiting attendance for the last four months averaged just under a hundred
and forty. Divide by four – call it thirty-five Visiting Brethren a time. Our record's seventy-one, but we have packed in
as many as eighty-four at Banquets. You can see for yourself
what a potty little hole we are!'

'Banquets too!' I cried. 'It must cost like anything. May
the Visiting Brethren –'

The Doctor – his name was Keede – laughed. 'No, a Visiting Brother may *not*.'

'But when a man has had an evening like this, he wants
to –'

'That's what they all say. That makes our difficulty. They
do exactly what you were going to suggest, and they're
offended if we don't take it.'

'Don't you?' I asked.

'My dear man – what *does* it come to? They can't all stay
to Banquet. Say one hundred suppers a week – fifteen quid –
sixty a month – seven hundred and twenty a year. How much
are Lemming and Orton worth? And Ellis and McKnight –
that long big man over yonder – the provision dealers? How
much d'you suppose could Burges write a cheque for and not
feel? 'Tisn't as if he had to save for anyone now. I assure you
we have no scruple in calling on the Visiting Brethren when
we want anything. We couldn't do the work otherwise. Have
you noticed how the Lodge is kept – brass-work, jewels, furniture, and so on?'

'I have indeed,' I said. 'It's like a ship. You could eat your
dinner off the floor.'

'Well, come here on a bye-day and you'll often find half-a-dozen Brethren, with eight legs between 'em, polishing and ronuking and sweeping everything they can get at. I cured a shell-shocker this spring by giving him our jewels to look after. He pretty well polished the numbers off 'em, but – it kept him from fighting Huns in his sleep. And when we need Masters to take our duties – two matinées a week is rather a tax – we've the choice of P.M.'s from all over the world. The Dominions are much keener on Ritual than an average English Lodge. Besides that – Oh, we're going to adjourn. Listen to the greetings. They'll be interesting.'

The crack of the great gavel brought us to our feet, after some surging and plunging among the cripples. Then the Battery-Sergeant-Major, in a trained voice, delivered hearty and fraternal greetings to 'Faith and Works' from his tropical District and Lodge. The others followed, without order, in every tone between a grunt and a squeak. I heard 'Hauraki', 'Inyanga-Umbezi', 'Aloha'. 'Southern Lights' (from somewhere Punta Arenas way), 'Lodge of Rough Ashlars' (and that Newfoundland Naval Brother looked it), two or three Stars of something or other, half-a-dozen cardinal virtues, variously arranged, hailing from Klondyke to Kalgoorlie, one Military Lodge on one of the fronts, thrown in with a severe Scots burr by my friend of the head-bandages, and the rest as mixed as the Empire itself. Just at the end there was a little stir. The silent Brother had begun to make noises; his companion tried to soothe him.

'Let him be! Let him be!' the Doctor called professionally. The man jerked and mouthed, and at last mumbled something unintelligible even to his friend, but a small dark P.M. pushed forward importantly.

'It iss all right,' he said. 'He wants to say – ' he spat out some yard-long Welsh name, adding, 'That means Pembroke Docks, Worshipful Sir. We haf good Masons in Wales, too.' The silent man nodded approval.

'Yes,' said the Doctor, quite unmoved. 'It happens that way sometimes. *Hespere panta fereis*, isn't it? The Star brings 'em all home. I must get a note of that fellow's case after

Lodge. I saw you didn't care for music,' he went on, 'but I'm afraid you'll have to put up with a little more. It's a paraphrase from Micah. Our organist arranged it. We sing it antiphonally, as a sort of dismissal.'

Even I could appreciate what followed. The singing seemed confined to half-a-dozen trained voices answering each other till the last line, when the full Lodge came in. I give it as I heard it:

> 'We have showèd thee, O Man,
>   What is good.
> What doth the Lord require of us?
> Or Conscience' self desire of us?
>   But to do justly —
>   But to love mercy,
> And to walk humbly with our God,
>   As every Mason should.'

Then we were played and sung out to the quaint tune of the 'Entered Apprentices' Song'. I noticed that the regular Brethren of the Lodge did not begin to take off their regalia till the lines:

> 'Great Kings, Dukes, and Lords
> Have laid down their swords.'

They moved into the ante-room, now set for the Banquet, on the verse:

> 'Antiquity's pride
> We have on our side,
> Which maketh men just in their station.'

The Brother (a big-boned clergyman) that I found myself next to at table told me the custom was 'a fond thing vainly invented' on the strength of some old legend. He laid down that Masonry should be regarded as an 'intellectual abstraction'. An Officer of Engineers disagreed with him, and told us how in Flanders, a year before, some ten or twelve Brethren held Lodge in what was left of a Church. Save for the Emblems of Mortality and plenty of rough ashlars, there was no furniture.

'I warrant you weren't a bit the worse for that,' said the Clergyman. 'The idea should be enough without trappings.'

'But it wasn't,' said the other. 'We took a lot of trouble to make our regalia out of camouflage-stuff that we'd pinched, and we manufactured our jewels from old metal. I've got the set now. It kept us happy for weeks.'

'Ye were absolutely irregular an' unauthorized. Whaur was your Warrant?' said the Brother from the Military Lodge. 'Grand Lodge ought to take steps against –'

'If Grand Lodge had any sense,' a private three places up our table broke in, 'it 'ud warrant travelling Lodges at the front and attach first-class lecturers to 'em.'

'Wad ye confer degrees promiscuously?' said the scandalized Scot.

'Every time a man asked, of course. You'd have half the Army in.'

The speaker played with the idea for a little while, and proved that, on the lowest scale of fees, Grand Lodge would get huge revenues.

'I believe,' said the Engineer Officer thoughtfully, 'I could design a complete travelling Lodge outfit under forty pounds weight.'

'Ye're wrong. I'll prove it. We've tried ourselves,' said the Military Lodge man; and they went at it together across the table, each with his own note-book.

The 'Banquet' was simplicity itself. Many of us ate in haste so as to get back to barracks or hospitals, but now and again a Brother came in from the outer darkness to fill a chair and empty a plate. These were Brethren who had been there before and needed no examination.

One man lurched in – helmet, Flanders mud, accoutrements and all – fresh from the leave-train.

' 'Got two hours to wait for my train,' he explained. 'I remembered your night, though. My God, this *is* good!'

'What is your train and from what station?' said the Clergyman precisely. 'Very well. What will you have to eat?'

'Anything. Everything. I've thrown up a month's rations in the Channel.'

He stoked himself for ten minutes without a word. Then, without a word, his face fell forward. The Clergyman had him by one already limp arm and steered him to a couch, where he dropped and snored. No one took the trouble to turn round.

'Is that usual too?' I asked.

'Why not?' said the Clergyman. 'I'm on duty tonight to wake them for their trains. They do not respect the Cloth on those occasions.' He turned his broad back on me and continued his discussion with a Brother from Aberdeen by way of Mitylene where, in the intervals of mine-sweeping, he had evolved a complete theory of the Revelation of St John the Divine in the Island of Patmos.

I fell into the hands of a Sergeant-Instructor of Machine Guns – by profession a designer of ladies' dresses. He told me that Englishwomen as a class 'lose on their corsets what they make on their clothes', and that 'Satan himself can't save a woman who wears thirty-shilling corsets under a thirty-guinea costume.' Here, to my grief, he was buttonholed by a zealous Lieutenant of his own branch, and became a Sergeant again all in one click.

I drifted back and forth, studying the prints on the walls and the Masonic collection in the cases, while I listened to the inconceivable talk all round me. Little by little the company thinned, till at last there were only a dozen or so of us left. We gathered at the end of a table near the fire, the night-bird from Flanders trumpeting lustily into the hollow of his helmet, which someone had tipped over his face.

'And how did it go with you?' said the Doctor.

'It was like a new world,' I answered.

'That's what it *is* really.' Brother Burges returned the gold pince-nez to their case and re-shipped his silver spectacles. 'Or that's what it might be made with a little trouble. When I think of the possibilities of the Craft at this juncture I wonder – ' He stared into the fire.

'I wonder, too,' said the Sergeant-Major slowly, 'but – on

the whole – I'm inclined to agree with you. We could do much with Masonry.'

'As an aid – as an aid – not as a substitute for Religion,' the Clergyman snapped.

'Oh, Lord! Can't we give Religion a rest for a bit?' the Doctor muttered. 'It hasn't done so – I beg your pardon all round.'

The Clergyman was bristling. 'Kamerad!' the wise Sergeant-Major went on, both hands up. 'Certainly not as a substitute for a creed, but as an average plan of life. What I've seen at the front makes me sure of it.'

Brother Burges came out of his muse. 'There ought to be a dozen – twenty – other Lodges in London every night; conferring degrees too, as well as instruction. Why shouldn't the young men join? They practise what we're always preaching. Well! Well! We must all do what we can. What's the use of old Masons if they can't give a little help along their own lines?'

'Exactly,' said the Sergeant-Major, turning on the Doctor. 'And what's the darn use of a Brother if he isn't allowed to help?'

'Have it your own way then,' said the Doctor testily. He had evidently been approached before. He took something the Sergeant-Major handed to him and pocketed it with a nod. 'I was wrong,' he said to me, 'when I boasted of our independence. They get round us sometimes. This,' he slapped his pocket, 'will give a banquet on Tuesday. We don't usually feed at matinées. It will be a surprise. By the way, try another sandwich. The ham are best.' He pushed me a plate.

'They are,' I said. 'I've only had five or six. I've been looking for them.'

'Glad you like them,' said Brother Lemming. 'Fed him myself, cured him myself – at my little place in Berkshire. His name was Charlemagne. By the way, Doc, am I to keep another one for next month?'

'Of course,' said the Doctor with his mouth full. 'A little fatter than this chap, please. And don't forget your promise about the pickled nasturtiums. They're appreciated.' Brother Lemming nodded above the pipe he had lit as we began a second supper. Suddenly the Clergyman, after a glance at the clock, scooped up half-a-dozen sandwiches from under my nose, put them into an oiled paper bag, and advanced cautiously towards the sleeper on the couch.

'They wake rough sometimes,' said the Doctor. 'Nerves, y'know.' The Clergyman tip-toed directly behind the man's head, and at arm's length rapped on the dome of the helmet. The man woke in one vivid streak, as the Clergyman stepped back, and grabbed for a rifle that was not there.

'You've barely half an hour to catch your train.' The Clergyman passed him the sandwiches. 'Come along.'

'You're uncommonly kind and I'm very grateful,' said the man, wriggling into his stiff straps. He followed his guide into the darkness after saluting.

'Who's that?' said Lemming.

' 'Can't say,' the Doctor returned indifferently. 'He's been here before. He's evidently a P.M. of sorts.'

'Well! Well!' said Brother Burges, whose eyelids were drooping. 'We must all do what we can. Isn't it almost time to lock up?'

'I wonder,' said I, as we helped each other into our coats, 'what would happen if Grand Lodge knew about all this.'

'About what?' Lemming turned on me quickly.

'A Lodge of Instruction open three nights and two afternoons a week – and running a lodging-house as well. It's all very nice, but it doesn't strike me somehow as regulation.'

'The point hasn't been raised yet,' said Lemming. 'We'll settle it after the war. Meantime, we shall go on.'

'There ought to be scores of them,' Brother Burges repeated as we went out of the door. 'All London's full of the Craft, and no places for them to meet in. Think of the possibilities of it! Think what could have been done *by* Masonry *through* Masonry *for* all the world. I hope I'm not censorious, but it sometimes crosses my mind that Grand Lodge may have thrown away its chance in the war almost as much as the Church has.'

'Lucky for you the Padre is taking that chap to King's Cross,' said Brother Lemming, 'or he'd be down your throat. What really troubles him is our legal position under Masonic Law. I think he'll inform on us one of these days. Well, good night, all.' The Doctor and Lemming turned off together.

'Yes,' said Brother Burges, slipping his arm into mine. 'Almost as much as the Church has. But perhaps I'm too much of a Ritualist.'

I said nothing. I was speculating how soon I could steal a march on the Clergyman and inform against 'Faith and Works No. 5837 E.C.'

A Madonna of the Trenches

'Whatever a man of the sons of men
  Shall say to his heart of the lords above,
They have shown man, verily, once and again,
  Marvellous mercies and infinite love.

'O sweet one love, O my life's delight,
  Dear, though the days have divided us,
Lost beyond hope, taken far out of sight,
  Not twice in the world shall the Gods do thus.'
                        SWINBURNE, 'Les Noyades.'

SEEING how many unstable ex-soldiers came to the Lodge of Instruction (attached to Faith and Works E.C. 5837) in the years after the war, the wonder is there was not more trouble from Brethren whom sudden meetings with old comrades jerked back into their still raw past. But our round, torpedo-bearded local Doctor – Brother Keede, Senior Warden – always stood ready to deal with hysteria before it got out of hand; and when I examined Brethren unknown or imperfectly vouched for on the Masonic side, I passed on to him anything that seemed doubtful. He had had his experience as medical officer of a South London Battalion, during the last two years of the war; and, naturally, often found friends and acquaintances among the visitors.

Brother C. Strangwick, a young, tallish, new-made Brother, hailed from some South London Lodge. His papers and his answers were above suspicion, but his red-rimmed eyes had a puzzled glare that might mean nerves. So I introduced him particularly to Keede, who discovered in him a Headquarters Orderly of his old Battalion, congratulated him on his return to fitness – he had been discharged for some infirmity or other – and plunged at once into Somme memories.

'I hope I did right, Keede,' I said when we were robing before Lodge.

'Oh, quite. He reminded me that I had him under my

hands at Sampoux in 'Eighteen, when he went to bits. He was a Runner.'

'Was it shock?' I asked.

'Of sorts – but not what he wanted me to think it was. No, he wasn't shamming. He had Jumps to the limit – but he played up to mislead me about the reason of 'em. . . . Well, if we could stop patients from lying, medicine would be too easy, I suppose.'

I noticed that, after Lodge-working, Keede gave him a seat a couple of rows in front of us, that he might enjoy a lecture on the Orientation of King Solomon's Temple, which an earnest Brother thought would be a nice interlude between Labour and the high tea that we called our 'Banquet'. Even helped by tobacco it was a dreary performance. About half-way through, Strangwick, who had been fidgeting and twitching for some minutes, rose, drove back his chair grinding across the tessellated floor, and yelped: 'Oh, My Aunt! I can't stand this any longer.' Under cover of a general laugh of assent he brushed past us and stumbled towards the door.

'I thought so!' Keede whispered to me. 'Come along!' We overtook him in the passage, crowing hysterically and wringing his hands. Keede led him into the Tyler's Room, a small office where we stored odds and ends of regalia and furniture, and locked the door.

'I'm – I'm all right,' the boy began, piteously.

' 'Course you are.' Keede opened a small cupboard which I had seen called upon before, mixed sal volatile and water in a graduated glass, and, as Strangwick drank, pushed him gently on to an old sofa. 'There,' he went on. 'It's nothing to write home about. I've seen you ten times worse. I expect our talk has brought things back.'

He hooked up a chair behind him with one foot, held the patient's hands in his own, and sat down. The chair creaked.

'Don't!' Strangwick squealed. 'I can't stand it! There's nothing on earth creaks like they do! And – and when it thaws we – we've got to slap 'em back with a spa-ade! Re-

member those Frenchmen's little boots under the duck-
boards? . . . What'll I do? What'll I do about it?'

Someone knocked at the door, to know if all were well.

'Oh, quite, thanks!' said Keede over his shoulder. 'But I
shall need this room awhile. Draw the curtains, please.'

We heard the rings of the hangings that drape the passage
from Lodge to Banquet Room click along their poles,
and what sound there had been, of feet and voices, was
shut off.

Strangwick, retching impotently, complained of the frozen
dead who creak in the frost.

'He's playing up still,' Keede whispered. '*That's* not his
real trouble – any more than 'twas last time.'

'But surely,' I replied, 'men get those things on the brain
pretty badly. Remember in October –'

'This chap hasn't, though. I wonder what's really helling
him. What are you thinking of?' said Keede peremptorily.

'French End an' Butcher's Row,' Strangwick muttered.

'Yes, there were a few there. But suppose we face Bogey
instead of giving him best every time.' Keede turned towards
me with a hint in his eye that I was to play up to his leads.

'What was the trouble with French End?' I opened at a
venture.

'It was a bit by Sampoux, that we had taken over from the
French. They're tough, but you wouldn't call 'em tidy as a
nation. They had faced both sides of it with dead to keep the
mud back. All those trenches were like gruel in a thaw. Our
people had to do the same sort of thing – elsewhere; but
Butcher's Row in French End was the – er – show-piece.
Luckily, we pinched a salient from Jerry just then, an'
straightened things out – so we didn't need to use the Row
after November. You remember, Strangwick?'

'My God, yes! When the duckboard-slats were missin'
you'd tread on 'em, an' they'd creak.'

'They're bound to. Like leather,' said Keede. 'It gets on
one's nerves a bit, but –'

'Nerves? It's real! It's real!' Strangwick gulped.

'But at your time of life, it'll all fall behind you in a year or so. I'll give you another sip of – paregoric, an' we'll face it quietly. Shall we?'

Keede opened his cupboard again and administered a carefully dropped dark dose of something that was not sal volatile. 'This'll settle you in a few minutes,' he explained. 'Lie still, an' don't talk unless you feel like it.'

He faced me, fingering his beard.

'Ye–es. Butcher's Row wasn't pretty,' he volunteered. 'Seeing Strangwick here, has brought it all back to me again. Funny thing! We had a Platoon Sergeant of Number Two – what the deuce was his name? – an elderly bird who must have lied like a patriot to get out to the front at his age; but he was a first-class Non-Com., and the last person, you'd think, to make mistakes. Well, he was due for a fortnight's home leave in January, 'Eighteen. You were at B.H.Q. then, Strangwick, weren't you?'

'Yes. I was Orderly. It was January twenty-first'; Strangwick spoke with a thickish tongue, and his eyes burned. Whatever drug it was, had taken hold.

'About then,' Keede said. 'Well, this Sergeant, instead of coming down from the trenches the regular way an' joinin' Battalion Details after dark, an' takin' that funny little train for Arras, thinks he'll warm himself first. So he gets into a dug-out in Butcher's Row, that used to be an old French dressing-station, and fugs up between a couple of braziers of pure charcoal! As luck 'ud have it, that was the only dug-out with an inside door opening inwards – some French anti-gas fitting, I expect – and, by what we could make out, the door must have swung to while he was warming. Anyhow, he didn't turn up at the train. There was a search at once. We couldn't afford to waste Platoon Sergeants. We found him in the morning. He'd got his gas all right. A machine-gunner reported him, didn't he, Strangwick?'

'No, sir. Corporal Grant – o' the Trench Mortars.'

'So it was. Yes, Grant – the man with that little wen on his neck. Nothing wrong with your memory, at any rate. What was the Sergeant's name?'

'Godsoe – John Godsoe,' Strangwick answered.

'Yes, that was it. I had to see him next mornin' – frozen stiff between the two braziers – and not a scrap of private papers on him. *That* was the only thing that made me think it mightn't have been – quite an accident.'

Strangwick's relaxing face set, and he threw back at once to the Orderly Room manner.

'I give my evidence – at the time – to you, sir. He passed – overtook me, I should say – comin' down from supports, after I'd warned him for leaf. I thought he was goin' through Parrot Trench as usual; but 'e must 'ave turned off into French End, where the old bombed barricade was.'

'Yes. I remember now. You were the last man to see him alive. That was on the twenty-first of January, you say? Now, *when* was it that Dearlove and Billings brought you to me – clean out of your head?' ... Keede dropped his hand, in the style of magazine detectives, on Strangwick's shoulder. The boy looked at him with cloudy wonder, and muttered: 'I was took to you on the evenin' of the twenty-fourth of January. But you don't think I did him in, do you?'

I could not help smiling at Keede's discomfiture; but he recovered himself. 'Then what the dickens *was* on your mind that evening – before I gave you the hypodermic?'

'The – the things in Butcher's Row. They kept on comin' over me. You've seen me like this before, sir.'

'But I knew that it was a lie. You'd no more got stiffs on the brain then than you have now. You've got something, but you're hiding it.'

' 'Ow do *you* know, Doctor?' Strangwick whimpered.

'D'you remember what you said to me, when Dearlove and Billings were holding you down that evening?'

'About the things in Butcher's Row?'

'Oh, no! You spun me a lot of stuff about corpses creaking; but you let yourself go in the middle of it – when you pushed that telegram at me. What did you mean, f'rinstance, by asking what advantage it was for you to fight beasts of officers if the dead didn't rise?'

'Did I say "Beasts of Officers"?'

'You did. It's out of the Burial Service.'

'I suppose, then, I must have heard it. As a matter of fact, I 'ave.' Strangwick shuddered extravagantly.

'Probably. And there's another thing – that hymn you were shouting till I put you under. It was something about Mercy and Love. Remember it?'

'I'll try,' said the boy obediently, and began to paraphrase, as nearly as possible thus: ' "Whatever a man may say in his heart unto the Lord, yea, verily I say unto you – Gawd hath shown man, again and again, marvellous mercy an' an' somethin' or other love." ' He screwed up his eyes and shook.

'Now where did you get *that* from?' Keede insisted.

'From Godsoe – on the twenty-first Jan. . . . 'Ow could *I* tell what 'e meant to do?' he burst out in a high, unnatural key – 'Any more than I knew *she* was dead.'

'Who was dead?' said Keede.

'Me Auntie Armine.'

'The one the telegram came to you about, at Sampoux, that you wanted me to explain – the one that you were talking of in the passage out here just now when you began: "O Auntie," and changed it to "O Gawd," when I collared you?'

'That's her! I haven't a chance with you, Doctor. *I* didn't know there was anything wrong with those braziers. How could I? We're always usin' 'em. Honest to God, I thought at first go-off he might wish to warm himself before the leaf-train. I – I didn't know Uncle John meant to start – 'ouse-keepin'.' He laughed horribly, and then the dry tears came.

Keede waited for them to pass in sobs and hiccoughs before he continued: 'Why? Was Godsoe your Uncle?'

'No,' said Strangwick, his head between his hands. 'Only we'd known him ever since we were born. Dad 'ad known him before that. He lived almost next street to us. Him an' Dad an' Ma an' – an' the rest had always been friends. So we called him Uncle – like children do.'

'What sort of man was he?'

'One o' *the* best, sir. Pensioned Sergeant with a little money left him – quite independent – and very superior.

They had a sittin'-room full o' Indian curios that him and his wife used to let sister an' me see when we'd been good.'

'Wasn't he rather old to join up?'

'That made no odds to him. He joined up as Sergeant In-structor at the first go-off, an' when the Battalion was ready he got 'imself sent along. He wangled me into 'is Platoon when I went out – early in 'Seventeen. Because Ma wanted it, I suppose.'

'I'd no notion you knew him that well,' was Keede's comment.

'Oh, it made no odds to him. He 'ad no pets in the Platoon, but 'e'd write 'ome to Ma about me an' all the doin's. You see' – Strangwick stirred uneasily on the sofa – 'we'd known him all our lives – lived in the next street an' all. . . . An' him well over fifty. Oh dear me! *Oh* dear me! What a bloody mix-up things are, when one's as young as me!' he wailed of a sudden.

But Keede held him to the point. 'He wrote to your Mother about you?'

'Yes. Ma's eyes had gone bad followin' on air-raids. Blood-vessels broke behind 'em from sittin' in cellars an' bein' sick. She had to 'ave 'er letters read to her by Auntie. Now I think of it, that was the only thing that you might have called any-thing at all –'

'Was that the Aunt that died, and that you got the wire about?' Keede drove on.

'Yes – Auntie Armine – Ma's younger sister, an' she nearer fifty than forty. What a mix-up! An' if I'd been asked any time about it, I'd 'ave sworn there wasn't a single sol'tary item concernin' her that everybody didn't know an' hadn't known all along. No more conceal to her doin's than – than so much shop-front. She'd looked after sister an' me, when needful – whoopin' cough an' measles – just the same as Ma. We was in an' out of her house like rabbits. You see, Uncle Armine is a cabinet-maker, an' second-'and furniture, an' we liked playin' with the things. She 'ad no children, and when the war came, she said she was glad of it. But she never talked much of her feelin's. She kept herself to herself, you understand.' He stared most earnestly at us to help out our understandings.

'What was she like?' Keede inquired.

'A biggish woman, an' had been 'andsome, I believe, but, bein' used to her, we two didn't notice much—except, per'aps, for one thing. Ma called her 'er proper name, which was Bella; but Sis an' me always called 'er Auntie Armine. See?'

'What for?'

'We thought it sounded more like her – like somethin' movin' slow, in armour.'

'Oh! And she read your letters to your mother, did she?'

'Every time the post came in she'd slip across the road from opposite an' read 'em. An' – an' I'll go bail for it that that was all there was to it for as far back as *I* remember. Was I to swing tomorrow, I'd go bail for *that*! 'Tisn't fair of 'em to 'ave unloaded it all on me, because – because – if the dead *do* rise, why, what in 'ell becomes of me an' all I've believed all me life? I want to know *that*! I – I –'

But Keede would not be put off. 'Did the Sergeant give you away at all in his letters?' he demanded, very quietly.

'There was nothin' to give away – we was too busy – but his letters about me were a great comfort to Ma. I'm no good at writin'. I saved it all up for my leafs. I got me fourteen days every six months an' one over. .... I was luckier than most, that way.'

'And when you came home, used you to bring 'em news about the Sergeant?' said Keede.

'I expect I must have; but I didn't think much of it at the time. I was took up with me own affairs – naturally. Uncle John always wrote to me once each leaf, tellin' me what was doin' an' what I was li'ble to expect on return, an' Ma 'ud 'ave that read to her. Then o' course I had to slip over to his wife an' pass her the news. An' then there was the young lady that I'd thought of marryin' if I came through. We'd got as far as pricin' things in the windows together.'

'And you didn't marry her – after all?'

Another tremor shook the boy. '*No!*' he cried. ' 'Fore it ended, I knew what reel things reelly mean! I – I never dreamed such things could be! ... An' she nearer fifty than forty an' me own Aunt! ... But there wasn't a sign nor a hint from first to last, so 'ow *could* I tell? Don't you *see* it? All she said to me after me Christmas leaf in '18, when I come to say good-bye – all Auntie Armine said to me was: "You'll be seein' Mister Godsoe soon?" "Too soon for my likings," I says. "Well then, tell 'im from me," she says, "that I expect to be through with my little trouble by the twenty-first of next month, an' I'm dyin' to see him as soon as possible after that date." '

'What sort of trouble was it?' Keede turned professional at once.

'She'd 'ad a bit of a gatherin' in 'er breast, I believe. But she never talked of 'er body much to anyone.'

'*I* see,' said Keede. 'And she said to you?'

Strangwick repeated: ' "Tell Uncle John I hope to be finished of my drawback by the twenty-first, an' I'm dying to see 'im as soon as 'e can after that date." An' then she says, laughin': "But you've a head like a sieve. I'll write it down, an' you can give it him when you see 'im." So she wrote it on a bit o' paper an' I kissed 'er good-bye – I was always her favourite, you see – an' I went back to Sampoux. The thing hardly stayed in my mind at all, d'you see. But the next time I was up in the front line – I was a Runner, d'ye see – our platoon was in North Bay Trench an' I was up with a message to the Trench Mortar there that Corporal Grant was in charge of. Followin' on receipt of it, he borrowed a couple of men off the platoon, to slue 'er round or somethin'. I give Uncle John Auntie Armine's paper, an' I give Grant a fag, an' we warmed up a bit over a brazier. Then Grant says to me: "I don't like it"; an' he jerks 'is thumb at Uncle John in the bay studyin' Auntie's message. Well, *you* know, sir, you had to speak to Grant about 'is way of prophesyin' things – after Rankine shot himself with the Very light.'

'I did,' said Keede, and he explained to me: 'Grant had the Second Sight – confound him! It upset the men. I was glad when he got pipped. What happened after that, Strangwick?'

'Grant whispers to me: "Look, you damned Englishman. 'E's for it." Uncle John was leanin' up against the bay, an' hummin' that hymn I was tryin' to tell you just now. He looked different all of a sudden – as if 'e'd got shaved. *I* don't know anything of these things, but I cautioned Grant as to his style of speakin', if an officer 'ad 'eard him, an' I went on. Passin' Uncle John in the bay, 'e nods an' smiles, which he didn't often, an' he says, pocketin' the paper: "This suits *me*. I'm for leaf on the twenty-first, too." '

'He said that to you, did he?' said Keede.

'*Pre*cisely the same as passin' the time o' day. O' course I returned the agreeable about hopin' he'd get it, an' in due course I returned to 'Eadquarters. The thing 'ardly stayed in my mind a minute. That was the eleventh January – three days after I'd come back from leaf. You remember, sir, there wasn't anythin' doin' either side round Sampoux the first part o' the month. Jerry was gettin' ready for his March Push, an' as long as he kept quiet, we didn't want to poke 'im up.'

'I remember that,' said Keede. 'But what about the Sergeant?'

'I must have met him, on an' off, I expect, goin' up an' down, through the ensuin' days, but it didn't stay in me mind. Why needed it? And on the twenty-first Jan., his name was on the leaf-paper when I went up to warn the leaf-men. I noticed *that*, o' course. Now that very afternoon Jerry 'ad been tryin' a new trench-mortar, an' before our 'Eavies could out it, he'd got a stinker into a bay an' mopped up 'alf a dozen. They were bringin' 'em down when I went up to the supports, an' that blocked Little Parrot, same as it always did. *You* remember, sir?'

'Rather! And there was that big machine-gun behind the Half-House waiting for you if you got out,' said Keede.

'I remembered that too. But it was just on dark an' the fog was comin' off the Canal, so I hopped out of Little Parrot an' cut across the open to where those four dead Warwicks are heaped up. But the fog turned me round, an' the next thing I knew I was knee-over in that old 'alf-trench that runs west o'

Little Parrot into French End. I dropped into it – almost atop o' the machine-gun platform by the side o' the old sugar boiler an' the two Zoo-ave skel'tons. That gave me my bearin's, an' so I went through French End, all up those missin' duckboards, into Butcher's Row where the *poy-looz* was laid in six deep each side, an' stuffed under the duck-boards. It had froze tight, an' the drippin's had stopped, an' the creakin's had begun.'

'Did that really worry you at the time?' Keede asked.

'No,' said the boy with professional scorn. 'If a Runner starts noticin' such things he'd better chuck. In the middle of the Row, just before the old dressin'-station you referred to, sir, it come over me that somethin' ahead on the duckboards was just like Auntie Armine, waitin' beside the door; an' I thought to meself 'ow truly comic it would be if she could be dumped where I was then. In 'alf a second I saw it was only the dark an' some rags o' gas-screen, 'angin' on a bit of board, 'ad played me the trick. So I went on up to the supports an' warned the leaf-men there, includin' Uncle John. Then I went up Rake Alley to warn 'em in the front line. I didn't hurry because I didn't want to get there till Jerry 'ad quieted down a bit. Well, then a Company Relief dropped in – an' the officer got the wind up over some lights on the flank, an' tied 'em into knots, an' I 'ad to hunt up me leaf-men all over the blinkin' shop. What with one thing an' another, it must 'ave been 'alf-past eight before I got back to the supports. There I run across Uncle John, scrapin' mud off himself, havin' shaved – quite the dandy. He asked about the Arras train, an' I said, if Jerry was quiet, it might be ten o'clock. "Good!" says 'e. "I'll come with you." So we started back down the old trench that used to run across Halnaker, back of the support dug-outs. *You* know, sir.'

Keede nodded.

'Then Uncle John says something to me about seein' Ma an' the rest of 'em in a few days, an' had I any messages for 'em? Gawd knows what made me do it, but I told 'im to tell Auntie Armine I never expected to see anything like *her* up in our part of the world. And while I told him I laughed.

That's the last time I *'ave* laughed. "Oh – you've seen 'er, 'ave you?" says he, quite natural-like. Then I told 'im about the sand-bags an' rags in the dark, playin' the trick. "Very likely," says he, brushin' the mud off his putties. By this time, we'd got to the corner where the old barricade into French End was – before they bombed it down, sir. He turns right an' climbs across it. "No, thanks," says I. "I've been there once this evenin'." But he wasn't attendin' to me. He felt behind the rubbish an' bones just inside the barricade, an' when he straightened up, he had a full brazier in each hand.

' "Come on, Clem," he says, an' he very rarely give me me own name. "You aren't afraid, are you?" he says. "It's just as short, an' if Jerry starts up again he won't waste stuff here. He knows it's abandoned." "Who's afraid now?" I says. "Me for one," says he. "I don't want *my* leaf spoiled at the last minute." Then 'e wheels round an' speaks that bit you said come out o' the Burial Service.'

For some reason Keede repeated it in full, slowly: 'If after the manner of men I have fought with beasts at Ephesus, what advantageth it me, if the dead rise not?'

'That's it,' said Strangwick. 'So we went down French End together – everything froze up an' quiet, except for their creakin's. I remember thinkin' – ' his eyes began to flicker.

'Don't think. Tell what happened,' Keede ordered.

'Oh! Beg y' pardon! He went on with his braziers, hummin' his hymn, down Butcher's Row. Just before we got to the old dressin'-station he stops and sets 'em down an' says: "Where did you say she was, Clem? Me eyes ain't as good as they used to be."

' "In 'er bed at 'ome," I says. "Come on down. It's perishin' cold, an' *I'm* not due for leaf."

' "Well, I am," 'e says. "*I* am. . . ." An' then – 'give you me word I didn't recognize the voice – he stretches out 'is neck a bit, in a way 'e 'ad, an' he says: "Why, Bella!" 'e says. "Oh, Bella!" 'e says. "Thank Gawd!" 'e says. Just like that! An' then I saw – I tell you I *saw* – Auntie Armine herself standin' by the old dressin'-station door where first I'd thought I'd

142

seen her. He was lookin' at 'er an' she was lookin' at him. I
saw it, an' me soul turned over inside me because – because it
knocked out everything I'd believed in. I 'ad nothin' to lay
'old of, d'ye see? An' 'e was lookin' at 'er as though he could
'ave et 'er, an' she was lookin' at 'im the same way, out of 'er
eyes. Then he says: "Why, Bella," 'e says, "this must be only
the second time we've been alone together in all these years."
An' I saw 'er half hold out her arms to 'im in that perishin'
cold. An' she nearer fifty than forty an' me own Aunt! You
can shop me for a lunatic tomorrow, but I saw it – I *saw* 'er
answerin' to his spoken word! ... Then 'e made a snatch to
unsling 'is rifle. Then 'e cuts 'is hand away saying: "No!
Don't tempt me, Bella. We've all Eternity ahead of us. An
hour or two won't make any odds." Then he picks up the
braziers an' goes on to the dug-out door. He'd finished with
me. He pours petrol on 'em, an' lights it with a match, an'
carries 'em inside, flarin'. All that time Auntie Armine stood
with 'er arms out – an' a look in 'er face! *I* didn't know such
things was or could be! Then he comes out an' says: "Come
in, my dear"; an' she stoops an' goes into the dug-out with
that look on her face – that look on her face! An' then 'e
shuts the door from inside an' starts wedgin' it up. So 'elp me
Gawd, I saw an' 'eard all these things with my own eyes an'
ears!'

He repeated his oath several times. After a long pause
Keede asked him if he recalled what happened next.

'It was a bit of a mix-up, for me, from then on. I must have
carried on – they told me I did, but – but I was – I felt a – a
long way inside of meself, like – if you've ever had that feelin'.
I wasn't rightly on the spot at all. They woke me up sometime next morning, because 'e 'adn't showed up at the train;
an' some one had seen him with me. I wasn't 'alf cross-exam-
ined by all an' sundry till dinner-time.

'Then, I think, I volunteered for Dearlove, who 'ad a sore
toe, for a front-line message. I had to keep movin', you see,
because I hadn't anything to hold *on* to. Whilst up there,
Grant informed me how he'd found Uncle John with the
door wedged an' sand-bags stuffed in the cracks. I hadn't

waited for that. The knockin' when 'e wedged up was enough for me. Like Dad's coffin.'

'No one told *me* the door had been wedged.' Keede spoke severely.

'No need to black a dead man's name, sir.'

'What made Grant go to Butcher's Row?'

'Because he'd noticed Uncle John had been pinchin' charcoal for a week past an' layin' it up behind the old barricade there. So when the 'unt began, he went that way straight as a string, an' when he saw the door shut, he knew. He told me he picked the sand-bags out of the cracks an' shoved 'is hand through and shifted the wedges before any one come along. It looked all right. You said yourself, sir, the door must 'ave blown to.'

'Grant knew what Godsoe meant, then?' Keede snapped.

'Grant knew Godsoe was for it; an' nothin' earthly could 'elp or 'inder. He told me so.'

'And then what did you do?'

'I expect I must 'ave kept on carryin' on, till Headquarters give me that wire from Ma – about Auntie Armine dyin'.'

'When had your Aunt died?'

'On the mornin' of the twenty-first. The mornin' of the 21st! That tore it, d'ye see? As long as I could think, I had kep' tellin' myself it was like those things you lectured about at Arras when we was billeted in the cellars – the Angels of Mons, and so on. But that wire tore it.'

'Oh! Hallucinations! I remember. And that wire tore it?' said Keede.

'Yes! You see' – he half lifted himself off the sofa – 'there wasn't a single gor-dam thing left abidin' for me to take hold of, here or hereafter. If the dead *do* rise – and I saw 'em – why – why, *anything* can 'appen. Don't you understand?'

He was on his feet now, gesticulating stiffly.

'For I saw 'er,' he repeated. 'I saw 'im an' 'er – she dead since mornin' time, an' he killin' 'imself before my livin' eyes so's to carry on with 'er for all Eternity – an' she 'oldin' out 'er arms for it! I want to know where I'm *at*! Look 'ere, you two – why stand *we* in jeopardy every hour?'

'God knows,' said Keede to himself.

'Hadn't we better ring for some one?' I suggested. 'He'll go off the handle in a second.'

'No, he won't. It's the last kick-up before it takes hold. I know how the stuff works. Hul-lo!'

Strangwick, his hands behind his back and his eyes set, gave tongue in the strained, cracked voice of a boy reciting. 'Not twice in the world shall the Gods do thus,' he cried again and again.

'And I'm damned if it's goin' to be even once for me!' he went on with sudden insane fury. '*I* don't care whether we *'ave* been pricin' things in the windows. ... *Let* 'er sue if she likes! She don't know what reel things mean. *I* do – I've 'ad occasion to notice 'em. ... *No*, I tell you! I'll 'ave 'em when I want 'em, an' be done with 'em; but not till I see that look on a face ... that look. ... I'm not takin' any. The reel thing's life an' death. It *begins* at death, d'ye see. *She* can't under-stand. . . . Oh, go on an' push off to Hell, you an' your lawyers. I'm fed up with it – fed up!'

He stopped as abruptly as he had started, and the drawn face broke back to its natural irresolute lines. Keede, holding both his hands, led him back to the sofa, where he dropped like a wet towel, took out some flamboyant robe from a press, and drew it neatly over him.

'Ye-es. *That's* the real thing at last,' said Keede. 'Now he's got it off his mind he'll sleep. By the way, who introduced him?'

'Shall I go and find out?' I suggested.

'Yes; and you might ask him to come here. There's no need for us to stand to all night.'

So I went to the Banquet, which was in full swing, and was seized by an elderly, precise Brother from a South London Lodge, who followed me, concerned and apologetic. Keede soon put him at his ease.

'The boy's had trouble,' our visitor explained. 'I'm most

mortified he should have performed his bad turn here. I thought he'd put it be'ind him.'

'I expect talking about old days with me brought it all back,' said Keede. 'It does sometimes.'

'Maybe! Maybe! But over and above that, Clem's had post-war trouble, too.'

'Can't he get a job? He oughtn't to let that weigh on him, at his time of life,' said Keede cheerily.

'' Tisn't that – he's provided for – but' – he coughed confidentially behind his dry hand – 'as a matter of fact, Worshipful Sir, he's – he's implicated for the present in a little breach of promise action.'

'Ah! That's a different thing,' said Keede.

'Yes. That's his reel trouble. No reason given, you understand. The young lady in every way suitable, an' she'd make him a good little wife too, if I'm any judge. But he says she ain't his ideel or something. No getting at what's in young people's minds these days, is there?'

'I'm afraid there isn't,' said Keede. 'But he's all right now. He'll sleep. You sit by him, and when he wakes, take him home quietly. . . . Oh, we're used to men getting a little upset here. You've nothing to thank us for, Brother – Brother –'

'Armine,' said the old gentleman. 'He's my nephew by marriage.'

'That's all that's wanted!' said Keede.

Brother Armine looked a little puzzled. Keede hastened to explain. 'As I was saying, all he wants now is to be kept quiet till he wakes.'

The Bull that Thought

(1924)

WESTWARD from a town by the Mouths of the Rhône, runs a road so mathematically straight, so barometrically level, that it ranks among the world's measured miles and motorists use it for records.

I had attacked the distance several times, but always with a Mistral blowing, or the unchancy cattle of those parts on the move. But once, running from the East, into a high-piled, almost Egyptian, sunset, there came a night which it would have been sin to have wasted. It was warm with the breath of summer in advance; moonlit till the shadow of every rounded pebble and pointed cypress wind-break lay solid on that vast flat-floored waste; and my Mr Leggatt, who had slipped out to make sure, reported that the road-surface was unblemished.

'Now,' he suggested, 'we might see what she'll do under strict road-conditions. She's been pullin' like the Blue de Luxe all day. Unless I'm all off, it's her night out.'

We arranged the trial for after dinner – thirty kilometres as near as might be; and twenty-two of them without even a level crossing.

There sat beside me at table d'hôte an elderly, bearded Frenchman wearing the rosette of by no means the lowest grade of the Legion of Honour, who had arrived in a talkative Citroën. I gathered that he had spent much of his life in the French Colonial Service in Annam and Tonquin. When the war came, his years barring him from the front line, he had supervised Chinese wood-cutters who, with axe and dynamite, deforested the centre of France for trenchprops. He said my chauffeur had told him that I contemplated an experiment. He was interested in cars – had admired mine – would, in short, be greatly indebted to me if I permitted him to assist as an observer. One could not well refuse; and, knowing my Mr Leggatt, it occurred to me there might also be a bet in the background.

While he went to get his coat, I asked the proprietor his name. 'Voiron – Monsieur André Voiron,' was the reply. 'And his business?' 'Mon Dieu! He is Voiron! He is all those things, there!' The proprietor waved his hands at brilliant advertisements on the dining-room walls, which declared that Voiron Frères dealt in wines, agricultural implements, chemical manures, provisions and produce throughout that part of the globe.

He said little for the first five minutes of our trip, and nothing at all for the next ten – it being, as Leggatt had guessed, Esmeralda's night out. But, when her indicator climbed to a certain figure and held there for three blinding kilometres, he expressed himself satisfied, and proposed to me that we should celebrate the event at the hotel. 'I keep yonder,' said he, 'a wine on which I should value your opinion.'

On our return, he disappeared for a few minutes, and I heard him rumbling in a cellar. The proprietor presently invited me to the dining-room, where, beneath one frugal light, a table had been set with local dishes of renown. There was, too, a bottle beyond most known sizes, marked black on red, with a date. Monsieur Voiron opened it, and we drank to the health of my car. The velvety, perfumed liquor, between fawn and topaz, neither too sweet nor too dry, creamed in its generous glass. But I knew no wine composed of the whispers of angels' wings, the breath of Eden and the foam and pulse of Youth renewed. So I asked what it might be.

'It is champagne,' he said gravely.

'Then what have I been drinking all my life?'

'If you were lucky, before the War, and paid thirty shillings a bottle, it is possible you may have drunk one of our better-class *tisanes*.'

'And where does one get this?'

'Here, I am happy to say. Elsewhere, perhaps, it is not so easy. We growers exchange these real wines among ourselves.'

I bowed my head in admiration, surrender, and joy. There stood the most ample bottle, and it was not yet eleven o'clock. Doors locked and shutters banged throughout the establishment. Some last servant yawned on his way to bed. Monsieur Voiron opened a window and the moonlight flooded in from a small pebbled court outside. One could almost hear the town of Chambres breathing in its first sleep. Presently, there was a thick noise in the air, the passing of feet and hooves, lowings, and a stifled bark or two. Dust rose over the courtyard wall, followed by the strong smell of cattle.

'They are moving some beasts,' said Monsieur Voiron, cocking an ear. 'Mine, I think. Yes, I hear Christophe. Our beasts do not like automobiles – so we move at night. You do not know our country – the Crau, here, or the Camargue? I was – I am now, again – of it. All France is good; but this is the best.' He spoke, as only a Frenchman can, of his own loved part of his own lovely land.

'For myself, if I were not so involved in all these affairs' – he pointed to the advertisements – 'I would live on our farm with my cattle, and worship them like a Hindu. You know our cattle of the Camargue, Monsieur? No? It is not an acquaintance to rush upon lightly. There are no beasts like them. They have a mentality superior to that of others. They graze and they ruminate, by choice, facing our Mistral, which is more than some automobiles will do. Also they have in them the potentiality of thought – and when cattle think – I have seen what arrives.'

'Are they so clever as all that?' I asked idly.

'Monsieur, when your sportif chauffeur camouflaged your limousine so that she resembled one of your Army lorries, I would not believe her capacities. I bet him – ah – two to one – she would not touch ninety kilometres. It was proved that she could. I can give you no proof, but will you believe me if I tell you what a beast who thinks can achieve?'

'After the War,' said I spaciously, 'everything is credible.'

'That is true! Everything inconceivable has happened; but still we learn nothing and we believe nothing. When I was a child in my father's house – before I became a Colonial Administrator – my interest and my affection were among our cattle. We of the old rock live here – have you seen? – in big farms like castles. Indeed, some of them may have been Saracenic. The barns group round them – great white-walled barns, and yards solid as our houses. One gate shuts all. It is a world apart; an administration of all that concerns beasts. It was there I learned something about cattle. You see, they are our playthings in the Camargue and the Crau. The boy measures his strength against the calf that butts him in play among the manure-heaps. He moves in and out among the cows, who are – not so amiable. He rides with the herdsmen in the open to shift the herds. Sooner or later, he meets as bulls the little calves that knocked him over. So it was with me – till it became necessary that I should go to our Colonies.' He laughed. 'Very necessary. That is a good time in youth, Monsieur, when one does these things which shock our parents. Why is it always Papa who is so shocked and has never heard of such things – and Mamma who supplies the excuses? ... And when my brother – my elder who stayed and created the business – begged me to return and help him, I resigned my Colonial career gladly enough. I returned to our own lands, and my well-loved, wicked white and yellow cattle of the Camargue and the Crau. My Faith, I could talk of them all night, for this stuff unlocks the heart, without making repentance in the morning. ... Yes! It was after the War that this happened. There was a calf, among Heaven knows how many of ours – a bull-calf – an infant indistinguishable from his companions. He was sick, and he had been taken up with his mother into the big farmyard at home with us. Naturally the children of our herdsmen practised on him from the first. It is in their blood. The Spaniards make a cult of bull-fighting. Our little devils down here bait bulls as automatically as the English child kicks or throws balls. This calf would chase them with his eyes open, like a cow when she hunts a man. They would take refuge behind our tractors and wine-carts in the centre of the yard: he would chase them in and out as a dog hunts rats. More than that, he would study their psychology, his eyes in their eyes. Yes, he watched their faces to divine which way they would run. He himself, also, would pretend sometimes to charge directly at a boy. Then he would wheel right or left – one could never tell – and knock over some child pressed against a wall who thought himself safe. After this, he would stand over him, knowing that his companions must come to his aid; and when they were all together, waving their jackets across his eyes and pulling his tail, he would scatter them – how he would scatter them! He could kick, too, sideways like a cow. He knew his ranges as well as our gunners, and he was as quick on his feet as our Carpentier. I observed him often. Christophe – the man who passed just now – our chief herdsman, who had taught me to ride with our beasts when I was ten – Christophe told me that he was descended from a yellow cow of those days that had chased us once into the marshes. "He kicks just like her," said Christophe. "He can side-kick as he jumps. Have you seen, too, that he is not deceived by the jacket when a boy waves it? He uses it to find the boy. They think they are feeling him. He is feeling them always. He thinks, that one." I had come to the same con- clusion. Yes – the creature was a thinker along the lines necessary to his sport; and he was a humorist also, like so many natural murderers. One knows the type among beasts as well as among men. It possesses a curious truculent mirth – almost indecent but infallibly significant – '

Monsieur Voiron replenished our glasses with the great wine that went better at each descent.

'They kept him for some time in the yards to practise upon. Naturally he became a little brutal; so Christophe turned him out to learn manners among his equals in the grazing lands, where the Camargue joins the Crau. How old was he then? About eight or nine months, I think. We met again a few months later – he and I. I was riding one of our little half-wild horses, along a road of the Crau, when I found myself almost unseated. It was he! He had hidden himself behind a wind-break till we passed, and had then charged my horse from behind. Yes, he had deceived even my little horse! But I recognized him. I gave him the whip across the nose, and I said: "Apis, for this thou goest to Arles! It was unworthy of thee, between us two." But that creature had no shame. He went away laughing, like an Apache. If he had dismounted me, I do not think it is I who would have laughed – yearling as he was.'

'Why did you want to send him to Arles?' I asked.

'For the bull-ring. When your charming tourists leave us, we institute our little amusements there. Not a real bull-fight, you understand, but young bulls with padded horns, and our boys from hereabouts and in the city go to play with them. Naturally, before we send them we try them in our yards at home. So we brought up Apis from his pastures. He knew at once that he was among the friends of his youth – he almost shook hands with them – and he submitted like an angel to padding his horns. He investigated the carts and tractors in the yards, to choose his lines of defence and attack. And then – he attacked with an *élan*, and he defended with a tenacity and forethought that delighted us. In truth, we were so pleased that I fear we trespassed upon his patience. We desired him to repeat himself, which no true artist will tolerate. But he gave us fair warning. He went out to the centre of the yard, where there was some dry earth; he knelt down and – you have seen a calf whose horns fret him thrusting and rooting into a bank? He did just that, very deliberately, till he had rubbed the pads off his horns. Then he rose, dancing on those wonderful feet that tinkled, and he said: "Now, my friends, the buttons are off the foils. Who begins?" We understood. We finished at once. He was turned out again on the pastures till it should be time to amuse them at our little metropolis. But, some time before he went to Arles – yes, I think I have it correctly – Christophe, who had been out on the Crau, informed me that Apis had assassinated a young bull who had given signs of developing into a rival. That happens, of course, and our herdsmen should prevent it. But Apis had killed in his own style – at dusk, from the ambush of a wind-break – by an oblique

charge from behind which knocked the other over. He had
then disembowelled him. All very possible, *but* – the murder
accomplished – Apis went to the bank of a wind-break, knelt,
and carefully, as he had in our yard, cleaned his horns in the
earth. Christophe, who had never seen such a thing, at once
borrowed (do you know, it is most efficacious when taken
that way?) some Holy Water from our little chapel in those
pastures, sprinkled Apis (whom it did not affect), and rode in
to tell me. It was obvious that a thinker of that bull's type
would also be meticulous in his toilette; so, when he was sent
to Arles, I warned our consignees to exercise caution with
him. Happily, the change of scene, the music, the general
attention, and the meeting again with old friends – all our
bad boys attended – agreeably distracted him. He became for
the time a pure *farceur* again; but his wheelings, his rushes,
his rat-huntings were more superb than ever. There was in
them now, you understand, a breadth of technique that
comes of reasoned art, and, above all, the passion that arrives
after experience. Oh, he had learned, out there on the Crau!
At the end of his little turn, he was, according to local rules,
to be handled in all respects except for the sword, which was
a stick, as a professional bull who must die. He was
manoeuvred into, or he posed himself in, the proper atti-
tude; made his rush; received the point on his shoulder and
then – turned about and cantered towards the door by which
he had entered the arena. He said to the world: "My friends,
the representation is ended. I thank you for your applause. I
go to repose myself." But our Arlesians, who are – not so
clever as some, demanded an encore, and Apis was headed
back again. We others from this country, we knew what
would happen. He went to the centre of the ring, kneeled,
and, slowly, with full parade, plunged his horns alternately
in the dirt till the pads came off. Christophe shouts: "Leave
him alone, you straight-nosed imbeciles! Leave him before
you must." But they required emotion; for Rome has always
debauched her loved Provincia with bread and circuses. It
was given. Have you, Monsieur, ever seen a servant, with pan

and broom, sweeping round the base-board of a room? In a half-minute Apis has them all swept out and over the barrier. Then he demands once more that the door shall be opened to him. It is opened and he retires as though – which, truly, is the case – loaded with laurels.'

Monsieur Voiron refilled the glasses, and allowed himself a cigarette, which he puffed for some time.

'And afterwards?' I said.

'I am arranging it in my mind. It is difficult to do it justice. Afterwards – yes, afterwards – Apis returned to his pastures and his mistresses and I to my business. I am no longer a scandalous old "sportif" in shirt-sleeves howling encouragement to the yellow son of a cow. I revert to Voiron Frères – wines, chemical manures, *et cetera*. And next year, through some chicane which I have not the leisure to unravel, and also, thanks to our patriarchal system of paying our older men out of the increase of the herds, old Christophe possesses himself of Apis. Oh, yes, he proves it through descent from a certain cow that my father had given his father before the Republic. Beware, Monsieur, of the memory of the illiterate man! An ancestor of Christophe had been a soldier under our Soult against your Beresford, near Bayonne. He fell into the hands of Spanish guerrillas. Christophe and his wife used to tell me the details on certain Saints' Days when I was a child. Now, as compared with our recent war, Soult's campaign and retreat across the Bidassoa –'

'But did you allow Christophe just to annex the bull?' I demanded.

'You do not know Christophe. He had sold him to the Spaniards before he informed me. The Spaniards pay in coin – douros of very pure silver. Our peasants mistrust our paper. You know the saying: "A thousand francs paper; eight hundred metal, and the cow is yours." Yes, Christophe sold Apis, who was then two and a half years old, and to Christophe's knowledge thrice at least an assassin.'

'How was that?' I said.

'Oh, his own kind only; and always, Christophe told me, by the same oblique rush from behind, the same sideways over-

throw, and the same swift disembowelment, followed by this
levitical cleaning of the horns. In human life he would have
kept a manicurist – this Minotaur. And so, Apis disappears
from our country. That does not trouble me. I know in
due time I shall be advised. Why? Because, in this land,
Monsieur, not a hoof moves between Berre and the Saintes
Maries without the knowledge of specialists such as
Christophe. The beasts are the substance and the drama
of their lives to them. So when Christophe tells me, a
little before Easter Sunday, that Apis makes his début
in the bull-ring of a small Catalan town on the road to
Barcelona, it is only to pack my car and trundle there across
the frontier with him. The place lacked importance and
manufactures, but it had produced a matador of some reputation, who was condescending to show his art in his native
town. They were even running one special train to the place.
Now our French railway system is only execrable, but the
Spanish –'

'You went down by road, didn't you?' said I.

'Naturally. It was not too good. Villamarti was the matador's name. He proposed to kill two bulls for the honour of
his birthplace. Apis, Christophe told me, would be his
second. It was an interesting trip, and that little city by the
sea was ravishing. Their bull-ring dates from the middle of
the seventeenth century. It is full of feeling. The ceremonial
too – when the horsemen enter and ask the Mayor in his box
to throw down the keys of the bull-ring – that was exquis-
itely conceived. You know, if the keys are caught in the
horseman's hat, it is considered a good omen. They were perfectly caught. Our seats were in the front row beside the
gates where the bulls enter, so we saw everything.

'Villamarti's first bull was not too badly killed. The second
matador, whose name escapes me, killed his without dis-
tinction – a foil to Villamarti. And the third, Chisto, a labori-
ous, middle-aged professional who had never risen beyond a
certain dull competence, was equally of the background. Oh,
they are as jealous as the girls of the Comédie Française,
these matadors! Villamarti's troupe stood ready for his

second bull. The gates opened, and we saw Apis, beautifully balanced on his feet, peer coquettishly round the corner, as though he were at home. A picador – a mounted man with the long lance-goad – stood near the barrier on his right. He had not even troubled to turn his horse, for the capeadors – the men with the cloaks – were advancing to play Apis – to feel his psychology and intentions, according to the rules that are made for bulls who do not think. . . . I did not realize the murder before it was accomplished! The wheel, the rush, the oblique charge from behind, the fall of horse and man were simultaneous. Apis leaped the horse, with whom he had no quarrel, and alighted, all four feet together (it was enough), between the man's shoulders, changed his beautiful feet on the carcass, and was away, pretending to fall nearly on his nose. Do you follow me? In that instant, by that stumble, he produced the impression that his adorable assassination was a mere bestial blunder. Then, Monsieur, I began to comprehend that it was an artist we had to deal with. He did not stand over the body to draw the rest of the troupe. He chose to reserve that trick. He let the attendants bear out the dead, and went on to amuse himself among the capeadors. Now to Apis, trained among our children in the yards, the cloak was simply a guide to the boy behind it. He pursued, you understand, the person, not the propaganda – the proprietor, not the journal. If a third of our electors of France were as wise, my friend! . . . But it was done leisurely, with humour and a touch of truculence. He romped after one man's cloak as a clumsy dog might do, but I observed that he kept the man on his terrible left side. Christophe whispered to me: "Wait for his mother's kick. When he has made the fellow confident it will arrive." It arrived in the middle of a gambol. My God! He lashed out in the air as he frisked. The man dropped like a sack, lifted one hand a little towards his head, and – that was all. So you see, a body was again at his disposition; a second time the cloaks ran up to draw him off, but, a second time, Apis refused his grand scene. A second time he acted that his murder was accident and – he convinced his audience! It was as though he had knocked over a bridge-gate in the marshes by mistake. Unbelievable? I saw it.'

The memory sent Monsieur Voiron again to the champagne; and I accompanied him.

'But Apis was not the sole artist present. They say Villamarti comes of a family of actors. I saw him regard Apis with a new eye. He, too, began to understand. He took his cloak and moved out to play him before they should bring on another picador. He had his reputation. Perhaps Apis knew it. Perhaps Villamarti reminded him of some boy with whom he had practised at home. At any rate Apis permitted it – up to a certain point; but he did not allow Villamarti the stage. He cramped him throughout. He dived and plunged clumsily and slowly, but always with menace and always closing in. We could see that the man was conforming to the bull – not the bull to the man; for Apis was playing him towards the centre of the ring, and, in a little while – I watched his face – Villamarti knew it. But I could not fathom the creature's motive. "Wait," said old Christophe. "He wants that picador on the white horse yonder. When he reaches his proper distance he will get him. Villamarti is his cover. He used me once that way." And so it was, my friend! With the clang of one of our own Seventy-fives, Apis dismissed Villamarti with his chest – breasted him over – and had arrived at his objective near the barrier. The same oblique charge; the head carried low for the sweep of the horns; the immense sideways fall of the horse, broken-legged and half-paralysed; the senseless man on the ground, and – behold Apis between them, backed against the barrier – his right covered by the horse; his left by the body of the man at his feet. The simplicity of it! Lacking the carts and tractors of his early parade-grounds he, being a genius, had extemporized with the materials at hand, and dug himself in. The troupe closed up again, their left wing broken by the kicking horse, their right immobilized by the man's body which Apis bestrode with significance. Villamarti almost threw himself between the horns, but – it was more an appeal than an attack. Apis refused him. He held his base. A picador was sent at him – necessarily from the front, which alone was open. Apis charged – he who, till then, you realize, had not used the horn! The horse went over backwards, the man half beneath him. Apis halted, hooked him under the heart, and threw him to the barrier. We heard his head crack, but he was dead before he hit the wood. There was no demonstration from the audience. They, also, had begun to realize this Foch among bulls! The arena occupied itself again with the dead. Two of the troupe irresolutely tried to play him – God knows in what hope! – but he moved out to the centre of the ring. "Look!" said Christophe. "Now he goes to clean himself. That always frightened me." He knelt down; he began to clean his horns. The earth was hard. He worried at it in an ecstasy of absorption. As he laid his head along and rattled his ears, it was as though he were interrogating the Devils themselves upon their secrets, and always saying impatiently: "Yes, I know that – and *that* – and *that*! Tell me more – *more*!' In the silence that covered us, a woman cried: "He digs a grave! Oh, Saints, he digs a grave!" Some others echoed this – not loudly – as a wave echoes in a grotto of the sea.

'And when his horns were cleaned, he rose up and studied poor Villamarti's troupe, eyes in eyes, one by one, with the gravity of an equal in intellect and the remote and merciless resolution of a master in his art. This was more terrifying than his toilette.'

'And they – Villamarti's men?' I asked.

'Like the audience, were dominated. They had ceased to posture, or stamp, or address insults to him. They conformed to him. The two other matadors stared. Only Chisto, the oldest, broke silence with some call or other, and Apis turned his head towards him. Otherwise he was isolated, immobile – sombre – meditating on those at his mercy. Ah!

'For some reason the trumpet sounded for the *banderillas* – those gay hooked darts that are planted in the shoulders of bulls who do not think, after their neck-muscles are tired by lifting horses. When such bulls feel the pain, they check for an instant, and, in that instant, the men step gracefully

aside. Villamarti's banderillero answered the trumpet mechanically – like one condemned. He stood out, poised the darts
and stammered the usual patter of invitation. . . . And after?
I do not assert that Apis shrugged his shoulders, but he reduced the episode to its lowest elements, as could only a bull
of Gaul. With his truculence was mingled always – owing to
the shortness of his tail – a certain Rabelaisian abandon, especially when viewed from the rear. Christophe had often
commented upon it. Now, Apis brought that quality into
play. He circulated round that boy, forcing him to break up
his beautiful poses. He studied him from various angles, like
an incompetent photographer. He presented to him every
portion of his anatomy except his shoulders. At intervals he
feigned to run in upon him. My God, he was cruel! But his
motive was obvious. He was playing for a laugh from the
spectators which should synchronize with the fracture of the
human morale. It was achieved. The boy turned and ran
towards the barrier. Apis was on him before the laugh
ceased; passed him; headed him – what do I say? – herded
him off to the left, his horns beside and a little in front of his
chest: he did not intend him to escape into a refuge. Some of
the troupe would have closed in, but Villamarti cried: "If he
wants him he will take him. Stand!" They stood. Whether
the boy slipped or Apis nosed him over I could not see. But
he dropped, sobbing. Apis halted like a car with four brakes,
struck a pose, smelt him very completely and turned away. It
was dismissal more ignominious than degradation at the
head of one's battalion. The representation was finished. Remained only for Apis to clear his stage of the subordinate
characters.

'Ah! His gesture then! He gave a dramatic start – this
Cyrano of the Camargue – as though he was aware of them
for the first time. He moved. All their beautiful breeches
twinkled for an instant along the top of the barrier. He held
the stage alone! But Christophe and I, we trembled! For, observe, he had now involved himself in a stupendous drama of
which he only could supply the third act. And, except for an
audience on the razor-edge of emotion, he had exhausted his

material. Molière himself – we have forgotten, my friend, to drink to the health of that great soul – might have been at a loss. And Tragedy is but a step behind Failure. We could see the four or five Civil Guards, who are sent always to keep order, fingering the breeches of their rifles. They were but waiting a word from the Mayor to fire on him, as they do sometimes at a bull who leaps the barrier among the spectators. They would, of course, have killed or wounded several people – but that would not have saved Apis.'

Monsieur Voiron drowned the thought at once, and wiped his beard.

'At that moment Fate – the Genius of France, if you will – sent to assist in the incomparable finale, none other than Chisto, the eldest, and I should have said (but never again will I judge!) the least inspired of all; mediocrity itself, but at heart – and it is the heart that conquers always, my friend – at heart an artist. He descended stiffly into the arena, alone and assured. Apis regarded him, his eyes in his eyes. The man took stance, with his cloak, and called to the bull as to an equal: "Now, Señor, we will show these honourable caballeros something together." He advanced thus against this thinker who at a plunge – a kick – a thrust – could, we all knew, have extinguished him. My dear friend, I wish I could convey to you something of the unaffected bonhomie, the humour, the delicacy, the consideration bordering on respect even, with which Apis, the supreme artist, responded to this invitation. It was the Master, wearied after a strenuous hour in the atelier, unbuttoned and at ease with some not inexpert but limited disciple. The telepathy was instantaneous between them. And for good reason! Christophe said to me: "All's well. That Chisto began among the bulls. I was sure of it when I heard him call just now. He has been a herdsman. He'll pull it off." There was a little feeling and adjustment, at first, for mutual distances and allowances.

'Oh, yes! And here occurred a gross impertinence of Villamarti. He had, after an interval, followed Chisto – to retrieve his reputation. My Faith! I can conceive the elder Dumas slamming his door on an intruder precisely as Apis did. He raced Villamarti into the nearest refuge at once. He stamped his feet outside it, and he snorted: "Go! I am engaged with an artist." Villamarti went – his reputation left behind for ever.

'Apis returned to Chisto saying: "Forgive the interruption. I am not always master of my time, but you were about to observe, my dear confrère . . .?" Then the play began. Out of compliment to Chisto, Apis chose as his objective (every bull varies in this respect) the inner edge of the cloak – that nearest to the man's body. This allows but a few millimetres clearance in charging. But Apis trusted himself as Chisto trusted him, and, this time, he conformed to the man, with inimitable judgement and temper. He allowed himself to be played into the shadow or the sun, as the delighted audience demanded. He raged enormously; he feigned defeat; he despaired in statuesque abandon, and thence flashed into fresh paroxysms of wrath – but always with the detachment of the true artist who knows he is but the vessel of an emotion whence others, not he, must drink. And never once did he forget that honest Chisto's cloak was to him the gauge by which to spare even a hair on the skin. He inspired Chisto too. My God! His youth returned to that meritorious beef-sticker – the desire, the grace, and the beauty of his early dreams. One could almost see that girl of the past for whom he was rising, rising to these present heights of skill and daring. It was his hour too – a miraculous hour of dawn returned to gild the sunset. All he knew was at Apis' disposition. Apis acknowledged it with all that he had learned at home, at Arles and in his lonely murders on our grazing-grounds. He flowed round Chisto like a river of death – round his knees, leaping at his shoulders, kicking just clear of one side or the other of his head; behind his back, hissing as he shaved by; and once or twice – inimitable! – he reared wholly up before him while Chisto slipped back from beneath the avalanche of that instructed body. Those two, my dear friend, held five thousand people dumb with no sound but of their breathings – regular as pumps. It was unbearable. Beast and man realized together that we needed a change of

note – a *détente*. They relaxed to pure buffoonery. Chisto
fell back and talked to him outrageously. Apis pretended he
had never heard such language. The audience howled with
delight. Chisto slapped him; he took liberties with his short
tail, to the end of which he clung while Apis pirouetted; he
played about him in all postures; he had become the herdsman again – gross, careless, brutal, but comprehending. Yet
Apis was always the more consummate clown. All that time
(Christophe and I saw it) Apis drew off towards the gates of
the *toril* where so many bulls enter but – have you ever
heard of one that returned? *We* knew that Apis knew that
as he had saved Chisto, so Chisto would save him. Life is
sweet to us all; to the artist who lives many lives in one,
sweetest. Chisto did not fail him. At the last, when none
could laugh any longer, the man threw his cape across the
bull's back, his arm round his neck. He flung up a hand at
the gate, as Villamarti, young and commanding but *not* a
herdsman, might have raised it, and he cried: "Gentlemen,
open to me and my honourable little donkey." They opened –
I have misjudged Spaniards in my time! – those gates opened
to the man and the bull together, and closed behind them.
And then? From the Mayor to the Guardia Civil they went
mad for five minutes, till the trumpets blew and the fifth
bull rushed out – an unthinking black Andalusian. I suppose
some one killed him. My friend, my very dear friend, to
whom I have opened my heart, I confess that I did not watch.
Christophe and I, we were weeping together like children of
the same Mother. Shall we drink to Her?'

The Wish House

(1924)

THE new Church Visitor had just left after a twenty minutes' call. During that time, Mrs Ashcroft had used such English as an elderly, experienced, and pensioned cook should, who had seen life in London. She was the readier, therefore, to slip back into easy, ancient Sussex ('t's softening to 'd's as one warmed) when the 'bus brought Mrs Fettley from thirty miles away for a visit, that pleasant March Saturday. The two had been friends since childhood; but, of late, destiny had separated their meetings by long intervals.

Much was to be said, and many ends, loose since last time, to be ravelled up on both sides, before Mrs Fettley, with her bag of quilt-patches, took the couch beneath the window commanding the garden, and the football-ground in the valley below.

'Most folk got out at Bush Tye for the match there,' she explained, 'so there weren't no one for me to cushion agin, the last five mile. An' she *do* just-about bounce ye.'

'You've took no hurt,' said her hostess. 'You don't brittle by agein', Liz.'

Mrs Fettley chuckled and made to match a couple of patches to her liking. 'No, or I'd ha' broke twenty year back. You can't ever mind when I was so's to be called round, can ye?'

Mrs Ashcroft shook her head slowly – she never hurried – and went on stitching a sack-cloth lining into a list-bound rush tool-basket. Mrs Fettley laid out more patches in the spring light through the geraniums on the window-sill, and they were silent awhile.

'What like's this new Visitor o' yourn?' Mrs Fettley inquired, with a nod towards the door. Being very shortsighted, she had, on her entrance, almost bumped into the lady.

Mrs Ashcroft suspended the big packing-needle judicially on high, ere she stabbed home. 'Settin' aside she don't bring

163

much news with her yet, I dunno as I've anythin' special agin her.'

'Ourn, at Keyneslade,' said Mrs Fettley, 'she's full o' words an' pity, but she don't stay for answers. Ye can get on with your thoughts while she clacks.'

'This 'un don't clack. She's aimin' to be one o' those High Church nuns, like.'

'Ourn's married, but, by what they say, she've made no great gains of it ...' Mrs Fettley threw up her sharp chin. 'Lord! How they dam' cherubim do shake the very bones o' the place!'

The tile-sided cottage trembled at the passage of two specially chartered forty-seat charabancs on their way to the Bush Tye match; a regular Saturday 'shopping' 'bus, for the county's capital, fumed behind them; while, from one of the crowded inns, a fourth car backed out to join the procession, and held up the stream of through pleasure-traffic.

'You're as free-tongued as ever, Liz,' Mrs Ashcroft observed.

'Only when I'm with you. Otherwhiles, I'm Granny – three times over. I lay that basket's for one o' your gran'chiller – ain't it?'

' 'Tis for Arthur – my Jane's eldest.'

'But he ain't workin' nowheres, is he?'

'No. 'Tis a picnic-basket.'

'You're let off light. My Willie, he's allus at me for money for them aireated wash-poles folk puts up in their gardens to draw the music from Lunnon, like. An' I give it 'im – pore fool me!'

'An' he forgets to give you the promise-kiss after, don't he?' Mrs Ashcroft's heavy smile seemed to strike inwards.

'He do. No odds 'twixt boys now an' forty year back. Take all an' give naught – an' we to put up with it! Pore fool we! Three shillin' at a time Willie'll ask me for!'

'They don't make nothin' o' money these days,' Mrs Ashcroft said.

'An' on'y last week,' the other went on, 'me daughter, she ordered a quarter pound suet at the butchers's; an' she sent it back to 'im to be chopped. She said she couldn't bother with choppin' it.'

'I lay he charged her, then.'

'I lay he did. She told me there was a whisk-drive that afternoon at the Institute, an' she couldn't bother to do the choppin'.'

'Tck!'

Mrs Ashcroft put the last firm touches to the basket-lining. She had scarcely finished when her sixteen-year-old grandson, a maiden of the moment in attendance, hurried up the garden-path shouting to know if the thing were ready, snatched it, and made off without acknowledgement. Mrs Fettley peered at him closely.

'They're goin' picnickin' somewheres,' Mrs Ashcroft explained.

'Ah,' said the other, with narrowed eyes. 'I lay *he* won't show much mercy to any he comes across, either. Now 'oo the dooce do he remind me of, all of a sudden?'

'They must look arter theirselves – 'same as we did.' Mrs Ashcroft began to set out the tea.

'No denyin' *you* could, Gracie,' said Mrs Fettley.

'What's in your head now?'

'Dunno . . . But it come over me, sudden-like – about dat woman from Rye – I've slipped the name – Barnsley, wadn't it?'

'Batten – Polly Batten, you're thinkin' of.'

'That's it – Polly Batten. That day she had it in for you with a hay-fork – 'time we was all hayin' at Smalldene – for stealin' her man.'

'But you heered me tell her she had my leave to keep him?' Mrs Ashcroft's voice and smile were smoother than ever.

'I did – an' we was all looking that she'd prod the fork spang through your breastes when you said it.'

'No-oo. She'd never go beyond bounds – Polly. She shruck too much for reel doin's.'

'Allus seems to *me*,' Mrs Fettley said after a pause, 'that a man 'twixt two fightin' women is the foolishest thing on earth. Like a dog bein' called two ways.'

'Mebbe. But what set ye off on those times, Liz?'

'That boy's fashion o' carryin' his head an' arms. I haven't rightly looked at him since he's growed. Your Jane never showed it, but – him! Why, 'tis Jim Batten and his tricks come to life again! ... Eh?'

'Mebbe. There's some that would ha' made it out so – bein' barren-like, themselves.'

'Oho! Ah well! Dearie, dearie me, now! ... An' Jim Batten's been dead this –'

'Seven and twenty years,' Mrs Ashcroft answered briefly. 'Won't ye draw up, Liz?'

Mrs Fettley drew up to buttered toast, currant bread, stewed tea, bitter as leather, some home-preserved pears, and a cold boiled pig's tail to help down the muffins. She paid all the proper compliments.

'Yes. I dunno as I've ever owed me belly much,' said Mrs Ashcroft thoughtfully. 'We only go through this world once.'

'But don't it lay heavy on ye, sometimes?' her guest suggested.

'Nurse says I'm a sight liker to die o' me indigestion than me leg.' For Mrs Ashcroft had a long-standing ulcer on her shin, which needed regular care from the Village Nurse, who boasted (or others did, for her) that she had dressed it one hundred and three times already during her term of office.

'An' you that *was* so able, too! It's all come on ye before your full time, like. *I*'ve watched ye goin'.' Mrs Fettley spoke with real affection.

'Somethin's bound to find ye sometime. I've me 'eart left me still,' Mrs Ashcroft returned.

'You was always big-hearted enough for three. That's somethin' to look back on at the day's eend.'

'I reckon you've *your* back-lookin's, too,' was Mrs Ashcroft's answer.

'You know it. But I don't think much regardin' such matters excep' when I'm along with you, Gra'. 'Takes two sticks to make a fire.'

Mrs Fettley stared, with jaw half-dropped, at the grocer's

bright calendar on the wall. The cottage shook again to the roar of the motor-traffic, and the crowded football-ground below the garden roared almost as loudly; for the village was well set to its Saturday leisure.

Mrs Fettley had spoken very precisely for some time without interruption, before she wiped her eyes. 'And,' she concluded, 'they read 'is death-notice to me, out o' the paper last month. O' course it wadn't any o' *my* becomin' concerns – let be I 'adn't set eyes on him for so long. O' course *I* couldn't say nor show nothin'. Nor I've no rightful call to go to Eastbourne to see 'is grave, either. I've been schemin' to slip over there by the 'bus some day; but they'd ask questions at 'ome past endurance. So I 'aven't even *that* to stay me.'

'But you've 'ad your satisfactions?'

'Godd! Yess! Those four years 'e was workin' on the rail near us. An' the other drivers they gave him a brave funeral, too.'

'Then you've naught to cast-up about. 'Nother cup o' tea?'

The light and air had changed a little with the sun's descent, and the two elderly ladies closed the kitchen-door against chill. A couple of jays squealed and skirmished through the undraped apple-trees in the garden. This time, the word was with Mrs Ashcroft, her elbows on the tea-table, and her sick leg propped on a stool...

'Well I never! But what did your 'usband say to that?' Mrs Fettley asked, when the deep-toned recital halted.

' 'E said I might go where I pleased for all of 'im. But seein' 'e was bedrid, I said I'd 'tend 'im out. 'E knowed I wouldn't take no advantage of 'im in that state. 'E lasted eight or nine week. Then he was took with a seizure-like; an' laid stone-still for days. Then 'e propped 'imself up abed an' says: "You pray no man'll ever deal with you like you've dealed with some." "An' you?" I says, for *you* know, Liz, what a rover 'e was. "It cuts both ways," says 'e, "but *I*'m death-wise, an' I can see what's comin' to you." He died a-Sunday an' was buried a-Thursday. .... An' yet I'd set a heap by him – one time or – did I ever?'

'You never told me that before,' Mrs Fettley ventured.

'I'm payin' ye for what ye told me just now. Him bein' dead, I wrote up, sayin' I was free for good, to that Mrs Marshall in Lunnon – which gave me my first place as kitchen-maid – Lord, how long ago! She was well pleased, for they two was both gettin' on, an' I knowed their ways. You remember, Liz, I used to go to 'em in service between whiles, for years – when we wanted money, or – or my 'usband was away – on occasion.'

' 'E *did* get that six months at Chichester, didn't 'e?' Mrs Fettley whispered. 'We never rightly won to the bottom of it.'

' 'E'd ha' got more, but the man didn't die.'

'None o' your doin', was it, Gra'?'

'No! 'Twas the woman's husband this time. An' so, my man bein' dead, I went back to them Marshall's, as cook, to get me legs under a gentleman's table again, and be called with a handle to me name. That was the year you shifted to Portsmouth.'

'Cosham,' Mrs Fettley corrected. 'There was a middlin' lot o' new buildin' bein' done there. My man went first, an' got the room, an' I follered.'

'Well, then, I was a year-abouts in Lunnon, all at a breath, like, four meals a day an' livin' easy. Then, 'long towards autumn, they two went travellin', like, to France; keepin' me on, for they couldn't do without me. I put the house to rights for the caretaker, an' then I slipped down 'ere to me sister Bessie – me wages in me pockets, an' all 'ands glad to be 'old of me.'

'That would be when I was at Cosham,' said Mrs Fettley.

'*You* know, Liz, there wasn't no cheap-dog pride to folk, those days, no more than there was cinemas nor whisk-drives. Man or woman 'ud lay hold o' any job that promised a shillin' to the backside of it, didn't they? I was all peaked up after Lunnon, an' I thought the fresh airs 'ud serve me. So I took on at Smalldene, obligin' with a hand at the early potato-liftin', stubbin' hens, an' such-like. They'd ha' mocked me sore in my kitchen in Lunnon, to see me in men's boots, an' me petticoats all shorted.'

'Did it bring ye any good?' Mrs Fettley asked.

' 'Twadn't for that I went. You know, 's'well's me, that na'un happens to ye till it '*as* 'appened. Your mind don't warn ye before'and of the road ye've took, till you're at the far eend of it. We've only a backwent view of our proceedin's.'

' 'Oo was it?'

' 'Arry Mockler.' Mrs Ashcroft's face puckered to the pain of her sick leg.

Mrs Fettley gasped. ' 'Arry? Bert Mockler's son! An' *I* never guessed!'

Mrs Ashcroft nodded. 'An' I told myself – *an*' I beleft it – that I wanted field-work.'

'What did ye get out of it?'

'The usuals. Everythin' at first – worse than naught after. I had signs an' warning a-plenty, but I took no heed of 'em. For we was burnin' rubbish one day, just when we'd come to know how 'twas with – with both of us. 'Twas early in the year for burnin', an' I said so. "No!" says he. "The sooner dat old stuff's off an' done with," 'e says, "the better." 'Is face was harder'n rocks when he spoke. Then it come over me that I'd found me master, which I 'adn't ever before. I'd allus owned 'em, like.'

'Yes! Yes! They're yourn or you're theirn,' the other sighed. 'I like the right way best.'

'I didn't. But 'Arry did ... 'Long then, it come time for me to go back to Lunnon. I couldn't. I clean couldn't! So, I took an' tipped a dollop o' scaldin' water out o' the copper one Monday mornin' over me left 'and and arm. Dat stayed me where I was for another fortnight.'

'Was it worth it?' said Mrs Fettley, looking at the silvery scar on the wrinkled fore-arm.

Mrs Ashcroft nodded. 'An' after that, we two made it up 'twixt us so's 'e could come to Lunnon for a job in a liv'ry-stable not far from me. 'E got it. *I* 'tended to that. There wadn't no talk nowhere. His own mother never suspicioned how 'twas. He just slipped up to Lunnon, an' there we abode that winter, not 'alf a mile 'tother from each.'

'Ye paid 'is fare an' all, though'; Mrs Fettley spoke convincedly.

Again Mrs Ashcroft nodded. 'Dere wadn't much I didn't do for him. 'E was me master, an' – O God, help us! – we'd laugh over it walkin' together after dark in them paved streets, an' me corns fair wrenchin' in me boots! I'd never been like that before. Ner he! Ner he!'

Mrs Fettley clucked sympathetically.

'An' when did ye come to the eend?' she asked.

'When 'e paid it all back again, every penny. Then I knowed, but I wouldn't *suffer* meself to know. "You've been mortal kind to me," he says. "Kind!" I said. " 'Twixt *us*?" But 'e kep' all on tellin' me 'ow kind I'd been an' 'e'd never forget it all his days. I held it from off o' me for three evenin's, because I would *not* believe. Then 'e talked about not bein' satisfied with 'is job in the stables, an' the men there puttin' tricks on 'im, an' all they lies which a man tells when 'e's leavin' ye. I heard 'im out, neither 'elpin' nor 'inderin'. At the last, I took off a liddle brooch which he'd give me an' I says: "Dat'll do. *I* ain't askin' na'un'." An' I turned me round an' walked off to me own sufferin's. 'E didn't make 'em worse. 'E didn't come nor write after that. 'E slipped off 'ere back 'ome to 'is mother again.'

'An' 'ow often did ye look for 'en to come back?' Mrs Fettley demanded mercilessly.

'More'n once – more'n once! Goin' over the streets we'd used, I thought de very pave-stones 'ud shruck out under me feet.'

'Yes,' said Mrs Fettley. 'I dunno but dat don't 'urt as much as aught else. An' dat was all ye got?'

'No. 'Twadn't. That's the curious part, if you'll believe it, Liz.'

'I do. I lay you're further off lyin' now than in all your life, Gra'.'

'I am . . . An' I suffered, like I'd not wish my most arrantest enemies to. God's Own Name! I went through the hoop that spring! One part of it was 'eddicks which I'd never known all me days before. Think o' *me* with an 'eddick! But I come to be grateful for 'em. They kep' me from thinkin' ...'

' 'Tis like a tooth,' Mrs Fettley commented. 'It must rage an' rugg till it tortures itself quiet on ye; an' then – then there's na'un left.'

'*I* got enough lef' to last me all *my* days on earth. It come about through our charwoman's liddle girl – Sophy Ellis was 'er name – all eyes an' elbers an' hunger. I used to give 'er vittles. Otherwhiles, I took no special notice of 'er, an' a sight less, o' course, when me trouble about 'Arry was on me. But – you know how liddle maids first feel it sometimes – she come to be crazy-fond o' me, pawin' an' cuddlin' all whiles; an' I 'adn't the 'eart to beat 'er off. ... One afternoon, early in spring 'twas, 'er mother 'ad sent 'er round to scutchel up what vittles she could off of us. I was settin' by the fire, me apern over me head, half-mad with the 'eddick, when she slips in. I reckon I was middlin' short with 'er. "Lor'!" she says. "Is *that* all? I'll take it off you in two-twos!" I told her not to lay a finger on me, for I thought she'd want to stroke my forehead; an' – I ain't that make. "*I* won't tech ye," she says, an' slips out again. She 'adn't been gone ten minutes 'fore me old 'eddick took off quick as bein' kicked. So I went about my work. Prasin'ly, Sophy comes back, an' creeps into my chair quiet as a mouse. 'Er eyes was deep in 'er 'ead an' 'er face all drawed. I asked 'er what 'ad 'appened. "Nothin'," she says. "Only *I*'ve got it now." "Got what?" I says. "Your 'eddick," she says, all hoarse an' sticky-lipped. "I've took it on me." "Nonsense," I says, "it went of itself when you was out. Lay still an' I'll make ye a cup o' tea." " 'Twon't do no good," she says, "till your time's up. 'Ow long do *your* 'eddicks last?" "Don't talk silly," I says, "or I'll send for the Doctor." It looked to me like she might be hatchin' de measles. "Oh, Mrs Ashcroft," she says, stretchin' out 'er liddle thin arms. "I *do* love ye." There wasn't any holdin' agin that. I took 'er into me lap an' made much of 'er. "Is it truly gone?" she says. "Yes," I says, "an' if 'twas you took it away, I'm truly grateful." " '*Twas* me," she says, layin' 'er cheek to mine. "No one but me knows how." An' then she said she'd changed me 'eddick for me at a Wish 'Ouse.'

'Whatt?' Mrs Fettley spoke sharply.

'A Wish House. No! *I* 'adn't 'eard o' such things, either. I couldn't get it straight at first, but, puttin' all together, I made out that a Wish 'Ouse 'ad to be a house which 'ad stood unlet an' empty long enough for Some One, like, to come an' in'abit there. She said a liddle girl that she'd played with in the livery-stables where 'Arry worked 'ad told 'er so. She said the girl 'ad belonged in a caravan that laid up, o' winters, in Lunnon. Gipsy, I judge.'

'Ooh! There's no sayin' what Gippos know, but *I*'ve never 'eard of a Wish 'Ouse, an' I know – some things,' said Mrs Fettley.

'Sophy said there was a Wish 'Ouse in Wadloes Road – just a few streets off, on the way to our green-grocer's. All you 'ad to do, she said, was to ring the bell an' wish your wish through the slit o' the letter-box. I asked 'er if the fairies give it 'er? "Don't ye know," she says, "there's no fairies in a Wish 'Ouse? There's on'y a Token." '

'Goo' Lord A'mighty! Where did she come by *that* word?' cried Mrs Fettley; for a Token is a wraith of the dead or, worse still, of the living.

'The caravan-girl 'ad told 'er, she said. Well, Liz, it troubled me to 'ear 'er, an' lyin' in me arms she must ha' felt it. "That's very kind o' you," I says, holdin' 'er tight, "to wish me 'eddick away. But why didn't ye ask somethin' nice for yourself?" "You can't do that," she says. "All you'll get at a Wish 'Ouse is leave to take some one else's trouble. I've took Ma's 'eddicks, when she's been kind to me; but this is the first time I've been able to do aught for you. Oh, Mrs Ashcroft, I *do* just-about love you." An' she goes on all like that. Liz, I tell you my 'air e'en a'most stood on end to 'ear 'er. I asked 'er what like a Token was. "I dunno," she says, "but after you've ringed the bell, you'll 'ear it run up from the basement, to the front door. Then say your wish," she says, "an' go away." "The Token don't open de door to ye, then?" I says. "Oh no," she says. "You on'y 'ear gigglin', like, be'ind the front door. Then you say you'll take the trouble off of 'oo ever 'tis you've chose for your love; an' ye'll get it," she says. I didn't ask no more – she was too 'ot an' fevered. I made much of 'er till it come time to light de gas, an' a liddle after that, 'er 'eddick – mine, I suppose – took off, an she got down an' played with the cat.'

'Well, I never!' said Mrs Fettley. 'Did – did ye foller it up, anyways?'

'She askt me to, but I wouldn't 'ave no such dealin's with a child.'

'What *did* ye do, then?'

'Sat in me own room 'stid o' the kitchen when me 'eddicks come on. But it lay at de back o' me mind.'

' 'Twould. Did she tell ye more, ever?'

'No. Besides what the Gippo girl 'ad told 'er, she knew naught, 'cept that the charm worked. An', next after that – in May 'twas – I suffered the summer out in Lunnon. 'Twas hot an' windy for weeks, an' the streets stinkin' o' dried 'orse-dung blowin' from side to side an' lyin' level with the kerb We don't get that nowadays. I 'ad my 'ol'day just before hoppin';* an' come down 'ere to stay with Bessie again. She noticed I'd lost flesh, an' was all poochy under the eyes.'

'Did ye see 'Arry?'

Mrs Ashcroft nodded. 'The fourth–no, the fifth day. Wednesday 'twas. I knowed 'e was workin' at Smalldene again. I asked 'is mother in the street, bold as brass. She 'adn't room to say much, for Bessie – you know 'er tongue – was talkin' full-clack. But that Wednesday, I was walkin' with one o' Bessie's chillern hangin' on me skirts, at de back o' Chanter's Tot. Prasin'ly, I felt 'e was be'ind me on the footpath, an' I knowed by 'is tread 'e'd changed 'is nature. I slowed, an' I heard 'im slow. Then I fussed a piece with the child, to force him past me, like. So 'e 'ad to come past. 'E just says "Good-evenin'," and goes on, tryin' to pull 'isself together.'

'Drunk, was he?' Mrs Fettley asked.

'Never! S'runk an' wizen; 'is clothes 'angin' on 'im like
* Hop-picking.

173

bags, an' the back of 'is neck whiter'n chalk. 'Twas all I could do not to oppen my arms an' cry after him. But I swallered me spittle till I was back 'ome again an' the chillern abed. Then I says to Bessie, after supper, "What in de world's come to 'Arry Mockler?" Bessie told me 'e'd been a-Hospital for two months, 'long o' Cuttin' 'is foot wid a spade, muckin' out the old pond at Smalldene. There was poison in de dirt, an' it rooshed up 'is leg, like, an' come out all over him. 'E 'adn't been back to 'is job – carterin' at Smalldene – more'n a fort-night. She told me the Doctor said he'd go off, likely, with the November frostes; an' 'is mother 'ad told 'er that 'e didn't rightly eat nor sleep, an' sweated 'imself into pools, no odds 'ow chill 'e lay. An' spit terrible o' mornin's. "Dearie me," I says. "But, mebbe, hoppin' 'll set 'im right again," an' I licked me thread-point an' I fetched me needle's eye up to it an' I threads me needle under de lamp, steady as rocks. An' dat night (me bed was in de wash-house) I cried an' I cried. An' *you* know, Liz – for you've been with me in my throes – it takes summat to make me cry.'

'Yes; but chile-bearin' is on'y just pain,' said Mrs Fettley.

'I come round by cock-crow, an' dabbed cold tea on me eyes to take away the signs. Long towards nex' evenin' – I was settin' out to lay some flowers on me 'usband's grave, for the look 'o the thing – I met 'Arry over against where the War Memorial is now. 'E was comin' back from 'is 'orses, so 'e couldn't *not* see me. I looked 'im all over, an' " 'Arry," I says twix' me teeth, "come back an' rest-up in Lunnon." "I won't take it," he says, "for I can give ye naught." "I don't ask it," I says. "By God's Own Name, I don't ask na'un! On'y come up an' see a Lunnon doctor." 'E lifts 'is two 'eavy eyes at me: " 'Tis past that, Gra'," 'e says. "I've but a few months left." " 'Arry!" I says. "*My* man!" I says. I couldn't say no more. 'Twas all up in me throat. "Thank ye kindly Gra'," 'e says (but 'e never says "my woman"), an' 'e went on up-street an' 'is mother – Oh, damn 'er! – she was watchin' for 'im, an' she shut de door be'ind 'im.'

Mrs Fettley stretched an arm across the table, and made to

finger Mrs Ashcroft's sleeve at the wrist, but the other moved it out of reach.

'So I went on to the churchyard with my flowers, an' I remembered my 'usband's warnin' that night he spoke. 'E *was* death-wise, an' it *'ad* 'appened as 'e said. But as I was settin' down de jam-pot on the grave-mound, it come over me there was one thing I *could* do for 'Arry. Doctor or no Doctor, I thought I'd make a trial of it. So I did. Nex' mornin', a bill came down from our Lunnon green-grocer. Mrs Marshall, she'd lef' me petty cash for suchlike – o' course – but I tole Bess 'twas for me to come an' open the 'ouse. So I went up, afternoon train.'

'An' – but I know you 'adn't – 'adn't you no fear?'

'What for? There was nothin' front o' me but my own shame an' God's croolty. I couldn't ever get 'Arry – 'ow *could* I? I knowed it must go on burnin' till it burned me out.'

'Aie!' said Mrs Fettley, reaching for the wrist again, and this time Mrs Ashcroft permitted it.

'Yit 'twas a comfort to know I could try *this* for 'im. So I went an' I paid the green-grocer's bill, an' put 'is receipt in me hand-bag, an' then I stepped round to Mrs Ellis – our char – an' got the 'ouse-keys an' opened the 'ouse. First, I made me bed to come back to (God's Own Name! Me bed to lie upon!). Nex' I made me a cup o' tea an' sat down in the kitchen thinkin', till 'long towards dusk. Terrible close, 'twas. Then I dressed me an' went out with the receipt in me 'and-bag, feignin' to study it for an address, like. Fourteen, Wadloes Road, was the place – a liddle basement-kitchen 'ouse, in a row of twenty-thirty such, an' tiddy strips o' walled garden in front – the paint off the front door, an' na'un done to na'un since ever so long. There wasn't 'ardly no one in the streets 'cept the cats. *'Twas* 'ot, too! I turned into the gate bold as brass; up de steps I went an' I ringed the front-door bell. She pealed loud, like it do in an empty house. When she'd all ceased, I 'eard a cheer, like, pushed back on de floor o' the kitchen. Then I 'eard feet on de kitchen-stairs, like it might ha' been a heavy woman in slippers. They come up to de stair-head, acrost the hall – I 'eard the bare boards

creak under 'em – an' at de front door dey stopped. I stooped
me to the letter-box slit, an' I says: "Let me take everythin'
bad that's in store for my man, 'Arry Mockler, for love's
sake." Then, whatever it was 'tother side de door let its
breath out, like, as if it 'ad been holdin' it for to 'ear better.'

'Nothin' was *said* to ye?' Mrs Fettley demanded.

'Na'un. She just breathed out – a sort of *A-ah*, like. Then
the steps went back an' downstairs to the kitchen – all draggy
– an' I heard the cheer drawed up again.'

'An' you abode on de doorstep, throughout all, Gra'?'

Mrs Ashcroft nodded.

'Then I went away, an' a man passin' says to me: "Didn't
you know that house was empty?" "No," I says. "I must ha'
been give the wrong number." An' I went back to our 'ouse,
an' I went to bed; for I was fair flogged out. 'Twas too 'ot to
sleep more'n snatches, so I walked me about, lyin' down be-
tweens, till crack o' dawn. Then I went to the kitchen to
make me a cup o' tea, an' I hitted meself just above the ankle
on an old roastin'-jack o' mine that Mrs Ellis had moved out
from the corner, her last cleanin'. An' so – nex' after that – I
waited till the Marshalls come back o' their holiday.'

'Alone there? I'd ha' thought you'd 'ad enough of empty
houses,' said Mrs Fettley, horrified.

'Oh, Mrs Ellis an' Sophy was runnin' in an' out soon's I
was back, an' 'twixt us we cleaned de house again top-to-
bottom. There's allus a hand's turn more to do in every
house. An' that's 'ow 'twas with me that autumn an' winter,
in Lunnon.'

'Then na'un hap – overtook ye for your doin's?'

Mrs Ashcroft smiled. 'No. Not then. 'Long in November I
sent Bessie ten shillin's.'

'You was allus free-'anded,' Mrs Fettley interrupted.

'An' I got what I paid for, with the rest o' the news. She
said the hoppin' 'ad set 'im up wonderful. 'E'd 'ad six weeks of
it, and now 'e was back again carterin' at Smalldene. No odds
to me 'ow it 'ad 'appened – 'slong's it 'ad. But I dunno as my
ten shillin's eased me much. 'Arry bein' *dead*, like, 'e'd ha'
been mine, till Judgement. 'Arry bein' alive, 'e'd like as not

pick up with some woman middlin' quick. I raged over that. Come spring, I 'ad somethin' else to rage for. I'd growed a nasty little weepin' boil, like, on me shin, just above the boot-top, that wouldn't heal no shape. It made me sick to look at it, for I'm clean-fleshed by nature. Chop me all over with a spade, an' I'd heal like turf. Then Mrs Marshall she set 'er own doctor at me. 'E said I ought to ha' come to him at first go-off, 'stead o' drawin' all manner o' dyed stockin's over it for months. 'E said I'd stood up too much to me work, for it was settin' very close atop of a big swelled vein, like, behither the small o' me ankle. "Slow come, slow go," 'e says. "Lay your leg up on high an' rest it," he says, "an' 'twill ease off. Don't let it close up too soon. You've got a very fine leg, Mrs Ashcroft," 'e says. An' he put wet dressin's on it.'

' 'E done right.' Mrs Fettley spoke firmly. 'Wet dressin's to wet wounds. They draw de humours, same's a lamp-wick draws de oil.'

'That's true. An' Mrs Marshall was allus at me to make me set down more, an' dat nigh healed it up. An' then after a while they packed me off down to Bessie's to finish the cure; for I ain't the sort to sit down when I ought to stand up. You was back in the village then, Liz.'

'I was. I was, but – never did I guess!'

'I didn't desire ye to.' Mrs Ashcroft smiled. 'I saw 'Arry once or twice in de street, wonnerful fleshed up an' restored back. Then, one day I didn't see 'im, an' 'is mother told me one of 'is 'orses 'ad lashed out an' caught 'im on the 'ip. So 'e was abed an' middlin' painful. An' Bessie, she says to his mother, 'twas a pity 'Arry 'adn't a woman of 'is own to take the nursin' off 'er. And the old lady *was* mad! She told us that 'Arry 'ad never looked after any woman in 'is born days, an' as long as she was atop the mowlds, she'd contrive for 'im till 'er two 'ands dropped off. So I knowed she'd do watch-dog for me, 'thout askin' for bones.'

Mrs Fettley rocked with small laughter.

'That day,' Mrs Ashcroft went on, 'I'd stood on me feet nigh all the time, watchin' the doctor go in an' out; for they thought it might be 'is ribs, too. That made my boil break

again, issuin' an' weepin'. But it turned out 'twadn't ribs at
all, an' 'Arry 'ad a good night. When I heard that, nex'
mornin', I says to meself, "I won't lay two an' two together
yit. I'll keep me leg down a week, an' see what comes of it." It
didn't hurt me that day, to speak of – 'seemed more to draw
the strength out o' me like – an' 'Arry 'ad another good
night. That made me persevere; but I didn't dare lay two an'
two together till the week-end, an' then, 'Arry come forth
e'en a'most 'imself again – na'un hurt outside ner in of him. I
nigh fell on me knees in de wash-house when Bessie was up-
street. "I've got ye now, my man," I says. "You'll take your
good from me 'thout knowin' it till my life's end. O God, send
me long to live for 'Arry's sake!" I says. An' I dunno that
didn't still me ragin's.'

'For good?' Mrs Fettley asked.

'They come back, plenty times, but, let be how 'twould, I
knowed I was doin' for 'im. I *knowed* it. I took an' worked me
pains on an' off, like regulatin' my own range, till I learned to
'ave 'em at my commandments. An' that was funny, too.
There was times, Liz, when my trouble 'ud all s'rink an' dry
up, like. First, I used to try an' fetch it on again; bein' fearful
to leave 'Arry alone too long for anythin' to lay 'old of.
Prasin'ly I come to see that was a sign he'd do all right
awhile, an' so I saved myself.'

' 'Ow long for?' Mrs Fettley asked, with deepest interest.

'I've gone de better part of a year onct or twice with na'un
more to show than the liddle weepin' core of it, like. *All*
s'rinked up an' dried off. Then he'd inflame up – for a warnin'
– an' I'd suffer it. When I couldn't no more – an' I *'ad* to keep
on goin' with my Lunnon work – I'd lay me leg high on a
cheer till it eased. Not too quick. I knowed by the feel of it,
those times, dat 'Arry was in need. Then I'd send another five
shillin's to Bess, or somethin' for the chillern, to find out if,
mebbe, 'e'd took any hurt through my neglects. 'Twas *so*!
Year in, year out, I worked it dat way, Liz, an' 'e got 'is good
from me 'thout knowin' – for years and years.'

'But what did *you* get out of it, Gra'?' Mrs Fettley almost
wailed. 'Did ye see 'im reg'lar?'

'Times – when I was 'ere on me 'ol'days. An' more, now that I'm 'ere for good. But 'e's never looked at me, ner any other woman 'cept 'is mother. 'Ow I used to watch an' listen! So did she.'

'Years an' years!' Mrs Fettley repeated. 'An' where's 'e workin' at now?'

'Oh, 'e's give up carterin' quite a while. He's workin' for one o' them big tractorisin' firms – plowin' sometimes, an' sometimes off with lorries – fur as Wales, I've 'eard. He comes 'ome to 'is mother 'tween whiles; but I don't set eyes on him now, fer weeks on end. No odds! 'Is job keeps 'im from continuin' in one stay anywheres.'

'But – just for de sake o' sayin' somethin' – s'pose 'Arry *did* get married?' said Mrs Fettley.

Mrs Ashcroft drew her breath sharply between her still even and natural teeth. '*Dat* ain't been required of me,' she answered. 'I reckon my pains 'ull be counted agin that. Don't *you*, Liz?'

'It ought to be, dearie. It ought to be.'

'It *do* 'urt sometimes. You shall see it when Nurse comes. She thinks I don't know it's turned.'

Mrs Fettley understood. Human nature seldom walks up to the word 'cancer.'

'Be ye certain sure, Gra'?' she asked.

'I was sure of it when old Mr Marshall 'ad me up to 'is study an' spoke a long piece about my faithful service. I've obliged 'em on an' off for a goodish time, but not enough for a pension. But they give me a weekly 'lowance for life. I knew what *that* sinnified – as long as three years ago.'

'Dat don't *prove* it, Gra'.'

'To give fifteen bob a week to a woman 'oo'd live twenty year in the course o' nature? It *do*!'

'You're mistook! You're mistook!' Mrs Fettley insisted.

'Liz, there's *no* mistakin' when the edges are all heaped up, like – same as a collar. You'll see it. An' I laid out Dora Wickwood, too. *She* 'ad it under the arm-pit, like.'

Mrs Fettley considered awhile, and bowed her head in finality.

' 'Ow long d'you reckon 'twill allow ye, countin' from now, dearie?'

'Slow come, slow go. But if I don't set eyes on ye 'fore next hoppin', this'll be good-bye, Liz.'

'Dunno as I'll be able to manage by then – not 'thout I have a liddle dog to lead me. For de chillern, dey won't be troubled, an' – O Gra'! – I'm blindin' up – I'm blindin' up!'

'Oh, *dat* was why you didn't more'n finger with your quilt-patches all this while! I was wonderin' ... But the pain *do* count, don't ye think, Liz? The pain *do* count to keep 'Arry – where I want 'im. Say it can't be wasted, like.'

'I'm sure of it – sure of it, dearie. You'll 'ave your reward.'

'I don't want no more'n this – *if* de pain is taken into de reckonin'.'

' 'Twill be – 'twill be, Gra'.'

There was a knock on the door.

'That's Nurse. She's before 'er time,' said Mrs Ashcroft. 'Open to 'er.'

The young lady entered briskly, all the bottles in her bag clicking. 'Evenin', Mrs Ashcroft,' she began. 'I've come raound a little earlier than usual because of the Institute dance to-na-ite. You won't ma-ind, will you?'

'Oh, no. Me dancin' days are over.' Mrs Ashcroft was the self-contained domestic at once. 'My old friend, Mrs Fettley 'ere, has been settin' talkin' with me a while.'

'I hope she 'asn't been fatiguing you?' said the Nurse a little frostily.

'Quite the contrary. It 'as been a pleasure. Only – only – just at the end I felt a bit – a bit flogged out like.'

'Yes, yes.' The Nurse was on her knees already, with the washes to hand. 'When old ladies get together they talk a deal too much, I've noticed.'

'Mebbe we do,' said Mrs Fettley, rising. 'So now I'll make myself scarce.'

'Look at it first, though,' said Mrs Ashcroft feebly. 'I'd like ye to look at it.'

Mrs Fettley looked, and shivered. Then she leaned over,

and kissed Mrs Ashcroft once on the waxy yellow forehead, and again on the faded grey eyes.

'It *do* count, don't it – de pain?' The lips that still kept trace of their original moulding hardly more than breathed the words.

Mrs Fettley kissed them and moved towards the door.

The Eye of Allah

THE Cantor of St Illod's being far too enthusiastic a musician
to concern himself with its Library, the Sub-Cantor, who
idolized every detail of the work, was tidying up, after two
hours' writing and dictation in the Scriptorium. The copy-
ing-monks handed him in their sheets – it was a plain Four
Gospels ordered by an Abbot at Evesham – and filed out to
vespers. John Otho, better known as John of Burgos, took no
heed. He was burnishing a tiny boss of gold in his miniature
of the Annunciation for his Gospel of St Luke, which it was
hoped that Cardinal Falcodi, the Papal Legate, might later
be pleased to accept.

'Break off, John,' said the Sub-Cantor in an undertone.

'Eh? Gone, have they? I never heard. Hold a minute, Clement.'

The Sub-Cantor waited patiently. He had known John
more than a dozen years, coming and going at St Illod's, to
which monastery John, when abroad, always said he belonged. The claim was gladly allowed, for, more even than
other Fitz Othos, he seemed to carry all the Arts under his
hand, and most of their practical receipts under his hood.

The Sub-Cantor looked over his shoulder at the pinned-
down sheet where the first words of the Magnificat were built
up in gold washed with red-lac for a background to the
Virgin's hardly yet fired halo. She was shown, hands joined in
wonder, at a lattice of infinitely intricate arabesque, round
the edges of which sprays of orange-bloom seemed to load
the blue hot air that carried back over the minute parched
landscape in the middle distance.

'You've made her all Jewess,' said the Sub-Cantor, studying the olive-flushed cheek and the eyes charged with fore-
knowledge.

'What else was Our Lady?' John slipped out the pins.
'Listen, Clement. If I do not come back, this goes into my
Great Luke, whoever finishes it.' He slid the drawing be-
tween its guard-papers.

'Then you're for Burgos again – as I heard?'

'In two days. The new Cathedral yonder – but they're slower than the Wrath of God, those masons – is good for the soul.'

'*Thy* soul?' The Sub-Cantor seemed doubtful.

'Even mine, by your permission. And down south – on the edge of the Conquered Countries – Granada way – there's some Moorish diaper-work that's wholesome. It allays vain thought and draws it towards the picture – as you felt, just now, in my Annunciation.'

'She – it was very beautiful. No wonder you go. But you'll not forget your absolution, John?'

'Surely.' This was a precaution John no more omitted on the eve of his travels than he did the recutting of the tonsure which he had provided himself with in his youth, somewhere near Ghent. The mark gave him privilege of clergy at a pinch, and a certain consideration on the road always.

'You'll not forget, either, what we need in the Scriptorium. There's no more true ultramarine in this world now. They mix it with that German blue. And as for vermilion – '

'I'll do my best always.'

'And Brother Thomas' (this was the Infirmarian in charge of the monastery hospital) 'he needs – '

'He'll do his own asking. I'll go over his side now, and get me re-tonsured.'

John went down the stairs to the lane that divides the hospital and cook-house from the back-cloisters. While he was being barbered, Brother Thomas (St Illod's meek but deadly persistent Infirmarian) gave him a list of drugs that he was to bring back from Spain by hook, crook, or lawful purchase. Here they were surprised by the lame, dark Abbot Stephen, in his fur-lined night-boots. Not that Stephen de Sautré was any spy; but as a young man he had shared an unlucky Crusade, which had ended, after a battle at Mansura, in two years' captivity among the Saracens at Cairo where men learn to walk softly. A fair huntsman and hawker, a reasonable disciplinarian, but a man of science above all, and a

Doctor of Medicine under one Ranulphus, Canon of St Paul's, his heart was more in the monastery's hospital work than its religious. He checked their list interestedly, adding items of his own. After the Infirmarian had withdrawn, he gave John generous absolution, to cover lapses by the way; for he did not hold with chance-bought Indulgences.

'And what seek you *this* journey?' he demanded, sitting on the bench beside the mortar and scales in the little warm cell for stored drugs.

'Devils, mostly,' said John, grinning.

'In Spain? Are not Abana and Pharpar – ?'

John, to whom men were but matter for drawings, and well-born to boot (since he was a de Sanford on his mother's side), looked the Abbot full in the face and – 'Did *you* find it so?' said he.

'No. They were in Cairo too. But what's your special need of 'em?'

'For my Great Luke. He's the master-hand of all Four when it comes to devils.'

'No wonder. He was a physician. You're not.'

'Heaven forbid! But I'm weary of our Church-pattern devils. They're only apes and goats and poultry conjoined. Good enough for plain red-and-black Hells and Judgement Days – but not for me.'

'What makes you so choice in them?'

'Because it stands to reason and Art that there are all musters of devils in Hell's dealings. Those Seven, for example, that were haled out of the Magdalene. They'd be she-devils – no kin at all to the beaked and horned and bearded devils-general.'

The Abbot laughed.

'And see again! The devil that came out of the dumb man. What use is snout or bill to *him*? He'd be faceless as a leper. Above all – God send I live to do it! – the devils that entered the Gadarene swine. They'd be – they'd be – I know not yet what they'd be, but they'd be surpassing devils. I'd have 'em diverse as the Saints themselves. But now, they're all one pattern, for wall, window, or picture-work.'

'Go on, John. You're deeper in this mystery than I.'

'Heaven forbid! But I say there's respect due to devils, damned tho' they be.'

'Dangerous doctrine.'

'My meaning is that if the shape of anything be worth man's thought to picture to man, it's worth his best thought.'

'That's safer. But I'm glad I've given you Absolution.'

'There's less risk for a craftsman who deals with the outside shapes of things – for Mother Church's glory.'

'Maybe so, but, John' – the Abbot's hand almost touched John's sleeve – 'tell me, now, is – is she Moorish or – or Hebrew?'

'She's mine,' John returned.

'Is that enough?'

'I have found it so.'

'Well – ah well! It's out of my jurisdiction, but – how do they look at it down yonder?'

'Oh, they drive nothing to a head in Spain – neither Church nor King, bless them! There's too many Moors and Jews to kill them all, and if they chased 'em away there'd be no trade nor farming. Trust me, in the Conquered Countries, from Seville to Granada, we live lovingly enough together – Spaniard, Moor, and Jew. Ye see, *we* ask no questions.'

'Yes – yes,' Stephen sighed. 'And always there's the hope she may be converted.'

'Oh yes, there's always hope.'

The Abbot went on into the hospital. It was an easy age before Rome tightened the screw as to clerical connections. If the lady were not too forward, or the son too much his father's beneficiary in ecclesiastical preferments and levies, a good deal was overlooked. But, as the Abbot had reason to recall, unions between Christian and Infidel led to sorrow. None the less, when John with mule, mails, and man, clattered off down the lane for Southampton and the sea, Stephen envied him.

He was back, twenty months later, in good hard case, and loaded down with fairings. A lump of richest lazuli, a bar of orange-hearted vermilion, and a small packet of dried beetles which make most glorious scarlet, for the Sub-Cantor. Besides that, a few cubes of milky marble, with yet a pink flush in them, which could be slaked and ground down to incomparable background-stuff. There were quite half the drugs that the Abbot and Thomas had demanded, and there was a long deep-red cornelian necklace for the Abbot's Lady – Anne of Norton. She received it graciously, and asked where John had come by it.

'Near Granada,' he said.

'You left all well there?' Anne asked. (Maybe the Abbot had told her something of John's confession.)

'I left all in the hands of God.'

'Ah me! How long since?'

'Four months less eleven days.'

'Were you – with her?'

'In my arms. Childbed.'

'And?'

'The boy too. There is nothing now.'

Anne of Norton caught her breath.

'I think you'll be glad of that,' she said after a while.

'Give me time, and maybe I'll compass it. But not now.'

'You have your handiwork and your art, and – John – remember there's no jealousy in the grave.'

'Ye-es! I have my Art, and Heaven knows I'm jealous of none.'

'Thank God for that at least,' said Anne of Norton, the always ailing woman who followed the Abbot with her sunk eyes. 'And be sure I shall treasure this' – she touched the beads – 'as long as I shall live.'

'I brought – trusted – it to you for that,' he replied, and took leave. When she told the Abbot how she had come by it, he said nothing, but as he and Thomas were storing the drugs that John handed over in the cell which backs on to the hospital kitchen-chimney, he observed, of a cake of dried poppy-juice: 'This has power to cut off all pain from a man's body.'

'I have seen it,' said John.

'But for pain of the soul there is, outside God's Grace, but one drug; and that is a man's craft, learning, or other helpful motion of his own mind.'

'That is coming to me, too,' was the answer.

John spent the next fair May day out in the woods with the monastery swineherd and all the porkers; and returned loaded with flowers and sprays of spring, to his own carefully kept place in the north bay of the Scriptorium. There, with his travelling sketch-books under his left elbow, he sunk himself past all recollections in his Great Luke.

Brother Martin, Senior Copyist (who spoke about once a fortnight), ventured to ask, later, how the work was going.

'All here!' John tapped his forehead with his pencil. 'It has been only waiting these months to – ah God! – be born. Are ye free of your plain-copying, Martin?'

Brother Martin nodded. It was his pride that John of Burgos turned to him, in spite of his seventy years, for really good page-work.

'Then see!' John laid out a new vellum – thin but flawless. 'There's no better than this sheet from here to Paris. Yes! Smell it if you choose. Wherefore – give me the compasses and I'll set it out for you – if ye make one letter lighter or darker than its next, I'll stick ye like a pig.'

'Never, John!' The old man beamed happily.

'But I will! Now, follow! Here and here, as I prick, and in script of just this height to the hair's-breadth, ye'll scribe the thirty-first and thirty-second verses of Eighth Luke.'

'Yes, the Gadarene Swine! *"And they besought him that he would not command them to go out into the abyss. And there was a herd of many swine"* ' – Brother Martin naturally knew all the Gospels by heart.

'Just so! Down to *"and he suffered them."* Take your time to it. My Magdalene has to come off my heart first.'

Brother Martin achieved the work so perfectly that John

stole some soft sweetmeats from the Abbot's kitchen for his reward. The old man ate them; then repented; then confessed and insisted on penance. At which, the Abbot, knowing there was but one way to reach the real sinner, set him a book called *De Virtutibus Herbarum* to fair-copy. St Illod's had borrowed it from the gloomy Cistercians, who do not hold with pretty things, and the crabbed text kept Martin busy just when John wanted him for some rather specially spaced letterings.

'See now,' said the Sub-Cantor improvingly. 'You should not do such things, John. Here's Brother Martin on penance for your sake –'

'No – for my Great Luke. But I've paid the Abbot's cook. I've drawn him till his own scullions cannot keep straight-faced. *He*'ll not tell again.'

'Unkindly done! And you're out of favour with the Abbot too. He's made no sign to you since you came back – never asked you to high table.'

'I've been busy. Having eyes in his head, Stephen knew it. Clement, there's no Librarian from Durham to Torre fit to clean up after you.'

The Sub-Cantor stood on guard; he knew where John's compliments generally ended.

'But outside the Scriptorium –'

'Where I never go.' The Sub-Cantor had been excused even digging in the garden, lest it should mar his wonderful book-binding hands.

'In all things outside the Scriptorium you are the master-fool of Christendie. Take it from me, Clement. I've met many.'

'I take everything from you,' Clement smiled benignly. 'You use me worse than a singing-boy.'

They could hear one of that suffering breed in the cloister below, squalling as the Cantor pulled his hair.

'God love you! So I do! But have you ever thought how I lie and steal daily on my travels – yes, and for aught you know, murder – to fetch you colours and earths?'

'True,' said just and conscience-stricken Clement. 'I have

often thought that were I in the world – which God forbid! –
I might be a strong thief in some matters.'

Even Brother Martin, bent above his loathed *De Virtutibus*, laughed.

But about mid-summer, Thomas the Infirmarian conveyed
to John the Abbot's invitation to supper in his house that
night, with the request that he would bring with him anything that he had done for his Great Luke.

'What's toward?' said John, who had been wholly shut up
in his work.

'Only one of his "wisdom" dinners. You've sat at a few
since you were a man.'

'True: and mostly good. How would Stephen have us – ?'

'Gown and hod over all. There will be a doctor from
Salerno – one Roger, an Italian. Wise and famous with the
knife on the body. He's been in the Infirmary some ten days,
helping me – even me!'

'Never heard the name. But our Stephen's *physicus*
before *sacerdos*, always.'

'And his Lady has a sickness of some time. Roger came
hither in chief because of her.'

'Did he? Now I think of it, I have not seen the Lady Anne
for a while.'

'Ye've seen nothing for a long while. She has been housed
near a month – they have to carry her abroad now.'

'So bad as that, then?'

'Roger of Salerno will not yet say what he thinks. But—'

'God pity Stephen! . . . Who else at table, besides thee?'

'An Oxford friar. Roger is his name also. A learned and
famous philosopher. And he holds his liquor too, valiantly.'

'Three doctors – counting Stephen. I've always found that
means two atheists.'

Thomas looked uneasily down his nose. 'That's a wicked
proverb,' he stammered. 'You should not use it.'

'Hoh! Never come you the monk over me, Thomas!
You've been Infirmarian at St Illod's eleven years – and a

lay-brother still. Why have you never taken orders, all this while?'

'I – I am not worthy.'

'Ten times worthier than that new fat swine – Henry Who's-his-name – that takes the Infirmary Masses. He bullocks in with the Viaticum, under your nose, when a sick man's only faint from being bled. So the man dies – of pure fear. Ye know it! I've watched your face at such times. Take Orders, Didymus. You'll have a little more medicine and a little less Mass with your sick then; and they'll live longer.'

'I am unworthy – unworthy,' Thomas repeated pitifully.

'Not you – but – to your own master you stand or fall. And now that my work releases me for awhile, I'll drink with any philosopher out of any school. And, Thomas,' he coaxed, 'a hot bath for me in the Infirmary before vespers.'

When the Abbot's perfectly cooked and served meal had ended, and the deep-fringed naperies were removed, and the Prior had sent in the keys with word that all was fast in the Monastery, and the keys had been duly returned with the word, 'Make it so till Prime,' the Abbot and his guests went out to cool themselves in an upper cloister that took them, by way of the leads, to the South Choir side of the Triforium. The summer sun was still strong, for it was barely six o'clock, but the Abbey Church, of course, lay in her wonted darkness. Lights were being lit for choir-practice thirty feet below.

'Our Cantor gives them no rest,' the Abbot whispered. 'Stand by this pillar and we'll hear what he's driving them at now.'

'Remember, all!' the Cantor's hard voice came up. 'This is the soul of Bernard himself, attacking our evil world. Take it quicker than yesterday, and throw all your words cleanbitten from you. In the loft there! Begin!'

The organ broke out for an instant, alone and raging. Then the voices crashed together into that first fierce line of the *'De Contemptu Mundi.'**

'*Hora novissima – tempora pessima*' – a dead pause till the

* Hymn No. 226, A. and M., 'The world is very evil.'

assenting *sunt* broke, like a sob, out of the darkness, and one boy's voice, clearer than silver trumpets, returned the long-drawn *vigilemus*.

'*Ecce minaciter, imminet Arbiter*' (organ and voices were leashed together in terror and warning, breaking away liquidly to the '*ille supremus*'). Then the tone-colours shifted for the prelude to – '*Imminet, imminet, ut mala terminet –*'

'Stop! Again!' cried the Cantor; and gave his reasons a little more roundly than was natural at choir-practice.

'Ah! Pity o' man's vanity! He's guessed we are here. Come away!' said the Abbot. Anne of Norton, in her carried chair, had been listening too, further along the dark Triforium, with Roger of Salerno. John heard her sob. On the way back, he asked Thomas how her health stood. Before Thomas could reply the sharp-featured Italian doctor pushed between them. 'Following on our talk together, I judged it best to tell her,' said he to Thomas.

'What?' John asked simply enough.

'What she knew already.' Roger of Salerno launched into a Greek quotation to the effect that every woman knows all about everything.

'I have no Greek,' said John stiffly. Roger of Salerno had been giving them a good deal of it, at dinner.

'Then I'll come to you in Latin. Ovid hath it neatly. "*Utque malum late solet immedicabile cancer –* " but doubtless you know the rest, worthy Sir.'

'Alas! My school-Latin's but what I've gathered by the way from fools professing to heal sick women. "*Hocus-pocus –* " but doubtless you know the rest, worthy Sir.'

Roger of Salerno was quite quiet till they regained the dining-room, where the fire had been comforted and the dates, raisins, ginger, figs, and cinnamon-scented sweetmeats set out, with the choicer wines, on the after-table. The Abbot seated himself, drew off his ring, dropped it, that all might hear the tinkle, into an empty silver cup, stretched his feet towards the hearth, and looked at the great gilt and carved rose in the barrel-roof. The silence that keeps from Com-

pline to Matins had closed on their world. The bull-necked
Friar watched a ray of sunlight split itself into colours on the
rim of a crystal salt-cellar; Roger of Salerno had re-opened
some discussion with Brother Thomas on a type of spotted
fever that was baffling them both in England and abroad;
John took note of the keen profile, and – it might serve as a
note for the Great Luke – his hand moved to his bosom. The
Abbot saw, and nodded permission. John whipped out silver-
point and sketch-book.

'Nay – modesty is good enough – but deliver your own
opinion,' the Italian was urging the Infirmarian. Out of
courtesy to the foreigner nearly all the talk was in table-
Latin; more formal and more copious than monk's patter.
Thomas began with his meek stammer.

'I confess myself at a loss for the cause of the fever unless –
as Varro saith in his *De Re Rustica* – certain small animals
which the eye cannot follow enter the body by the nose and
mouth, and set up grave diseases. On the other hand, this is
not in Scripture.'

Roger of Salerno hunched head and shoulders like an
angry cat. 'Always *that*!' he said, and John snatched down
the twist of the thin lips.

'Never at rest, John.' The Abbot smiled at the artist. 'You
should break off every two hours for prayers, as we do. St
Benedict was no fool. Two hours is all that a man can carry
the edge of his eye or hand.'

'For copyists – yes. Brother Martin is not sure after one
hour. But when a man's work takes him, he must go on till it
lets him go.'

'Yes, that is the Demon of Socrates,' the Friar from Oxford
rumbled above his cup.

'The doctrine leans towards presumption,' said the Abbot.
'Remember, "Shall mortal man be more just than his
Maker?"'

'There is no danger of justice'; the Friar spoke bitterly.
'But at least Man might be suffered to go forward in his
Art or his thought. Yet if Mother Church sees or hears
him move anyward, what says she? "No!" Always "No."'

'But if the little animals of Varro be invisible' – this was Roger of Salerno to Thomas – 'how are we any nearer to a cure?'

'By experiment' – the Friar wheeled round on them suddenly. 'By reason and experiment. The one is useless without the other. But Mother Church –'

'Ay!' Roger de Salerno dashed at the fresh bait like a pike. 'Listen, Sirs. Her bishops – our Princes – strew our roads in Italy with carcasses that they make for their pleasure or wrath. Beautiful corpses! Yet if I – if we doctors – so much as raise the skin of one of them to look at God's fabric beneath, what says Mother Church? "Sacrilege! Stick to your pigs and dogs, or you burn!"'

'And not Mother Church only!' the Friar chimed in. '*Every* way we are barred – barred by the words of some man, dead a thousand years, which are held final. Who is any son of Adam that his one say-so should close a door towards truth? I would not except even Peter Peregrinus, my own great teacher.'

'Nor I Paul of Aegina,' Roger of Salerno cried. 'Listen, Sirs! Here is a case to the very point. Apuleius affirmeth, if a man eat fasting of the juice of the cut-leaved buttercup – *sceleratus* we call it, which means 'rascally'' – this with a condescending nod towards John – 'his soul will leave his body laughing. Now this is the lie more dangerous than truth, since truth of a sort is in it.'

'He's away!' whispered the Abbot despairingly.

'For the juice of that herb, I know by experiment, burns, blisters, and wries the mouth. I know also the *rictus*, or pseudo-laughter, on the face of such as have perished by the strong poisons of herbs allied to this ranunculus. Certainly that spasm resembles laughter. It seems then, in my judgement, that Apuleius, having seen the body of one thus poisoned, went off at score and wrote that the man died laughing.'

'Neither staying to observe, nor to confirm observation by experiment,' added the Friar, frowning.

Stephen the Abbot cocked an eyebrow towards John.

'How think *you*?' said he.

'I'm no doctor,' John returned, 'but I'd say Apuleius in all these years might have been betrayed by his copyists. They take short-cuts to save 'emselves trouble. Put case that Apuleius wrote the soul *seems to* leave the body laughing, after this poison. There's not three copyists in five (*my* judgement) would not leave out the "seems to". For who'd question Apuleius? If it seemed so to him, so it must be. Otherwise any child knows cut-leaved buttercup.'

'Have you knowledge of herbs?' Roger of Salerno asked curtly.

'Only that, when I was a boy in convent, I've made tetters round my mouth and on my neck with buttercup-juice, to save going to prayer o' cold nights.'

'Ah!' said Roger. 'I profess no knowledge of tricks.' He turned aside, stiffly.

'No matter! Now for your own tricks, John,' the tactful Abbot broke in. 'You shall show the doctors your Magdalene and your Gadarene Swine and the devils.'

'Devils? Devils? *I* have produced devils by means of drugs; and have abolished them by the same means. Whether devils be external to mankind or immanent, I have not yet pronounced.' Roger of Salerno was still angry.

'Ye dare not,' snapped the Friar from Oxford. 'Mother Church makes Her own devils.'

'Not wholly! Our John has come back from Spain with brand-new ones.' Abbot Stephen took the vellum handed to him, and laid it tenderly on the table. They gathered to look. The Magdalene was drawn in palest, almost transparent, grisaille, against a raging, swaying background of woman-faced devils, each broke to and by her special sin, and each, one could see, frenziedly straining against the Power that compelled her.

'I've never seen the like of this grey shadowwork,' said the Abbot. 'How came you by it?'

'*Non nobis!* It came to me,' said John, not knowing he was a generation or so ahead of his time in the use of that medium.

'Why is she so pale?' the Friar demanded.

'Evil has all come out of her – she'd take any colour now.'

'Ay, like light through glass. *I* see.'

Roger of Salerno was looking in silence – his nose nearer and nearer the page. 'It is so,' he pronounced finally. 'Thus it is in epilepsy – mouth, eyes, and forehead – even to the droop of her wrist there. Every sign of it! She will need restoratives, that woman, and, afterwards, sleep natural. No poppy-juice, or she will vomit on her waking. And thereafter – but I am not in my Schools.' He drew himself up. 'Sir,' said he, 'you should be of Our calling. For, by the Snakes of Aesculapius, you *see!*'

The two struck hands as equals.

'And how think you of the Seven Devils?' the Abbot went on.

These melted into convoluted flower- or flame-like bodies, ranging in colour from phosphorescent green to the black purple of outworn iniquity, whose hearts could be traced beating through their substance. But, for sign of hope and the sane workings of life, to be regained, the deep border was of conventionalized spring flowers and birds, all crowned by a kingfisher in haste, atilt through a clump of yellow iris.

Roger of Salerno identified the herbs and spoke largely of their virtues.

'And now, the Gadarene Swine,' said Stephen. John laid the picture on the table.

Here were devils dishoused, in dread of being abolished to the Void, huddling and hurtling together to force lodgement by every opening into the brute bodies offered. Some of the swine fought the invasion, foaming and jerking; some were surrendering to it, sleepily, as to a luxurious back-scratching; others, wholly possessed, whirled off in bucking droves for the lake beneath. In one corner the freed man stretched out his limbs all restored to his control, and Our Lord, seated, looked at him as questioning what he would make of his deliverance.

'Devils indeed!' was the Friar's comment. 'But wholly a new sort.'

Some devils were mere lumps, with lobes and pro-tuberances — a hint of a fiend's face peering through jelly-like walls. And there was a family of impatient, globular devillings who had burst open the belly of their smirking parent, and were revolving desperately towards their prey. Others patterned themselves into rods, chains and ladders, single or conjoined, round the throat and jaws of a shrieking sow, from whose ear emerged the lashing, glassy tail of a devil that had made good his refuge. And there were granu-lated and conglomerate devils, mixed up with the foam and slaver where the attack was fiercest. Thence the eye carried on to the insanely active backs of the downward-racing swine, the swineherd's aghast face, and his dog's terror.

Said Roger of Salerno, 'I pronounce that these were be-gotten of drugs. They stand outside the rational mind.'

'Not these,' said Thomas the Infirmarian, who as a servant of the Monastery should have asked his Abbot's leave to speak. 'Not *these* – look! – in the bordure.'

The border to the picture was a diaper of irregular but balanced compartments or cellules, where sat, swam, or wel-tered, devils in blank, so to say – things as yet uninspired by Evil – indifferent, but lawlessly outside imagination. Their shapes resembled, again, ladders, chains, scourges, diamonds, aborted buds, or gravid phosphorescent globes – some well-nigh star-like.

Roger of Salerno compared them to the obsessions of a Churchman's mind.

'Malignant?' the Friar from Oxford questioned.

' "Count everything unknown for horrible," ' Roger quoted with scorn.

'Not I. But they are marvellous – marvellous. I think –'

The Friar drew back. Thomas edged in to see better, and half opened his mouth.

'Speak,' said Stephen, who had been watching him. 'We are all in a sort doctors here.'

'I would say then' – Thomas rushed at it as one putting out his life's belief at the stake – 'that these lower shapes in the bordure may not be so much hellish and malignant as models and patterns upon which John has tricked out and embellished his proper devils among the swine above there!'

'And that would signify?' said Roger of Salerno sharply.

'In my poor judgement, that he may have seen such shapes – without help of drugs.'

'Now who – *who*,' said John of Burgos, after a round and unregarded oath, 'has made thee so wise of a sudden, my Doubter?'

'I wise? God forbid! Only John, remember – one winter six years ago – the snow-flakes melting on your sleeve at the cookhouse-door. You showed me them through a little crystal, that made small things larger.'

'Yes. The Moors call such a glass the Eye of Allah,' John confirmed.

'You showed me them melting – six-sided. You called them, then, your patterns.'

'True. Snow-flakes melt six-sided. I have used them for diaper-work often.'

'Melting snow-flakes as seen through a glass? By art optical?' the Friar asked.

'Art optical? *I* have never heard!' Roger of Salerno cried.

'John,' said the Abbot of St Illod's commandingly, 'was it – is it so?'

'In some sort,' John replied, 'Thomas has the right of it. Those shapes in the bordure were my workshop-patterns for the devils above. In *my* craft, Salerno, we dare not drug. It kills hand and eye. My shapes are to be seen honestly, in nature.'

The Abbot drew a bowl of rose-water towards him. 'When I was prisoner with – with the Saracens after Mansura,' he began, turning up the fold of his long sleeve, 'there were certain magicians – physicians – who could show – ' he dipped his third finger delicately in the water – 'all the firmament of Hell, as it were, in – ' he shook off one drop from his polished nail on to the polished table – 'even such a supernaculum as this.'

'But it must be foul water – not clean,' said John.

'Show us then – all – all,' said Stephen. 'I would make sure – once more.' The Abbot's voice was official.

John drew from his bosom a stamped leather box, some six or eight inches long, wherein, bedded on faded velvet, lay what looked like silver-bound compasses of old box-wood, with a screw at the head which opened or closed the legs to minute fractions. The legs terminated, not in points, but spoon-shapedly, one spatula pierced with a metal-lined hole less than a quarter of an inch across, the other with a half-inch hole. Into this latter John, after carefully wiping with a silk rag, slipped a metal cylinder that carried glass or crystal, it seemed, at each end.

'Ah! Art optic!' said the Friar. 'But what is that beneath it?'

It was a small swivelling sheet of polished silver no bigger than a florin, which caught the light and concentrated it on the lesser hole. John adjusted it without the Friar's proffered help.

'And now to find a drop of water,' said he, picking up a small brush.

'Come to my upper cloister. The sun is on the leads still,' said the Abbot, rising.

They followed him there. Half-way along, a drip from a gutter had made a greenish puddle in a worn stone. Very carefully, John dropped a drop of it into the smaller hole of the compass-leg, and, steadying the apparatus on a coping, worked the screw in the compass-joint, screwed the cylinder, and swung the swivel of the mirror till he was satisfied.

'Good!' He peered through the thing. 'My Shapes are all here. Now look, Father! If they do not meet your eye at first, turn this nicked edge here, left- or right-handed.'

'I have not forgotten,' said the Abbot, taking his place. 'Yes! They are here – as they were in my time – my time past. There is no end to them, I was told.... There *is* no end!'

'The light will go. Oh, let me look! Suffer me to see, also!' the Friar pleaded, almost shouldering Stephen from the eyepiece. The Abbot gave way. His eyes were on time past. But the Friar, instead of looking, turned the apparatus in his capable hands.

'Nay, nay,' John interrupted, for the man was already fiddling at the screws. 'Let the Doctor see.'

Roger of Salerno looked, minute after minute. John saw his blue-veined cheek-bones turn white. He stepped back at last, as though stricken.

'It is a new world – a new world, and – Oh, God Unjust! – I am old!'

'And now Thomas,' Stephen ordered.

John manipulated the tube for the Infirmarian, whose hands shook, and he too looked long. 'It is Life,' he said presently in a breaking voice. 'No Hell! Life created and rejoicing – the work of the Creator. They live, even as I have dreamed. Then it was no sin for me to dream. No sin – O God – no sin!'

He flung himself on his knees and began hysterically the *Benedicite omnia Opera*.

'And now I will see how it is actuated,' said the Friar from Oxford, thrusting forward again.

'Bring it within. The place is all eyes and ears,' said Stephen.

They walked quietly back along the leads, three English counties laid out in evening sunshine around them; church upon church, monastery upon monastery, cell after cell, and the bulk of a vast cathedral moored on the edge of the banked shoals of sunset.

When they were at the after-table once more they sat down, all except the Friar, who went to the window and huddled bat-like over the thing. 'I see! I see!' he was repeating to himself.

'He'll not hurt it,' said John. But the Abbot, staring in front of him, like Roger of Salerno, did not hear. The Infirmarian's head was on the table between his shaking arms.

John reached for a cup of wine.

'It was shown to me,' the Abbot was speaking to himself,

'in Cairo, that man stands ever between two Infinities – of greatness and littleness. Therefore, there is no end – either to life – or –'

'And *I* stand on the edge of the grave,' snarled Roger of Salerno. 'Who pities *me*?'

'Hush!' said Thomas the Infirmarian. 'The little creatures shall be sanctified – sanctified to the service of His sick.'

'What need?' John of Burgos wiped his lips. 'It shows no more than the shapes of things. It gives good pictures. I had it at Granada. It was brought from the East, they told me.'

Roger of Salerno laughed with an old man's malice. 'What of Mother Church? Most Holy Mother Church? If it comes to Her ears that we have spied into Her Hell without Her leave, where do we stand?'

'At the stake,' said the Abbot of St Illod's, and, raising his voice a trifle, 'You hear that? Roger Bacon, heard you that?'

The Friar turned from the window, clutching the compasses tighter.

'No, no!' he appealed. 'Not with Falcodi – not with our English-hearted Foulkes made Pope. He's wise – he's learned. He reads what I have put forth. Foulkes would never suffer it.'

' "Holy Pope is one thing, Holy Church another," ' Roger quoted.

'But I – I can bear witness it is no Art Magic,' the Friar went on. 'Nothing is it, except Art optical – wisdom after trial and experiment, mark you. I can prove it, and – my name weighs with men who dare think.'

'Find them!' croaked Roger of Salerno. 'Five or six in all the world. That makes less than fifty pounds by weight of ashes at the stake. I have watched such men – reduced.'

'I will not give this up!' The Friar's voice cracked in passion and despair. 'It would be to sin against the Light.'

'No, no! Let us – let us sanctify the little animals of Varro,' said Thomas.

Stephen leaned forward, fished his ring out of the cup, and

frame it. Our John here returns from the Moors, and shows us a hell of devils contending in the compass of one drop of water. Magic past clearance! You can hear the faggots crackle.'

'But thou knowest! Thou hast seen it all before! For man's poor sake! For old friendship's sake – Stephen!' The Friar was trying to stuff the compasses into his bosom as he appealed.

'What Stephen de Sautré knows, you his friends know also. I would have you, now, obey the Abbot of St Illod's. Give to me!' He held out his ringed hand.

'May I – may John here – not even make a drawing of one – one screw?' said the broken Friar, in spite of himself.

'Nowise!' Stephen took it over. 'Your dagger, John. Sheathed will serve.'

He unscrewed the metal cylinder, laid it on the table, and with the dagger's hilt smashed some crystal to sparkling dust which he swept into a scooped hand and cast behind the hearth.

'It would seem,' said he, 'the choice lies between two sins. To deny the world a Light which is under our hand, or to enlighten the world before her time. What you have seen, I saw long since among the physicians at Cairo. And I know what doctrine they drew from it. Hast *thou* dreamed, Thomas? I also – with fuller knowledge. But this birth, my sons, is untimely. It will be but the mother of more death, more torture, more division, and greater darkness in this dark age. Therefore I, who know both my world and the Church, take this Choice on my conscience. Go! It is finished.'

He thrust the wooden part of the compasses deep among the beech logs till all was burned.

slipped it on his finger. 'My sons,' said he, 'we have seen what we have seen.'

'That it is no magic but simple Art,' the Friar persisted.

' 'Avails nothing. In the eyes of Mother Church we have seen more than is permitted to man.'

'But it was Life – created and rejoicing,' said Thomas.

'To look into Hell as we shall be judged – as we shall be proved – to have looked, is for priests only.'

'Or green-sick virgins on the road to sainthood who, for cause any midwife could give you –'

The Abbot's half-lifted hand checked Roger of Salerno's outpouring.

'Nor may even priests see more in Hell than Church knows to be there. John, there is respect due to Church as well as to Devils.'

'My trade's the outside of things,' said John quietly. 'I have my patterns.'

'But you may need to look again for more,' the Friar said.

'In my craft, a thing done is done with. We go on to new shapes after that.'

'And if we trespass beyond bounds, even in thought, we lie open to the judgement of the Church,' the Abbot continued.

'But thou knowest – *knowest!*' Roger of Salerno had returned to the attack. 'Here's all the world in darkness concerning the causes of things – from the fever across the lane to thy Lady's – thine own Lady's – eating malady. Think!'

'I have thought upon it, Salerno! I have thought indeed.'

Thomas the Infirmarian lifted his head again; and this time he did not stammer at all. 'As in the water, so in the blood must they rage and war with each other! I have dreamed these ten years – I thought it was a sin – but my dreams and Varro's are true! Think on it again! Here's the Light under our very hand!'

'Quench it! You'd no more stand to roasting than – any other. I'll give you the case as Church – as I myself – would

The Gardener

(1926)

One grave to me was given,
  One watch till Judgement Day;
And God looked down from Heaven
  And rolled the stone away.

One day in all the years,
  One hour in that one day,
His Angel saw my tears,
  And rolled the stone away!

EVERYONE in the village knew that Helen Turrell did her
duty by all her world, and by none more honourably than by
her only brother's unfortunate child. The village knew, too,
that George Turrell had tried his family severely since early
youth, and were not surprised to be told that, after many
fresh starts given and thrown away, he, an Inspector of
Indian Police, had entangled himself with the daughter of a
retired non-commissioned officer, and had died of a fall from
a horse a few weeks before his child was born. Mercifully,
George's father and mother were both dead, and though
Helen, thirty-five and independent, might well have washed
her hands of the whole disgraceful affair, she most nobly
took charge, though she was, at the time, under threat of
lung trouble which had driven her to the South of France.
She arranged for the passage of the child and a nurse from
Bombay, met them at Marseilles, nursed the baby through
an attack of infantile dysentery due to the carelessness of the
nurse, whom she had had to dismiss, and at last, thin and
worn but triumphant, brought the boy late in the autumn,
wholly restored, to her Hampshire home.

All these details were public property, for Helen was as
open as the day, and held that scandals are only increased by
hushing them up. She admitted that George had always been
rather a black sheep, but things might have been much
worse if the mother had insisted on her right to keep the boy.

Luckily, it seemed that people of that class would do almost anything for money, and, as George had always turned to her in his scrapes, she felt herself justified – her friends agreed with her – in cutting the whole non-commissioned officer connection, and giving the child every advantage. A christening, by the Rector, under the name of Michael, was the first step. So far as she knew herself, she was not, she said, a child-lover, but, for all his faults, she had been very fond of George, and she pointed out that little Michael had his father's mouth to a line; which made something to build upon.

As a matter of fact, it was the Turrell forehead, broad, low, and well-shaped, with the widely spaced eyes beneath it, that Michael had most faithfully reproduced. His mouth was somewhat better cut than the family type. But Helen, who would concede nothing good to his mother's side, vowed he was a Turrell all over, and, there being no one to contradict, the likeness was established.

In a few years Michael took his place, as accepted as Helen had always been – fearless, philosophical, and fairly good-looking. At six, he wished to know why he could not call her 'Mummy,' as other boys called their mothers. She explained that she was only his auntie, and that aunties were not quite the same as mummies, but that, if it gave him pleasure, he might call her 'Mummy' at bedtime, for a pet-name between themselves.

Michael kept his secret most loyally, but Helen, as usual, explained the fact to her friends; which when Michael heard, he raged.

'Why did you tell? *Why* did you tell?' came at the end of the storm.

'Because it's always best to tell the truth,' Helen answered, her arm round him as he shook in his cot.

'All right, but when the troof's ugly I don't think it's nice.'

'Don't you, dear?'

'No, I don't, and' – she felt the small body stiffen – 'now you've told, I won't call you "Mummy" any more – not even at bedtimes.'

'But isn't that rather unkind?' said Helen softly.

'I don't care! I don't care! You've hurted me in my insides and I'll hurt you back. I'll hurt you as long as I live!'

'Don't, oh, don't talk like that, dear! You don't know what –'

'I will! And when I'm dead I'll hurt you worse!'

'Thank goodness, I shall be dead long before you, darling.'

'Huh! Emma says, " 'Never know your luck." ' (Michael had been talking to Helen's elderly, flat-faced maid.) 'Lots of little boys die quite soon. So'll I. *Then* you'll see!'

Helen caught her breath and moved towards the door, but the wail of 'Mummy! Mummy!' drew her back again, and the two wept together.

At ten years old, after two terms at a prep. school, something or somebody gave him the idea that his civil status was not quite regular. He attacked Helen on the subject, breaking down her stammered defences with the family directness.

' 'Don't believe a word of it,' he said, cheerily, at the end. 'People wouldn't have talked like they did if my people had been married. But don't you bother, Auntie. I've found out all about my sort in English Hist'ry and the Shakespeare bits. There was William the Conqueror to begin with, and – oh, heaps more, and they all got on first-rate. 'Twon't make any difference to you, my being *that* – will it?'

'As if anything could –' she began.

'All right. We won't talk about it any more if it makes you cry.' He never mentioned the thing again of his own will, but when, two years later, he skilfully managed to have measles in the holidays, as his temperature went up to the appointed one hundred and four he muttered of nothing else, till Helen's voice, piercing at last his delirium, reached him with assurance that nothing on earth or beyond could make any difference between them.

The terms at his public school and the wonderful Christmas, Easter, and Summer holidays followed each other, variegated and glorious as jewels on a string; and as jewels Helen treasured them. In due time Michael developed his own interests, which ran their courses and gave way to others; but his interest in Helen was constant and increasing throughout. She repaid it with all that she had of affection or could command of counsel and money; and since Michael was no fool, the War took him just before what was like to have been a most promising career.

He was to have gone up to Oxford, with a scholarship, in October. At the end of August he was on the edge of joining the first holocaust of public-school boys who threw themselves into the Line; but the captain of his O.T.C., where he had been sergeant for nearly a year, headed him off and steered him directly to a commission in a battalion so new that half of it still wore the old Army red, and the other half was breeding meningitis through living overcrowdedly in damp tents. Helen had been shocked at the idea of direct enlistment.

'But it's in the family,' Michael laughed.

'You don't mean to tell me that you believed that old story all this time?' said Helen. (Emma, her maid, had been dead now several years.) 'I gave you my word of honour – and I give it again – that – that it's all right. It is indeed.'

'Oh, *that* doesn't worry me. It never did,' he replied valiantly. 'What I meant was, I should have got into the show earlier if I'd enlisted – like my grandfather.'

'Don't talk like that! Are you afraid of its ending so soon, then?'

'No such luck. You know what K. says.'

'Yes. But my banker told me last Monday it couldn't *possibly* last beyond Christmas – for financial reasons.'

' 'Hope he's right, but our Colonel – and he's a Regular – says it's going to be a long job.'

Michael's battalion was fortunate in that, by some chance which meant several 'leaves', it was used for coast-defence among shallow trenches on the Norfolk coast; thence sent north to watch the mouth of a Scotch estuary, and, lastly, held for weeks on a baseless rumour of distant service. But, the very day that Michael was to have met Helen for four whole hours at a railway junction up the line, it was hurled out, to help make good the wastage of Loos, and he had only just time to send her a wire of farewell.

In France luck again helped the battalion. It was put down near the Salient, where it led a meritorious and unexacting life, while the Somme was being manufactured; and enjoyed the peace of the Armentieres and Laventie sectors when that battle began. Finding that it had sound views on protecting its own flanks and could dig, a prudent Commander stole it out of its own Division, under pretence of helping to lay telegraphs, and used it round Ypres at large.

A month later, and just after Michael had written Helen that there was nothing special doing and therefore no need to worry, a shell-splinter dropping out of a wet dawn killed him at once. The next shell uprooted and laid down over the body what had been the foundation of a barn wall, so neatly that none but an expert would have guessed that anything unpleasant had happened.

By this time the village was old in experience of war, and, English fashion, had evolved a ritual to meet it. When the postmistress handed her seven-year-old daughter the official telegram to take to Miss Turrell, she observed to the Rector's gardener: 'It's Miss Helen's turn now.' He replied, thinking of his own son: 'Well, he's lasted longer than some.' The child herself came to the front door weeping aloud, because Master Michael had often given her sweets. Helen, presently, found herself pulling down the house-blinds one after one with great care, and saying earnestly to each: 'Missing *always* means dead.' Then she took her place in the dreary procession that was impelled to go through an inevitable series of unprofitable emotions. The Rector, of course, preached hope and prophesied word, very soon, from a prison camp. Several friends, too, told her perfectly truthful tales, but always about other women, to whom, after months and months of silence, their missing had been miraculously restored. Other people urged her to communicate with infallible Secretaries of organizations who could communicate

with benevolent neutrals, who could extract accurate information from the most secretive of Hun prison com-
mandants. Helen did and wrote and signed everything that
was suggested or put before her.

Once, on one of Michael's leaves, he had taken her over a
munition factory, where she saw the progress of a shell from
blank-iron to the all but finished article. It struck her at the
time that the wretched thing was never left alone for a single
second; and 'I'm being manufactured into a bereaved next of
kin,' she told herself, as she prepared her documents.

In due course, when all the organizations had deeply or
sincerely regretted their inability to trace, etc., something
gave way within her and all sensation – save of thankfulness
for the release – came to an end in blessed passivity. Michael
had died and her world had stood still and she had been one
with the full shock of that arrest. Now she was standing still
and the world was going forward, but it did not concern her –
in no way or relation did it touch her. She knew this by the
ease with which she could slip Michael's name into talk and
incline her head to the proper angle, at the proper murmur
of sympathy.

In the blessed realization of that relief, the Armistice with
all its bells broke over her and passed unheeded. At the end
of another year she had overcome her physical loathing of
the living and returned young, so that she could take them
by the hand and almost sincerely wish them well. She had no
interest in any aftermath, national or personal, of the war,
but, moving at an immense distance, she sat on various relief
committees and held strong views – she heard herself delivering them – about the site of the proposed village War
Memorial.

Then there came to her, as next of kin, an official inti-
mation, backed by a page of a letter to her in indelible pencil,
a silver identity-disc, and a watch, to the effect that the body
of Lieutenant Michael Turrell had been found, identified,
and re-interred in Hagenzeele Third Military Cemetery –
the letter of the row and the grave's number in that row duly
given.

So Helen found herself moved on to another process of the manufacture – to a world full of exultant or broken relatives, now strong in the certainty that there was an altar upon earth where they might lay their love. These soon told her, and by means of time-tables made clear, how easy it was and how little it interfered with life's affairs to go and see one's grave.

'*So* different,' as the Rector's wife said, 'if he'd been killed in Mesopotamia, or even Gallipoli.'

The agony of being waked up to some sort of second life drove Helen across the Channel, where, in a new world of abbreviated titles, she learnt that Hagenzeele Third could be comfortably reached by an afternoon train which fitted in with the morning boat, and that there was a comfortable little hotel not three kilometres from Hagenzeele itself, where one could spend quite a comfortable night and see one's grave next morning. All this she had from a Central Authority who lived in a board and tar-paper shed on the skirts of a razed city full of whirling lime-dust and blown papers.

'By the way,' said he, 'you know your grave, of course?'

'Yes, thank you,' said Helen, and showed its row and number typed on Michael's own little typewriter. The officer would have checked it, out of one of his many books; but a large Lancashire woman thrust between them and bade him tell her where she might find her son, who had been corporal in the A.S.C. His proper name, she sobbed, was Anderson, but, coming of respectable folk, he had of course enlisted under the name of Smith; and had been killed at Dickiebush, in early 'Fifteen. She had not his number nor did she know which of his two Christian names he might have used with his alias; but her Cook's tourist ticket expired at the end of Easter week, and if by then she could not find her child she should go mad. Whereupon she fell forward on Helen's breast; but the officer's wife came out quickly from a little bedroom behind the office, and the three of them lifted the woman on to the cot.

'They are often like this,' said the officer's wife, loosening the tight bonnet-strings. 'Yesterday she said he'd been killed at Hooge. Are you sure you know your grave? It makes such a difference.'

'Yes, thank you,' said Helen, and hurried out before the woman on the bed should begin to lament again.

Tea in a crowded mauve and blue striped wooden structure, with a false front, carried her still further into the nightmare. She paid her bill beside a stolid, plain-featured Englishwoman, who, hearing her inquire about the train to Hagenzeele, volunteered to come with her.

'I'm going to Hagenzeele myself,' she explained. 'Not to Hagenzeele Third; mine is Sugar Factory, but they call it La Rosière now. It's just south of Hagenzeele Three. Have you got your room at the hotel there?'

'Oh yes, thank you. I've wired.'

'That's better. Sometimes the place is quite full, and at others there's hardly a soul. But they've put bathrooms into the old Lion d'Or – that's the hotel on the west side of Sugar Factory – and it draws off a lot of people, luckily.'

'It's all new to me. This is the first time I've been over.'

'Indeed! This is my ninth time since the Armistice. Not on my own account. *I* haven't lost anyone, thank God – but, like everyone else, I've a lot of friends at home who have. Coming over as often as I do, I find it helps them to have someone just look at the – the place and tell them about it afterwards. And one can take photos for them, too. I get quite a list of commissions to execute.' She laughed nervously and tapped her slung Kodak. 'There are two or three to see at Sugar Factory this time, and plenty of others in the cemeteries all about. My system is to save them up, and arrange them, you know. And when I've got enough commissions for one area to make it worth while, I pop over and execute them. It *does* comfort people.'

'I suppose so,' Helen answered, shivering as they entered the little train.

'Of course it does. (Isn't it lucky we've got window-seats?) It must do or they wouldn't ask one to do it, would they? I've a list of quite twelve or fifteen commissions here' – she tapped the Kodak again – 'I must sort them out tonight. Oh, I forgot to ask you. What's yours?'

'My nephew,' said Helen. 'But I was very fond of him.'

'Ah, yes! I sometimes wonder whether *they* know after death? What do you think?'

'Oh, I don't – I haven't dared to think much about that sort of thing,' said Helen, almost lifting her hands to keep her off.

'Perhaps that's better,' the woman answered. 'The sense of loss must be enough, I expect. Well, I won't worry you any more.'

Helen was grateful, but when they reached the hotel Mrs Scarsworth (they had exchanged names) insisted on dining at the same table with her, and after the meal, in the little, hideous salon full of low-voiced relatives, took Helen through her 'commissions' with biographies of the dead, where she happened to know them, and sketches of their next of kin. Helen endured till nearly half past nine, ere she fled to her room.

Almost at once there was a knock at her door and Mrs Scarsworth entered; her hands, holding the dreadful list, clasped before her.

'Yes – yes – *I* know,' she began. 'You're sick of me, but I want to tell you something. You – you aren't married, are you? Then perhaps you won't. . . . But it doesn't matter. I've *got* to tell some one. I can't go on any longer like this.'

'But please – ' Mrs Scarsworth had backed against the shut door, and her mouth worked dryly.

'In a minute,' she said. 'You – you know about these graves of mine I was telling you about downstairs, just now? They really *are* commissions. At least several of them are.' Her eye wandered round the room. 'What extraordinary wall-papers they have in Belgium, don't you think? . . . Yes. I swear they are commissions. But there's *one*, d'you see, and – and he was more to me than anything else in the world. Do you understand?'

Helen nodded.

'More than any one else. And, of course, he oughtn't to have been. He ought to have been nothing to me. But he *was*. He *is*. That's why I do the commissions you see. That's all.'

'But why do you tell me?' Helen asked desperately.

'Because I'm *so* tired of lying. Tired of lying – always lying – year in and year out. When I don't tell lies I've got to act 'em and I've got to think 'em, always. *You* don't know what that means. He was everything to me that he oughtn't to have been – the one real thing – the only thing that ever happened to me in all my life; and I've had to pretend he wasn't. I've had to watch every word I said, and think out what lie I'd tell next, for years and years!'

"How many years?' Helen asked.

'Six years and four months before, and two and three-quarters after. I've gone to him eight times, since. Tomorrow'll make the ninth, and – and I can't – I *can't* go to him again with nobody in the world knowing. I want to be honest with some one before I go. Do you understand? It doesn't matter about *me*. I was never truthful, even as a girl. But it isn't worthy of *him*. So – so I – I had to tell you. I can't keep it up any longer. Oh, I can't!'

She lifted her joined hands almost to the level of her mouth, and brought them down sharply, still joined, to full arms' length below her waist. Helen reached forward, caught them, bowed her head over them, and murmured: 'Oh, my dear! My dear!' Mrs Scarsworth stepped back, her face all mottled.

'My God!' said she. 'Is *that* how you take it?'

Helen could not speak, and the woman went out; but it was a long while before Helen was able to sleep.

Next morning Mrs Scarsworth left early on her round of commissions, and Helen walked alone to Hagenzeele Third. The place was still in the making, and stood some five or six feet above the metalled road, which it flanked for hundreds of yards. Culverts across a deep ditch served for entrances through the unfinished boundary wall. She climbed a few wooden-faced earthen steps and then met the entire crowded level of the thing in one held breath. She did not know that Hagenzeele Third counted twenty-one thousand dead already. All she saw was a merciless sea of black crosses, bearing little strips of stamped tin at all angles across their faces. She could distinguish no order or arrangement in their mass; nothing but a waist-high wilderness as of weeds stricken dead, rushing at her. She went forward, moved to the left and the right hopelessly, wondering by what guidance she should ever come to her own. A great distance away there was a line of whiteness. It proved to be a block of some two or three hundred graves whose headstones had already been set, whose flowers were planted out, and whose new-sown grass showed green. Here she could see clear-cut letters at the ends of the rows, and, referring to her slip, realized that it was not here she must look.

A man knelt behind a line of headstones – evidently a gardener, for he was firming a young plant in the soft earth. She went towards him, her paper in her hand. He rose at her approach and without prelude or salutation asked: 'Who are you looking for?'

'Lieutenant Michael Turrell – my nephew,' said Helen slowly and word for word, as she had many thousands of times in her life.

The man lifted his eyes and looked at her with infinite compassion before he turned from the fresh-sown grass towards the naked black crosses.

'Come with me,' he said, 'and I will show you where your son lies.'

When Helen left the Cemetery she turned for a last look. In the distance she saw the man bending over his young plants; and she went away, supposing him to be the gardener.

Dayspring Mishandled

(1928)

C'est moi, c'est moi, c'est moi!
Je suis la Mandragore!
La fille des beaux jours qui s'éveille à l'aurore –
Et qui chante pour toi!

C. NODIER

In the days beyond compare and before the Judgements, a
genius called Graydon foresaw that the advance of education
and the standard of living would submerge all mind-marks in
one mudrush of standardized reading-matter, and so created
the Fictional Supply Syndicate to meet the demand.

Since a few days' work for him brought them more money
than a week's elsewhere, he drew many young men – some
now eminent – into his employ. He bade them keep their
eyes on the Sixpenny Dream Book, the Army and Navy
Stores Catalogue (this for backgrounds and furniture as they
changed), and *The Hearthstone Friend*, a weekly publication
which specialized unrivalledly in the domestic emotions. Yet,
even so, youth would not be denied, and some of the collaborated love-talk in 'Passion Hath Peril,' and 'Ena's Lost
Lovers,' and the account of the murder of the Earl in 'The
Wickwire Tragedies' – to name but a few masterpieces now
never mentioned for fear of blackmail – was as good as anything to which their authors signed their real names in more
distinguished years.

Among the young ravens driven to roost awhile on Graydon's ark was James Andrew Manallace – a darkish, slow
northerner of the type that does not ignite, but must be de-
tonated. Given written or verbal outlines of a plot, he was
useless; but, with a half-dozen pictures round which to write
his tale, he could astonish.

And he adored that woman who afterwards became the
mother of Vidal Benzaquen,* and who suffered and died be-

* 'The Village that voted the Earth was Flat.' *A Diversity of Creatures.*

cause she loved one unworthy. There was, also, among the company a mannered, bellied person called Alured Castorley, who talked and wrote about 'Bohemia', but was always afraid of being 'compromised' by the weekly suppers at Neminaka's Café in Hestern Square, where the Syndicate work was apportioned, and where everyone looked out for himself. He, too, for a time, had loved Vidal's mother, in his own way.

Now, one Saturday at Neminaka's, Graydon, who had given Manallace a sheaf of prints – torn from an extinct children's book called *Philippa's Queen* – on which to improvise, asked for results. Manallace went down into his ulster-pocket, hesitated a moment, and said the stuff had turned into poetry on his hands.

'Bosh!'

'That's what it isn't,' the boy retorted. 'It's rather good.'

'Then it's no use to us.' Graydon laughed. 'Have you brought back the cuts?'

Manallace handed them over. There was a castle in the series; a knight or so in armour; an old lady in a horned head-dress; a young ditto; a very obvious Hebrew; a clerk, with pen and inkhorn, checking wine-barrels on a wharf; and a Crusader. On the back of one of the prints was a note, 'If he doesn't want to go, why can't he be captured and held to ransom?' Graydon asked what it all meant.

'I don't know yet. A comic opera, perhaps,' said Manallace.

Graydon, who seldom wasted time, passed the cuts on to someone else, and advanced Manallace a couple of sovereigns to carry on with, as usual; at which Castorley was angry and would have said something unpleasant but was suppressed. Half-way through supper, Castorley told the company that a relative had died and left him an independence; and that he now withdrew from 'hackwork' to follow 'Literature.' Generally, the Syndicate rejoiced in a comrade's good fortune, but Castorley had gifts of waking dislike. So the news was received with a vote of thanks, and he went out before the end, and, it was said, proposed to 'Dal

Benzaquen's mother, who refused him. He did not come back. Manallace, who had arrived a little exalted, got so drunk before midnight that a man had to stay and see him home. But liquor never touched him above the belt, and when he had slept awhile, he recited to the gas-chandelier the poetry he had made out of the pictures; said that, on second thoughts, he would convert it into comic opera; deplored the Upas-tree influence of Gilbert and Sullivan; sang somewhat to illustrate his point; and – after words, by the way, with a negress in yellow satin – was steered to his rooms.

In the course of a few years, Graydon's foresight and genius were rewarded. The public began to read and reason upon higher planes, and the Syndicate grew rich. Later still, people demanded of their printed matter what they expected in their clothing and furniture. So, precisely as the three guinea hand-bag is followed in three weeks by its thirteen and sevenpence ha'penny, indistinguishable sister, they enjoyed perfect synthetic substitutes for Plot, Sentiment, and Emotion. Graydon died before the Cinema-caption school came in, but he left his widow twenty-seven thousand pounds.

Manallace made a reputation, and, more important, money for Vidal's mother when her husband ran away and the first symptoms of her paralysis showed. His line was the jocundly-sentimental Wardour Street brand of adventure, told in a style that exactly met, but never exceeded, every expectation.

As he once said when urged to 'write a real book': 'I've got my label, and I'm not going to chew it off. If you save people thinking, you can do anything with 'em.' His output apart, he was genuinely a man of letters. He rented a small cottage in the country and economized on everything, except the care and charges of Vidal's mother.

Castorley flew higher. When his legacy freed him from 'hackwork,' he became first a critic – in which calling he loyally scalped all his old associates as they came up – and then looked for some speciality. Having found it (Chaucer was the prey), he consolidated his position before he occupied it, by his careful speech, his cultivated bearing, and the whispered words of his friends whom he, too, had saved the trouble of thinking. It followed that, when he published his first serious articles on Chaucer, all the world which is interested in Chaucer said: 'This is an authority.' But he was no impostor. He learned and knew his poet and his age; and in a month-long dog-fight in an austere literary weekly, met and mangled a recognized Chaucer expert of the day. He also, 'for old sake's sake,' as he wrote to a friend, went out of his way to review one of Manallace's books with an intimacy of unclean deduction (this was before the days of Freud) which long stood as a record. Some member of the extinct Syndicate took occasion to ask him if he would – for old sake's sake – help Vidal's mother to a new treatment. He answered that he had 'known the lady very slightly and the calls on his purse were so heavy that,' etc. The writer showed the letter to Manallace, who said he was glad Castorley hadn't interfered. Vidal's mother was then wholly paralysed. Only her eyes could move, and those always looked for the husband who had left her. She died thus is Manallace's arms in April of the first year of the War.

During the War he and Castorley worked as some sort of departmental dishwashers in the Office of Co-ordinated Supervisals. Here Manallace came to know Castorley again. Castorley, having a sweet tooth, cadged lumps of sugar for his tea from a typist, and when she took to giving them to a younger man, arranged that she should be reported for smoking in unauthorized apartments. Manallace possessed himself of every detail of the affair, as compensation for the review of his book. Then there came a night when, waiting for a big air-raid, the two men had talked humanly, and Manallace spoke of Vidal's mother. Castorley said something in reply, and from that hour – as was learned several years later – Manallace's real life-work and interests began.

The War over, Castorley set about to make himself Supreme Pontiff on Chaucer by methods not far removed from the employment of poison-gas. The English Pope was silent, through private griefs, and influenza had carried off the learned Hun who claimed continental allegiance. Thus Castorley crowed unchallenged from Upsala to Seville, while Manallace went back to his cottage with the photo of Vidal's mother over the mantelpiece. She seemed to have emptied out his life, and left him only fleeting interests in trifles. His private diversions were experiments of uncertain outcome, which, he said, rested him after a day's gadzooking and vital-stapping. I found him, for instance, one weekend, in his toolshed-scullery, boiling a brew of slimy barks which were, if mixed with oak-galls, vitriol and wine, to become an ink-powder. We boiled it till the Monday, and it turned into an adhesive stronger than birdlime, and entangled us both.

At other times, he would carry me off, once in a few weeks, to sit at Castorley's feet, and hear him talk about Chaucer. Castorley's voice, bad enough in youth, when it could be shouted down, had, with culture and tact, grown almost insupportable. His mannerisms, too, had multiplied and set. He minced and mouthed, postured and chewed his words throughout those terrible evenings; and poisoned not only Chaucer, but every shred of English literature which he used to embellish him. He was shameless, too, as regarded self-advertisement and 'recognition' – weaving elaborate intrigues; forming petty friendships and confederacies, to be dissolved next week in favour of more promising alliances; fawning, snubbing, lecturing, organizing and lying as unrestingly as a politician, in chase of the Knighthood due not to him (he always called on his Maker to forbid such a thought) but as tribute to Chaucer. Yet, sometimes, he could break from his obsession and prove how a man's work will try to save the soul of him. He would tell us charmingly of copyists of the fifteenth century in England and the Low Countries, who had multiplied the Chaucer MSS., of which there remained – he gave us the exact number – and how each scribe could by him (and, he implied, by him alone) be distinguished from every other by some peculiarity of letter-formation, spacing or like trick of pen-work; and how he could fix the dates of their work within five years. Sometimes he would give us an hour of really interesting stuff and then return to his overdue 'recognition'. The changes sickened me, but Manallace defended him, as a master in his own line who had revealed Chaucer to at least one grateful soul.

This, as far as I remembered, was the autumn when Manallace holidayed in the Shetlands or the Faroes, and came back with a stone 'quern' – a hand corn-grinder. He said it interested him from the ethnological standpoint. His whim lasted till next harvest, and was followed by a religious spasm which, naturally, translated itself into literature. He showed me a battered and mutilated Vulgate of 1485, patched up the back with bits of legal parchments, which he had bought for thirty-five shillings. Some monk's attempt to rubricate chapter-initials had caught, it seemed, his forlorn fancy, and he dabbled in shells of gold and silver paint for weeks.

That also faded out, and he went to the Continent to get local colour for a love-story, about Alva and the Dutch, and the next year I saw practically nothing of him. This released me from seeing much of Castorley, but, at intervals, I would go there to dine with him, when his wife – an unappetizing, ash-coloured woman – made no secret that his friends wearied her almost as much as he did. But at a later meeting, not long after Manallace had finished his Low Countries' novel, I found Castorley charged to bursting-point with triumph and high information hardly withheld. He confided to me that a time was at hand when great matters would be made plain, and 'recognition' would be inevitable. I assumed, naturally, that there was fresh scandal or heresy afoot in Chaucer circles, and kept my curiosity within bounds.

In time, New York cabled that a fragment of a hitherto unknown Canterbury Tale lay safe in the steel-walled vaults of the seven-million-dollar Sunnapia Collection. It was news on an international scale – the New World exultant – the Old deploring the 'burden of British taxation which drove such treasures, etc.,' and the lighter-minded journals disporting themselves according to their publics; for 'our Dan,' as one earnest Sunday editor observed, 'lies closer to the national

heart than we wot of.' Common decency made me call on
Castorley, who, to my surprise, had not yet descended into
the arena. I found him, made young again by joy, deep in
just-passed proofs.

Yes, he said, it was all true. He had, of course, been in it
from the first. There had been found one hundred and seven
new lines of Chaucer tacked on to an abridged end of *The
Persone's Tale*, the whole the work of Abraham Mentzius,
better known as Mentzel of Antwerp (1388–1438/9) – I might
remember he had talked about him – whose distinguishing
peculiarities were a certain Byzantine formation of his g's,
the use of a 'sickle-slanted' reed-pen, which cut into the
vellum at certain letters; and, above all, a tendency to spell
English words on Dutch lines, whereof the manuscript carried one convincing proof. For instance (he wrote it out for
me), a girl praying against an undesired marriage, says:

> 'Ah Jesu-Moder, pitie my oe peyne.
> Daiespringe mishandeelt cometh nat agayne'.

Would I, please, note the spelling of 'mishandeelt'? Stark
Dutch and Mentzel's besetting sin! But in *his* position one
took nothing for granted. The page had been part of the
stiffening of the side of an old Bible, bought in a parcel by
Dredd, the big dealer, because it had some rubricated chapter-initials, and by Dredd shipped, with a consignment of
similar odds and ends, to the Sunnapia Collection, where
they were making a glass-cased exhibit of the whole history
of illumination and did not care how many books they
gutted for that purpose. There, someone who noticed a crack
in the back of the volume had unearthed it. He went on:
'They didn't know what to make of the thing at first. But
they knew about *me*! They kept quiet till I'd been consulted.
You might have noticed I was out of England for three
months.

'I was over there, of course. It was what is called a "spoil" –
a page Mentzel had spoiled with his Dutch spelling – I
expect he had had the English dictated to him – then had
evidently used the vellum for trying out his reeds; and then,

I suppose, had put it away. The "spoil" had been doubled,
pasted together, and slipped in as stiffening to the old book-
cover. I had it steamed open, and analysed the wash. It gave
the flour-grains in the paste - coarse, because of the old mill-
stone – and there were traces of the grit itself. What? Oh,
possibly a handmill of Mentzel's own time. He may have
doubled the spoilt page and used it for part of a pad to steady
wood-cuts on. It may have knocked about his workshop for
years. That, indeed, is practically certain because a beginner
from the Low Countries has tried his reed on a few lines of
some monkish hymn – not a bad lilt tho' – which must have
been common form. Oh yes, the page may have been used in
other books before it was used for the Vulgate. That doesn't
matter, but *this* does. Listen! I took a wash, for analysis,
from a blot in one corner – that would be after Mentzel had
given up trying to make a possible page of it, and had grown
careless – and I got the actual *ink* of the period! It's a practically eternal stuff compounded on – I've forgotten his name
for the minute – the scribe at Bury St Edmunds, of course –
hawthorn bark and wine. Anyhow, on *his* formula. *That*
wouldn't interest you either, but, taken with all the other
testimony, it clinches the thing. (You'll see it all in my Statement to the Press on Monday.) Overwhelming, isn't it?'

'Overwhelming,' I said, with sincerity. 'Tell me what the
tale was about, though. That's more in my line.'

'I know it; but *I* have to be equipped on all sides. The
verses are relatively easy for one to pronounce on. The fresh-
ness, the fun, the humanity, the fragrance of it all, cries – no,
shouts – itself as Dan's work. Why "Daiespringe mis-
handled" alone stamps it from Dan's mint. Plangent as
doom, my dear boy – plangent as doom! It's all in my Statement. Well, substantially, the fragment deals with a girl
whose parents wish her to marry an elderly suitor. The
mother isn't so keen on it, but the father, an old Knight, is.
The girl, of course, is in love with a younger and a poorer
man. Common form? Granted. Then the father, who doesn't
in the least want to, is ordered off to a Crusade and, by way of
passing on the kick, as we used to say during the War, orders

the girl to be kept in duress till his return or her consent to
the old suitor. Common form, again? Quite so. That's too
much for her mother. She reminds the old Knight of his age
and infirmities, and the discomforts of Crusading. Are you
sure I'm not boring you?'

'Not at all,' I said, though time had begun to whirl back-
ward through my brain to a red-velvet, pomatum-scented,
side-room at Neminaka's and Manallace's set face intoning
to the gas.

'You'll read it all in my Statement next week. The sum is
that the old lady tells him of a certain Knight-adventurer on
the French coast, who, for a consideration, waylays Knights
who don't relish crusading and holds them to impossible
ransoms till the trooping-season is over or they are returned
sick. He keeps a ship in the Channel to pick 'em up and
transfers his birds to his castle ashore, where he has a reputation for doing 'em well. As the old lady points out:

> "And if perchance thou fall into his honde
> By God how canstow ride to Holilonde?"

'You see? Modern in essence as Gilbert and Sullivan, but
handled as only Dan could! And she reminds him that
"Honour and olde bones" parted company long ago. He
makes one splended appeal for the spirit of chivalry:

> "Lat all men change as Fortune may send,
> But Knighthood beareth service to the end,"

and *then*, of course, he gives in:

> "For what his woman willeth to be don
> Her manne must or wauken Hell anon."

'Then she hints that the daughter's young lover, who is in
the Bordeaux wine-trade, could open negotiations for a kid-
napping without compromising him. And *then* that careless
brute Mentzel spoils his page and chucks it! But there's
enough to show what's going to happen. You'll see it all in
my Statement. Was there ever anything in literary finds to

hold a candle to it? . . . And they give grocers Knighthoods for selling cheese!'

I went away before he could get into his stride on that course. I wanted to think, and to see Manallace. But I waited till Castorley's Statement came out. He had left himself no loophole. And when, a little later, his (nominally the Sunnapia people's) 'scientific' account of their analyses and tests appeared, criticism ceased, and some journals began to demand 'public recognition.' Manallace wrote me on this subject, and I went down to his cottage, where he at once asked me to sign a Memorial on Castorley's behalf. With luck, he said, we might get him a K.B.E. in the next Honours List. Had I read the Statement?

'I have,' I replied. 'But I want to ask you something first. Do you remember the night you got drunk at Neminaka's, and I stayed behind to look after you?'

'Oh, *that* time,' said he, pondering. 'Wait a minute! I remember Graydon advancing me two quid. He was a generous paymaster. And I remember – now, who the devil rolled me under the sofa – and what for?'

'We all did,' I replied. 'You wanted to read us what you'd written to those Chaucer cuts.'

'I don't remember that. No! I don't remember anything after the sofa-episode. . . . *You* always said that you took me home – didn't you?'

'I did, and you told Kentucky Kate outside the old Empire that you had been faithful, Cynara, in your fashion.'

'Did I?' said he. 'My God! Well, I suppose I have.' He stared into the fire. 'What else?'

'Before we left Neminaka's you recited me what you had made out of the cuts – the whole tale! So – you see?'

'Ye–es.' He nodded. 'What are you going to do about it?'

'What are *you*?'

'I'm going to help him get his Knighthood – first.'

'Why?'

'I'll tell you what he said about 'Dal's mother – the night there was that air-raid on the offices.'

He told it.

'That's why,' he said. 'Am I justified?'

He seemed to me entirely so.

'But after he gets his Knighthood?' I went on.

'That depends. There are several things I can think of. It interests me.'

'Good Heavens! I've always imagined you a man without interests.'

'So I was. I owe my interests to Castorley. He gave me every one of 'em except the tale itself.'

'How did *that* come?'

'Something in those ghastly cuts touched off something in me – a sort of possession, I suppose. I was in love too. No wonder I got drunk that night. I'd *been* Chaucer for a week! Then I thought the notion might make a comic opera. But Gilbert and Sullivan were too strong.'

'So I remember you told me at the time.'

'I kept it by me, and it made me interested in Chaucer – philologically and so on. I worked on it on those lines for years. There wasn't a flaw in the wording even in '14. I hardly had to touch it after that.'

'Did you ever tell it to anyone except me?'

'No, only 'Dal's mother – when she could listen to any-thing – to put her to sleep. But when Castorley said – what he did about her, I thought I might use it. 'Twasn't difficult. *He* taught me. D'you remember my birdlime experiments, and the stuff on our hands? I'd been trying to get that ink for more than a year. Castorley told me where I'd find the formula. And your falling over the quern, too?'

'That accounted for the stone-dust under the micro-scope?'

'Yes. I grew the wheat in the garden here, and ground it myself. Castorley gave me Mentzel complete. He put me on to an MS. in the British Museum which he said was the finest sample of his work. I copied his "Byzantine *g*'s" for months.'

'And what's a "sickle-slanted" pen?' I asked.

'You nick one edge of your reed till it drags and scratches on the curves of the letters. Castorley told me about Mentzel's spacing and margining. I only had to get the hang of his script.'

'How long did that take you?'

'On and off – some years. I was too ambitious at first – I wanted to give the whole poem. That would have been risky. Then Castorley told me about spoiled pages and I took the hint. I spelt "Dayspring mishandeelt" Mentzel's way – to make sure of him. It's not a bad couplet in itself. Did you see how he admires the "plangency" of it?'

'Never mind him. Go on!' I said.

He did. Castorley had been his unfailing guide throughout, specifying in minutest detail every trap to be set later for his own feet. The actual vellum was an Antwerp find, and its introduction into the cover of the Vulgate was begun after a long course of amateur bookbinding. At last, he bedded it under pieces of an old deed, and a printed page (1686) of Horace's *Odes*, legitimately used for repairs by different owners in the seventeenth and eighteenth centuries; and at the last moment, to meet Castorley's theory that spoiled pages were used in workshops by beginners, he had written a few Latin words in fifteenth century script – the Statement gave the exact date – across an open part of the fragment. The thing ran: '*Illa alma Mater ecca, secum afferens me acceptum. Nicolaus Atrib.*' The disposal of the thing was easiest of all. He had merely hung about Dredd's dark bookshop of fifteen rooms, where he was well known, occasionally buying but generally browsing, till, one day, Dredd Senior showed him a case of cheap black-letter stuff, English and Continental – being packed for the Sunnapia people – into which Manallace tucked his contribution, taking care to wrench the back enough to give a lead to an earnest seeker.

'And then?' I demanded.

'After six months or so Castorley sent for me. Sunnapia had found it, and as Dredd had missed it, and there was no money-motive sticking out, they were half convinced it was genuine from the start. But they invited him over. He conferred with their experts, and suggested the scientific tests. *I* put that into his head, before he sailed. That's all. And now, will you sign our Memorial?'

I signed. Before we had finished hawking it round there was a host of influential names to help us, as well as the impetus of all the literary discussion which arose over every detail of the glorious trove. The upshot was a K.B.E.* for Castorley in the next Honours List; and Lady Castorley, her cards duly printed, called on friends that same afternoon.

Manallace invited me to come with him, a day or so later, to convey our pleasure and satisfaction to them both. We were rewarded by the sight of a man relaxed and ungirt – not to say wallowing naked – on the crest of Success. He assured us that 'The Title' should not make any difference to our future relations, seeing it was in no sense personal, but, as he had often said, a tribute to Chaucer; 'and, after all,' he pointed out, with a glance at the mirror over the mantelpiece, 'Chaucer was the prototype of the "veray parfit gentil Knight" of the British Empire so far as that then existed.'

On the way back, Manallace told me he was considering either an unheralded revelation in the baser Press which should bring Castorley's reputation about his own ears some breakfast-time, or a private conversation, when he would make clear to Castorley that he must now back the forgery as long as he lived, under threat of Manallace's betraying it if he flinched.

He favoured the second plan. 'If I pull the string of the shower-bath in the papers', he said, 'Castorley might go off his veray parfit gentil nut. I want to keep his intellect.'

'What about your own position? The forgery doesn't matter so much. But if you tell this you'll kill him,' I said.

'I intend that. Oh – my position? I've been dead since – April, Fourteen, it was. But there's no hurry. What was it *she* was saying to you just as we left?'

'She told me how much your sympathy and understanding

---

* Officially it was on account of his good work in the Departmental of Co-ordinated Supervisals, but all true lovers of literature knew the real reason, and told the papers so.

had meant to him. She said she thought that even Sir Alured did not realize the full extent of his obligations to you.'

'She's right, but I don't like her putting it that way.'

'It's only common form – as Castorley's always saying.'

'Not with *her*. She can hear a man think.'

'She never struck me in that light.'

'*You* aren't playing against her.'

' 'Guilty conscience, Manallace?'

'H'm! I wonder. Mine or hers? I *wish* she hadn't said that. "More even than *he* realizes it." I won't call again for a while.'

He kept away till we read that Sir Alured, owing to slight indisposition, had been unable to attend a dinner given in his honour.

Inquiries brought word that it was but natural reaction, after strain, which, for the moment, took the form of nervous dyspepsia, and he would be glad to see Manallace at any time. Manallace reported him as rather pulled and drawn, but full of his new life and position, and proud that his efforts should have martyred him so much. He was going to collect, collate, and expand all his pronouncements and inferences into one authoritative volume.

'I must make an effort of my own,' said Manallace. 'I've collected nearly all his stuff about the Find that has appeared in the papers, and he's promised me everything that's missing. I'm going to help him. It will be a new interest.'

'How will you treat it?' I asked.

'I expect I shall quote his deductions on the evidence, and parallel 'em with my experiments – the ink and the paste and the rest of it. It ought to be rather interesting.'

'But even then there will only be your word. It's hard to catch up with an established lie,' I said. 'Especially when you've started it yourself.'

He laughed. 'I've arranged for *that* – in case anything happens to me. Do you remember the "Monkish Hymn"?'

'Oh yes! There's quite a literature about it already.'

'Well, you write those ten words above each other, and

read down the first and second letters of 'em; and see what you get.* My Bank has the formula.'

He wrapped himself lovingly and leisurely round his new task, and Castorley was as good as his word in giving him help. The two practically collaborated, for Manallace suggested that all Castorley's strictly scientific evidence should be in one place, with his deductions and dithyrambs as appendices. He assured him that the public would prefer this arrangement, and, after grave consideration, Castorley agreed.

'That's better,' said Manallace to me. 'Now I sha'n't have so many hiatuses in my extracts. Dots always give the reader the idea you aren't dealing fairly with your man. I shall merely quote him solid, and rip him up, proof for proof, and date for date, in parallel columns. His book's taking more out of him than I like, though. He's been doubled up twice with tummy attacks since I've worked with him. And he's just the sort of flatulent beast who may go down with appendicitis.'

We learned before long that the attacks were due to gall-stones, which would necessitate an operation. Castorley bore the blow very well. He had full confidence in his surgeon, an old friend of theirs; great faith in his own constitution; a strong conviction that nothing would happen to him till the book was finished, and, above all, the Will to Live.

He dwelt on these assets with a voice at times a little out of pitch and eyes brighter than usual beside a slightly sharpening nose.

I had only met Gleeag, the surgeon, once or twice at Castorley's house, but had always heard him spoken of as a most

*Illa
alma
Mater
ecca
secum
afferens
me
acceptum
Nicolaus
Atrib.

capable man. He told Castorley that his trouble was the price exacted, in some shape or other, from all who had served their country; and that, measured in units of strain, Castorley had practically been at the front through those three years he had served in the Office of Co-ordinated Supervisals. However, the thing had been taken betimes, and in a few weeks he would worry no more about it.

'But suppose he dies?' I suggested to Manallace.

'He won't. I've been talking to Gleeag. He says he's all right.'

'Wouldn't Gleeag's talk be common form?'

'I *wish* you hadn't said that. But, surely, Gleeag wouldn't have the face to play with me – or her.'

'Why not? I expect it's been done before.'

But Manallace insisted that, in this case, it would be impossible.

The operation was a success and, some weeks later, Castorley began to recast the arrangement and most of the material of his book. 'Let me have my way,' he said, when Manallace protested. 'They are making too much of a baby of me. I really don't need Gleeag looking in every day now.' But Lady Castorley told us that he required careful watching. His heart had felt the strain, and fret or disappointment of any kind must be avoided. 'Even,' she turned to Manallace, 'though you know ever so much better how his book should be arranged than he does himself.'

'But really,' Manallace began. 'I'm very careful not to fuss – '

She shook her finger at him playfully. 'You don't think you do; but, remember, he tells me everything that you tell him, just the same as he told me everything that he used to tell *you*. Oh, I don't mean the things that men talk about. I mean about his Chaucer.'

'I didn't realize that,' said Manallace, weakly.

'I thought you didn't. He never spares me anything; but *I* don't mind,' she replied with a laugh, and went off to Gleeag, who was paying his daily visit. Gleeag said he had no objection to Manallace working with Castorley on the book for a

229

given time – say, twice a week – but supported Lady Castorley's demand that he should not be over-taxed in what she
called 'the sacred hours.' The man grew more and more
difficult to work with, and the little check he had heretofore
set on his self-praise went altogether.

'He says there has never been anything in the History of
Letters to compare with it,' Manallace groaned. 'He wants
now to inscribe – he never dedicates, you know – inscribe it to
me, as his "most valued assistant". The devil of it is that *she*
backs him up in getting it out soon. Why? How much do you
think she knows?'

'Why should she know anything at all?'

'You heard her say he had told her everything that he had
told me about Chaucer? (I *wish* she hadn't said that!) If she
puts two and two together, she can't help seeing that every
one of his notions and theories has been played up to. But
then – but then. . . . Why is she trying to hurry publication?
She talks about me fretting him. *She's* at him, all the time,
to be quick.'

Castorley must have over-worked, for, after a couple of
months, he complained of a stitch in his right side, which
Gleeag said was a slight sequel, a little incident of the operation. It threw him back awhile, but he returned to his work
undefeated.

The book was due in the autumn. Summer was passing,
and his publisher urgent, and – he said to me, when after a
longish interval I called – Manallace had chosen this time, of
all, to take a holiday. He was not pleased with Manallace,
once his indefatigable *aide*, but now dilatory, and full of
time-wasting objections. Lady Castorley had noticed it,
too.

Meantime, with Lady Castorley's help, he himself was
doing the best he could to expedite the book; but Manallace
had mislaid (did I think through jealousy?) some essential
stuff which had been dictated to him. And Lady Castorley
wrote Manallace, who had been delayed by a slight motor
accident abroad, that the fret of waiting was prejudicial to

her husband's health. Manallace, on his return from the Continent, showed me that letter.

'He has fretted a little, I believe,' I said.

Manallace shuddered. 'If I stay abroad, I'm helping to kill him. If I help him to hurry up the book, I'm expected to kill him. *She* knows,' he said.

'You're mad. You've got this thing on the brain.'

'I have not! Look here! You remember that Gleeag gave me from four to six, twice a week, to work with him. She called them the "sacred hours". You heard her? Well, they *are*! They are Gleeag's and hers. But she's so infernally plain, and I'm such a fool, it took me weeks to find it out.'

'That's their affair,' I answered. 'It doesn't prove she knows anything about the Chaucer.'

'She *does*! He told her everything that he had told me when I was pumping him, all those years. She put two and two together when the thing came out. She saw exactly how I had set my traps. I know it! She's been trying to make me admit it.'

'What did you do?'

' 'Didn't understand what she was driving at, of course. And then she asked Gleeag, before me, if he didn't think the delay over the book was fretting Sir Alured. He didn't think so. He said getting it out might deprive him of an interest. He had that much decency. *She's* the devil!'

'What do you suppose is her game, then?'

'If Castorley knows he's been had, it'll kill him. She's at me all the time, indirectly, to let it out. I've told you she wants to make it a sort of joke between us. Gleeag's willing to wait. He knows Castorley's a dead man. It slips out when they talk. They say "He was", not "He is". Both of 'em know it. But *she* wants him finished sooner.'

'I don't believe it. What are you going to do?'

'What *can* I? I'm not going to have him killed, though.'

Manlike, he invented compromises whereby Castorley might be lured up by-paths of interest, to delay publication. This was not a success. As autumn advanced Castorley fretted more, and suffered from returns of his distressing colics. At last, Gleeag told him that he thought they might be due to an overlooked gallstone working down. A second comparatively trivial operation would eliminate the bother once and for all. If Castorley cared for another opinion, Gleeag named a surgeon of eminence. 'And then,' said he, cheerily, 'the two of us can talk you over.' Castorley did not want to be talked over. He was oppressed by pains in his side, which, at first, had yielded to the liver-tonics Gleeag prescribed; but now they stayed – like a toothache – behind everything. He felt most at ease in his bedroom-study, with his proofs round him. If he had more pain than he could stand, he would consider the second operation. Meantime Manallace – 'the meticulous Manallace,' he called him – agreed with him in thinking that the Mentzel page-facsimile, done by the Sunnapia Library, was not quite good enough for the great book, and the Sunnapia people were, very decently, having it reprocessed. This would hold things back till early spring, which had its advantages, for he could run a fresh eye over all in the interval.

One gathered these news in the course of stray visits as the days shortened. He insisted on Manallace keeping to the 'sacred hours', and Manallace insisted on my accompanying him when possible. On these occasions he and Castorley would confer apart for half an hour or so, while I listened to an unendurable clock in the drawing-room. Then I would join them and help wear out the rest of the time, while Castorley rambled. His speech, now, was often clouded and uncertain – the result of the 'liver-tonics'; and his face came to look like old vellum.

It was a few days after Christmas – the operation had been postponed till the following Friday – that we called together. She met us with word that Sir Alured had picked up an irritating little winter cough, due to a cold wave, but we were not, therefore, to abridge our visit. We found him in steam perfumed with Friar's Balsam. He waved the old Sunnapia facsimile at us. We agreed that it ought to have been more worthy. He took a dose of his mixture, lay back and asked us to lock the door. There was, he whispered, something wrong somewhere. He could not lay his finger on it, but it was in the air. He felt he was being played with. He did not like it. There was something wrong all round him. Had we noticed it? Manallace and I severally and slowly denied that we had noticed anything of the sort.

With no longer break than a light fit of coughing, he fell into the hideous, helpless panic of the sick – those worse than captives who lie at the judgement and mercy of the hale for every office and hope. He wanted to go away. Would we help him to pack his Gladstone? Or, if that would attract too much attention in certain quarters, help him to dress and go out? There was an urgent matter to be set right, and now that he had The Title and knew his own mind it would all end happily and he would be well again. *Please* would we let him go out, just to speak to – he named her; he named her by her 'little' name out of the old Neminaka days? Manallace quite agreed, and recommended a pull at the 'liver-tonic' to brace him after so long in the house. He took it, and Manallace suggested that it would be better if, after his walk, he came down to the cottage for a week-end and brought the revise with him. They could then re-touch the last chapter. He answered to that drug and to some praise of his work, and presently simpered drowsily. Yes, it *was* good – though he said it who should not. He praised himself awhile till, with a puzzled forehead and shut eyes, he told us that *she* had been saying lately that it was too good – the whole thing, if we understood, was *too* good. He wished us to get the exact shade of her meaning. She had suggested, or rather implied, this doubt. She had said – he would let us draw our own inferences – that the Chaucer find had 'anticipated the wants of humanity', Johnson, of course. No need to tell *him* that. But what the hell was her implication? Oh God! Life had always been one long innuendo! *And* she had said that a man could do anything with anyone if he saved him the trouble of thinking. What did she mean by that? *He* had never shirked thought. He had thought sustainedly all his life. It *wasn't* too good was it? Manallace didn't think it was too good – did he? But this pick-pick-picking at a man's brain and work was too bad, wasn't it? *What* did she mean? Why did she always bring in Manallace, who was only a friend – no scholar, but a lover of the game – Eh? – Manallace could confirm this if he were here, instead of loafing on the Continent just when he was most needed.

'I've come back,' Manallace interrupted, unsteadily. 'I can confirm every word you've said. You've nothing to worry about. It's *your* find – *your* credit – *your* glory and – all the rest of it.'

'Swear you'll tell her so then,' said Castorley. 'She doesn't believe a word I say. She told me she never has since before we were married. Promise!'

Manallace promised, and Castorley added that he had named him his literary executor, the proceeds of the book to go to his wife. 'All profits without deduction,' he gasped. 'Big sales if it's properly handled. *You* don't need money. ... Graydon'll trust *you* to any extent. It'ud be a long ...'

He coughed, and, as he caught breath, his pain broke through all the drugs, and the outcry filled the room. Manallace rose to fetch Gleeag, when a full, high, affected voice, unheard for a generation, accompanied, as it seemed, the clamour of a beast in agony, saying: 'I wish to God someone would stop that old swine howling down there! *I* can't ... I was going to tell you fellows that it would be a dam' long time before Graydon advanced *me* two quid ...'

We escaped together, and found Gleeag waiting, with Lady Castorley, on the landing. He telephoned me, next morning, that Castorley had died of bronchitis, which his weak state made it impossible for him to throw off. 'Perhaps it's just as well,' he added, in reply to the condolences I asked him to convey to the widow. 'We might have come across something we couldn't have coped with.'

Distance from that house made me bold.

'You knew all along, I suppose? What was it, really?'

'Malignant kidney-trouble – generalized at the end. 'No use worrying him about it. We let him through as easily as possible. Yes! A happy release. . . . What? . . . Oh! Cremation. Friday, at eleven.'

There, then, Manallace and I met. He told me that she had asked him whether the book need now be published; and he had told her this was more than ever necessary, in her interests as well as Castorley's.

'She is going to be known as his widow – for a while, at any rate. Did I perjure myself much with him?'

'Not explicitly,' I answered.

'Well, I have now – with *her* – explicitly,' said he, and took out his black gloves . . .

As, on the appointed words, the coffin crawled sideways through the noiselessly-closing door-flaps, I saw Lady Castorley's eyes turn towards Gleeag.

The Church that was at Antioch
(1929)

'But when Peter was come to Antioch, I withstood him to the face, because he was to be blamed.' – St Paul's Epistle to the Galatians, ii. 11.

HIs mother, a devout and well-born Roman widow, decided that he was doing himself no good in an Eastern Legion so near to free-thinking Constantinople, and got him seconded for civil duty in Antioch, where his uncle, Lucius Sergius, was head of the urban Police. Valens obeyed as a son and as a young man keen to see life, and, presently, cast up at his uncle's door.

'That sister-in-law of mine,' said the elder, 'never remembers me till she wants something. What have you been doing?'

'Nothing, Uncle.'

'Meaning everything?'

'That's what mother thinks. But I haven't.'

'We shall see. Your quarters are across the inner court-yard. Your – er – baggage is there already.... Oh, I shan't interfere with your private arrangements! I'm not the uncle with the rough tongue. Get your bath. We'll talk at supper.'

But before that hour 'Father Serga', as the Prefect of Police was called, learned from the Treasury that his nephew had marched overland from Constantinople in charge of a treasure-convoy which, after a brush with brigands in the pass outside Tarsus, he had duly delivered.

'Why didn't you tell me about it?' his uncle asked at the meal.

'I had to report to the Treasury first,' was the answer.

Serga looked at him. 'Gods! You *are* like your father,' said he. 'Cilicia is scandalously policed.'

'So I noticed. They ambushed us not five miles from Tarsus town. Are we given to that sort of thing here?'

'You make yourself at home early. No. *We* are not, but Syria is a Non-regulation Province – under the Emperor – not the Senate. We've the entire unaccountable East to one side; the scum of the Mediterranean on the other; and all hellicat Judaea southward. Anything can happen in Syria. D'you like the prospect?'

'I shall – under you.'

'It's in the blood. The same with men as horses. Now what have you done that distresses your mother so?'

'She's a little behind the times, sir. She follows the old school, of course – the home-worships, and the strict Latin Trinity. I don't think she recognizes any gods outside Jupiter, Juno, and Minerva.'

'I don't either – officially.'

'Nor I, as an officer, sir. But one wants more than that, and – and – what I learned in Byzant squared with what I saw with the Fifteenth.'

'You needn't go on. All Eastern Legions are alike. You mean you follow Mithras – eh?'

The young man bowed his head slightly.

'No harm, boy. It's a soldier's religion, even if it comes from outside.'

'So I thought. But Mother heard of it. She didn't approve and – I suppose that's why I'm here.'

'Off the trident and into the net! Just like a woman! All Syria is stuffed with Mithraism. *My* objection to fancy religions is that they mostly meet after dark, and that means more work for the Police. We've a College here of stiff-necked Hebrews who call themselves Christians.'

'I've heard of them,' said Valens. 'There isn't a ceremony or symbol they haven't stolen from the Mithras ritual.'

' 'No news to *me!* Religions are part of my office-work; and they'll be part of yours. Our Synagogue Jews are fighting like Scythians over this new faith.'

'Does that matter much?'

'So long as they fight each other, we've only to keep the ring. Divide and rule – especially with Hebrews. Even these

Christians are divided now. You see – one part of their worship is to eat together.'

'Another theft! The Supper is the essential Symbol with us,' Valens interrupted.

'With *us*, it's the essential symbol of trouble for your uncle, my dear. Anyone can become a Christian. A Jew may; but he still lives by his Law of Moses (I've had to master that cursed code, too), and it regulates all his doings. Then he sits down at a Christian love feast beside a Greek or Westerner, who doesn't kill mutton or pig – No! No! Jews don't touch pork – as the Jewish Law lays down. Then the tables are broken up – but not by laughter – No! No! Riot!'

'That's childish,' said Valens.

' 'Wish it were. But my lictors are called in to keep order, and I have to take the depositions of Synagogue Jews, denouncing Christians as traitors to Caesar. If I chose to act on half the stuff their Rabbis swear to, I'd have respectable little Jew shop-keepers up every week for conspiracy. *Never* decide on the evidence, when you're dealing with Hebrews! Oh, you'll get your bellyful of it! You're for Market-duty tomorrow in the Little Circus ward, all among 'em. And now, sleep you well! I've been on this frontier as far back as anyone remembers – that's why they call me the Father of Syria – and oh – it's good to see a sample of the old stock again!'

Next morning, and for many weeks after, Valens found himself on Market-inspection duty with a fat Aedile, who flew into rages because the stalls were not flushed down at the proper hour. A couple of his uncle's men were told off to him, and, of course, introduced him to the thieves' and prostitutes' quarters, to the leading gladiators and so forth.

One day, behind the Little Circus, near Singon Street, he ran into a mob, where a race-course gang were trying to collect, or evade, some bets on recent chariot-races. The Aedile said it was none of his affair and turned back. The lictors closed up behind Valens, but left the situation in his charge. Then a small hard man with eyebrows was punted on to his chest, amid howls from all around that he was the ringleader of a conspiracy. 'Yes,' said Valens, 'that was an old trick in Byzant; but I think we'll take *you*, my friend.' Turning the small man loose, he gathered in the loudest of his accusers to appear before his uncle.

'You were quite right,' said Serga next day. 'That gentleman was put up to the job – by someone else. I ordered him one Roman dozen. Did you get the name of the man they were trying to push off on to you?'

'Yes. Gaius Julius Paulus. Why?'

'I guessed as much. He's an old acquaintance of mine, a Cilician from Tarsus. Well-born – a citizen by descent, and well-educated, but his people have disowned him. So he works for his living.'

'He spoke like a well-born. He's in splendid training, too. 'Felt him. All muscle.'

'Small wonder. He can outmarch a camel. He is really the Prefect of this new sect. He travels all over our Eastern Provinces starting their Colleges and keeping them up to the mark. That's why the Synagogue Jews are hunting him. If they could run him in on the political charge, it would finish him.'

'Is he seditious, then?'

'Not in the least. Even if he were, I wouldn't feed him to the Jews just because they wanted it. One of our Governors tried that game down-coast – for the sake of peace – some years ago. He didn't get it. Do you like your Market-work, my boy?'

'It's interesting. D'you know, uncle, I think the Synagogue Jews are better at their slaughter-house arrangements than we.'

'They are. That's what makes 'em so tough. A dozen stripes are nothing to Apella, though he'll howl the yard down while he's getting 'em. You've the Christians' College in your quarter. How do they strike you?'

'Quiet enough. They're worrying a bit over what they ought to eat at their love-feasts.'

'I know it. Oh, I meant to tell you – we mustn't try 'em too high just now, Valens. My office reports that Paulus, your small friend, is going down-country for a few days to meet another priest of the College, and bring him back to help smooth over their difficulties about their victuals. That means their congregation will be at loose ends till they return. Mass without mind always comes a cropper. So, *now* is when the Synagogue Jews will try to compromise them. I don't want the poor devils stampeded into what can be made to look like a political crime. 'Understand?'

Valens nodded. Between his uncle's discursive evening talks, studded with kitchen-Greek and out-of-date Roman society-verses; his morning tours with the puffing Aedile; and the confidences of his lictors at all hours; he fancied he understood Antioch.

So he kept an eye on the rooms in the colonnade behind the Little Circus, where the new faith gathered. One of the many Jew butchers told him that Paulus had left affairs in the hands of some man called Barnabas, but that he would come back with one, Petrus – evidently a well-known character – who would settle all the food-differences between Greek and Hebrew Christians. The butcher had no spite against Greek Christians as such, if they would only kill their meat like decent Jews.

Serga laughed at this talk, but lent Valens an extra man or two, and said that this lion would be his to tackle, before long.

The boy found himself rushed into the arena one hot dusk, when word had come that this was to be a night of trouble. He posted his lictors in an alley within signal, and entered the common-room of the College, where the love-feasts were held. Everyone seemed as friendly as a Christian – to use the slang of the quarter – and Barnabas, a smiling, stately man by the door, specially so.

'I am glad to meet you,' he said. 'You helped our Paulus in that scuffle the other day. We can't afford to lose *him*. I wish he were back!'

He looked nervously down the hall, as it filled with people, of middle and low degree, setting out their evening meal on the bare tables, and greeting each other with a special gesture.

'I assure you,' he went on, his eyes still astray, '*we've* no intention of offending any of the brethren. Our differences can be settled if only –'

As though on a signal, clamour rose from half a dozen tables at once, with cries of 'Pollution! Defilement! Heathen! The Law! The Law! Let Caesar know!' As Valens backed against the wall, the crowd pelted each other with broken meats and crockery, till at last stones appeared from nowhere.

'It's a put-up affair,' said Valens to Barnabas.

'Yes. They come in with stones in their breasts. Be careful! They're throwing your way,' Barnabas replied. The crowd was well-embroiled now. A section of it bore down to where they stood, yelling for the Justice of Rome. His two lictors slid in behind Valens, and a man leaped at him with a knife.

Valens struck up the hand, and the lictors had the man helpless as the weapon fell on the floor. The clash of it stilled the tumult a little. Valens caught the lull, speaking slowly: ', citizens,' he called, '*must* you begin your love-feasts with battle? Our tripe-sellers' burial-club has better manners.'

A little laughter relieved the tension.

'The Synagogue has arranged this,' Barnabas muttered. 'The responsibility will be laid on me.'

'Who is the Head of your College?' Valens called to the crowd.

The cries rose against each other.

'Paulus! Saul! *He* knows the world – No! No! Petrus! Our Rock! *He* won't betray us. Petrus, the Living Rock.'

'When do they come back?' Valens asked. Several dates were given, sworn to, and denied.

'Wait to fight till they return. I'm not a priest; but if you don't tidy up these rooms, our Aedile (Valens gave him his gross nick-name in the quarter) will fine the sandals off your feet. And you mustn't trample good food either. When you've finished, I'll lock up after you. Be quick. *I* know our Prefect if you don't.'

They toiled, like children rebuked. As they passed out with baskets of rubbish, Valens smiled. The matter would not be pressed further.

'Here is our key,' said Barnabas at the end. 'The Synagogue will swear I hired this man to kill you.'

'Will they? Let's look at him.'

The lictors pushed their prisoner forward.

'Ill-fortune!' said the man. 'I owed you for my brother's death in Tarsus Pass.'

'Your brother tried to kill me,' Valens retorted.

The fellow nodded.

'Then we'll call it even-throws,' Valens signed to the lictors, who loosed hold. 'Unless you *really* want to see my uncle?'

The man vanished like a trout in the dusk. Valens returned the key to Barnabas, and said:

'If I were you, I shouldn't let your people in again till your leaders come back. You don't know Antioch as I do.'

He went home, the grinning lictors behind him, and told his uncle, who grinned also, but said that he had done the right thing – even to patronizing Barnabas.

'Of course, *I* don't know Antioch as you do; but, seriously, my dear, I think you've saved their Church for the Christians this time. I've had three depositions already that your Cilician friend was a Christian hired by Barnabas. 'Just as well for Barnabas that you let the brute go.'

'You told me you didn't want them stampeded into trouble. Besides, it was fair-throws. I may have killed his brother after all. We had to kill two of 'em.'

'Good! You keep a level head in a tight corner. You'll need it. There's no lying about in secluded parks for *us*! I've got to see Paulus and Petrus when they come back, and find out what they've decided about their infernal feasts. Why can't they all get decently drunk and be done with it?'

'They talk of them both down-town as though they were

Gods. By the way, uncle, all the riot was worked up by Synagogue Jews sent from Jerusalem – not by our lot at all.'

'You *don't* say so? Now, perhaps, you understand why I put you on market-duty with old Sow-Belly! You'll make a Police-officer yet.'

Valens met the scared, mixed congregation round the fountains and stalls as he went about his quarter. They were rather relieved at being locked out of their rooms for the time; as well as by the news that Paulus and Petrus would report to the Prefect of Police before addressing them on the great food-question.

Valens was not present at the first part of that interview, which was official. The second, in the cool, awning-covered courtyard, with drinks and *hors-d'oeuvre*, all set out beneath the vast lemon and lavender sunset, was much less formal.

'You have met, I think,' said Serga to the little lean Paulus as Valens entered.

'Indeed, yes. Under God, we are twice your debtors,' was the quick reply.

'Oh, that was part of my duty. I hope you found our roads good on your journey,' said Valens.

'Why, yes. I think they were.' Paulus spoke as if he had not noticed them.

'We should have done better to come by boat,' said his companion, Petrus, a large fleshy man, with eyes that seemed to see nothing, and a half-palsied right hand that lay idle in his lap. .

'Valens came overland from Byzant,' said his uncle. 'He rather fancies his legs.'

'He ought to at his age. What was your best day's march on the Via Sebaste?' Paulus asked interestedly, and before he knew, Valens was reeling off his mileage on mountain-roads every step of which Paulus seemed to have trod.

'That's good,' was the comment. 'And I expect you march in heavier order than I.'

'What would you call your best day's work?' Valens asked in turn.

'I have covered . . .' Paulus checked himself. 'And yet not I but the God,' he muttered. 'It's hard to cure oneself of boasting.'

A spasm wrenched Petrus' face.

'Hard indeed,' said he. Then he addressed himself to Paulus as though none other were present. 'It is true I have eaten with Gentiles and as the Gentiles ate. Yet, at the time, I doubted if it were wise.'

'That is behind us now,' said Paulus gently. 'The decision has been taken for the Church – that little Church which you saved, my son.' He turned on Valens with a smile that half-captured the boy's heart. 'Now – as a Roman and a Police-officer – what think you of us Christians?'

'That I have to keep order in my own ward.'

'Good! Caesar must be served. But – as a servant of Mithras, shall we say – how think you about our food-disputes?'

Valens hesitated. His uncle encouraged him with a nod. 'As a servant of Mithras I eat with any initiate, so long as the food is clean,' said Valens.

'But,' said Petrus, '*that* is the crux.'

'Mithras also tells us,' Valens went on, 'to share a bone covered with dirt, if better cannot be found.'

'You observe no difference, then, between peoples at your feasts?' Paulus demanded.

'How dare we? We are all His children. Men make laws. Not Gods,' Valens quoted from the old Ritual.

'Say that again, child!'

'Gods do not make laws. They change men's hearts. The rest is the Spirit.'

'You heard it, Petrus? You heard that? It is the utter Doctrine itself!' Paulus insisted to his dumb companion.

Valens, a little ashamed of having spoken of his faith, went on:

'They tell me the Jew butchers here want the monopoly of killing for your people. Trade feeling's at the bottom of most of it.'

'A little more than that perhaps,' said Paulus. 'Listen a

minute.' He threw himself into a curious tale about the God of the Christians, Who, he said, had taken the shape of a Man, and Whom the Jerusalem Jews, years ago, had got the authorities to deal with as a conspirator. He said that he himself, at that time a right Jew, quite agreed with the sentence, and had denounced all who followed the new God. But one day the Light and the Voice of the God broke over him, and he experienced a rending change of heart – precisely as in the Mithras creed. Then he met, and had been initiated by, some men who had walked and talked and, more particularly, had eaten, with the new God before He was killed, and who had seen Him after, like Mithras, He had risen from His grave. Paulus and those others – Petrus was one of them – had next tried to preach Him to the Jews, but that was no success; and, one thing leading to another, Paulus had gone back to his home at Tarsus, where his people disowned him for a renegade. There he had broken down with overwork and despair. Till then, he said, it had never occurred to any of them to show the new religion to any except right Jews; for their God had been born in the shape of a Jew. Paulus himself only came to realize the possibilities of outside work, little by little. He said he had all the foreign preaching in his charge now, and was going to change the whole world by it.

Then he made Petrus finish the tale, who explained, speaking very slowly, that he had, some years ago, received orders from the God to preach to a Roman officer of Irregulars down-country; after which that officer and most of his people wanted to become Christians. So Petrus had initiated them the same night, although none of them were Hebrews. 'And,' Petrus ended, 'I saw there is nothing under heaven that we dare call unclean.'

Paulus turned on him like a flash and cried:

'You admit it! Out of your own mouth it is evident.' Petrus shook like a leaf and his right hand almost lifted.

'Do *you* too twit me with my accent?' he began, but his face worked and he choked.

'Nay! God forbid! And God once more forgive *me*!' Paulus

seemed as distressed as he, while Valens stared at the extraordinary outbreak.

'Talking of clean and unclean,' his uncle said tactfully,
'there's that ugly song come up again in the City. They were
singing it on the city-front yesterday, Valens. Did you
notice?'

He looked at his nephew, who took the hint.

'If it was "Pickled Fish," sir, they were. Will it make
trouble?'

'As surely as these fish' – a jar of them stood on the table –
'make one thirsty. How does it go? Oh yes.' Serga
hummed:

Oie-eaah!

From the Shark and the Sardine – the clean and the unclean –
To the Pickled Fish of Galilee, said Petrus, shall be mine.

He twanged it off to the proper gutter-drawl.

(Ha-ow?)
In the nets or on the line,
Till the Gods Themselves decline.
(Whe-en?)
When the Pickled Fish of Galilee ascend the Esquiline!

That'll be something of a flood – worse than live fish in trees!
Hey?'

'It will happen one day,' said Paulus.

He turned from Petrus, whom he had been soothing tenderly, and resumed in his natural, hardish voice:

'Yes. We owe a good deal to that Centurion being converted when he was. It taught us that the whole world could
receive the God; and it showed *me* my next work. I came over
from Tarsus to teach here for a while. And I shan't forget
how good the Prefect of Police was to us then.'

'For one thing, Cornelius was an early colleague,' Serga
smiled largely above his strong cup. ' "Prime companion" –
how does it go? – "we drank the long, long Eastern day out
together," and so on. For another, I know a good workman
when I see him. That camel-kit you made for my desert-

tours, Paul, is as sound as ever. And for a third – which to a man of my habits is most important – that Greek doctor you recommended me is the only one who understands my tumid liver.'

He passed a cup of all but unmixed wine, which Paulus handed to Petrus, whose lips were flaky white at the corners.

'But your trouble,' the Prefect went on, 'will come from your own people. Jerusalem never forgives. They'll get you run in on the charge of *laesa majestatis* soon or late.'

'Who knows better than I?' said Petrus. 'And the decision we *all* have taken about our love-feasts may unite Hebrew and Greek against us. As I told you, Prefect, we are asking Christian Greeks not to make the feasts difficult for Christian Hebrews by eating meat that has not been lawfully killed. (Our way is much more wholesome, anyhow.) Still, we may get round that. But there's *one* vital point. Some of our Greek Christians bring food to the love-feasts that they've bought from your priests, after your sacrifices have been offered. That we can't allow.'

Paulus turned to Valens imperiously.

'You mean they buy Altar-scraps,' the boy said. 'But only the very poor do it; and it's chiefly block-trimmings. The sale's a perquisite of the Altar-butchers. They wouldn't like its being stopped.'

'Permit separate tables for Hebrew and Greek, as I once said,' Petrus spoke suddenly.

'That would end in separate churches. There shall be but *one* Church,' Paulus spoke over his shoulder, and the words fell like rods. 'You think there may be trouble, Valens?'

'My uncle –' Valens began.

'No, no!' the Prefect laughed. 'Singon Street Markets are your Syria. Let's hear what our Legate thinks of his Province.'

Valens flushed and tried to pull his wits together.

'Primarily,' he said, 'it's pig, I suppose. Hebrews hate pork.'

'Quite right, too. Catch *me* eating pig east the Adriatic! *I* don't want to die of worms. Give me a young Sabine tush-ripe boar! I have spoken!'

Serga mixed himself another raw cup and took some pickled Lake fish to bring out the flavour.

'But, still,' Petrus leaned forward like a deaf man, 'if we admitted Hebrew and Greek Christians to separate tables we should escape –'

'Nothing, except salvation,' said Paulus. 'We have broken with the whole Law of Moses. We live in and through and by our God only. Else we are nothing. What is the sense of hark-ing back to the Law at meal-times? Whom do we deceive? Jerusalem? Rome? The God? You yourself have eaten with Gentiles! You yourself have said –'

'One says more than one means when one is carried away,' Petrus answered, and his face worked again.

'This time you will say precisely what is meant,' Paulus spoke between his teeth. 'We will keep the Churches *one* – in and through the Lord. You dare not deny this?'

'I dare nothing – the God knows! But I have denied Him. . . . I denied Him. . . . And He said – He said I was the Rock on which His Church should stand.'

'*I* will see that it stands, and yet not I – ' Paulus' voice dropped again. 'Tomorrow you will speak to the one Church of the one Table the world over.'

'That's *your* business,' said the Prefect. 'But I warn you again, it's your own people who will make you trouble.'

Paulus rose to say farewell, but in the act he staggered, put his hand to his forehead and, as Valens steered him to a divan, collapsed in the grip of that deadly Syrian malaria which strikes like a snake. Valens, having suffered, called to his rooms for his heavy travelling-fur. His girl, whom he had bought in Constantinople a few months before, fetched it. Petrus tucked it awkwardly round the shivering little figure; the Prefect ordered lime-juice and hot water, and Paulus thanked them and apologized, while his teeth rattled on the cup.

'Better today than tomorrow,' said the Prefect. 'Drink –

sweat – and sleep here the night. Shall I send for my doctor?'

But Paulus said that the fit would pass naturally, and as soon as he could stand he insisted on going away with Petrus, late though it was, to prepare their announcement to the Church.

'Who was that big, clumsy man?' his girl asked Valens as she took up the fur. 'He made more noise than the small one, who was really suffering.'

'He's a priest of the new College by the Little Circus, dear. He believes, uncle told me, that he once denied his God, Who, he says, died for him.'

She halted in the moonlight, the glossy jackal skins over her arm.

'Does he? *My* God bought me from the dealers like a horse. Too much, too, he paid. Didn't he? 'Fess, thou?'

'No, thee!' emphatically.

'But I wouldn't deny *my* God – living or dead! . . . Oh – but *not* dead! My God's going to live – for me. Live – live Thou, my heart's blood, for ever!'

It would have been better had Paulus and Petrus not left the Prefect's house so late; for the rumour in the city, as the Prefect knew, and as the long conference seemed to confirm, was that Caesar's own Secretary of State in Rome was, through Paulus, arranging for a general defilement of the Hebrew with the Greek Christians, and that after this had been effected, by promiscuous eating of unlawful foods, all Jews would be lumped together as Christians – members, that is, of a mere free-thinking sect instead of the very particular and troublesome 'Nation of Jews within the Empire'. Eventually, the story went, they would lose their rights as Roman citizens, and could then be sold on any slave-stand.

'Of course,' Serga explained to Valens next day, 'that has been put about by the Jerusalem Synagogue. Our Antioch Jews aren't clever enough. Do you see their game? Petrus is a defiler of the Hebrew nation. If he is cut down tonight by some properly primed young zealot so much the better.'

'He won't be,' said Valens. 'I'm looking after him.'

' 'Hope so. But, if he isn't knifed,' Serga went on, 'they'll try to work up city riots on the grounds that, when all the Jews have lost their civil rights, he'll set up as a sort of King of the Christians.'

'At Antioch? In the present year of Rome? That's crazy, Uncle.'

'*Every* crowd is crazy. What else do we draw pay for? But, listen. Post a Mounted Police patrol at the back of the Little Circus. Use 'em to keep the people moving when the congregation comes out. Post two of your men in the Porch of their College itself. Tell Paulus and Petrus to wait there with them, till the streets are clear. Then fetch 'em both over here. Don't hit till you have to. Hit hard *before* the stones fly. Don't get my little horses knocked about more than you can help, and – look out for "Pickled Fish"!'

Knowing his own quarter, it seemed to Valens as he went on duty that evening, that his uncle's precautions had been excessive. The Christian Church, of course, was full, and a large crowd waited outside for word of the decision about the feasts. Most of them seemed to be Christians of sorts, but there was an element of gesticulating Antiochene loafers, and like all crowds they amused themselves with popular songs while they waited. Things went smoothly, till a group of Christians raised a rather explosive hymn, which ran:

> 'Enthroned above Caesar and Judge of the Earth!
> We wait on Thy coming – oh tarry not long!
>   As the Kings of the Sunrise
>   Drew sword at Thy Birth,
> So we arm in this midnight of insult and wrong!'

'Yes – and if one of their fish-stalls is bumped over by a camel – it's *my* fault!' said Valens. 'Now they've started it!'

Sure enough, voices on the outskirts broke into 'Pickled Fish', but before Valens could speak, they were suppressed by someone crying:

'Quiet there, or you'll get your pickle before your fish.'

It was close on twilight when a cry rose from within the

packed Church, and its congregation breasted out into the crowd. They all talked about the new orders for their love-feasts, most of them agreeing that they were sensible and easy. They agreed, too, that Petrus (Paulus did not seem to have taken much part in the debate) had spoken like one inspired, and they were all extremely proud of being Christians. Some of them began to link arms across the alley, and strike into the 'Enthroned above Caesar' chorus.

'And this, I *think*,' Valens called to the young Commandant of the Mounted Patrol, 'is where we'll begin to steer 'em home. Oh! And "Let night also have her well-earned hymn", as Uncle 'ud say.'

There filed out from behind the Little Circus four blaring trumpets, a standard, and a dozen Mounted Police. Their wise little grey Arabs sidled, passaged, shouldered, and nosed softly into the mob, as though they wanted petting, while the trumpets deafened the narrow street. An open square, near by, eased the pressure before long. Here the Patrol broke into fours, and gridironed it, saluting the images of the Gods at each corner and in the centre. People stopped, as usual, to watch how cleverly the incense was cast down over the withers into the spouting cressets; children reached up to pat horses which they said they knew; family groups re-found each other in the smoky dusk; hawkers offered cooked suppers; and soon the crowd melted into the main traffic avenues. Valens went over to the Church porch, where Petrus and Paulus waited between his lictors.

'That was well done,' Paulus began.

'How's the fever?' Valens asked.

'I was spared for today. I think, too, that by The Blessing we have carried our point.'

'Good hearing! My uncle bids me say you are welcome at his house.'

'That is always a command,' said Paulus, with a quick down-country gesture. 'Now that this day's burden is lifted, it will be a delight.'

Petrus joined up like a weary ox. Valens greeted him, but he did not answer.

'Leave him alone,' Paulus whispered. 'The virtue has gone out of me – him – for the while.' His own face looked pale and drawn.

The street was empty, and Valens took a short cut through an alley, where light ladies leaned out of windows and laughed. The three strolled easily together, the lictors behind them, and far off they heard the trumpets of the Night Horse saluting some statue of a Caesar, which marked the end of their round. Paulus was telling Valens how the whole Roman Empire would be changed by what the Christians had agreed to about their love-feasts, when an impudent little Jew boy stole up behind them, playing 'Pickled Fish' on some sort of desert bag-pipe.

'Can't you stop that young pest, one of you?' Valens asked laughing. 'You shan't be mocked on this great night of yours, Paulus.'

The lictors turned back a few paces, and shook a torch at the brat, but he retreated and drew them on. Then they heard Paulus shout, and when they hurried back, found Valens prostrate and coughing – his blood on the fringe of the kneeling Paul's robe. Petrus stooped, waving a helpless hand above them.

'Someone ran out from behind that well-head. He stabbed him as he ran, and ran on. Listen!' said Paulus.

But there was not even the echo of a footfall for clue, and the Jew boy had vanished like a bat. Said Valens from the ground:

'Home! Quick! I have it!'

They tore a shutter out of a shop-front, lifted and carried him, while Paulus walked beside. They set him down in the lighted inner courtyard of the Prefect's house, and a lictor hurried for the Prefect's physician.

Paulus watched the boy's face, and, as Valens shivered a little, called to the girl to fetch last night's fur rug. She brought it, laid the head on her breast, and cast herself beside Valens.

'It isn't bad. It doesn't bleed much. So it *can't* be bad – can it?' she repeated. Valens' smile reassured her, till the Prefect came and recognized the deadly upward thrust under the ribs. He turned on the Hebrews.

'Tomorrow you will look for where your Church stood,' said he.

Valens lifted the hand that the girl was not kissing.

'No – no!' he gasped. 'The Cilician did it! For his brother! He said it.'

'The Cilician you let go to save these Christians because I – ?' Valens signed to his uncle that it was so, while the girl begged him to steal strength from her till the doctor should come.

'Forgive me,' said Serga to Paulus. 'None the less I wish your God in Hades once for all. . . . But what am I to write his mother? Can't either of you two talking creatures tell me what I'm to tell his mother?'

'What has *she* to do with him?' the slave-girl cried. 'He is mine – mine! I testify before all Gods that he bought me! I am his. He is mine.'

'We can deal with the Cilician and his friends later,' said one of the lictors. 'But what now?'

For some reason, the man, though used to butcher-work, looked at Petrus.

'Give him drink and wait,' said Petrus. 'I have – seen such a wound.' Valens drank and a shade of colour came to him. He motioned the Prefect to stoop.

'What is it? Dearest of lives, what troubles?'

'The Cilician and his friends. . . . Don't be hard on them. . . . They get worked up. . . . They don't know what they are doing. . . . Promise!'

'This is not I, child. It is the Law.'

' 'No odds. You're Father's brother. . . . Men make laws – not Gods. . . . Promise! . . . It's finished with me.'

Valens' head eased back on its yearning pillow.

Petrus stood like one in a trance. The tremor left his face as he repeated:

' "Forgive them, for they know not what they do." Heard you *that*, Paulus? He, a heathen and an idolator, said it!'

'I heard. What hinders now that we should baptize him?' Paulus answered promptly.

Petrus stared at him as though he had come up out of the sea.

'Yes,' he said at last. 'It is the little maker of tents. . . . And what does he *now* – command?'

Paulus repeated the suggestion.

Painfully, that other raised the palsied hand that he had once held up in a hall to deny a charge.

'Quiet!' said he. 'Think you that one who has spoken Those Words needs such as *we* are to certify him to any God?'

Paulus cowered before the unknown colleague, vast and commanding, revealed after all these years.

'As you please – as you please,' he stammered, overlooking the blasphemy. 'Moreover there is the concubine.'

The girl did not heed, for the brow beneath her lips was chilling, even as she called on her God who had bought her at a price that he should not die but live.

T. E. LAWRENCE

Seven Pillars of Wisdom

Winston Churchill said that this celebrated narrative of
T. E. Lawrence's Arabian adventures 'ranks with the great-
est books ever written in the English language.' Lawrence
went to the Middle East with an archaeological expedi-
tion. When World War I broke out, he led Arab tribes-
men in their revolt against Turkish domination. Using an
Arab force of only a few thousand, his brilliant campaign
succeeded in immobilizing huge Turkish armies. *Seven
Pillars of Wisdom* is much more than a soldier's account
of his tactics, however; it is also an intimate self-portrait
by one of the century's most unusual and complex person-
alities. '*Seven Pillars of Wisdom* is a superbly intelligent
and complex work' — Paul Zweig, *The New York Times*.